OUR LIZZIE

He came across and sat down beside her on the sofa,
taking her hand and keeping hold of it, patting it from
time to time as if to emphasise what he was saying.
'Well, Lizzie Kershaw? Are you going to give me a
chance to court you or not?'

She stared down at their linked hands and cast a quick
glance sideways at him, feeling warmed by the
expression on his face. 'Well – all right. But nothing's
settled, mind. It's just – we'll see how we go, eh?'

He beamed at her and gave her a rib-cracking hug.
'Eh, I'm that glad.'

Our Lizzie

Anna Jacobs

CORONET BOOKS
Hodder & Stoughton

Copyright © 1999 by Anna Jacobs

The right of Anna Jacobs to be identified as the Author of
the Work has been asserted by her in accordance with the
Copyright, Designs and Patents Act 1988.

First published in Great Britain in 1999 by Hodder and Stoughton
First published in paperback in 1999 by Hodder and Stoughton
A division of Hodder Headline

A Coronet Paperback

14

A CIP catalogue record for this title is available
from the British Library.

ISBN 0 340 69301 0

Printed and bound in Great Britain by
Mackays of Chatham plc, Chatham, Kent.

Hodder and Stoughton
A division of Hodder Headline
338 Euston Road
London NW1 3BH

ACKNOWLEDGEMENTS

For Sharon Micenko – a wonderful, steadfast friend and another of those writing women!

And I would also like to express my grateful thanks to Margaret Mendelawitz who kindly lent me the World War I memorabilia of her grandfather Edward Peyton Whitfield which gave me such a vivid window on the times in which Lizzie lived.

CONTACTING ANNA JACOBS

Anna is always delighted to hear from readers and can be contacted:

BY MAIL

*PO Box 628
Mandurah
Western Australia 6210*

If you'd like a reply, please enclose a self-addressed envelope – stamped from inside Australia or with an international reply coupon from outside Australia.

VIA THE INTERNET

Anna Jacobs now has her own web domain, with details of her books and excerpts to read. She'd love to have you visit at http://www.annajacobs.com

She can also be contacted by e-mail on anna@annajacobs.com

If you'd like to receive e-mail news about Anna and her books (once every few weeks only) you are cordially invited to join her announcements list. Your e-mail address will not be passed on to anyone. E-mail Anna and ask to be put on the list, or there is a link from her web page.

CHAPTER ONE

September 1908

'Eeh, our Lizzie, don't do it! You'll get what for if Mam finds out.'

Her sister Eva's words were all Lizzie needed to push her into accepting the dare. She tossed back her straight dark hair, half of which had fallen out of its plaits as usual, and scrambled up on top of the wall which kept the end of their street from sliding down the hill — at least, her dad said it did. The wall was only three feet high, but the drop on the other side was about twenty feet and suddenly, as she stood there wobbling and staring down, she wondered if this was a good idea.

Glancing over her shoulder, however, she saw the triumphant expression on Mary Holden's face and gritted her teeth. She wasn't going to back out now, not when her arch-enemy had dared her to walk right along the top of the wall.

Straightening up, she spread out her arms. That felt better. Glancing back again at the other girl, who was watching her now with a tight, annoyed expression on her plump face, she jeered, 'It's no worse than walking along the edge of the pavement. See! Easy! Your turn next.'

But it wasn't easy and Lizzie had a funny, shivery feeling in her stomach as she faced the narrow line of bricks. Taking a deep breath and keeping her eyes off the drop on her right, she began to walk slowly forward, one foot in its scuffed shoe edging into place in front of the other. There was nothing in the dare about doing it quickly, after all, just getting to the far end without falling off.

As Lizzie continued to move, her confidence rose. Ha! She would do it all right and then wouldn't Mary Holden look stupid? Because she wouldn't dare do this. She had a big mouth on her, but no guts. Five steps completed. Ten. It helped to count them, made her forget the drop tugging at her from the right.

Fifteen steps. Nearly halfway there. 'Nothin' to it!' she jeered, but she didn't dare turn her head, not now. She could hear her sister's soft breathing over to her left – well, everything about Eva was soft and soppy – and she could feel the anger beating out from Mary behind her, as it had beaten at her many times before, for they'd been enemies from birth, even though their families lived opposite one another in Bobbin Lane. She let out her breath slowly, glad she'd made it a condition nobody spoke while she was walking the wall. That helped. A bit.

In the distance, she could hear the sound of clogs clattering over the cobblestones towards them. Oh, no! If it was a grown-up, she'd be for it. The sound kept coming closer, but although the footsteps slowed down at the corner, no voice called out to her to get off. Sighing in relief, she took another careful step forward.

Three-quarters of the way there now. She was going to make it. She was. But her legs felt stiff, sweat was trickling down her neck and she hated, absolutely *hated*, that drop. This was a dead stupid idea, but Mary had made her so angry, mocking the whole Kershaw family, especially Eva for being the teacher's pet! Well, Eva *was* a teacher's pet, but no one else was going to say that when Lizzie was around.

The footsteps had stopped now, but she didn't turn her head to see who was watching her. No one in her family, that was sure, for the Kershaws didn't wear clogs. Her mam took pride in turning out her children in proper shoes, even if they were bought second hand and pinched, as Lizzie's did, or let in water, as her younger brother Johnny's did.

Thirty steps. She wobbled, but regained her balance.

'Thirty-three an' I'm there!' she called in sudden triumph as her toe touched the wall of the first house in Carters Row. Then she wobbled again and this time lost her balance as she tried to get off the wall. She shrieked in terror, sure she was going to crash twenty feet down to the cobblestones of Mill Road – but hands grabbed her, snatching her into the air, away from the drop. *Safe!* For a moment, she couldn't speak, couldn't breathe with the relief of it all, just held on to her rescuer for dear life, shuddering.

'You lost!' Mary's voice crowed behind her. 'You lost the dare, Lizzie Kershaw. Now you have to carry my books to school.'

She came out of her brief paralysis, struggling to get away from the hands that were still holding her. 'I did not lose! I touched that wall with my toe *and* my hand. It was only when I was jumpin' down that I lost my balance.'

'Did not!'

'Did so!'

'Be quiet, the pair of you!' roared a loud voice.

Only then did Lizzie realise who had rescued her – Sam Thoxby, who lived in the narrow alley at the end of her street. He was only a bit older than their Percy, but he was a big fellow and she'd never seen him look so angry!

Even as she stared up at him, he took her by the shoulders and shook her hard. 'Stay there, you! I'll skin you alive if you move one step!'

With a gasp, Mary turned to flee but Sam caught hold of her skirt and dragged her back to his other side. 'You, too, young lady! You can stay right here till I've done with you. An' you,' a nod across at Eva, 'had better not move, either!'

Lizzie saw how frightened her sister looked. Though even now, after a whole day at school, Eva's dark, wavy hair was neat and tidy and there was hardly a speck of dirt on her pinny. It wasn't fair how pretty and tidy she always looked.

A heavy hand on each girl's shoulder pulled them round to face one another. 'You two are going nowhere,' another

3

shake, 'till you've promised me never, *ever* to try that stupid trick again.'

Mary stopped struggling to smile up at her captor, her voice soft now. 'I won't if you say not to, Sam.'

Lizzie closed her mouth firmly. *She* wasn't going to promise him anything. He might work with her brother, but he wasn't family and he had no right, *no right at all*, to interfere.

His fingers dug into her shoulder. 'I'm waiting, Lizzie Kershaw. An' I'm not moving a step till I hear you promise.'

She scowled up at him. 'Shan't, then.'

He gave Mary a push. 'I shall know if you break your promise. Get off home with you.' The look he turned upon Lizzie was severe in the extreme. 'You could have been killed, you silly little fool.'

'What have you been doing now, our Lizzie?'

Oh, no! Their Percy would have to turn up. He was always trying to boss her around. If she had to have a big brother, why couldn't she have a tall, good-looking one like Peter Dearden, who gave his little brother sweets from the shop and never had a cross word for anyone? Lizzie scowled at Percy, who looked so thin and faded next to other men, especially a huge fellow like Sam Thoxby.

'What have you been doing now, Lizzie Kershaw?' he repeated, catching hold of her arm.

'Nothin'.' She tried to twist away, but was held fast between the two men.

Sam's fingers tightened. 'You can stop that wriggling, young lady. You're going nowhere till you've promised.' Without taking his eyes off her, he said to Percy, 'She were walking along the top of that there wall. If I hadn't caught her, she'd have fell down on to Mill Road.'

Lizzie saw Percy turn pale. He was nervous of heights, always had been. 'It was a dare,' she explained sullenly. 'An' it was Mary Holden what dared me, not me her, an' I'm not letting her tell folk I'm afraid of owt, 'cos I'm not. An' – an' you're just a big bully, Sam Thoxby. Let *go* of me, will you?'

But the fingers were still digging into her shoulder and she couldn't shake them off, though her brother let go of her when she pushed at him again.

Percy turned to his other sister, still hovering nearby. 'You should have run to fetch someone when this started, our Eva.'

'We don't tell on one another.' She hunched her shoulders and walked off down the street.

Lizzie glared up at Percy. Same features as Eva, same dark wavy hair – but he always looked worried about something, sighing over his tea, poring over his books. She knew he was a good son, because people were always saying so, but she just wished he wasn't so *soft*.

'If you don't promise me an' Sam not to do it again,' his voice sounded thin and weary, 'I'll have to tell Mam about this. Or Dad.'

Tears came into Lizzie's eyes. She was always in trouble with Mam and Percy knew it, though Eva was Mam's pet. And their dad worked so hard at the brewery he was tired out by evening and didn't need extra worries. But if she promised – and she always kept her promises, always – Mary Holden would crow at her and goad her. 'I hate you, our Percy!'

'Promise!' Sam gave her another little shake.

'Oh, all right, then. I promise I won't do it again.' They let her go, but she waited till she was a few paces away before yelling, 'Yer a pair of silly bloody sheep, you two are! So there!'

'I'll wash your mouth out with soap when you come home, Lizzie Kershaw!' Percy roared, ashamed of being shown up in front of his workmate.

She danced around, pulling faces at them. 'Ya, ya, ya! You'll have to catch me first, won't you?' And when he took a step towards her she was off again, running down Bobbin Lane, as lithe and graceful as a young colt Sam had seen frolicking in a field on the last works picnic.

Percy sighed and turned to the man next to him. Sam was older, twenty-three to his twenty, and towered over him by a good six inches, for none of the Kershaws was tall. 'Thanks for stoppin' her.'

5

Sam watched the child disappear round a corner, admiration on his face. 'She's a lively one.'

'Too lively. There's only Dad can keep her in order an' he's been so tired lately. That new manager at the brewery's a right slave-driver.'

'Your Lizzie's going to be pretty, too, when she grows up.' Sam frowned. 'No, not pretty exactly, but she'll attract the fellows, you'll see.' She attracted him, if truth be told, for all her scrawny child's body. She had such bright eyes and she was so alive compared to other lasses. He had seen her several times lately; seen and stopped to watch.

'Our Lizzie? You've got to be joking! It's Eva as is the pretty one.'

Sam looked at him thoughtfully. Everyone knew that Percy Kershaw was as soft as butter and a worrier. You couldn't help taking to him, though. He'd do anything to help you and was well respected at the works, knew his job better than most and was studying to learn more at night classes. 'Come an' have a drink, lad. We need one after that.'

'Thanks, but I can't.' He'd have loved to go into the warmth and bustle of the pub after a hard day's work, especially with a big confident fellow like Sam, but Percy didn't allow himself luxuries like beer at the moment. He had to watch every farthing if he was to save enough money to go to Technical School part-time next year. Mr Pilby himself had given permission for Percy to work part-time in order to do that. It was all arranged.

'The drink's on me,' Sam offered. 'I had a win on the horses.'

But Percy was stubborn as well as soft. 'No. Thanks all the same, but I couldn't afford to buy you one back, an' I prefer to pay my own way.'

'Just a half, then. I don't like drinking alone.' Sam took a grip on his companion's arm and led him firmly, still protesting, into the Hare and Hounds. They passed a woman with soft dark hair and green eyes, and for a moment he was reminded of Lizzie. But this woman's eyes were dull and she was slouching along.

As he chuckled at the memory of the little lass spitting fury at him, Sam knew suddenly that he wanted her. Not now, but later. He didn't lust after children, and for all her lively wits Lizzie was a child still, but when she grew up – ah, then he'd be waiting for her. Something in her wild, defiant nature appealed to him, as other girls' flattery and admiring glances never did. He'd enjoy taming her, wooing her first and then mastering her, as all women loved to be mastered. Marrying her, perhaps. Yes, that idea pleased him. He didn't want his sons mothered by a whining fool like that other lass. And Sam was going to have sons, lots of them.

He waited to be served, brow creased in thought. The Kershaws were well respected in Southlea, the district at the bottom end of the low hill across which the small town of Overdale sprawled. Mrs Kershaw was a cut above her neighbours, for she'd been a housemaid to the gentry before she married, and she talked better and ran her home better than most. So would her daughters, with her training, which would suit Sam just fine. He had ambitions for his future. Oh, yes. Big ambitions.

He grinned as he paid for the two half-pints and pondered on his tactics. He was about to become Percy Kershaw's best mate, and all for the sake of that cheeky little brat! And he'd better soft-soap the mother a bit, as well. He enjoyed making folk do what he wanted, setting his sights on something and getting it, too. He hadn't done badly for a whore's bastard – he scowled briefly as he thought of the mother he'd never met, but heard of, oh, aye, heard of and been taunted about many a time.

The two young men's glasses of light ale were only half-empty when someone came pounding into the pub. 'There's been an accident down at the brewery!' he gasped, then his eyes fell on Percy, sitting at the back, glass halfway to his mouth. 'Oh, you're there, Percy!' His voice became gentle. 'Eeh, I'm that sorry, lad. It's your dad, I'm afraid.'

Several weeks before the accident at the brewery, another man had died suddenly in a comfortable house on the edge of the moors. Bonamy Harper had been haranguing his two daughters, a pastime in which he often indulged, playing out all the tricks of a domestic tyrant and shouting at them for their extravagance – though indeed they had no capacity for extravagance with the meagre amount he gave them on which to keep house. Suddenly he clutched his throat, his face turned an even darker red than usual and he keeled over.

It was a moment before they bent over him and then, after another moment of startled disbelief, the main emotion each felt was relief.

The next morning the family lawyer paid a hurried visit to warn them to keep the funeral costs down. 'There are debts to be cleared, you see, due to some rather rash investments your father made.'

'How much is owed?' Emma asked.

'Several hundred pounds, I'm afraid.' Mr Peelby inclined his head towards Blanche. 'Your annuity from your godmother is safe, of course, Miss Harper. However, that only amounts to about fifty pounds a year . . . Um, you'll have to sell this house and its contents, I'm afraid, but I can tell you now they'll barely cover the debts. You can stay on here till it's sold, but don't remove anything apart from your personal effects – though you can give your father's clothes away, if you like. None of the debtors will want those.'

Blanche, white and trembling, clutched at her sister's hand. 'But – where shall we live?'

'With your aunt, I suppose. I'm sure Mrs Reed will offer you a home when she hears how things stand.'

Emma groaned. 'Oh, no! Not Aunt Gertrude.' For their sole surviving relative was as domineering as their father had been.

Mr Peelby spoke somewhat impatiently. 'Times are hard. Poorer people lack work and whole families are starving. You're lucky to have someone to turn to.'

Immediately he'd left, Emma turned to Blanche. 'Whatever happens, I'm not going to live with Aunt Gertrude. You can if you wish, but I absolutely refuse.'

'But what else can we do?'

'I don't know, but I'll find something. For a start, I'm not going to give Father's clothes away, I'm going to sell them. Even if they're only worth a pound or two, it'll help.'

'But how . . . ?'

Emma pondered for a moment, then said slowly, 'Sam Thoxby will probably know what to do. I'll send him a message.'

'But the debts . . .'

'Are Father's, not ours.'

That evening, when Sam turned up at the house he'd been in and out of since the days his gran had done the rough charring work for Mrs Harper, he said the wardrobe of fine suits and hats was worth something and agreed to sell the stuff. Emma was a little older than he was and Blanche older still. They and their mother had been kind to him as a lad, feeding him leftovers and giving him old scarves and gloves of Mr Harper's to keep him warm in winter. He never forgot a kindness because he hadn't known many. Mind you, that wouldn't stop him turning a penny out of this.

'What about selling some of the other stuff as well?' he asked, looking round at the furniture and ornaments.

Emma shook her head. 'This all belongs to the creditors now.'

'Only if they get their hands on it.'

The two women stared at him, then at each other. It was Emma who nodded. 'I suppose we could sort out a few things.'

'Smaller stuff would be best. I'll come back with my handcart after dark.'

Only when he'd left did Blanche ask, 'Should we?'

'We need to. And,' Emma added thoughtfully, 'we'll keep Mother's jewellery for ourselves.'

'I don't like to think of leaving debts unpaid.'

'Well, I don't like to think of us not having something to fall back on.'

'My annuity—'

'Is not enough, dear. You know it isn't.'

That night, Sam and a friend brought a handbarrow round to the back door and took away three loads of stuff. Some of it would be sold, the rest kept to give the sisters a start in their new home.

Emma worked herself to exhaustion sorting it all out. Blanche wept almost continuously and was of little use.

Lizzie was in the children's playground when their neighbour found her. She was letting the swing move gently to and fro as she dreamed about a story she'd read at school. *She was an orphan, the lost child of a duchess, kidnapped when she was very young by gypsies. She had long, curly golden hair, and*—

'There you are, Lizzie Kershaw! I've been looking all over for you.'

She jerked out of her daydream and scowled at Mrs Preston from across the street. 'Well, now you've found me, haven't you?'

That should have earned her a scolding, or at the least a muttered, 'Cheeky young madam!' but all Mrs Preston did was mop her eyes and pat Lizzie's shoulder. 'Eeh, you poor thing!'

Lizzie jerked to her feet, leaving the swing rocking to and fro behind her. 'What do you mean?' she demanded, arms akimbo. 'We're not poor.' Poor people only had bread and dripping for tea. They wore clogs and their clothes smelled sour. How dare anyone call her that?

Mrs Preston's hand dropped from her shoulder. 'You'll be cheeking the angels as folk lower your coffin into the grave, you will!' Then her mouth trembled and she flourished a handkerchief. 'Look, lass, there's been an accident. At the brewery. You're wanted at home. Your father's—'

'*Dad!*'

Before the explanation was complete, Lizzie set off running, twisting between the iron posts at the entrance to the playground with barely a pause and haring off down the road as if she were being chased by a mad dog. When she arrived home, she found a knot of people gathered near the front door, as always happened when there was trouble. She pushed her way past them and they started saying, 'Poor lass!' as well.

The fear became stark terror and she stopped for a minute at the door, suddenly afraid to go inside. Why were the blinds pulled down in the front room? It wasn't dark yet. She went into the long narrow hall and pushed the front door to behind her with her foot, then stopped again, not daring to take another step.

Percy appeared in the doorway of the front room. 'Oh, Lizzie,' his voice broke, 'our Dad's – he's been killed.'

She stood there for a moment with the words echoing inside her head, then started bawling, sobbing as loudly as any five-year-old child.

Her mother's voice was sharp. 'Lizzie Kershaw, you can just stop that!'

With a gulp, she forced back the tears and the panic. She'd never seen her mother look so white and sad, not even when their Timmy, who had been older than her, died. 'M-mam? Dad isn't – he *can't* be dead!'

Her mother's voice was dull. 'He is.'

As Percy's grasp slackened, the girl moved forward. 'Where is he?'

'In the front room.'

Lizzie took a deep breath. 'I want to see him.'

Meg Kershaw closed her eyes for a minute and prayed for strength, finding it briefly in Percy's quick hug, then she gestured her daughter past her into the front room.

Her son stayed in the hall.

Lizzie found Gran Thoxby in the front room. She always helped out when someone died, thought Lizzie wasn't sure what she did. 'I want to see my dad.'

The old woman looked questioningly at Meg, received a nod of assent and lifted up a corner of the blanket.

Hesitantly Lizzie stretched out one hand to touch her father's cheek. She'd always been his favourite, always known he loved her whatever she did. As she let her hand drop, she half-expected him to wink at her, but he didn't. He lay so still she wanted to shake him, force him to move again. 'He feels cold.'

'Aye.' Gran drew the blanket back across the face. 'They allus do. An' he'll get colder yet.'

'What happened, Mam?' It was a whisper.

It was Gran who answered, for Meg was weeping into her handkerchief again. 'An accident at the brewery.'

'It's not fair! We need our Dad!'

Gran looked sympathetically at the child, who was as taut as a bow-string, her eyes seeming huge in the whiteness of her thin face. 'Think on, lass. I never even met *my* father. At least you had yours with you for twelve year. At least you'll never forget him.'

Lizzie was distracted for a moment. 'You never met your own father?'

'No. Not once. An' our Sam's never met his, neither.' Well, how could he have? Even her daughter hadn't known who the father was. 'Nor he hasn't seen his mother since he were three.' Trust her Janey to run out on them. One daughter, she'd had, just the one, and a right heartless little bitch she'd turned out to be. But Sam was a good lad.

Meg gave Lizzie a push and gestured towards the door. 'Go and look after the others. I want to spend a few moments alone with my Stanley.'

Lizzie walked outside into the hall where her brother was waiting for her. Only then did it occur to her that she didn't know what had happened to her father. 'What sort of accident was it?'

'It were that new dray horse. Dad said it were a bugger, but Mr Beckins insisted on buyin' it because it looked good. Somethin' frit the damned thing and it trampled our Dad down in a corner of the stable yard before anyone could get to it.' Percy had seen the bloody mess below his father's waist and knew with shuddering certainty that no man would want to live on like that. He could only be thankful that the horse had finished off what it had started and that his dad had died quickly of a massive blow to the back of his head.

Lizzie looked round blindly. She hated to think of a horse trampling on her father. 'It must have hurt him.'

'They said it were over very quick.' Percy suddenly leaned against the wall, feeling sick.

She saw how close to tears he was, so put her arm round his waist. 'I'll brew us all some tea, shall I? I expect Mam'll be glad of a cup, too.'

In the kitchen, Eva was sitting at the table, with Polly cuddled up beside her and Johnny on her other side. For once, even clever Eva didn't seem to know what to do. They all three looked at Percy, but when he just stood there, they turned a questioning gaze upon their eldest sister instead.

Lizzie stepped forward and took charge. 'You put the kettle on, our Eva. Polly, get out the cups an' teaspoons. Johnny, you fetch the milk jug. We'll all have a nice cup of tea. That'll make us feel a – a bit better.' Her voice choked on the last word.

After that, it was comings and goings, strangers knocking on their door, neighbours coming to see if they could help, some men carrying a coffin into the front room. Lizzie hated the idea of her dad being shut up inside a big box.

For once, she was glad to go to bed. She hesitated in the hall, then whispered, 'Good night, Dad!' not liking to leave him on his own.

Years afterwards, Lizzie realised she'd suddenly and very painfully left her carefree childhood behind her that night. Afterwards, things were never the same. And she was never the same, either.

Gertrude Reed turned up for Bonamy Harper's funeral in a brand-new motor car. As an affluent widow, she could afford to indulge herself in such luxuries – and the gardener was only too happy to drive her around.

Afterwards she came back to the house and took a quick cup of tea with her nieces, questioning them about why her brother's funeral had been such a shabby affair, with no one invited back for refreshments afterwards.

Emma explained about the debts and the sale.

There was a long silence, followed by, 'You'll have to come and live with me, then, I suppose. I can let the parlourmaid go and you two can take over her duties. She's always been a flighty piece. Mind, I'll expect the cleaning to be done thoroughly.'

Emma tried not to let her indignation show. 'We're grateful for your offer, Aunt Gertrude, but we'd rather find somewhere of our own to live, thank you.'

'You can't afford it on Blanche's fifty pounds a year, and I'm not giving you any money. You're used to living in some style and comfort, not dwelling in the slums.'

'We're not used to that much comfort, actually.' Emma held her aunt's gaze. 'Father was very stingy with us towards the end.'

'Nonetheless, you'll come to me.' Gertrude heaved herself to her feet and glared at them. 'It wouldn't be fitting for a Harper to live somewhere like Southlea.' She added sharply, 'And I'd have expected a bit of gratitude from you, I would indeed. Beggars can't afford to be choosers.'

It was Blanche who stepped forward then, surprising herself as much as the others, for she was usually the quiet one. 'As Emma has told you, Aunt, we *both* prefer to live on our own. And – and we don't appreciate being bullied.'

'Bullied! *Bullied!* How dare you speak to me like that? Apologise at once.'

Blanche shook her head.

'Then you can get yourselves out of this mess.' Gertrude stormed from the room, pausing in the hallway, expecting one of them to run after her, but neither moved. So she muttered something and left. They'd soon realise which side their bread was buttered on.

Both the Harper sisters were delighted with the results of the sales. And Sam was equally delighted with his share, but that didn't stop him accepting the gift of Bonamy Harper's second pocket watch, a battered silver piece, in return for his help.

'Silly buggers!' he said as he walked home. Then, as his fingers stroked the watch case, he grew thoughtful. 'I wonder if they have owt else tucked away? Old Mrs Harper used to have quite a few pieces of jewellery. I reckon I'd better keep an eye on them two. They may need my help again.' He threw back his head and laughed, chuckling all the way home at his own cleverness.

CHAPTER TWO

After Stanley Kershaw's funeral was over, the invited guests walked back from the cemetery behind the widow and her family, their faces solemn and their conversation subdued.

When they reached Bobbin Lane, they relaxed a little, however, and everyone came into number thirty to offer their advice to the bereaved family and enjoy the feast to which all the neighbours had contributed a plate of something. The family had provided great platters of sandwiches containing wafer thin slices of ham, because it was unthinkable to Meg that her Stanley should not have the dignity of being 'buried with ham', as folk called it. When Percy had remonstrated about this extravagance, given their reduced income, she had burst into tears and insisted on it, getting so hysterical he had given in.

Lizzie had survived the funeral by feeling angry. She stayed angry, hating the crowd of people sitting or standing in the front room, clustering in the kitchen and spilling out on to the doorstep.

Percy hovered near their mother, who was looking white and ill in her black skirt and blouse, bought second-hand from Pettit's pawnbroker's, for Meg had also been adamant about being properly attired in her grief. She kept an eye on what was happening around her while she tried to listen politely to Mrs Preston from across the street, who didn't seem to have stopped talking since they got back from the cemetery.

When Eva came over to join them, Meg slipped her arm round her daughter's shoulders. She felt Eva tense up, because she wasn't one for cuddling, but then her arm went round her mother's waist and Meg sighed in gratitude for this unspoken support. Folk said you shouldn't have favourites, but how could you help it? This child had been easy to bear and easy to rear, unlike Lizzie. She and Stanley had had such hopes for their clever second daughter.

'They'll be a comfort to you.' Mrs Preston stuffed another sandwich into her mouth, wishing the ham were cut a bit thicker. Meg watched her wagging her head up and down as she chewed it, like a fat old hen pecking at scattered grain, and nodded weary agreement. 'Yes.'

'And your Percy's old enough to bring in a man's wage, at least. He's a good son, that one is. He'll look after you.'

Meg nodded again. People had been saying that to her ever since Stanley was killed. As if it helped. As if anything could help now. She had lain sleepless in her bed last night, absolutely terrified of the responsibilities she'd now have to shoulder.

'Good thing you was in the Funeral Club, eh? They put on a nice penny funeral, don't they?'

Meg breathed deeply. Of course everyone knew how much their neighbours spent on this and that, but only Fanny Preston would have said it aloud.

At last the neighbours began to leave, one after the other murmuring ritual phrases of encouragement to the widow and taking with them their plates, cups and chairs, lent for the occasion.

When the last person – Fanny Preston, of course! – had closed the front door behind her, Meg sighed and said in a tight, hard voice, 'Let's go and sit in the kitchen, shall we, Eva?'

There they found the door to the back scullery open, and Polly and Lizzie washing up, with little Johnny putting the cups and plates away.

Meg straightened her shoulders and tried to look calm. 'We have to t-talk about how we're going to manage. When you've finished the washing up, c-come and sit down at the table with me, all of you.'

Lizzie, who was still standing near the sink, looked up quickly.

Mam only stuttered when she was nervous. She watched her mother hesitate, then move to take Dad's place at the head of the table. She saw how Mam's hand lingered for a moment on the chair back before she pulled it out, and how her face twisted as she sat down and dragged the chair back up to the table.

When they'd all sat down, that left one empty chair and somehow they couldn't help staring at it. Percy muttered something and got up to shove it into the corner. When he sat down again, Lizzie saw that his eyes were bright with unshed tears and felt her own fill up yet again.

It was Percy who broke the silence. 'I've got some savings, Mam. We'll be all right for a bit.'

'That money's for your schooling, Percy.'

He looked at his mother, his expression bleak. 'We both know there'll be no more schooling for me, not now.'

It was then that Lizzie suddenly realised why everyone kept calling her 'poor child'. It hadn't occurred to her before that they'd have to manage without her dad's weekly wage packet. Some of the children at school came from really poor families. They didn't have any sandwiches to eat at lunchtime and weren't allowed to go home, either, so they just hung around the playground, grateful for any scraps they could scrounge and willing to do the silliest tricks if rewarded by a mouthful of food. Horror flooded through her. Would the Kershaws go short of food now?

'I've been thinking hard, trying to work it out,' Meg said at last, and if her voice wobbled a bit, no one let on they'd noticed. 'We're going to miss your dad's money coming in, so I think the best thing will be to take in lodgers. If you boys go up into the attic, I can have your room and we can fit a couple in.'

Lizzie frowned. With three bedrooms on the first floor they'd never needed the old weavers' attic, so had used the big space upstairs only to dry clothes on wet days and the smaller attic next to it to store a few bits and pieces. It'd be cold up there.

'We could move to a smaller house, then we could manage on my money,' Percy offered.

Meg sucked in her breath sharply. '*No*. I'd do anything rather than move from here. *Anything*. It'd be like l–losing the last memories of my Stanley. And anyhow, there'll be no need to m–move if we can get some lodgers.'

Percy patted her hand. 'All right, Mam. All right. An' I've got a steady job, so we don't need to panic.'

Lizzie suddenly realised how she could help. 'I could get a job, too. I turn thirteen this year, so they'd let me go half-time at school.'

'No!' This time two voices spoke as one, her mother's and Percy's.

'Why not?' She hated school, always had, hated being trapped behind a desk, having to waste time chanting silly rhymes and tables.

Her mother's voice was quiet and tired. 'Because – as you very well know, young lady – your dad wanted both you girls to get a good schooling, go on to do a secretarial course, perhaps, or,' she looked at Eva, 'learn to be a teacher, even.'

Lizzie hung her head and confessed, 'I can't do that, Mam. I'm not a good enough scholar. An' anyway, I don't like school. I'd *rather* start work.'

There was silence, then Percy said, 'But perhaps if you tried harder—'

She scowled across at him. 'I *can't* try harder! I'm no good at lessons, an' I'm not interested in them stuffy old books! It's our Eva what likes that sort of thing, not me. She's the teacher's pet, she is. Miss Blake hates me.'

Percy sighed. 'Dad would be so disappointed, Lizzie. He had his heart set on his girls bettering themselves.'

Lizzie could feel tears spill from the corners of her eyes and blinked rapidly to prevent more forming, sagging in relief as someone knocked on the front door and attention shifted from her.

Meg sighed. 'You'd think they'd leave us alone now the funeral's over.'

Percy stood up. 'I'll go an' see who it is, Mam.'

There was the sound of voices, then he came back with Sam

Thoxby, who had been in and out of the house ever since the accident, helping, though he hadn't come to the funeral itself, even though it was a Saturday, due to a 'prior engagement' with a man who was buying some of the Harpers' remaining bits and pieces.

He bobbed his head at Meg. 'Sorry to intrude at a time like this, Mrs Kershaw, but I have a bit of good news for you. At least, I think it's good news.'

'Come in. Polly, get Sam that other chair.'

His eyes flickered briefly towards Lizzie and she glared at him. He'd needn't think she'd forgiven him for interfering between her and Mary, because she hadn't.

He smiled and turned back to her mother. 'I know you'll be a bit short of money now, Mrs Kershaw, and I was speaking to the foreman yesterday. They need help in the packing room. They'd be willing to take your Lizzie on half-time, till she can leave school. See how she goes, like.'

Lizzie stared at him in horror. If she went to work at Pilby's, she'd never be out of sight of Percy – or of Sam. And anyway, she hated Pilby's. The works were big and dark, even worse than school. She'd feel trapped if she had to spend her days shut up in there.

She bounced to her feet and set her hands on her hips. 'Well, I don't *want* to work at Pilby's!' As she caught sight of Percy's shocked face, she tossed her head. 'An' I'm not goin' to, so there!'

Her mother jerked upright. '*Lizzie Kershaw!* Apologise at once for talking to Sam like that.'

Lizzie pressed her lips together and said nothing.

Meg's expression promised later retribution as she turned towards her visitor. 'She's not thinking straight at the moment, Sam. Can we let you know tomorrow?'

'Aye, of course.' He stood up, hesitating in the doorway, not wanting to leave. There was a sense of togetherness in the room that he envied, something he'd never had in his own home, though his gran did her best for him. His house had never been shiny with polish like this one, nor had Gran ever done much cooking. She preferred to get fish and chips from down the road – which people like Mrs Kershaw considered 'common' – or a hot pie from the baker's. He'd often made his tea on jam butties in his childhood, or just plain bread sometimes. But Gran had always found him something to eat, he'd give her that, and in return he would never let her want as long as she lived.

Hardly had Sam left than there was another knock on the front door, a loud one this time, repeated almost immediately. Lizzie went to open it. 'It's Mr Cuttler, Mam!' she called from the hall, to give them warning.

The rent man came in. 'Sorry about your trouble, Mrs Kershaw. I need to know if you'll be staying on here or wanting somewhere smaller? I have another place just come empty down in Mill Road. Cheaper than this.'

'We'll be staying here, if that's all right, Mr Cuttler? I'm going to take in lodgers, so we'll need the extra space.'

He shrugged. 'All right by me.' He jingled his leather satchel meaningfully. 'Might as well collect the rent while I'm here, eh? It's due today.'

Meg went and put her hand up on the mantelpiece, feeling for the coins, frowning when she didn't find them. 'I know I put them up there.' She fumbled further along for her purse and couldn't find that either. In sudden panic, she turned to Percy. 'I *did* put the rent here! And my purse has gone, too.'

He went to search the mantelpiece, but shook his head.

Lizzie stood up to watch. 'Ooh, someone must have took them!'

Meg's face crumpled. 'No! They wouldn't! Surely they w-wouldn't, not on the d-day of the funeral?' Suddenly it was all too much for her and she sank down on her chair, head in hands, sobbing.

Percy fumbled in his pocket, but found only a couple of shillings and a few coppers, after the various expenses of the past day or two. He held out the silver coins. 'Here, Mr Cuttler, take this on account. I'll get the rest to you on Monday. I've got some money in the savings bank.'

Meg's weeping grew louder and even through her handkerchief the words, 'Never been late with the rent. Never!' could be distinguished.

There was another knock on the front door. With an exclamation of annoyance, Lizzie stamped along the corridor again. 'What do you want now?' she asked Sam, still furious with him for trying to get her a job at Pilby's.

'I forgot my hat.' The sound of Meg's weeping echoed down the narrow hall. 'Summat wrong?'

'Someone's took the rent money off the mantelpiece an' Mam's purse as well. An' Mr Cuttler's here wantin' the rent. Only our Percy didn't have enough to pay him, so Mam started cryin'.'

Sam fumbled in his pocket. 'How much do you need?'

She looked down at the big callused hand, not wanting to touch him for some strange reason. 'Percy's got some money in the savings bank, thank you. We don't need anything.'

'Don't be daft! Better owe me than Cuttler. How much more does your mam need?'

'Two an' six. It's four and six a week.'

He took hold of her hand and dropped the coins into it, closing her fingers on them. 'Here. Tell Percy he can pay me back any time.'

Lizzie stared down at the coins, then up at his face. After a moment, she nodded and her expression became a shade less hostile. 'All right.' She took a quick step backwards, feeling threatened by the way he was standing over her. He was such a big man. Staring up at him, she decided she'd never liked ginger hair. It looked funny against the pink of his neck. Even the hairs in his nostrils were orange-coloured. Ugh! And she wished he wouldn't always stare at her like that.

The feel of the coins in her hand reminded her of her manners and she managed to say, 'Thank you!' in a scratchy voice as she turned towards the kitchen.

'I'll come round tomorrow night, Lizzie. Give you time to think things over. It's not bad working at Pilby's. There's be other lasses to pal on with, you know.'

Somehow, Lizzie swallowed another blunt refusal. She wasn't going to work at Pilby's, she was absolutely determined about that. But she'd have to have a good reason for refusing, or they'd push her into it. Why was Sam Thoxby taking such an interest in them all of a sudden?

He picked up the bowler hat he had left behind on purpose and walked out, whistling softly, mightily pleased with himself. It had been easy to take the rent money and purse while he was helping Percy get the house ready. No one had noticed a thing. Eeh, they were a soft lot, the Kershaws, when it came to looking out for themselves. Fancy leaving money lying around like that with a house full of people coming and going!

He beamed up at the blue sky. And now the Kershaws would have even more cause to be grateful to him. Like the Harpers. He strolled back home where his good humour evaporated rapidly. Gran wasn't in, of course, the sink was piled high with dirty dishes and there was nothing in the house for tea, not even a loaf. It'd have to be the chip shop again. When he was married, he'd make sure his wife always had his tea waiting for him. And kept the place nice, too. He wasn't going to live like this for ever.

It was then that he decided to extend his additional activities, remembering how easily he'd diddled the Harpers out of half the proceeds of the sales, and how easily he'd picked up the purse and rent money at the Kershaws. Folk were just asking to be robbed, they were so trusting. And only fools worked themselves into an early grave.

He looked round and anger mounted in his throat and belly. This place was a sodding mess! He was going to get himself something better before he was through, a lot better. And he was going to marry Lizzie Kershaw, too. She'd really taken his fancy, that cheeky little lass had. He could afford to wait for her to grow up, though. In fact, it wouldn't be convenient for him to get wed now.

By the time Sam had dumped a paper full of fish and chips on the kitchen table and started eating its contents with his fingers, he had cheered up. When he wanted something, he

usually got it. One way or the other. He just had to work it
out in his head and make a few plans.

An hour later, Lizzie decided she couldn't stand being cooped
up indoors any longer. She went to see her mother, who was
sitting in the front room, looking lost and weary. 'Can I go out
for a breath of fresh air, Mam?'

'No.'

Percy, sitting in their dad's armchair opposite, frowned at
his sister.

'Please, Mam. Just for a few minutes.' Tears filled Lizzie's
eyes. 'I feel,' she patted her thin chest, 'as if I haven't been able
to breathe properly all day.'

Meg roused herself to look at her eldest daughter, noting
the drooping shoulders and reddened eyes. For once, she let
the child have her way because she'd felt like that today as
well when the house was full of people. 'All right, then, you
can run me an errand. Percy, have you still got a few coppers?
Thanks. Go down to Dearden's, Lizzie, and get me some more
milk. It all got drunk up this afternoon. I was going to use a tin
of condensed, but it never tastes the same.'

'Thanks, Mam.' She was out of the house before anyone
could change their mind.

Meg gulped back a sob and looked sideways at her son. 'I'm
s-sorry about the Technical School, love. I know how set you
were on going there. Maybe in a year or two we'll manage
something.'

'Maybe.' He went to sit beside her, putting his arm round
her thin shoulders. 'I know you'll miss Dad, but I'll look after
you. Always.' *Look after your mam*, his dad had often said. *Don't
let her tire herself out. She's not strong.*

It was up to him, Percy, to keep an eye on things now. The
children would need supporting for years yet. He wouldn't even
be able to marry, he realised suddenly. Well, not unless he met
someone who got on with his mother and wouldn't mind her
living with them. And Meg Kershaw wasn't an easy woman to

deal with – look at the way Lizzie always managed to get on the wrong side of her. Face facts, Percy, he told himself sternly. But it was hard, indeed it was, because he'd had his dreams just like the next fellow.

Lizzie wandered down Bobbin Lane, crossing the street to avoid a group of young fellows who all turned round to stare at her, but thank goodness didn't shout out after her. They were like that, lads were, as soon as they started work. They stood around street corners in the evenings and you kept away from them if you were a lass, because the things they said made you blush.

She went past the little corner shop. Her mother didn't buy milk from Minter's, said they didn't scour out the milk churn well enough and sometimes didn't cover it up properly, allowing bits of dust and dirt to blow in. The Kershaws always went down to Dearden's for their milk, even though it was twice as far to York Road, where the posh shops were. Today Lizzie was glad of that, dawdling along in the dusk, trying not to attract attention to herself.

The lights were still on in Dearden's, but they were clearing up the counters ready to close at eight o'clock. She stopped outside for a moment to watch them bustling, envying them their busy cheerfulness. It was then that she saw the notice, written on a piece of card hanging inside the window:

HELP WANTED, SUIT HALF-TIMER

She froze where she stood for a minute as she realised that this might be the answer to her problem. Then she pushed open the shop door, shaking her head in refusal as Jack Dearden, who was a year older than her at school, tried to serve her.

'I need to see your mother,' she said, breathless with excitement. 'About the job.'

He cast a knowledgeable eye towards a customer and her pile of packages assembled on the long, polished wooden counter. 'She's nearly done.'

Lizzie went to wait at the rear. It was no use asking for Mr Dearden, because it was common knowledge in town that Mrs Dearden made all the decisions nowadays. Her husband spent most of his time out at the back in the warehouse, roasting the coffee and blending the teas to make *Dearden's Best*. He wheezed like a pair of leaky bellows and Lizzie had heard folk say that he wouldn't make old bones.

At last the customer said goodnight and walked out, then Mrs Dearden turned to Lizzie, her voice softer than usual. 'What can I do for you, lass?'

'It's about the job, Mrs Dearden. I saw the card.' She waved one hand towards the window. A phrase she'd heard at school came into her head. 'I'd like to apply for the position, please.'

There was silence and a frown, then the shopkeeper's lips pursed. 'Hmm. Does your mother know you've come?'

'She knows I need to find a job, but she doesn't know about this one because I've only just seen the card.' Lizzie gestured around the big, brightly lit shop, filled with rows of fascinating goods. 'I'd really like to work here, and I don't want to work at Pilby's.'

'Oh? Why not?'

'It's dark an' shut in, an' they do the same thing all day long in that packing room. I like to see the sunshine an' talk to people an' – an' move about. It'd be so interesting here, with all the different things to sell. I bet I'd soon learn all the prices. I can learn quick when it's real things what make sense. It doesn't make any sense, what we have to write about at school.' Lizzie took a deep breath, half-closed her eyes and started to recite the piece they'd just been learning by heart. '"*Describe the shape of the earth. The earth is a huge spheroid with a diameter of nearly 8,000 miles and a circumference of nearly 25,000 miles.*"' She paused and added indignantly, 'What does that mean? Nowt!'

Sally Dearden tried in vain to hide a smile. 'All right, all right. I get enough of that stuff with our Jack.' The words Lizzie had recited hadn't made much sense to her, either, but she wasn't going to admit that to a potential employee. Actually they'd been meaning to take on a lad and train him up in the trade. Her husband had complained last time she took on a lass because he said grocery was men's business, though Susan was much neater in her ways than young Fred. But it was a poor look out if you couldn't help a family in trouble. She leaned forward and said quietly, 'I'm right sorry about your father, lass.'

Lizzie had forgotten for a minute, but at that the grief all rushed back in on her like one of those black express trains roaring through the station and she had to gulp back a sudden desire to weep. 'Yes,' she managed. 'Yes, th-thank you.'

Sally waited a minute, then got down to business. 'What are you like at adding up?'

'I'm good at arithmetic, but,' Lizzie stared down at her feet, 'I'm not so good at problems. I can't see what furlongs and farmers' fields and one man walking twice as fast as his brother have to do with anything.'

'What's threepence halfpenny plus fourpence three-farthings?'

'Eightpence farthing,' Lizzie replied without the slightest hesitation.

'And if the customer gave you a shilling to pay that, how much change would you give her?'

'Threepence three-farthings.'

'And are you an honest child?'

Lizzie nodded, looking at her in slight puzzlement.

Sally's face relaxed infinitesimally. She knew that, really. The Kershaws were a decent family, well respected in the Southlea district. The father been a fine figure of a man, with his thick black hair and burly body. She'd often seen him in church, with his pretty little wife beside him. After another long silence, she said slowly, 'Come back here tomorrow with your mother. We'll have to see what she thinks about it.'

It wasn't till she was halfway home that Lizzie realised she'd forgotten the milk. She hesitated then decided not to go back. It wouldn't look good, forgetting something, not when you wanted a job, and she did want the job at Dearden's. It was a nice shop. All the posh folk from the top of the hill and from the new houses over in Northlea shopped there, and there was always someone passing the window. Well, there would be in the main street of the town, wouldn't there?

When she got home, she forgot about being quiet and erupted into the house, shouting, 'Mam, Mam, guess what's happened?'

Meg listened to her daughter in silence and didn't say anything about the empty milk jug. It'd be a good chance for Lizzie, working at Dearden's would. A better class of job than Pilby's. She stared at the child disapprovingly. Scrawny, not at all pretty like Eva, a real disappointment in so many ways – and wilful with it. Why Stanley had thought the world of her, Meg didn't know. She found Lizzie a real trial, with her slapdash ways and her cheekiness.

She sniffed and dabbed at her eyes. Even her clever little Eva wouldn't be able to stay on at school now and they'd have to watch every farthing they spent. Terror lanced through her and for a moment or two she just stood there, her breath rasping in her throat, wishing she had died with Stanley, wishing she didn't have all these terrifying responsibilities.

Percy frowned at his sister. 'But Sam's got you the offer of a job at the works, Lizzie.'

'I told you an' I told him – I don't want to work at Pilby's. It's horrid, your works is, all dark an' gloomy, an' the girls in the packing room do the same thing all day long. I'd go mad working there.' She turned to her mother. 'I can go an' work at Dearden's, can't I, Mam?'

'If they take you on. I think your father would have preferred you to work in a shop. Well, I know he would.'

So far as Lizzie was concerned, it was all settled. And maybe, just maybe, her mother would let her keep a penny or two from her earnings. Images of buying her very own copy of *Girl's Best Friend* every week and reading it over and over made her sigh with pleasure. At the moment, she had to club together with other girls to afford it, and although she got the occasional copy back, it was always dog-eared by then.

When she went to bed, she lay staring bleakly into the darkness. The house seemed very quiet without the rumble of her father's voice from downstairs, and the murmur of her mother's answers. It wasn't fair. Why did her dad have to get killed? Who'd call her 'my bonny little lass' now? Who'd care about what happened to her?

She rolled over and when Eva protested sleepily, poked her backside out so that she shoved Eva and Polly closer together. But it was a while before she slept.

CHAPTER THREE

The next morning, Lizzie's mother put on the new black clothes again and smoothed them down self-consciously, before sighing at her reflection in the front room mirror.

Lizzie walked across to peer at herself. 'I don't see why I should have to wear this.' She tugged at the black armband which had been sewn for the funeral and which her mother had handed her after breakfast.

'You'll wear that for the first month to show respect for your father!' Meg snapped.

'I don't need to show other people how I feel!' Lizzie felt the desperate need for her dad surge up again and pounded her chest. 'It's inside me – all the time.'

'Don't you cheek me like that! You know your father wouldn't have stood for it.'

Meg turned away, trying to calm down, when all she felt like was rushing back upstairs to weep in private. It seemed as if she couldn't weep enough to clear her grief, somehow. That morning she had woken up alone in the big bed and felt the shock of bereavement all over again at finding no Stanley lying beside her. She had had to force herself out of bed to get the family ready for school and work.

Normally, by now, everyone was out and she could have her little sit-down, as she always thought of it. She would get a cup of tea and take a bit of time to catch her breath before the next lot of jobs had to be done. But now – now she didn't know how she would cope with everything. Lodgers would make far more work, but that was the only way she could see of earning money, so somehow she must find the energy to do it.

'Come on!' she snapped. 'I don't want to take all day about this.'

She and Lizzie went first to Dearden's, walking side by side through the streets, not saying anything. Outside the big corner grocery store with its maroon paint and gold lettering they both paused instinctively.

Lizzie looked for the card to show her mother and gasped. 'It's gone! The card's not there. What's happened to it?'

'They'll have taken it out of the window till they've seen us.' At least, Meg hoped that was what had happened. She squared her shoulders. 'Well, let's go in, then.' She knew Sally Dearden slightly from church, but today she was here to ask a favour and felt stiff and awkward, for she hated being beholden to anyone.

They waited for Mrs Dearden to serve a customer, Lizzie watching everything with bright-eyed interest, Meg with her shoulders slumping dispiritedly, though she didn't realise it.

Just as that customer was leaving, there was a noise outside and a motor car drew up in front of the shop. People in the street stopped to stare as a lady was helped down.

Sally moved forward at once, saying to Meg, 'Excuse me. I always serve Mrs Pilby myself.' The girl serving the other customer rushed forward to open the door and place a chair for the wife of the richest man in Overdale.

As Lizzie and her mother moved to the back of the shop, a door opened behind them and a lad peeped out. 'She's got the Wolsely Cavallos today, I see,' he said to Lizzie with an air of superiority. 'Do you know, they drove one of those all the way from Land's End to John O'Groats without a single engine stop? They're the most reliable cars around, they are, but I still prefer Mr Pilby's Rover. One of those won the International Tourist Trophy last year. Wouldn't I like to see him open the throttle on it! I'm going to drive one myself when I grow up. Fast.'

Lizzie scowled because she hadn't much idea what he was talking about. She was later to find that the warehouse lad was car crazy. He left a few months after she started at Dearden's to go and work for a firm making motor cars in Manchester.

While Mrs Pilby was tasting a piece of the new cheese, Mrs Dearden turned to frown in their direction and Fred disappeared smartly through the door. Lizzie and her mother hovered at the back, trying not to look as if they were listening to what was being said, but listening avidly, all the same. Everyone in town knew the people from the big house, by sight at least, especially 'the second Mrs P' as Sam had called this one the other day, rolling his eyes to indicate his scorn for her fancy ways.

Lizzie agreed with him. She had seen Mr Pilby's second and much younger wife riding around in her swanky motor car, looking down her nose at people on foot. Like many other children, Lizzie had pulled faces at the car as it passed and had minced along the street more than once, holding a stick and mocking the way Mrs Pilby tapped her long handled parasol on the ground as she strolled through the town centre.

She looked at the lady's wide-brimmed hat with its heaped feathers and flowers, wondering what kept that huge edifice sitting so straight and steady on her head. Her mother's elbow jabbing into her ribs made her realise that she was staring, so she turned round and examined the display of teas on the shelves at the rear. She hadn't realised there were so many sorts of tea, or that you could pay so much for a packet of the fancy stuff.

It was a further fifteen minutes before Mrs Dearden was free to attend to the Kershaws, by which time Mrs Pilby had considered several items but had made only a couple of personal purchases, for Mr Dearden visited her housekeeper every week for the grocery order.

Lizzie edged a bit closer as Mrs Pilby stood up to leave. If I was rich like her, I wouldn't look so sulky, she thought. What's *she* got to be miserable about? I bet she has cream cake every day for tea an' she can buy all the comics she wants.

When the lady turned and picked up her parasol, Lizzie saw that the girl behind the other counter was just cutting a pound of butter and had her hands all greasy, so she hurried forward to open the door, though she received not a word of thanks for doing so.

But Sally noticed and nodded to herself. Good manners.

It all helped. 'Well, then, Mrs Kershaw, you'd better come through into the back before anyone else wants serving.'

Behind the shop was a long narrow L-shaped room, built on a few years previously to connect the warehouse which lay across the back yard with the shop. It provided a packing space to divide the bulk deliveries into more manageable amounts. Here, the lad who'd peeped out at the car was weighing sugar and putting it into blue paper bags, then folding the top of each down neatly.

'Smarten up, Fred Ross!' Mrs Dearden snapped as they passed him. 'I thought you'd be on to the currants by now. An' who asked you to peep out when Mrs Pilby came in, pray?'

'I just wanted to see the car, Mrs D.'

'You and your cars!' But it was said without any real heat. 'Just make sure you give full measure. We don't want the inspector to find our stuff underweight.'

'Right you are, Mrs D.'

'But don't be over-generous, either. We're not here to give stuff away.'

Lizzie watched Fred pour sugar on to the scales, then use the narrowed end of the brass weighing pan to pour it into a bag, spilling some as he did so. He's all fingers and thumbs, that one, she thought scornfully. I could do better than that. She followed her mother into the office in the corner, standing beside her as the two women sat down to discuss details.

'I've decided to give your Lizzie a month's trial,' Mrs Dearden announced. 'The pay's five shillings a week, for half days and all day Saturday, and she'll get a cup of tea and a bun mid-morning or mid-afternoon, whenever there's a free moment, and dinner at mid-day on Saturdays, though she'll have to eat it quickly whenever there's a lull. Oh, and your family gets ten per cent off any groceries bought here and first chance to buy damaged stuff cheaply. But if the lass breaks or spills things by handling them carelessly, the cost will be docked from her wages. Accidents happen and you can't prevent them, but I will not have any fooling around in my shop.'

'That's very kind of you, Mrs Dearden,' Meg said, in her

best accent, the one she had learned to use as a maid. 'I'm sure Lizzie will do her very best.'

'If she doesn't, she won't be staying.' Sally fixed the girl with an eagle eye and noted with interest that she didn't flinch or look cowed. In fact, she liked the way the lass held her head up and looked you straight in the eyes. She wouldn't hire an assistant with shifty eyes, no matter how sorry she felt for the family.

She turned back to the mother. 'You have to get a paper from the school to say it's all right for her to work here half-time.' She frowned to see Mrs Kershaw's thin white face and hear her rasping breath. Not a strong woman, and not the sort to cope well with adversity, she decided. Got a die-away air about her already. Well, the lass doesn't breathe funny, at least, though she has the same thin face and dark hair, but her eyes are green not washed-out blue. And life hasn't hit her so hard yet. It will, though, it always does. There's few of us come through unscathed. She thought of her own husband, with his chest getting worse by the year. He no longer had the stamina to stand on his feet all day. If she hadn't been around to take over the front shop, she didn't know what they'd have done – though her son, Peter, was starting to shape up now.

'I'll supply the pinnies,' she said, turning to practical matters once more. After all, she had a pile of aprons left from when her niece had worked in the shop, though Helen was married now with a baby on the way. Providing the aprons would be a way of helping the widow without seeming to offer charity. 'You'll wash them yourself,' she added firmly, 'and I expect them to be properly starched and ironed, mind. You'll need a clean one every day, child, an' you'd better keep an extra one here as well, in case something gets spilled.'

Lizzie nodded eagerly, her smile lighting up her face like a beacon. 'When can I start?'

At the works that morning, Sam stopped next to Percy. 'How's things going at home, lad?'

'All right. Mam coped this morning without getting too

upset an' I put a notice in Minter's window on my way here, offering lodgings. Let's hope we find someone soon.' That would, he hoped, take his mother's mind off her loss.

Sam looked at him thoughtfully. Mrs Kershaw would suit the Harpers much better than Mrs Blackburn did. He'd speak to them. It tickled him that two fine ladies should rely on him as they were doing. But it'd been a profitable connection so far and who knew what it'd do for him in the future? 'Need any help moving your stuff up to the attic?'

'No. There won't be much an' our Lizzie's stronger than she looks.'

'Need any more furniture?'

Percy shrugged. 'We'll see how we go. I'll put up some hooks in the attic for me an' Johnny to hang our clothes on. An' we'll manage with a mattress on the floor for now, just get a new one for the lodgers. We have to watch our pennies.' Percy cleared his throat and said huskily, 'An' I'd just like to thank you for being such a good friend to me.'

Sam shrugged, feeling a brief trickle of guilt about taking the purse, then telling himself not to be so bleedin' soft. He clapped Percy on the back. 'Well, if you can't help a mate when he's in trouble, who can you help? I'll come round to see your mam tonight about that job for Lizzie.'

Percy blushed bright red.

Sam stared at him, eyes narrowed. 'What's up?'

'She's – um – found herself another job, at least we think she has. Mam's gone over to Dearden's with her this morning. They want a half-timer in the shop.'

'Oh, do they?'

Percy laid his hand on his friend's arm. 'Mam an' I both appreciate what you tried to do, but I don't think Lizzie would fit in here at Pilby's. The work's not all that interesting, an' when she's bored, she can be a young devil. So I reckon it's best if she goes to Dearden's. She won't have time to be bored there. I hope you won't take offence? I mean, it was very kind of you to—'

The foreman strolled over. 'Nothing to do, Percy lad?'

'Oh, sorry, Mr Symes.'

Sam moved on, whistling through his teeth, and Ben Symes stood watching him, a frown on his plump face. He was sorry to see Percy Kershaw taking up with that one, but there was no accounting for friendships. Even he tried to avoid outright confrontations with Thoxby, though he'd never admit that to anyone. There was something about him that made you feel nervous, something just a bit threatening underneath all those easy smiles.

Both the Kershaws stopped dead by unspoken consent at the school gate, Lizzie to scowl at the building where she had spent so many unhappy hours, Meg to catch her breath.

Mr Dacing, the headmaster, looked out of the window and saw them coming, so stripped off his sleeve protectors and left his class to the next-door teacher's supervision. As the classroom was right next to his office he had no worries about the pupils misbehaving. Which was more than could be said for young Lizzie. He'd lost count of the number of times she'd been in trouble, though mostly just from high spirits or boredom. She wasn't a sly or nasty child.

Eva was a different kettle of fish entirely, a good little worker and the cleverest girl in the school. Alice Blake thought a lot of her and they had hoped she'd get to secondary school next year, but that was probably out of the question now. Life could be very hard at times.

He didn't allow himself to dwell on that. The world was full of troubles and let alone you couldn't take your pupils' troubles on yourself, there were worse cases than the Kershaws' in times like these: children who grew thinner by the week, who fell asleep over their lessons, who came to school hungry day after day. He'd asked the Council about getting up a subscription from the wealthier citizens of the town to provide free breakfasts for those in need, and the Mayor had given his approval, on condition that no food went to the undeserving whose parents drank up their earnings. But what the Council didn't know, the Council wouldn't worry about. Mr Dacing wasn't going to refuse a pupil a meal because of a father's sins. He hated to see hunger in a child's eyes.

When he greeted the Kershaws, he noticed how tired the mother looked and how full of herself Lizzie was. 'Please come this way, Mrs Kershaw. May I offer you my sincere condolences on your loss? And those of my staff.'

'Thank you.' Meg's voice was a mere whisper. She felt intimidated by the headmaster, so tall and gentlemanly, with his white upright collar and dark suit. She had never liked coming here to the school, never, and had left it to Stanley whenever she could.

'How may I help you?' Mr Dacing indicated a chair.

'I'd like – if you agree – my Lizzie's been offered a job, you see – but she needs your permission to – it's part-time, of course. She's only t-twelve, though she turns thirteen in March.'

He nodded and smiled encouragingly. 'And where is this job?'

Lizzie could see that Mam had gone breathless, like she did sometimes when she was nervous. 'It's at Dearden's, sir. Working in the shop.' She could not prevent a smile at the thought of it.

He was surprised. 'I see. A good opportunity, Dearden's. Well, I only hope you'll apply yourself better there than you have done here, Lizzie.' His tone said he wasn't very optimistic about that.

She stifled a sigh. 'Yessir.'

He went to the big cupboard at the back of the room and pulled out a piece of paper headed PERMISSION TO WORK HALF-TIME, smoothing it carefully as he laid it down on his blotter. There was always something very satisfying about making the first marks on a pristine sheet. He took out his new fountain pen, unscrewed it carefully and tested out the nib on his blotter, before beginning to write in immaculate copperplate script.

His two companions waited, not daring to interrupt.

When he had finished, Mr Dacing passed the paper to Mrs

Kershaw. 'You have to sign it.' She read it and nodded, then signed with the steel-nibbed ordinary pen he passed her. After that, he signed at the bottom, blotting the paper gently to make sure the ink was completely dry before he folded it, for he could not abide smudges.

He allus messes around, Lizzie thought, standing half behind her mother and glowering down at her shoes, which were hurting her after all the walking. He can't do nothin' quick, he can't.

'Listen to me, Lizzie.'

She jerked to attention. 'Sir?'

'You are to work harder in future on your half-days at school.' He gestured to the piece of paper. 'This doesn't mean you're stopping learning, you know. You'll still be coming here half-time.'

'No, sir. I mean, yes, sir.' But she would be able to learn real things at the shop, she thought, quickly cheering up. Not silly stuff like Miss Blake taught them.

'When is Lizzie required to start work, Mrs Kershaw?' he asked, folding the paper carefully into three and slipping it into an envelope, before passing it to her.

'Tomorrow, if that's all right with you, Mr Dacing? The sooner the better, really.'

Eva watched Lizzie come into the class and make her apologies to the teacher. They were both in the same standard because she was better at schoolwork than Lizzie was, but they didn't sit together. Eva sat next to Clara Grey at the back, with the top scholars, while her sister sat at the front where Miss Blake could keep an eye on her. And from now on Lizzie would be sitting with the part-timers at the side, which was even worse in her sister's opinion.

For a moment, looking at the sunshine streaming in through the tall, narrow windows, Eva wished she too had been out walking round town, then she looked down at her page and smiled. No, she didn't. It'd mean she'd have to go part-time and she didn't want to do that. She dipped the pen nib carefully into the ink and drew another stroke, enjoying the way the line of ink curved down the page.

'Very good, Eva,' Miss Blake's voice approved from behind her. 'You're developing a fine hand.'

From behind the teacher's back, Lizzie beamed across the room and nodded her head vigorously to indicate success – till her deskmate jabbed her in the ribs.

Not wanting to get into trouble, Eva ignored her sister. Next year, she thought gloomily, she'd probably have to go part-time herself and sit at the side of the class as if she didn't matter any more. It wasn't fair. She wanted quite desperately to go to the secondary school. If her father hadn't been killed, he would have managed the fees and the cost of the uniform somehow, she knew that. It just wasn't *fair!*

When Meg arrived home from the visit to the school, she made herself a cup of tea and allowed herself a ten-minute sit down, for she felt exhausted already. Just as she had poured the boiling water into her own little teapot, however, someone knocked on the front door. 'Oh, bother!' she muttered and put a tea cosy over the pot.

At the door she found Mr Beckins, the new manager from the brewery, with two men standing behind him, shuffling their feet and looking embarrassed. She scowled at them all impartially. If Mr Beckins hadn't insisted on buying that horse, her Stanley would be alive now.

He nodded. 'Mrs Kershaw.'

She nodded back and folded her arms.

'I wonder if we could come in? I – we have something for you.'

She could guess what it was so she led the way into the parlour, feeling a pang as she went inside it. She was even going to lose this, the room that was her pride and joy, because the lodgers would want somewhere to sit. Manners obliged her to offer the men seats, but she kept Stanley's big armchair for herself, feeling comforted by the shape of it, as if he were still nearby, somehow, watching over her. 'What can I do for you, Mr Beckins?'

'I . . .' He cleared his throat. 'That is, the owners of the brewery want you to take this.' He got up and walked across to press an envelope into her hand. 'It's something to help you out till you get on your feet again.'

'I'll never get on my feet properly again without my Stanley,' she said, but took the envelope. Pride kept her from looking inside it, but she hoped they'd been generous.

Frank Beckins turned to one of the men. 'Peter?'

'The lads took up a collection as well, Mrs Kershaw,' he said, standing up and twisting his checked cap round in his big calloused hands as he spoke. 'We thought a lot of your Stanley.' He could not resist a sideways scowl at the new foreman. They none of them thought much of this new fellow and his penny-pinching ways, but he was thick as thieves with the owners. 'So we'd like you to accept this, with our *sincere* sympathy.'

Meg accepted a second, heavier envelope, full of coins. 'Thank you, Peter. I'm grateful to you all. Tell the men thank you for me. It's going to be a – a bit hard. With the children still so young.'

'But your Percy is, I believe, working at Pilby's?' Frank Beckins said, angry that she was not showing more gratitude. 'At least you'll have a man's wage coming into the house still.'

'And my Percy was going to take a year on half-time, to get himself some more schooling. He won't be able to do that now, will he? And it's all *your* fault.' Suddenly Meg couldn't bear to see him sitting there in her parlour, looking down his nose at her. 'If you hadn't insisted on buying that animal . . . my Stanley *told* you it was a bad 'un . . .' Her voice broke and she buried her head in her hands, sobbing.

Peter stared at the floor. She was right about that, and Beckins was still insisting on keeping that brute, which was just asking for trouble. It was the most edgy drayhorse he'd ever seen, for all its good looks. Twitched at the mere sight of a dog coming towards it in the street. No one liked driving it. Suddenly, hearing her sobbing, realising how much trouble his own wife would be in if anything happened to him – for none of their four children was near working age – he said gruffly, 'We're getting rid of that horse.'

Meg gaped at him. 'Is it still there? Haven't you had it put down?'

Beckins glared at them all. 'That's a valuable animal. We can't just buy and sell horses all the time, or what would happen to the owners' profits?'

Meg's voice came out shrilly and she made no effort to moderate it. 'And what are you going to do about the *next* man that brute kills? Or maybe it'll be one of the stable boys another time.'

Peter exchanged glances and nods with his companion. 'Well, none of us'll drive it, Mrs Kershaw. Nor shall we let the yard boys near it.'

Beckins coughed sharply. 'This is *not* the time to discuss something like that!'

Peter stood up. 'No, but I think Mrs Kershaw deserves reassuring that we're going to get rid of it.' He bobbed his head awkwardly to Meg and walked towards the door, remembering with a shudder the mess the horse had made of Stanley's lower body.

Beckins gave her a sour look and followed him out.

Meg had to make a huge effort to force herself upright. 'Please thank the owners for their kindness,' she said formally at the front door, but as she turned to Peter, her voice softened. 'And thank the men, too. For everything.'

When she had shut the door behind them, she trailed into the kitchen and freshened up her tea with some hot water, before opening the envelope.

'Five pounds! The mean devils! Is that all the value the owners set on my Stanley's life?'

The other envelope, from the men, contained over ten pounds, much of it in loose change. She was touched, knowing how much it had cost men who had their own families to look after to give so generously.

She felt a bit shaky still, after her anger, and her breath was rasping in her throat as it did sometimes, but the money was comforting, sitting there in little piles on the table. Then she remembered suddenly that someone had stolen her purse from this very room and scooped the coins into her apron, rushing upstairs to hide this money in her best hat box.

'I'll have to get on or the children will be home for their dinner,' she muttered afterwards as she finished drinking the last of the stewed tea. But it was a while before she started her housework. What was the point? What was the point of anything now?

At dinner time, the two sisters walked home together, with Lizzie boasting of all she had seen in the shop and how much she was looking forward to working there. Eva was silent over the meal, and when they met some other girls on the way back to afternoon school, she managed to drop behind a bit and get away from Lizzie's talk about the shop. She didn't feel like chatting. She felt plain miserable about everything.

That afternoon, when the final bell rang, the pupils tidied up their desks enthusiastically and rushed off as soon as Miss Blake nodded permission. Eva gestured to Lizzie to go ahead without her and lingered. She didn't want to go home and have her mother weep all over her again. So she rearranged the books on a shelf and dusted the window ledge absent-mindedly.

'No home to go to, Eva?'

She jumped in shock. 'Ooh! I didn't hear you come back in, miss.'

Alice Blake hesitated. You shouldn't have favourites, but she couldn't help it with this child. If she had ever had a daughter – which she hadn't and never would now that she was forty-five – she'd have wanted one like this. Clever and yet gentle. Thoughtful, too. 'Are you all right, dear?'

Eva nodded, but to her dismay, tears suddenly flooded her eyes.

Alice looked down at the big blue eyes, bright with tears, and was betrayed into giving her pupil a quick hug, something she would not normally have done. But the girl was suffering. You got them every now and then, special ones like Eva. As if God had given you a reward for all the 'unspecial' ones you had to deal with the rest of the time.

'Did I get on the list for going to secondary school, miss? Did Mr Dacing say it was all right?'

'Of course you got on the list.'

'I won't be able to go there now, but — I'd like to think I was good enough. So could you leave my name on the list, please?'

Alice Blake nodded.

'Don't tell Mam, though, will you? She'll only ask you to cross my name out, say it's a waste of time.'

'No, I won't withdraw your name.'

'I bet I'll have to go part-time next year, like our Lizzie,' Eva whispered, staring down at her clenched hands. 'But I want to go to secondary school and learn to be a teacher, like you. I want it so *much*. It's just not fair!'

'We'll have to see if we can think of something before then.' She felt sure Eva would be offered a scholarship to secondary school — the child was quite exceptional. It would be a crying shame if she lost her one big chance to make something of her life.

Frowning, Alice Blake decided to go and see her old friend, Mavis Pilby, to ask whether the family could see their way to doing anything to help this most deserving case. The Pilbys did a lot of good in this town — well, they owned half of it, didn't they? — so why not seek their help for Eva? And she could talk to the manager of the brewery. Mr Kershaw had worked there a long time. Surely they'd be prepared to help the children?

Eva was fiddling with a pencil. 'Mam says I have to look for a Saturday job.'

Alice sighed. That would be the beginning of the end. It'd

be just Saturdays at first, then skipping school to 'help out' wherever Eva worked when things got busy or some other worker was ill. She had seen it happen time and time again with the needy families. It would be terrible if it happened to this child!

It was then that she had the idea. She didn't say anything about it, of course. She always liked to think things through first. But if – no, she'd wait till later to work it all out. 'Get off home, now, child,' she said gently. 'And try not to worry. Something'll turn up. It usually does.'

Eva trailed out, feeling comforted. She'd never seen Miss Blake hug anyone before, not even when Jimmy Pikely broke his arm. She knew she was the teacher's pet and she liked that. Who cared what the others said? Miss Blake was wonderful, with her gored skirts and her crisp white blouses. Even the dark aprons she wore at school were more elegant than other teachers' aprons. Miss Blake had *style*.

And it didn't matter if she wasn't good–looking. Where did being good–looking get you anyway? Eva sniffed scornfully. It got you into trouble with the lads, being good–looking did, like Mary Holden's sister Flo. And then you had to get married and have babies and stay at home all day looking after them. Well, she wasn't going to do that! She'd go mad with nothing to do but housework. If she couldn't become a teacher, she'd find some other way to escape her mother. She didn't much like their mam, whatever it said in the Bible about honouring your parents.

Tears filled her eyes again and the world turned to a blur of colours. Why did her dad have to die like that? Life wasn't fair. And it was only going to get more unfair, so far as she could see.

That night, Sam went out on the prowl. He wanted to see what the town was like after everything had shut down. He strolled along as the Town Hall clock struck two, enjoying himself. There was a moon to light his way and the only sound was his own footsteps, though once a dog barked as he walked past a house.

He stopped and frowned down at his feet. He hadn't worn his work clogs, but even his best shoes had metal heel and toe tips to make the leather last longer and they made too much noise. He'd have to buy a pair of shoes with rubber soles. Hmm. His preference for clogs was well known at work and in Fowler's shoe shop on York Road. He'd better go over to Manchester and buy some quiet shoes there. No one knew who you were in Manchester – or cared.

What about Gran, though? She'd notice the new shoes and wonder why he needed them. He'd have to hide them somewhere she couldn't reach. Eeh, there were a lot of things to think about. He wasn't like Josh Lumb. He liked to think things out and plan for them. Whatever Josh said about its being easy pickings, so long as you didn't go out thieving too often, Sam intended to tread very carefully at first.

And any road, it wasn't just a question of getting the stuff, but of selling it for a decent price. He had to sort out that side of things, too. Though on the other hand, he had a few contacts already from his buying and selling of this and that – so maybe it'd all fit in quite well. If he took a bit of care. And he would. Josh might only go for money when he broke into a house, but there were other things you could take which sold well, things like fancy clocks. Look at the prices he'd got for the Harpers' oddments.

A noise alerted Sam long before he saw the bobby in the distance. He slipped down a back alley and watched the fellow pass. Stupid sods, policemen. Listen to the row that one's boots were making. You could hear him coming a mile off.

When he got home, Sam lay in bed, wide awake and excited, for all he'd have to be up early to get to work. He was going to do it. Oh, yes. And he was going to make himself a lot of money. By the time that little lass grew old enough to marry, he'd be in a position to look after her properly. Funny, the way he'd taken to the idea of wedding Lizzie. But he had. And he always got what he wanted.

CHAPTER FOUR

When Percy got home that evening, a bit late after a quick visit to the pub with Sam after work, the children had already eaten but Meg had a place set for his tea, with the remains of a loaf covered by a cloth in the middle of the table and a big helping of hearty stew bubbling gently on the gas stove. She looked red-eyed, but a little brighter than before.

'Come and have your tea, Percy love. The children have eaten. I sent them out to play because I wanted to talk to you.'

'Eva doesn't like playing out,' he joked. 'She'd rather bury her head in a book.'

Meg's voice was grim. 'She's playing out today. And she's helping out round the house more from now on. So is our Lizzie.'

So far as he could see, Lizzie already did quite a bit round the house, and usually quite cheerfully, too, but he didn't waste his breath saying so, just went to wash his hands in the scullery behind the kitchen, calling over his shoulder as he went, 'I got the money out of the savings bank at lunch time and paid Sam what we owed him. I got a bit extra out for you, too.'

'What? Oh, yes, the rent. I'd forgotten about that. And someone found my purse in the park today — empty, of course — and brought it round. Stealing my money at a time like that . . .' Her voice broke and she set the dish of stew on the table, then went to fuss over the stove. She knew how hungry men always were when they came home from a hard day's work, how they didn't like to talk until they'd had time to relax a bit, though from the smell of his breath, Percy had already relaxed

47

with a sup of ale on the way home. She wouldn't mention that now, though she'd keep an eye on it. What they'd all do if he took up drinking, she didn't know.

A few minutes later, seeing he'd taken the edge off his appetite, she brought him a big mug of tea and some for herself in the china cup and saucer she always insisted on, because tea tasted better in it.

Sitting down, she said abruptly, 'Mr Beckins came round to see me.'

Percy stopped eating to look sideways at her. 'Oh?'

'An' the brewery owners sent us some money to help tide us over.' Her voice became bitter. '*Five pounds!*'

'The mean buggers!' He saw her look of shock. 'Sorry for the language, Mam, but it is mean after all the years Dad worked there.'

She nodded. 'The men took up a collection as well. Just over ten pounds, they gave me.'

'That was kind of 'em.'

Meg began to fiddle with her teaspoon. 'I've been thinking. About the lodgers, you know.'

He laid his hand over hers. 'I've been thinking about that, too. There's no need for you to do it, Mam. We can move to a smaller house and manage on my money. I don't want you wearing yourself out.'

'We'll have what Lizzie earns now, as well as your money. It's only a few shillings, but it'll make a difference.'

He stared at her, mug halfway to his lips. 'She did get the job, then?' Since his mother had not mentioned it, he'd assumed Lizzie had been unsuccessful.

'Oh, yes. Mrs Dearden was very kind. But – the thing is, I don't want to leave this house, Percy.' She looked around and tears filled her eyes. 'We've been happy here. And it's got memories of my Stanley.' It was also better than most other houses in the Southlea district. She liked that, too.

'But—'

'I think if I take two lodgers, women perhaps, friends who would share a room – if I do that, then we can manage all right here if we're careful.' She glanced quickly sideways at him. 'If you don't mind giving me some of your money every week, that is?'

'You know I don't mind. You can have most of it.'

She let out a sigh. She had known she could rely on him, but it still made her feel better to hear him say it. 'Thanks, love. If you and Johnny move into the attic, I'll take your room and that'll leave the big front bedroom for the lodgers.'

Percy sat frowning. 'Hmm. I'll get some paper out and we'll do this properly, work out what money we'll need.' You couldn't beat seeing the proof in figures, so far as he was concerned. He'd always liked arithmetic. He pushed away the empty plate. 'That was lovely, Mam. No one makes stew like you do.' While she cleared up, he found an old exercise book and pencil, then made her sit down and help him with the calculations.

'All right,' he said when they'd gone through the money side of it twice, just to be sure, 'let's see if we can find two lodgers. Women, mind, since they'll be less work for you. Then we'll give it a try, see how we go. If it's too much for you, we can still move to a smaller house.'

'Yes, Percy.'

Although neither of them realised it at the time, from that evening she treated him as head of the household, deferred to him, gave him the biggest chop, the armchair that had been his father's. But Eva noticed. And Lizzie. Their mother had never fussed over her daughters the way she had over her menfolk and now it was, 'Get our Percy a cup of tea!' or 'Pass our Percy the paper.' Even when Lizzie's feet were killing her after working in the shop, or Eva had homework to do, they still had to get up and serve their brother.

Two evenings later, there was a knock on the front door and when Eva opened it, she found her teacher standing there. She couldn't help beaming. 'Miss Blake!' Then the smile faded. 'There's nothing wrong, is there?'

'Nothing's wrong, no. I'd just like to speak to your mother about an idea I've had. Would it be convenient for me to see her now?'

'Oh, yes.' She showed the visitor into the front room and went rushing into the kitchen.

Meg's heart sank when she heard it was the teacher. 'What have you been doing now?' she asked Lizzie.

'I haven't been doing nothing!'

'Haven't been doing *anything*!' Eva corrected automatically. 'And she isn't in trouble, Mam. I'd have known if she was.'

In the front room, Meg sat down opposite her visitor and Eva stood behind her mother. Lizzie crept into the hall to listen. She knew she hadn't misbehaved, but teachers got mad at you for nothing, so she wanted to know what was being said.

'I'm so sorry about your loss, Mrs Kershaw,' Miss Blake began.

Meg nodded, because every time someone said that a big lump came into her throat and she found it hard to speak.

'Eva was telling me she hoped to find herself a little Saturday job.' She cocked her head on one side and gazed at Mrs Kershaw questioningly.

'Oh. Well, yes. I'm afraid we shall need every penny. They all have to p-pull their weight.' Lizzie had complained that her shoes were too tight and it made her feet hurt to stand up in them all the time at the shop, but there was good wear left in them still so she wasn't going to replace them yet.

'I was wondering if I could hire your Eva to come and help me out at home on Saturdays? I could pay her a shilling and give her a good meal at midday.'

Meg blinked. This was the last thing she'd expected to hear from Miss Blake. 'Doing what?'

'Housework, running errands, washing my china bits and pieces. Whatever needs doing.'

Eva nudged her mother and Meg looked back to see a radiant face behind her.

'Well – I can't see any objection.'

'I'd *love* to help you, Miss Blake.' Eva's eyes were glowing. 'I'll work ever so hard.'

Alice smiled at her. 'I know you will, dear. I've been meaning to look for some help for a while and when you said you were seeking a Saturday job, I knew you'd be ideal. I couldn't have a noisy person clattering around. I do enjoy my peace and quiet at weekends.'

'Well, that's settled, then,' Meg said, pleased at the prospect of more money coming in.

Outside in the hall, Lizzie scowled. Trust their Eva to get a soft job like that. She winced as she turned and her shoe rubbed a blister on her heel. If her dad had been alive, he wouldn't have expected her to wear shoes that were too small. She went out across the yard to the lav and sat there alone in the darkness until the urge to weep had passed. It didn't do any good crying, she told herself. No one cared how she felt now.

Three days later, on Saturday, Peter Dearden noticed that the new girl was limping. She was a nice lass, very willing and quick to learn, but today she seemed a bit slower than usual. At first he wondered if her early enthusiasm for the new job was wearing off. After a while, however, he noticed the limp she was trying to hide, the way she stood on one foot when she thought no one was looking, and decided that her feet must be hurting. He went to whisper in his mother's ear and she, too, began to watch Lizzie.

When there was a lull, Sally sent Lizzie out to the back for a quick cup of tea and a bun. She'd always found that if you fed your staff mid-morning, they worked better. And she had an arrangement with the baker's across the road to buy stale buns or cake left over from the previous day, so it didn't cost much. After a minute, she followed Lizzie out to the packing area and, not seeing her, raised one eyebrow at young Fred. 'Where is she?'

'In the lav.'

Sally peered outside, saw a movement in the corner and

marched across the yard, to find Lizzie with her black stocking off dabbing at her foot with a handkerchief dampened under the outside tap. 'What—' she began, then she noticed the foot. A huge blister on the heel, broken and weeping, and another on the big toe. How on earth had the child put up with that all morning?

'Your shoes are too tight,' she said in a firm voice. 'You must get some more.'

Lizzie hung her head. 'I'm sorry, Mrs Dearden. I asked Mam and she said there was still a lot of wear in these.'

Sally drew in a long slow breath. You didn't blame a mother in front of a child, but it made her feel angry that Mrs Kershaw hadn't even checked her daughter's feet before refusing, as she herself would have done. 'You can't put that shoe back on again. I've got some slippers you can use for the rest of the day. They're black, so no one will notice. Come with me.'

'I'm that sorry, Mrs Dearden.' Lizzie limped after the broad figure of her employer up the stairs into the family's living quarters, a place she'd never been before. 'I won't let it stop me working. I'll make up for—'

'Here. Sit down on that chair and let me put some sticking plasters on your foot. What's the other foot like?'

'Oh, not as bad.'

'Show me.' She inspected it. 'It's just as bad.' But the lass hadn't complained. Not so much as a whimper. If Peter wasn't so sharp-eyed, no one would even have known.

'I'm sorry to be such a trouble,' Lizzie said miserably, sure she was going to lose her lovely new job.

Sally guessed instantly what had brought tears to those big green eyes. 'I'm not going to sack you, you silly child. But from now on, you're to come and tell me if anything's troubling you. *Anything.* Is that clear?'

'Yes, Mrs Dearden.'

'And wipe those tears away!'

Lizzie fumbled through her pockets. 'I – I've lost my handkerchief.'

'Tch!' Sally went into her bedroom and came out with a perfectly folded and ironed handkerchief. 'Here, use this!'

Lizzie mopped her face and blew her nose, then looked down in dismay at the soggy square of material. 'I'll w-wash this before I bring it back.' Her voice wobbled, because the kindness was shaking her self-control.

'Right, then, go down and eat your bun, then get back to work.'

'I can go straight back to make up for the time I've lost,' Lizzie offered, but her stomach growled and betrayed her.

Sally could not help smiling. 'I think we can afford the time for you to eat a bun, child.'

'Yes, Mrs Dearden. And – and thank you for helping me. I'll ask Mam again about the shoes tonight.'

When Lizzie had gone, Sally sat on for a moment, lost in thought. Meg Kershaw couldn't be that short of money. She'd heard that the owners of the brewery had given her something, and the men had taken up a collection, too. It must be just a reluctance to spend and the child would have difficulty changing that. Lips pressed into a thin, tight line, she took out a piece of notepaper and penned a short letter. When she went downstairs, she gave it to young Fred and ordered him to call in at Lizzie's house when he took the next lot of local deliveries out on his bicycle.

Meg heard the knock at the door and grunted in exasperation. Just when she was in the middle of making Percy's favourite cake, too! She wiped her hands and went to open the front door. 'Yes?'

The lad held out an envelope. 'Mrs Dearden sent this. I'm to wait for an answer.'

Meg took the missive with a sinking heart. Lizzie must be in trouble. Already! Could that child do nothing right?

The note was quite brief:

Dear Mrs Kershaw

Lizzie's shoes are too tight and have given her blisters. I would like to supply her with a new pair immediately, ones which fit so that she can do her work properly. She's given satisfaction so far and will be continuing here after her month's trial. I can take the cost out of her wages at a shilling a week, if you like.

However, I do not approve of the shoes obtainable from the Clothing Club. My assistants are on their feet all day and good shoes wear better in these circumstances and are gentler on the feet. I have an arrangement with Fowler's Shoe Store for a discount on my staff's footwear purchases, so I shall take Lizzie across in a quiet moment and get her a new pair, if you do not object? You may tell the errand boy your answer.

Sally Dearden

Meg stared at the piece of paper angrily. Lizzie must have been complaining. There was plenty of wear left in those shoes. Plenty. However, you couldn't offend an employer. Grudgingly, she told the lad to thank Mrs Dearden and say it was all right to get the shoes.

But it wasn't all right. She felt angry and shamed. And it was all Lizzie's fault. Stanley had spoiled that child, but Meg had no intention of doing so. Her eldest daughter had to learn to buckle down and work hard now, and above all to make things last. They all had. Tears came into her eyes again and she brushed them away wearily. What use was it crying? It didn't change anything. Stanley was gone and she'd be alone now for the rest of her life. And if she didn't keep Percy happy, she'd have no one to look after her in her old age. Even to pass the poor house terrified her, always had. They weren't going to put her in there. She'd hang herself first.

When Lizzie came home, still limping, carrying her old shoes wrapped in brown paper, she went straight to show the new ones to her mother.

Meg ignored them. 'How could you shame me like that in

front of Sally Dearden?' The anger that had been bubbling inside her all day overflowed and she slapped her daughter's face.

The other children, who'd gathered to inspect the shiny new shoes, stared at their mother in shock.

Lizzie stood frozen for a minute, then said in a wobbly voice, 'W-what did you do that for, Mam?'

'To teach you not to complain to Mrs Dearden in future.'

Lizzie burst into noisy, gulping tears.

The noise brought Percy in from the back yard. 'What's the matter?'

'She's been complaining about her shoes, that's what. And got Sally Dearden to buy her some new ones – expensive ones, too. Shoes we can't afford!'

He turned to his sister. 'Eeh, our Lizzie, have you no sense?'

'I *didn't* complain. Peter Dearden saw me limping and told his mother.'

Meg gave a scornful laugh. 'Oh, yes. It's a good way to get attention, limping is.'

Eva came forward and put an arm round her sister. 'She's got blisters from those shoes, Mam. Bad ones. I was going to ask you about new shoes myself tonight.'

'She'll complain about anything, that one will!' Meg turned round abruptly and went into the parlour, from whence issued the sound of muffled weeping.

Percy shook his head. 'You'll have to stop causing trouble, Lizzie. Mam can't cope with it.'

She smeared away the tears. 'An' I suppose I can? Does that mean running around all day with blisters on my feet?'

'A blister's nothing.' He cocked an ear. His mother's weeping had died down, but she was still sobbing and he needed to go and comfort her. 'Go and get your tea.'

Lizzie walked over to the cooker to find her food cold and congealing on a plate beside it, not even kept warm as usual. She carried it over to the table and sat picking at it, tears still trickling down her face at the injustice of her mother's accusations. Eva went to sit beside her, not saying anything, just staying with her.

'Mam's still grieving,' she murmured as she watched Lizzie push the half-empty plate away. 'She doesn't mean it.'

'She does, you know. She's never liked me. Never. Only it didn't matter so much when Dad was alive. Now, I can't do nothing right for *her*.'

Eva pulled the plate back towards her sister. 'Eat it. You need to keep up your strength. You're not the only one to suffer, you know. I was going to go on to secondary school. Miss Blake was sure I'd get a scholarship.'

Lizzie looked at her and managed a half-smile. 'Fancy wanting to stay on at school!'

'Well, I did. More than anything.'

'Sorry.' Lizzie reached out one hand and the two sisters held on to one another for a minute.

When she'd eaten what she could, Lizzie scraped the leftovers into the fire so there'd be no scolding about wasting good food, her movements slow and weary.

Percy came in, frowning. 'Mam's gone to lie down. You two girls will have to clear up tonight and get the kitchen ready for morning. An' I don't want you upsetting her again, Lizzie. Do you hear me? You're the eldest daughter and should have a bit more sense.' He scowled at them and went to sit down in a chair, picking up the evening paper with a sigh. When his dad had been alive, the evenings had been pleasant times, but now each one seemed worse than the one before, so that he dreaded coming home after work.

Lizzie banged around, clearing his plate away with hers, glaring at his bent head. It wasn't fair! Men made more work than anyone, but they never helped clear the mess up, didn't even lift a finger to help. When she and Eva had finished the washing-up, she said, 'I'm going up to bed now. I'm tired.' She was trying to hide how close she still was to tears, and was annoyed when her voice came out gruffly.

Eva waited a minute then followed her up. She found Lizzie easing off a pair of socks sticky with blood. 'Those will have to be soaked. It's a good job they're black ones.'

'I'll do it in the morning.'

'I'll do it for you now. Give them to me.'

Percy looked up as Eva came back into the kitchen. Realising he'd been a bit harsh on the girls, he opened his mouth to tell her about the new player for the Overdale football team, by way of a peace offer, but the words remained unspoken as his eyes fell on the socks. 'What are you doing?'

'Putting these to soak.'

He looked down at her feet. 'They're not yours.'

They're Lizzie's.'

His mother's complaints about Lizzie shirking her chores came back to him. 'She can do her own.'

'She's upstairs crying.' Eva went to wave the socks in his face. 'And this stickiness is blood from where her blisters have burst. You only listened to Mam's side of the story, our Percy, and that's not fair. Go up and *look* at Lizzie's feet. She's not imagining those blisters.'

He tossed the paper aside. 'I'll do just that. She's probably exaggerating to get your sympathy.'

'I'm not that stupid.' Eva led the way upstairs, determined to see justice done, peeped in to see if Lizzie was decent, then ushered their elder brother in. Lizzie took one look at him and turned her back.

'Show me your feet,' he ordered.

'It's got nowt to do with you.'

He put one hand on her shoulder, surprised at how bony it felt, and turned her round. When he knelt to examine her feet, he was shocked at what he saw. 'Eeh, lass, why didn't you say something sooner?'

'I *did!* I told Mam.'

From downstairs, Meg listened in fury to the exchange. Trust Lizzie to put her in the wrong! From her fear of getting on the wrong side of her son, a new grievance against her eldest daughter was born. A grievance that festered within her.

Percy stood up. 'I'll go and get some methylated spirit. You'll need to dab it on night and morning till your feet harden up.' He gave Lizzie a quick hug by way of an apology, then went off to get the bottle from his father's shelf of tools.

After he'd taken it upstairs, he got out one of his books but couldn't settle to it. What was the point? He'd never get that schooling now, never lift himself 'out of the ranks', as the foreman, an old soldier, called it.

He sat there for a long time, staring into the fire, wishing he had his father to talk to and ask advice of. His mother couldn't say a good word for Lizzie and yet his little sister had cheerfully gone out and got herself a job to help the family. Well, it was up to him to keep an eye on things from now on. Lizzie could be a bit silly at times and was definitely wilful, but she had a good heart. And she'd miss their father more than anyone. Except Mam, of course.

The book lay unheeded on his lap, but when Eva came to hang Lizzie's socks over the fireguard, he picked it up again and pretended to read. He didn't want to discuss his mother with her, didn't want to do anything but sit quietly by the fire tonight. When the two youngest children came in from playing out, Eva gave them a jam butty each and sent them off to bed, warning Polly not to wake Lizzie, then sat down opposite him.

'It's not going to be easy, is it?' she said, showing that she, too, did not have her mind on her book.

'No.'

'Mam isn't very good at coping, is she?'

'No. She relied on Dad a lot.'

Eva looked at him, her face set firm and looking older than her years. 'I'd better tell you now that I'm determined to get a decent education, Percy.'

He looked across at her. 'We'll have to see how we go with the lodgers. But maybe—'

'I'm still in for a scholarship. I know I have no hope of becoming a teacher now, but even an offer of a place at secondary school might help me to get something better later.'

'Maybe you could train for clerical work,' he offered.

'Maybe.' Anything would be better than working at Pilby's. She agreed with Lizzie about that.

She would talk it over with Miss Blake, Eva decided as she

sat staring into the fire. Maybe her teacher would have some idea what else she could do. A smile curved her lips at the thought of going to work at Miss Blake's neat little cottage on Saturdays. It was a bit of a walk out of town and she didn't have a bicycle like her teacher did, but it'd be worth it. And in the meantime she'd better get on with her reading. Miss Blake said you couldn't know too much. She went to sit at the table, where the gas light shone brightest.

If Percy had looked at her, he'd have seen signs of the strong woman she would one day become. But he didn't. He was too engrossed in his own worries.

Upstairs, Lizzie turned her back on her younger sister and snarled at Polly to leave her alone, then sobbed herself to sleep. Mrs D, as all the employees called her, had given her the slippers to keep and a packet of sticking plasters for under the new shoes. On Monday she'd start her first full week, doing afternoons again because it suited her employer. But Mrs D's kindness only showed her how little her own mother cared. And that was what she was crying about.

CHAPTER FIVE

September – December, 1908

The following Monday morning, after everyone had left, there was a knock on the front door of number thirty Bobbin Lane. 'What next?' Meg sighed and went to answer it, to find two ladies standing on the doorstep. They were well-dressed by local standards. Meg stiffened. She didn't need charity from anyone.

The elder of the two, a rather plain woman with the yellowish complexion of someone who wasn't well, said in a posh voice, 'I believe you're offering lodgings?'

Meg relaxed a little, but she was still wary. What did ladies like this want with lodgings in Bobbin Lane? 'Yes. Won't you come in?'

'Thank you. I'm Miss Harper and this is my sister, Miss Emma Harper. You are, I believe, Mrs Kershaw?'

'That's right.' Meg led them into the front room and lifted the blind a little; not enough to let sunlight fall on her precious square of carpet and fade it, but enough to enable her to study the visitors. Come down in the world, was her first thought, for on second inspection she saw how shabby their clothes were. But still ladies from the way they talked and moved. She rather liked the idea of having real ladies for lodgers – so long as they could pay.

Emma Harper took charge of the interview. 'What sort of accommodation are you offering, Mrs Kershaw?'

'The big front bedroom and use of this room as a sitting-room. But we haven't got anything sorted out yet, furniture and such. My husband only d-died last week.'

Both of them looked embarrassed and Emma said gruffly, 'We didn't realise – Sam didn't tell us your loss was so recent. Please accept our condolences. Would you rather we came back another day?'

'No. No, of course not.' Meg didn't want them finding somewhere else to live.

'We wouldn't need the room until next week. May we just take a glimpse at it now, though?'

Meg hadn't missed the way the other lady had been studying her surroundings. Well, stare your eyes out, she thought. You won't find any dust in my house. 'Could you give me a minute to check that everything's tidy?'

They both nodded.

Meg went slowly upstairs. It wouldn't be so much of a come-down to take *them* in. *My lady lodgers*, she'd call them.

She paused to rest at the top, because going upstairs always made her breathless, then she went into her bedroom, looking round it regretfully, feeling as if she were saying goodbye to it. She'd known it was tidy, of course she had, but she'd wanted a minute to herself here, where she and Stanley had loved one another. 'Eeh, my lad!' she whispered, looking at the photo of him as a young man which stood beside the bed. Then, taking a deep breath, she pushed the thought of her husband resolutely away. She had to be businesslike today, if she wanted to keep this house. And she did want to. Desperately.

'Would you like to come upstairs now?' she called down.

'The houses on this side of Bobbin Lane are larger than most of the others round here, aren't they?' Miss Emma commented brightly.

'Yes. These were old weavers' cottages. We have three bedrooms *and* a big second-floor attic, where the looms used to stand a hundred years ago before all the weaving got done in mills.' Well, that's what the vicar had told her once, anyway. But Meg thought the big attic windows very wasteful. They made it so hard to keep the room warm. She opened the door of her bedroom and drew back to let them pass. 'My sons will be moving up to the attic and I'll be taking their bedroom to give you this one.'

Miss Harper moved in and studied the room. 'It's larger than our present place. And your house is much cleaner, too, Mrs Kershaw, if you don't mind my saying so?'

'I used to be in service. I think I know how to look after things – though it isn't always easy with children. You'd be having this bed, so why don't you try it?'

The ladies sat down on the edge of the bed, looking very stiff and self-conscious.

'It's much comfier than our present one.' Miss Emma bounced a little, sighed and closed her eyes for a moment. Then she patted her hair into place and looked sympathetically across at her hostess. 'But I feel bad about taking your bed. And your room.'

Meg shrugged. 'I don't need a double one now.'

'Is the other furniture staying?'

Meg looked around. 'Not the ornaments, of course, but yes, if you want.'

'We have quite a few bits and pieces of our own,' Miss Emma said hesitantly. 'We wondered if you'd mind us bringing them?' Then she went very still and looked at her sister. 'I just had a thought. Mrs Kershaw, the attic – is it larger than this room?'

'Well, yes. Twice as large, actually. It runs the length of the front.'

'Is it furnished?'

'Not yet. We haven't needed to use it before.'

'Could we see it, then, please?'

Meg looked at her in puzzlement.

'It might suit our purposes better to rent that and bring our own furniture. If you didn't mind?'

'I suppose it'd be all right.' Meg led the way upstairs and opened the attic door. 'It's warmer up here in summer, but colder in winter.'

'It's a nice large room,' said Miss Harper thoughtfully.

'And look at those windows!' Emma went straight across to

stare out of them, while her sister studied the room. Then they exchanged glances and nods.

'Would you consider letting us rent this room instead?' Emma asked.

'There's no fire here, and the boards aren't even stained, let alone a carpet—' Meg wouldn't want to sleep up here herself. She always felt a creepy sensation in the back of her neck when she came up to check there were no leaks – as if someone were staring at her. 'And I couldn't carry trays up and down all those stairs. It makes me wheeze, going upstairs does.' But her mind was racing. If they took this place, she needn't move out of her own bedroom. And if they had their own furniture, she needn't even lay out her money to buy more.

Emma smiled at her. 'It would be nice to have the boards stained, but we have some rugs – they're rather worn, or they'd have been sold with the rest of my father's possessions – and we have some old curtains, too. I think they'll fit these windows if we sew them together.' She hesitated then said frankly, 'Our father died in debt, you see, Mrs Kershaw. We have enough money to live on, but not much to spare.'

Tears came into Blanche's eyes at her sister's words and the memory of all they'd had to do since their father died. One dreadful thing after another. Worst of all, to her, had been the condescension of the creditors at the meetings they'd held to discuss what to do with Bonamy Harper's possessions. They'd even asked his daughters to give up their jewellery – but Emma had been ready with a story about having to sell things over the past few years and had cried so prettily over her mother's brooch, 'our last memento of her', that one gentleman had told her gruffly to keep it and when another creditor objected had said the ladies weren't their debtors, dammit, and he wasn't so poor he had to steal from them.

Blanche knew she had been of little use at that meeting, sitting there stiff and angry, but Emma had been wonderful, playing on the gentlemen's sympathies! Most of the furniture had been sold, especially the fine mahogany pieces that had been her mother's pride and joy. But, again at Emma's pleading, they had been allowed to keep their own beds and a few battered pieces from the nursery which hadn't sold. As well as the smaller items Sam had taken away for them. She had felt as though she were stealing, doing that, for all her sister's reassurances. Well, it *was* stealing, no denying that. But their need was so great, surely the Lord would forgive them?

Meg looked at her visitors thoughtfully. She could see they were dying to talk to one another. 'I'll go down and put the kettle on. You have a think, decide what you want to do, then come down and join me in the kitchen. You can definitely have this room, if you prefer it, and for the same price as the other, if you bring your own furniture. And we could maybe have a gas fire put in for the winter. One with a penny slot meter, so you could use it as much as you wanted.' And so she wouldn't have to pay. 'We'll talk about it over a nice cup of tea.'

Miss Harper raised one hand to stop her. 'How much are you asking? Sam Thoxby didn't say.' Her face grew pink. 'And we can't afford too much.'

Meg frowned at them suddenly as understanding dawned. 'Are you in Mrs Blackburn's?'

Miss Harper's lips tightened. 'Yes.'

Peggy Blackburn had taken in some lady lodgers and wasn't best pleased with their finicky ways, but then Meg knew how slapdash Peggy was.

'You didn't say how much, Mrs Kershaw?'

'Oh. Well, I hadn't quite decided.' She had, but mentally added two shillings. 'That's for this room, breakfast and evening meal, with use of the front room to sit in at night, though you'd have to pay extra for coal for that in the winter – and we'll need to join you there every now and then – like at Christmas and on Sundays, perhaps.' She wasn't giving it up completely, not for anyone. 'But the rest of the time, it'd be yours. So long as you look after my things.' Meg named her price, adding, 'And I can find you a shelf in the pantry to keep a few things for your dinners – I don't cook in the middle of the day – and for snacks, if you want them. You wouldn't want to keep food up here in the attic. It'd encourage mice.'

Miss Harper frowned, for this was more than they were paying now, then she looked at her sister and nodded. 'Very well.'

Meg realised with a lifting of the heart that she had found her two lodgers and that they were exactly the sort of people she would have chosen. 'Then you can move your stuff in next week.' She cast a look around her, assessing what needed doing. 'My son will stain the floorboards and distemper the walls. And we'll need to get your curtains altered and hung, as well. You can come round any time to fit them.' If she made these two women happy here, she'd have money coming in from them for a long time. Two ladies like these, short of money but with finicky ways, wouldn't be easily suited for lodgings in Overdale. But Meg knew exactly how ladies liked to live.

Miss Emma sighed in audible relief. 'Oh, I'm so glad. Would it be too much trouble if we moved in here the minute you have it ready, Mrs Kershaw? Things are very – difficult at Mrs Blackburn's, and even though we've paid in advance for the coming week, I'd rather leave as soon as possible. Sam said he'd help us move. Well, he's got our bits of furniture stored at his house.'

Thank goodness for Blanche's annuity, though it was barely enough to manage on. She didn't know what they'd have done without it. And if anything happened to her sister, Emma would be in trouble, for the annuity would die with Blanche. It was at that moment that the vague idea she had formed of seeking employment of some sort became firmly fixed.

When Mrs Kershaw left, the two sisters looked at one another and sighed in relief.

'We can afford it, just,' Emma said.

'I still think we were right to find lodgings. It'd cost much more to take a house of our own – even if we had enough furniture, which we don't.'

'Yes, I know, and you're not well enough to manage the housework.'

'No.' Blanche sighed and belched discreetly behind her

hand. Mrs Blackburn's greasy food wasn't helping her digestive troubles.

Emma was back looking out of the window. 'And as soon as we're settled, I've decided to learn to type and find myself a clerical job.'

For the first time, Blanche Harper's severe expression softened. 'You don't need to do that, dear. We can manage.'

'I've nearly gone mad with boredom since we left home. I'd much rather keep busy. And the annuity's yours, really. I'd rather earn some money of my own.'

'Yes.' Blanche stared blindly out of the window. She, too, had found the hours passing very slowly. She didn't miss her father ordering her about, but she did miss her beautiful home and garden quite dreadfully.

When they went downstairs, Meg called out to them from the kitchen, having decided in the interim that she didn't want to start by waiting on them hand and foot, and they could eat downstairs with the family. 'I'm in here. The tea's just brewing.'

They went into the back room, Blanche noting with pleasure that it was as clean as the rest of the house. Unlike Mrs Blackburn's establishment, where she had had her first experience with bed bugs and where the landlady had not thought that anything worth making a fuss about.

'Do sit down, Miss Harper. We all eat in here. You'll find my children know their table manners.'

'I shall enjoy their company,' Emma said at once.

Meg brought the teapot across to the table and poured some of the steaming liquid into her best cups. Like her, the lodgers would be using the good crockery.

'China cups!' Emma sighed happily. 'Oh, I've missed that at Mrs Blackburn's. I don't know why tea tastes so much better out of china, but it does.'

Meg smiled. 'I always say that myself.'

'And such pretty cups, too,' Blanche added, quite sincerely. Her new landlady's smile became a beam. 'They were a wedding present from my last employer and I've not broken a single piece. I was with her for four years before I married my Stanley.'

When they had finished the tea, Miss Emma asked for a tape measure and went upstairs to measure the windows, and Miss Harper pulled out her purse. 'I presume you'll want us to pay you weekly in advance?'

'Well – yes.' Meg accepted the money eagerly, though she couldn't help noticing how little it left in the purse. After showing them out, she smiled round the kitchen and poured the last of the tea into her cup. 'Couldn't be better!' she said as she sat sipping it. She had been dreading having lodgers, but rather thought she'd enjoy looking after these two ladies. For the first time since her husband's death, she hummed as she washed up the cups and saucers in the scullery at the rear.

When Percy came home that evening, he found his mother sitting by the kitchen fire, looking happier than she had for a while. Eva had her head in a book at the table as usual, Polly was just sitting there, quiet as ever, staring into the fire, and there was no sign of little Johnny. Lizzie wouldn't be home from the shop for an hour or two yet.

Meg jumped to her feet. 'Tea won't be long. I've got it all ready for you, love.'

He sniffed appreciatively. 'I could tell that as soon as I opened the front door. Cottage pie?'

She nodded.

'Lovely.' He went through into the scullery to wash his hands and face, sighing with tiredness. There seemed to be more dirty crockery here than usual – he pushed a pile of plates aside carefully – but perhaps Mam had had a busy day and had left it all for one big wash-up after tea.

When he went through into the kitchen again, she was stirring something on the stove.

'Guess what?'

Clearly good news from her expression. 'What?'

'I've found two lodgers, and they couldn't suit us better. Well,' she amended, 'it was Sam who sent them round, actually. That lad's been a good friend to us, Percy, a very good friend.'

'Aye, I know he has. Who are they?'

'Miss Harper and Miss Emma Harper.'

'Oh, he's spoken of them two. They come from outside the town, Harcup way. Why are they looking for lodgings? I thought they'd gone to Mrs Blackburn's?'

'They don't like it there. Well, Peggy Blackburn's no housewife. They've obviously come down in the world.'

Percy sat down at the table, waiting for her to bring his food. He could sympathise with the two ladies' problems, he could indeed. There were many ways of coming down in the world. Today he'd had to tell the foreman that he couldn't go to Technical School next year to study. Ben Symes had understood and sympathised, but that hadn't made Percy feel any better. You could study other things at night classes, but to do the course he wanted you had to go part-time, which meant your employer had to be agreeable to it. He realised his mother was still talking and the other children were sitting listening to her with interest. 'Sorry. What did you say?'

'I said they want to rent the attic, not my bedroom, so we won't have to move out of our rooms, and they have some furniture of their own they want to bring. That'll save us ever so much money. But we'll need to stain the floorboards up there and paint the walls before they can move in and they want to move in as soon as they can. Do you think you could do that for me, love? I swept the place out carefully today and gave it a bit of a mop to get rid of the dust, then I went and bought some stain. Dark walnut. I can get some distemper for the walls tomorrow. Pink, I thought. Is that all right?' Meg was exhausted now, absolutely exhausted, but pleased with her efforts.

'Yes. I'll go up and have a look at that floor after tea.'

She nodded to Polly. 'Go an' call Johnny in. I told him not to go past the corner.' She didn't like her girls being out on their own after dark, but it was different with lads. Still smiling, she began to dish up.

Percy frowned round the table. 'I don't like Lizzie eating on her own every night. Maybe we could have our tea later when she's on afternoons?'

'Goodness, no! She doesn't get back till well after eight and I need to get Johnny to bed before then. Besides, you're always hungry when you come in. A man needs a good dinner after a hard day's work.'

Eva put her book away and sat down. Tonight the little room seemed hot and overcrowded. She thought with longing of Miss Blake's pretty kitchen and elegant little parlour. What it'd be like here with two lodgers sitting at the table as well didn't bear thinking of. For a moment, she almost envied her elder sister, eating on her own in the evenings. Then she thought of the lukewarm leftovers that sat on a plate by the fire waiting for Lizzie to come home and changed her mind.

Having the Misses Harper living with them made life a bit easier for Lizzie, because her mother didn't shout at her or slap her in front of the boarders. Mam had never slapped them like this when Dad was alive, but she was always doing it now – well, she slapped Lizzie and Johnny a lot, and Polly sometimes – though usually only when Percy was out. She never slapped Eva, though she shouted at her. It wasn't fair.

Lizzie continued to miss her father very keenly as the weeks passed. It seemed to the grieving child that no one really cared about her now. Her mother only spoke to order her to do jobs around the house or to tell her off about something. When Percy was at home, Mam usually hovered near him, but quite often nowadays he went out for a drink in the evening with Sam, saying if there was no point studying, he might as well enjoy himself a bit, and he could make a half last all evening.

Polly was her usual quiet self, rarely speaking up, just watching everything the family did with her wide, pale blue eyes. And Johnny was a typical little boy of four going on five.

He had started school in the babies' class at the beginning of the year because their mother said it got him off the streets. But the little children all had to have a nap in the afternoons, so when he came home at tea-time, he was always full of beans, rushing out to play with his friends or coming back in bawling to have an injury bathed or else to whine for something to eat. And if Lizzie was around she was the one who had to see to him. In fact, if she was around in the afternoons, her mother hardly lifted a finger.

Sometimes it all got to be too much for the child, this strange new life. It was at those times she went out and sat in the lav by herself, the darker the night the better, because there was something comforting about darkness and people didn't disturb her there. Well, not unless they were desperate to go.

Even her sister Eva, with whom she had previously been quite close, now spent a lot of time round at Miss Blake's, since the teacher was giving her private coaching in return for more help in the house. And since Miss Blake lived quite a way away, she had lent Eva an old bike and Mam had given her permission to be out after dark – so long as she came back by the main road and didn't cut through the back lanes.

Only – when Eva wasn't there to do the chores, Mam always gave the extra work to Lizzie. So much work. Would it never end? What with Dearden's and school and housework, not to mention the extra washing up, Lizzie was always exhausted by bedtime. She would go up to bed early sometimes and lie there in the darkness, listening to the quiet murmurings from the lodgers upstairs, vaguely comforted by them. Sometimes she would try to tell herself stories like the ones she used to read in the comics – only Mam wouldn't let her buy comics now. And she took all the money Lizzie earned at Dearden's, every farthing. Life was rotten.

At the beginning of December, Miss Blake came to Bobbin Lane again to speak to Mrs Kershaw about Eva and school. On her pupil's advice, she chose a time when Percy would be at home.

Meg showed the teacher into the chilly front room, rarely used because the lodgers always sat up in their attic room in the evenings.

'I've come to speak to you about Eva and the scholarship,' Alice Blake began.

'She's going half-time next year, so she won't need to sit for it,' Meg said promptly. She was looking forward to having another addition to the family income and had even started to build up the savings account her husband had once opened and rarely paid into. Money was much safer in the bank than sitting on your mantelpiece where people could pinch it.

'That's what I've come to ask you about – does she have to go part-time? If she did get a scholarship, couldn't she stay on at school for a year or two?'

'No, she couldn't. You know how we're situated.'

Percy looked at his mother sideways, frowned, then turned back to the teacher. 'Why do you ask?'

'Eva is such a clever child, it's a pity to take her away from school. Is there no way . . .' Alice paused delicately.

'What would be the point of her staying on?'

'She wants to train as a teacher, and I think she'd make a good one. It'd be such a shame to waste her talents, Mr Kershaw.'

Percy could see his mother shaking her head and sat for a moment, thinking. He'd lost his chance in life, but surely they were managing all right, even without Eva's earnings as a part-timer? 'What exactly would all this entail?'

Meg leaned forward. 'It doesn't matter, Percy. She can't—'

'Shh, Mam. Let Miss Blake tell us.'

Alice explained about how a teacher was trained, and he nodded, asking occasional questions, proving, though he didn't realise it, that Eva wasn't the only clever one in the family.

'We'll have to think about it for a few days,' he said when she had finished speaking. 'It's not something you decide in a hurry.'

Meg breathed in deeply, feeling betrayed, but she wasn't going to argue with him in front of a guest.

'Let me show you out, Miss Blake,' said Percy, standing up.

As he fumbled with the front door, he whispered, 'Leave it to me. Give me a few days to talk Mam round.'

She clasped his hand and nodded. 'Eva *is* worth it. She's one of the cleverest girls I've ever taught.'

He went back to face a tirade from his mother about how careful they had to be nowadays and how they couldn't possibly afford for Eva to stay on at school.

Only when she'd run herself down did he say mildly, 'It does bear thinking about, you know.'

'Have you been listening to a word I've said, Percy Kershaw? It's not just her staying on, there's the uniform to buy – and books and other things, too. We simply can't afford it.'

'I know it'd be hard, Mam. But teachers earn good money, you know. Our Eva would be better placed to help you in your old age if she was a teacher, don't you think?'

Clearly, that possibility had not occurred to Meg. She gaped at him for a moment, then said sourly, 'Well, we still can't afford it. It takes them years to become teachers nowadays. They can't go as monitors first, as they did in the old days. And anyway, she's a pretty lass. She'll get married as soon as she's finished, whatever she says now, and then all that schooling will be wasted. They can't stay teachers if they get married, you know.'

'Not everyone gets married, though teachers meet a better class of person to marry, don't you think? It wouldn't be a chap like me.' One with no prospects. 'So she'd still be better placed to help you.' And if he knew their Eva, she'd not do anything stupid with her life. She wasn't a madcap like Lizzie.

His mother's face crumpled. 'Oh, Percy lad, it's *you* who should be getting some more schooling, not a lass.'

'Leave it, Mam. That's over and done with.'

'But—'

'Leave it, I said!'

But he had the satisfaction over the next few days of seeing his mother studying Eva, looking thoughtful. And she stopped complaining when his sister got her schoolbooks out.

In the end, it was decided just to see how they went. After all, as Mam said, Eva still had to get the scholarship.

Listening to the discussions, Lizzie felt more left out than ever. Eva spent most of her spare time, apart from helping round the house, with Miss Blake, now that she had that bicycle.

Life was rotten. The only time Lizzie felt happy was at Dearden's – and that was partly because of young Jack Dearden. He was only a bit older than she was, and was going to leave school that summer, to work in the shop full-time. He was such fun, Jack was, and could make you laugh when everything seemed black. And he didn't mock you because you were a girl, like other lads did. In fact, all the Deardens were nice, really lovely people.

So long as you worked hard. There was no place at the shop for slackers and when Fred left to go and work with cars, Mrs D said it was good riddance. But Lizzie enjoyed shop work. It was all so interesting, even the packing and sorting, because stuff came from all over the world. Mr Dearden had told her one day about how tea was grown, and Peter had told her about coffee plantations. He was nice, Peter was. Jack was so lucky having a family like that.

Twenty lessons for twenty shillings, the advert said. *Next course begins in January*. Emma knew it wasn't a very good commercial school, and in fact 'school' was an ambitious term for two rooms over a shop, but they could afford fees like this without dipping too deeply into their savings.

'Are you sure?' Blanche worried. 'I don't like the thought of you going out to work.'

'I need to earn my living, dear, you know I do. I'll go and see about the lessons this afternoon.'

Miss Aspinall, who ran the school, was a very plain woman with a tired face, but she seemed to know a lot about office work and Emma took to her at once.

'I can probably help you find you a position afterwards, as well,' the proprietor said as she wrote out a receipt. 'Employers know I train the girls properly and some come to me for staff.'

'I'm a bit older than your usual pupils, I think. Will that make a difference?'

'Not at all – so long as you don't mind working at the same things the other girls do?'

'I can't afford to mind.' Emma hesitated. 'And you can really get me a job afterwards?'

'Oh, yes. It won't be a good position, because you've never worked before, but I'll find you one where you'll be able to get some useful experience and at least you'll be earning something while you learn, even if it's only fifteen shillings a week.'

'As little as that? I thought people got about a pound a week for office work.'

'They do when they're experienced. Still, with your looks and background, you'll not have too much trouble finding something better once you know the work.'

So Emma walked home feeling she'd taken a positive step – and bought herself a quarter of her favourite caramels to celebrate.

CHAPTER SIX

December 1908 – March 1909

Lizzie missed her dad even worse at Christmas. Her mam kept crying and they only had a small present each, because Mam said they couldn't afford to spend much this year. Miss Harper looked terrible after a bout of influenza, and even Miss Emma wasn't as cheerful as usual.

Lizzie, who had been run off her feet at Dearden's where she was working full-time over the holidays, was glad to sit quietly once the special dinner had been served – a lovely roast chicken their Percy had brought home. Mrs D had given her a box of chocolates, one with the corner bashed in, but she didn't show it to her mam or the chocolates would have vanished into the sideboard to be kept for guests and she'd be lucky to get any of them for herself. She waited until everyone had gathered in the front room, opened the box in the kitchen, selected a couple of her favourites and ate them slowly, with great relish. Only then did she take the box in to hand round.

Mam glared at her, of course. 'Where did you get those?'

'Mrs D gave them me for a Christmas present. She gave us all something.'

'You didn't have to open them, though.'

'The box was already broken in one corner.'

'We could still have kept them for guests.'

Lizzie swelled with indignation. 'We never have any guests. And anyway, the chocolates are *mine*.'

'You mind how you talk to me, young woman, or you'll go up to bed, Christmas or no Christmas.'

Percy stepped in yet again to keep the peace and saw Miss Emma looking at him sympathetically from across the fireplace. Even the lodgers couldn't help noticing how down Mam was on her eldest daughter sometimes. Well, everyone in the street knew that. 'Let her eat her chocolates, Mam. It is Christmas and they were her present. It's kind of her to bring them in and share them.'

Meg looked sour. 'They're opened now, anyway.'

Lizzie tossed her head and took another chocolate, cramming it into her mouth before offering the box to her mother – who took the two biggest! – then offering the box round.

For the first time, as they were all sitting there lazily in front of the fire, talking of this and that, Lizzie found herself really talking to Miss Emma, who asked her what it was like to work in the shop.

'It's lovely. Ever so interesting. Of course, I don't serve in the shop most of the time. I work in the packing area because stuff comes in big crates and boxes, an' we have to pack it in small amounts ready for selling. Mr Dearden,' whose name nobody shortened, for some strange reason, 'goes round to the big houses in the pony trap for the orders, all dressed up smart. An' he sees the trade reps, too, though Peter sees some of them now. An' I have to make tea for everyone – the fellows in the stables as well – an' go across to the baker's for our buns in the morning. Oh, there's always somethin' needs doing. But we've been a bit busy this week, I can tell you, so I've helped out in the shop an' we've had to stay back some nights to stock the shelves. On Saturday we didn't close till after ten.' Lizzie thought about that. 'I like it when we're busy, though.'

'I like to keep busy, too. I'm going to take a commercial course after Christmas and then find myself a job, so that'll make two of us women working.' Emma smiled at the child, who always looked so sullen and unhappy, and was delighted to win a hesitant smile back from her.

'What do you do on a commercial course?'

'Don't pester Miss Emma with stupid questions!' Meg snapped from the end of the sofa.

Tears came into Lizzie's eyes again, and she stared down at the chocolates, which suddenly tasted like cardboard.

Not until Percy had got his mother talking did Emma say quietly, 'I'm going to study typing and bookkeeping and things like that, so that I can work in an office. I went to pay for my lessons this week and I'll be starting in the New Year.' She chuckled. 'I'll be the oldest student by far.'

Lizzie took another chocolate and offered the box to Polly, sitting quietly on the rug at her feet. 'I didn't know ladies went out to work.'

'They do if they need to earn some money.'

Lizzie saw her mother frowning at her again and slumped down on the couch.

Emma closed her eyes and prayed for patience. When the chocolates were finished, she fumbled in her pocket and produced a paper bag of caramels. Two bags in one week – of such things were her Christmases made now. This was her one remaining extravagance. She went into Dearden's specially to buy them, and had seen for herself how happy Lizzie looked there and how even the grumpiest of customers would be drawn into a shared smile or two as the smallest assistant bustled round, helping the seniors and opening the door for customers with an air of triumph as if she had accomplished something marvellous. But Lizzie looked very different at home, really downtrodden.

Later on, Blanche roused herself to lead them in singing carols.

Lizzie joined in the general chorus and smiled at Polly, who loved to sing – though her mam didn't like them singing round the house since Dad had died. Miss Harper was doing the descant while Polly's voice led the rest in the tune, and it sounded really nice.

It was strange that Miss Harper had such a lovely voice, because nothing else about her was lovely. She was so thin she looked as if underneath she was made of sticks with no flesh on. She had started going to church with them and had joined the choir there. Lizzie loved listening to her sing, which she did sometimes on special occasions like this evening, though she always said it'd be better if she had a piano accompaniment. They'd had to sell theirs when their father died.

Horrid things happened to everyone, it seemed, when their fathers died, Lizzie had decided, not just to her and her family. She found that thought vaguely comforting.

To Polly, watching everything as she always did, the singing was the best part of Christmas and it also stopped Mam from scolding Lizzie.

'Your voice is developing very nicely, Polly,' Miss Harper said after one song. 'You'll have a lovely voice when you grow up.'

Polly treasured that compliment. It wasn't often anyone praised her. She loved singing, but not like they did it at Sunday School. The mixed-up noises the other children made there hurt your ears. Why couldn't they hear the right notes?

Meg muttered that nice voices didn't earn you your daily bread, but no one paid any attention to that.

Polly nudged her sister's leg and winked.

Lizzie stared down at her for a moment, then smiled. Her little sister was a great comfort to her lately.

As if she knew that Lizzie was thinking about her, Mam looked across the room. 'I think we could all do with a nice cup of tea.' There was a chorus of agreement. 'Lizzie, go and put the kettle on and get the tea things out.'

'Why can't Eva do it? Me an' Polly did the washing up.'

Eva began to get up, but Mam snapped, 'Stay there! An' you can just stop cheeking me, Lizzie Kershaw. You act like a baby sometimes, not a big girl of nearly thirteen.'

Lizzie dragged herself to her feet, feeling left out again.

Then the kitchen door opened. 'I'll help you, shall I?' said Polly.

'Thanks.' Lizzie felt better not being on her own. She started telling Polly about the decorations in Mrs D's sitting room upstairs and the huge pile of presents on the sideboard there for the family. No one in Bobbin Lane had decorations like that, so bright and beautiful, or so many presents.

Shortly after Christmas, Sam was drinking in the Carter's Rest one night when his friend Josh murmured, 'Fancy earning a bit extra tonight?'

'I allus fancy earning a bit extra. What's the job?'

Josh winked. 'Tell you later. Don't drink too much. You'll need your wits about you.'

At closing time they left together, with Josh explaining in a low voice what he'd noticed. They called in at his place to get his special tools. His wife and children were in bed already. Sam waited in the kitchen, staring round in disgust. She was a slattern, that Dora. He'd not put up with this sort of thing. Even Gran managed better. And the whole place smelled sour. He was glad to get out into the fresh air again.

When they got to the warehouse, it looked deserted. The office window at the side was, as Josh had said, a bit loose. It was the work of a moment to jemmy it open and climb inside.

Sam felt alert and excited, enjoying this as he hadn't enjoyed anything for a while. He'd never have thought of doing a warehouse but as Josh said there was some good stuff stored here.

It was as they were carrying it back to the office that they bumped into the watchman. It happened so quickly that Sam was caught off guard for a moment, but Josh lashed out with his jemmy and the old fellow toppled with only a gurgle of protest.

'Hell! You didn't tell me they had someone keeping watch!' Sam snapped.

'I didn't bloody know, did I?'

'We'll have to be a damn' sight more careful next time.'

And they were.

It was a pity the old fellow died, but at least it meant he couldn't identify them. They didn't do any more jobs till all the fuss had settled down, but the stuff they'd taken brought in a nice bit of cash.

★　　★　　★

The week after Lizzie turned thirteen, Sam found a piano going cheap and offered it to the two ladies. After much anxious thought, Miss Harper asked if she could put it in the front room so that she could offer singing lessons. She'd pay extra for using the room and to make up for the noise.

Meg brightened and said yes at once, wondering how much extra she could charge.

'I won't take a lot of pupils, just a few, but it will help pay for the piano. And it'll give me an interest.' You could grow tired of reading library books and sewing.

In fact, there was soon a trail of children coming for lessons, girls mostly, from higher up the hill. Folk up there weren't finding times as hard as people in the Southlea district.

Meg didn't mind the noise, because Miss Harper played the piano so beautifully and she seemed to have a gift for teaching the girls to sing nicely. When the lodger offered to teach Polly for free, as well, saying again that the child had a lovely voice, Meg hesitated and consulted Percy. But he said why not, so she agreed to the lessons. Singing wouldn't bring in any more money, but it wouldn't cost anything, either – unlike this daft idea of Eva's going to secondary school, which Meg did not favour at all but which Percy was proving really stubborn about. She didn't know what had got into him lately, she really didn't.

Polly now helped Lizzie out with the jobs round the house whenever she could. The two of them would chat as they worked and that seemed to get things done faster. She'd teach Lizzie the words of some of her songs and they'd sing them together, though only quietly, so as not to upset Mam. And they knew a few music hall songs, too, though Miss Harper hadn't taught them those and some of the words were a bit cheeky.

She was, Polly felt, getting to be quite good friends with her big sister now. Before Dad died, Lizzie had been more friendly with Eva, but nowadays she either had her head in a book or was round at her teacher's 'helping out'.

After a week of worrying about Lizzie and thinking the situation over carefully, Polly got up one evening after tea and started doing the dishes in the scullery, setting the enamel washing-up bowl in the big, shallow slopstone, and pouring the hot water into it carefully from the kettle so that she wouldn't splash herself or spill any on the floor.

'What do you think you're doing?' a voice shouted suddenly in her ear.

The plate Polly was holding fell back into the soapy water, but fortunately didn't break. 'I'm doing the dishes, Mam.'

'What's the point of doing the dishes when your sister hasn't eaten yet?'

'Lizzie's tired when she comes home after work. She can wash her own things up then. And I don't mind doing the dishes, really I don't.'

'Well, I mind, so you can just leave them be. Lizzie will do them after she's eaten. If she makes extra work, it's only right that she clears it up.'

Polly stood stock still, frightened at the words that were forming inside her head. But for once, they wouldn't be held back. 'It isn't fair of you to make her do all the washing up. An' I—'

Meg gasped in outrage and slapped Polly on the side of her head, then cracked her again on the other side as well.

Polly wailed loudly and this time she knocked a plate off the wooden draining board and it shattered on the slopstone.

'Look what you've done now!' Meg shrieked, for the lodgers were safely up in the attic after tea. 'You can just clear that mess up and then do as you're told and leave this for your sister! I get no respect since your father died, none at all, and I'm *not having it!*' Another slap made Polly cry out again. 'If you've nothing better to do with yourself, there's plenty of mending in the basket.'

Percy's voice made them both jump. 'What's the matter,

Mam?' He couldn't remember anyone ever having to shout at Polly like this, for she was always so quiet and eager to please, more like a little ghost round the house, he sometimes thought, though she was a bit plump for a ghost.

Meg turned to him. 'Our Lizzie's got Polly doing her chores for her now. I don't know how she managed that. And when I told this one to leave things for her sister, she answered me back. I'm not having that from any of them.' It had become a point of honour to her since Stanley's death to keep control of her children.

Polly stopped sobbing and in the heat of the moment allowed more words to escape. 'It's not fair, leaving the whole day's dishes for Lizzie to do. She's tired when she comes home. And she didn't *make* me wash up. I *wanted* to do it, to help her.'

'Well, listen to that!' Meg moved forward again, hand upraised.

Polly ducked, clutching her reddened cheek with one soapy hand and continuing to sob.

Percy grabbed his mother's hand and stepped between them. 'Leave her to me, Mam. You're tired out. Why don't you go and have a sit-down, eh?'

Meg glared at her daughter. 'I shan't forget this, Polly Kershaw!' She clutched her son's arm, trying hard not to sob as well. 'I'm not having cheek from them. I'm not!'

Percy turned her gently round towards the kitchen. 'Mam, please go and sit down.'

When she'd left, he shut the door between the scullery and kitchen and looked sternly at Polly. 'What's got into you today, upsetting Mam like that?' Then he looked at the piles of dishes and frowned. Now he came to think of it, there did seem to be rather a lot of them.

'Mam leaves everything for our Lizzie to wash up after work.'

'Perhaps she was busy today?'

Polly shook her head. 'No. There's allus a pile like this. So I thought I'd help out. I don't mind, really I don't. And Lizzie never asked me to do it. It was my own idea.'

He made no further comment. 'Well, it's very kind of you to help your sister, love. You'd better get on with it while the water's hot. Shall I dry the dishes for you?'

'Eeh, no! Mam'd have a fit at you doing that, then she'd get mad all over again. She's allus mad at our Lizzie since Dad died. You go back into the kitchen an' talk to her. She'll like that.' Polly picked up the pieces of broken plate then took the dishrag and plunged her hands into the hot water again. She had meant what she said. She did enjoy housework of all sorts, though she didn't like schoolwork much.

Still upset by the red fingermarks on his little sister's cheeks, Percy went back into the kitchen.

His mother greeted him with, 'Have you found out what that young madam's been saying to make Polly do her work for her?'

'She hasn't been saying anything. It's Polly's own idea.'

'Ha! You don't know our Lizzie if you think that.'

'You're very hard on her lately, Mam. What's the matter?'

'Nothing's the matter. I'm just seeing she buckles down.' Meg stared at him defiantly. 'An' I don't want you interfering in how I bring up the girls, Percy Kershaw.'

'I'm not interfering, but it can't do any harm to let Polly help out, if she wants. I dare say there won't be as many things to do tomorrow. You must have been too busy to wash up today.'

She breathed deeply but did not pursue the matter, though she mentally added it to her growing list of grievances against her eldest daughter. 'Children are supposed to be a comfort to you,' she said bitterly, 'but Lizzie's no comfort at all, and Eva's just as bad nowadays. Always round at that schoolteacher's or doing her homework. And for what? We can't afford her to go to secondary school, whatever you say. I keep telling you that. I sit here on my own evening after evening, with no one to talk to, and when I do say something, no one listens.'

Percy immediately put down the newspaper.

'Oh, go on with you! It's no use buying that if no one reads it.'

She dabbed at her eyes and hunched her shoulder at him, so he picked up the newspaper again.

How was he going to persuade Mam to give Eva her chance? It had become something of an obsession with Percy. If he could help his clever sister, then he'd feel he'd won something, at least, from the ruin of their lives. His own future looked very bleak, tied to his mother. And she wasn't easy to live with since his father had died. Well, she never had been, but she was worse now.

At half-past eight Lizzie came in from work and Percy studied her surreptitiously. Polly was right. Their sister did look tired. He set himself to distract his mother from nagging the poor lass, and had the happy idea of inviting Mam to come out for a glass of shandy with himself and Sam.

Meg gaped at him. 'Go into a public house! What do you think I am? It's not respectable. Why, I've never been inside one in my whole life.'

'Things are changing, Mam. They've got a ladies' room at the Hare and Hounds now. You already know one or two of the women who go there, so you could sit with them. Fanny Preston from across the road for one, and Rosie Holden for another.'

She looked at him, clearly tempted.

'I wouldn't ask you to go into the Carter's Rest or the other pubs down the south end, but the Hare and Hounds is very respectable nowadays, I promise you. Mrs Sampson, the landlady, keeps a very quiet house.' Which was why he preferred it, though Sam liked the Carter's Rest better.

In the end Meg agreed and went upstairs to put on her second-best hat, for she was not one to go out with only a shawl flung over her head.

Lizzie breathed a sigh of relief as the front door closed on them and went to get her dinner. She found the usual dried-up mess congealing on a plate in front of the fire.

When she had finished eating what she could, Polly came

across and took the plate from her. 'You never eat your tea when you're on afternoons.'

'It's never worth eating.' Lizzie hauled herself to her feet. 'I'd better get the washing-up done or she'll go mad at me again.'

'I've done most of it already.'

They walked into the narrow scullery together and tears came into Lizzie's eyes at the sight of the piles of clean crockery on the shelves. 'Oh, Polly, you are a love!' And she hugged her younger sister again.

They heard footsteps and turned to find Miss Emma standing in the kitchen doorway. 'Our alarm clock's broken, so I wonder if one of you could wake me up early in the morning? I have to go out tomorrow to see about a job and I want to look my best.'

Lizzie nodded politely. She was always awake early. 'Yes, Miss Emma. I can do that. I hope you get your job.' Since their Christmas chat, she'd listened with interest to tales of the commercial college lessons and the difficulties of learning to type, feeling a new kinship with their younger lodger.

'Thank you so much, dear. I must say, it's a relief to have that course over.' Emma had worked hard and had paid 'practice money' to go back to the school at weekends and use the typewriter, as some girls did, feeling that twenty lessons weren't enough to learn to type accurately.

Yesterday Miss Aspinall had told her about a job that was going. 'They work their staff hard, but it's a place where you'll get a good range of office experience.'

Emma realised that she'd been lost in thought and the two girls were staring at her, so she winked at them. 'Do you still like caramels?'

They nodded.

She reached into the pocket of her skirt. 'I just happen to have a couple to spare.' In her opinion, both of them looked as if they needed a treat and the older girl looked absolutely worn out.

So the two sisters spent a companionable half hour sitting

by the fire, seeing how long they could make their caramels last. Lizzie enjoyed the rare luxury of talking about her day and Polly just enjoyed being the focus of someone's attention, because Eva was in the front room as usual, doing her school work, saying that being cold there was better than suffering the noise of the warm kitchen, and Johnny had gone up to bed, grumbling all the way, but not daring disobey orders about what was his proper bedtime.

By the time their mother came home, flushed with enjoyment from her first evening out since Stanley's death, Lizzie and Polly were both in bed and the younger girl, at least, was sound asleep. It was much longer before Lizzie got off. She heard Eva close the front room door, say goodnight to her mother, then tiptoe up the stairs. As Eva climbed over her, she pretended to be sleeping, so she wouldn't have to talk. Her sister was asleep in minutes, but Lizzie was wide awake for some reason. She heard the low voices of the two lodgers from the attic room above and wondered what they were talking about, remembering with a pang what the low rumble of her father's voice used to sound like.

Downstairs, she heard her mother making a cup of cocoa and chatting to Percy. Mam sounded happier tonight. Lizzie only hoped that would last, but she wasn't building her hopes on it. Nothing satisfied Mam nowadays, nothing!

The next morning, Emma Harper admitted to herself that she felt nervous as she walked along York Street. What if they laughed at her at Sevley's? Twenty commercial lessons and no experience at her age.

Miss Aspinall had said to wear dark, plain clothes to the interview, but the only dark clothes Emma had in her wardrobe were her old tweed walking skirt and the dark brown jacket she used to wear with it, and she didn't think they would look smart enough. Well, she knew they wouldn't. The skirt had a mend on it where she'd caught it on some brambles, and she'd had the jacket for five years, which meant she was now twenty-four years old.

She sighed as a couple of kids ran past her, shouting. She'd expected to be married and have at least one child by the time she reached this age. But it was no use repining. When she was younger, her father had discouraged admirers, and anyway, she'd known even then that she couldn't leave Blanche to cope with him on her own. It was a small comfort that one or two young men had shown an interest, but to tell the truth it hadn't broken her heart to discourage them because she hadn't been particularly smitten.

When he was in one of his hurtful moods, their father had sometimes said his elder daughter looked just like his own mother: plain as a plank. His younger daughter, on the other hand, favoured his wife, the woman he had idolised and grieved for ever since her early death, and he'd usually treated her more gently because of that. Emma couldn't even remember her mother, who had died when she was three. It was Blanche who had brought her up, Blanche who had done everything for her, Blanche whom she loved dearly.

She was kept waiting at Sevley's, sitting on a bench in a draughty outer room, then brought in with a peremptory command. She didn't take to the owner or to his wife, who managed the office, but kept reminding herself that she had no experience and that beggars couldn't be choosers and managed to hold her tongue.

When she returned home, she had the job, though she knew already that she wasn't going to like it. Mr Sevley had a look in his eyes she mistrusted. If his wife hadn't been the one running the office, Emma wouldn't have accepted the job under any circumstances. And the wages were only fifteen shillings a week: 'Because although you're older than our usual sort of girl, you're nobbut a beginner at office work and we'll have it all to teach you.' But fifteen shillings would make a big difference to their meagre budget, a very big difference, and this job was only a start, after all.

And Miss Aspinall said that Mrs Sevley knew her job. 'You'll learn more there than anywhere else in town. Ask for more money next year. She'll give you a bit more, probably. Then, later on, I'll help you find another job.' She had blushed. 'If you wish it, that is.'

'You're being very kind to me, Miss Aspinall.'

'Well, we're both single women with our living to earn and that isn't easy, is it? It's a man's world.' A flush stained her thin cheeks. 'And why don't you call me Millie – now that you're no longer a student? If you want to, that is?'

Emma realised that here was an offer of friendship and didn't hesitate to accept it. 'I'd love to. And my name's Emma. Um – perhaps you'd like to come to tea with me and my sister one weekend? I'm sure you'd get on well with Blanche.'

'Oh, I'd like that. I'd like it very much indeed. I don't care to leave Mother alone in the evenings, and I teach at Sunday school, but a Saturday afternoon – yes, that'd be very nice.'

'Next Saturday, perhaps?'

'Delightful.' She would look forward to it all week and enjoy telling Mother about it afterwards.

CHAPTER SEVEN

May 1909 – June 1911

In May, Eva heard that she'd got a scholarship to the secondary school and all hell broke out in the Kershaw household. Percy insisted she was to take it up and was not swayed by tears from his mother or pleas that they couldn't afford this, that they'd all end up in debt and in the workhouse. For once in his life, he held firm.

'Thank you, Percy,' Eva said the first night. The crumpled letter from the school was safely in his pocket, only one corner singed where Meg had tried to throw it on the fire. Their mother was now upstairs, sobbing into her pillow. 'I won't waste this chance, I promise you. If you can only persuade her to . . .'

They both paused to listen.

'I've never heard her go on like this before,' Eva said in a worried voice, when the weeping didn't stop.

'Me neither. What our lodgers must be thinking, I don't know. Eeh, we can't let her carry on making that row.' He went upstairs, flinging open his mother's bedroom door without knocking. 'That's enough!' he roared in a voice so loud he surprised himself.

The sobs abated only a little.

He went across to the bed and jerked her upright, giving her a good shake.

Meg gulped. 'Percy—'

'*Enough*, I said! I'm the one bringing the wages into this

house and I'm telling you now, if you don't let Eva go to that school, I'm leaving.' He let go of her and folded his arms, his expression grim. 'I wasn't able to take up my chance, but she's going to get hers, by hell she is!'

Terror replaced the anger in Meg's heart. If he left, she'd lose everything, for the money from the lodgers would not be enough to keep a family.

'I mean it!' He glared down at her. Then, because it was not in his nature to bully and demand things, he turned round before her tears could weaken his resolve, saying over his shoulder, 'I'm off to the pub and I don't want to hear any more about this after I get back – or you know what I'll do.'

They all suffered from their mam's bad temper for the next few days, but Eva did take up the scholarship. The knowledge that Miss Blake had persuaded the brewery to pay for the schoolbooks and had got the Pilbys to provide the school uniform helped with Meg. A little. But her fear of Percy's leaving helped far more.

At the same time as Eva was preparing to change schools, Lizzie was at last able to leave elementary school and work full-time at Dearden's. Her mam grudgingly agreed to let her buy some new clothes, and again Mrs D stepped in to prevent things from being obtained through the Clothing Club which sold only cheap stuff, with no wear in it. And anyway, she wanted her assistants turned out more smartly, if Mrs Kershaw didn't mind.

Mrs Kershaw did mind. Very much. But once again she was helpless to prevent such extravagance and did not dare protest openly.

So Lizzie purchased two neat navy serge skirts for work and four blouses, each with detachable high starched collars and sleeves which would roll up, rather like the ones Mrs D herself wore.

Her mam wanted to buy her some corsets as well, but the idea of being laced up absolutely horrified Lizzie. 'I don't *need* corsets! I'm thin enough already,' she protested. Then, seeing the determination on her mother's face, added, 'And what's more, I won't wear them.'

Meg breathed deeply for a moment, then shrugged. 'I suppose it would be a waste of money, when you're so scraggy.' But she always wore corsets herself, because it wasn't respectable to go without, in her opinion, and anyway they kept your chest warm. But you could never tell that Lizzie anything. A right madam, her eldest daughter, and heaven help the man who married her. *If* anyone ever did marry her. And if her figure got any bigger, she'd have the corsets, whether she liked the idea or not.

Lizzie had never had brand-new clothes before and when she got home, she ran upstairs and changed into them straight away, then came rushing down to show them off to Percy.

But as she sailed into the kitchen, calling, 'Look at me!' she was embarrassed to find that Sam Thoxby had come in while she was changing and was also part of the audience. He was indeed looking at her, but in that funny way he sometimes had, his eyes focusing for a moment on her breasts which had grown somewhat that year and then flicking up and down her figure, as if assessing her.

'You look very nice,' Percy told her, nodding approval.

'I like that blouse,' Sam said. 'Very grown-up.'

'Th-thank you.' Face scarlet, Lizzie escaped upstairs again.

'You're as large as you ever will be and no amount of staring will make you larger,' Meg said the next day when she caught Lizzie looking at a sideways view of her figure in the front room mirror. 'There's no denying you take after my side of the family and Eva takes after your father's. She's going to have a lovely little figure, our Eva is. But you're worse than me, you're all skin and bone.'

Lizzie tried not to show how that remark hurt. She'd far rather have lush curves like a lady on a postcard that had taken her fancy at the newsagent's. Everyone she knew had a collection of postcards, but she'd never wanted any before. She'd bought this one, however, instead of a comic, and kept it in her drawer, looking at it sometimes when she was on her own. Such a lovely, pillowy lady, with piled-up hair of a glorious blonde colour, not dull and black like Lizzie's, which fell straight down again if you tried to pile it up. Not that anyone would let her wear her hair up yet. Even Mrs D said she was too young for that and should just tie her hair back with a navy ribbon to match her skirt and wash it every week to keep it shiny. It wasn't fair keeping her looking like a child.

On Sam's next visit to Bobbin Lane, he looked so pleased with himself that Meg asked at once, 'What's the good news, then?' He was a great favourite with her nowadays and often called in on a Sunday, sitting with them in the front room, teasing her as no one else dared and chatting comfortably to the lodgers if they came down. He had remained on good terms with them on the principle that it never hurt to get on with folk.

'The news is . . .' He paused teasingly and grinned at a chorus of voices saying, 'Get on!'

'Well, the news is that my gran's going to get an old age pension now she's turned seventy – and they're going to give her the whole five shillings a week. Mr Lloyd George is in my good books, he is that.'

'Oh, that's wonderful!' said Meg at once.

Sam grinned reminiscently. 'Gran was so pleased she celebrated with a couple of extra glasses of porter last night and they had to call me to get her home. Danced down the street she did, seventy or not. She was a bit grumpy this morning, though.' Had screamed at him like a fishwife, actually, for making such a noise when her poor old head was aching fit to burst.

'I think the pension should be given to everyone when they get to be seventy,' Meg said. 'There's not that many who do live so long and no one can do a proper day's work by that age, can they?'

But the pensions were not given to everyone and those who 'had failed to work habitually, according to their ability and need' or 'to save money regularly' were excluded, she'd read that in the paper. She'd memorised the phrases in case those were still the rules when she got really old. At least she was earning some money with her lodgers and she was saving, too, so if they didn't change the rules, she'd qualify when her time came. 'I'm that glad for your gran, Sam. It must be a great comfort to her.'

'It is. Though I'd have looked after her when she got too old to do owt.' And actually, his gran had a knack of earning bits of money here and there, and even had some saved. But she kept most of that under a loose floorboard, with just a few pounds in the savings bank for show. She didn't really trust banks, but knew about the rules for getting the pension.

'There's a lot of changes going on in the world,' Percy said thoughtfully. 'Look at that Louis Bleriot, flying all the way across the English Channel.' The idea had really caught his imagination.

'He's a fool to risk his life in one of those rackety flying machines, when he could get across to England perfectly safely in a ship,' was Meg's comment.

'There's the cinema as well,' Lizzie chimed in. If she'd had more money, she'd have gone to the cinema every week. They had some lovely films. Jack had been telling her about his favourite. It was called 'The Great Train Robbery' and he'd seen it three times now. Ever so exciting it was.

'It's a lot of nonsense that cinema is,' Meg declared. 'It'll never last.'

Percy rolled his eyes at Sam and the two young men began talking about going for a walk. Everyone else found an excuse to go out so Meg was left alone again, which didn't please her at all.

As she worked in the shop, Lizzie often listened to the better off customers voice their resentment that their taxes were being 'given away' to old people in the form of these pensions, and she thought of Gran Thoxby, all twisted and worn, so grateful not to have to scrub floors any more though she still laid out dead people.

But Lizzie kept her thoughts to herself. You didn't argue with customers. They'd been saying the same thing since the beginning of the year when the pensions started, and she was fed up of the subject by now. But they'd only to hear of someone else getting the full five shillings and they'd be off again, grumbling away to one another.

Even Jack Dearden was driving her mad with his talk of aeroplanes. He was as bad as Fred had been about motor cars. During slack times in the shop, when they were making up packets of sugar or currants in the back room, he passed on to Lizzie all the latest news he'd garnered about flying, for he was allowed to read the newspaper at night, once his dad had finished with it.

Lizzie had a secret interest in what the suffragettes were doing, though of course she didn't let on to her mam or Mrs D about that, just talked about it with Miss Emma sometimes, who was also a secret supporter. Miss Emma couldn't talk about getting the vote for women in front of her sister, either, since Miss Harper disapproved as strongly of the suffragettes and their activities as Lizzie's mam did.

'Women have just as much sense as men and deserve the vote,' Emma said to Lizzie one evening when they were alone together in the kitchen. 'Not that I'd lower myself to make such a public fuss about it all.' She didn't think she'd have the courage to join the protests, either, for there was often a lot of unpleasantness attached and people threw rotten fruit at you, or flour – or worse.

'There was one chained herself to the railings down at the Town Hall today an' she shouted at the Mayor when he came out,' Lizzie said. 'I saw her with my own eyes. She was a lady from her clothes, an' yet she screeched an' kicked when them policemen dragged her off. Mind you, I saw one of them thump her. I don't think that was right, either.'

'That's shocking. The police have no right to hit anyone. They're there to serve the public, not abuse them.'

'I can't see what good it does anyone to get arrested and sent to prison, though,' Lizzie said thoughtfully. 'That won't get women no votes. Do you think we'll ever get them?'

'I certainly hope so.'

Lizzie really enjoyed talking to Miss Emma, who made her think about the world as no one had ever done before, and who lent her story books to read in her rare moments of leisure. Her mam said reading was a waste of time and gave Lizzie extra jobs to do if she caught her with a book, so she could only read them when Mam was round the pub with Percy and Sam. All Meg wanted to talk about was the rising prices.

Times were terrible hard, Mrs D said, but the shop still seemed very busy to Lizzie. As she walked to work, however, she often saw men who had no work standing around on street corners looking cold and miserable, or children with pinched faces going to school without breakfast. She knew she was lucky to have a job, and if only her mam would stop nagging her, life would be lovely. But Mam had been in a bit better mood lately, especially when it was her day to go to the pub.

In May 1910, just after Lizzie turned fourteen, the old King died and everyone went around talking about it in hushed voices. 'End of an era,' they said, or, 'Last real link with old Vicki.' Lizzie didn't see why they were making such a fuss. He was a fat old man, King or not, just the sort that tried to pinch your bum in the shop when Mrs D wasn't looking.

Halley's Comet blazed across the skies on the eve of the King's funeral, which some thought was a bad omen, others a good one. Peter Dearden said it was just a 'natural phenomenon' and so did Miss Harper, and certainly nothing seemed to come of it, but it made you feel funny to see it.

It was Peter who insisted on Dearden's buying a motor van to deliver goods to the outlying districts, and that caused great excitement among the staff. He said motors were the coming thing and made a lot less work and mess than horses did, though Lizzie liked to go and stroke the horses' noses in the stables and slip them a piece of carrot. They had such lovely velvety eyes.

Peter even gave Lizzie a ride home in the van one dark night, when it was pouring with rain. 'Your first ride in a motor vehicle?' he asked indulgently.

'Yes.' She beamed at him as the rain beat down on the roof. 'Thank you so much for bringing me home.'

'Well, it won't be your last ride, not by a long chalk, young lady. They're the thing of the future, motor cars are, and one day every family who now has a carriage will have a car instead.'

She gaped at him.

'I mean it, young Lizzie.'

She didn't like to contradict him, but she couldn't see these noisy smelly machines taking over from the horses her father had loved so much. She still thought of Dad sometimes when she saw a brewery dray in the street, and then she had to blink her eyes and quickly find something else to look at.

Lizzie saw Peter sometimes looking at his father with the same sorrow in his eyes. Mr D coughed a lot, and he looked all yellow and shrivelled up, like Miss Harper had when they first came to Bobbin Lane, though she was looking better now. Lizzie felt for Peter and Jack. It was a hard thing to lose your father.

But mostly Lizzie was too busy to stop and think about anything much. And that was how she liked it. She'd leave all the thinking to Eva, thank you very much.

In June of the following year, when Lizzie was fifteen, the Coronation of King George V took place, a great event for which most streets in Overdale were having parties. People were planning to bring out their tables and chairs, set them all in a long row and share their food and drink – but were keeping their fingers crossed that it would be a fine day.

All the shops had patriotic displays in the windows. Dearden's had 'Produce of Our Glorious Empire' taking up a whole window and a big golden crown outside, perched above the double shop doors. Peter had acquired that and arranged for it to be lit up at night by electric bulbs, but Mrs D didn't half complain about the cost.

Sam went round selling bunting, some of it obviously well used, but folk were buying it anyway and hanging it across the streets.

'He can always turn an extra penny, that lad can,' Meg said fondly. 'Why don't you go in with him on some of his jobs, our Percy? You could make a bit on the side.'

'I'm not the sort.'

'You'll have to be the sort with our Eva going to that school!'

So next time Sam offered him a chance to make a bit of money on the side, Percy swallowed his doubts. 'All right.'

Sam grinned. 'What's got into you, saying yes?'

'Didn't you mean it?' Percy felt relief wash through him, then saw he was being teased.

'A-course I did. This fellow from Rochdale's got a cartload of stuff to sell an' we need some help unloading it.'

Not until Percy was helping transfer things into two hand-carts in a dark area behind Pilby's did he realise from what the stranger was saying that the stuff was stolen. He froze where he stood, unable to lift another item.

Sam nudged him. 'Get on with it!'

But he couldn't. He just couldn't. He thought he heard someone coming along the street and his blood ran cold. 'It's stolen, isn't it? This stuff?'

His companion's teeth shone briefly for a moment in the fitful moonlight as he smiled. 'I wouldn't know. All I care about is it's going cheap an' I can make a profit.'

'I can't do it, Sam. I just can't.'

Sam grabbed his arm. 'What do you mean, you can't do it? We'll be finished in half an hour. Money for old rope.'

But for once Percy wasn't to be persuaded. 'No. I'm not doing owt dishonest.'

The stranger came over to them. 'What's up with him?'

'He's got a belly-ache.' Sam's fist jabbed suddenly into Percy's belly and he folded up in pain. 'Groan!' a voice hissed in his ear. 'Or he'll bash your brains in.'

So Percy groaned.

Sam clapped the stranger on the back. 'Ah, we'll manage fine without him. I shoulda knowed he'd get the gripes. He allus does when he's nervous. I shan't offer him work again.' He turned to Percy. 'An' don't come to me for payment afterwards.'

Percy turned and left abruptly, rushing off down the alley as if a pack of wild dogs was after him. Behind him, he heard laughter. When he saw someone coming down the street towards him, he forced himself to slow down and even nod a hello. But the man was drunk and greeting all the world, no one he knew, thank goodness.

He shivered all the way home and at every step half-expected a policeman to jump out from a dark doorway and ask what he was doing out so late. As he lay in the bed, vainly trying to fall asleep, all he could think of was that he would never, ever do business with Sam again. Did his friend often deal in stolen goods? Surely not?

Sam offered him a chance to make money several times after that. 'Guaranteed honest,' he said with a mocking grin each time.

But Percy just shook his head. 'Buying and selling isn't my sort of thing.'

'I thought you needed extra money for your Eva?'

'We're managing, thank you.'

After that, Percy went less often to the Carter's Rest. They were a rough crowd down there. And anyway, he was thinking of doing some studying at night classes. Emma (she said it was silly to keep calling her 'Miss Emma' when they were both folk who worked for their living) had told him there were some good classes being put on in the coming year. Elementary Bookkeeping, perhaps. He liked figures. Or Principles of Commerce. Not that a chap like him would ever get much chance to use such knowledge, but as Emma said, you could enjoy learning things for their own sake. And it'd cost no more than going to the pub.

She was learning shorthand now, because she didn't like the office where she worked, even though she'd learned a lot there. They were real slave drivers, apparently, the Sevleys, and the conditions in the yard outside were appalling, with rats running freely in the back privy they all had to use. She was looking for another job.

He both liked and admired their younger lodger. She was lively and pretty, kind to the children, especially Lizzie, who was often in the wars with their mother for something or other, poor lass.

Emma Harper dressed very carefully the next morning and for once could not face eating any of the breakfast which she had brought up to the attic on a tray because Blanche was at that delicate time of the month and wasn't feeling too well. Emma had asked Lizzie to call in at Sevley's on her way to Dearden's and tell them she was sick. She certainly felt sick at the moment, she was so nervous about the coming interview.

Millie Aspinall had told her about this job a few days ago. The man was a builder and needed more than just clerical help. He wanted someone who could speak nicely to clients when they came to his office. He'd apparently tried having a lad on the front desk and it hadn't worked. And his last typist had left in tears when he swore at her.

Well, he'd better not swear at me, Emma decided. I won't take that sort of language from anyone.

The builder's yard was about a mile away. She arrived there early, but decided to go inside anyway. They surely wouldn't count punctuality a fault!

When she opened the front door, she found herself in a large, untidy room with no one to be seen. She waited a few moments, then cleared her throat loudly. Still no one appeared. 'Is anyone there?' she called as the silence dragged on, her voice a bit wobbly with nervousness.

Just as she was wondering whether she'd made a mistake about the time, she heard footsteps from the back. The man who appeared looked to be in his mid-thirties, with a ruddy, healthy face and a shock of dark hair in dire need of a trim. He had such a confident air about him that she decided he must be Mr Cardwell, the owner.

'Sorry to keep you waiting, madam. The lad seems to have left his post. How can I help you?'

'I – er – I'm not a customer. My name's Emma Harper and I've come about the job. Miss Aspinall recommended me, I believe.'

'Oh, yes.'

He looked at her then, really looked, and his frown deepened. Her heart sank because he didn't seem pleased by what he saw.

'This isn't a job for a lady to play at.'

She gasped in shock. '*Play at!* I'm not playing at anything, I can assure you, Mr Cardwell. You *are* Mr James Cardwell?'

'Mmm-hmm.'

'I really need this job.'

His eyes lingered on her dress. 'You don't exactly look poverty-stricken to me. That's a rather fine dress for a clerk.' As fine as those his wife wore, though more flattering. You could always tell a quality material. Mind you, anything would be more flattering than what Edith wore. She had a real talent for picking unflattering shades of pink and dresses which made her hips look even bigger than they were.

Emma had come prepared to be subservient, to do her very best to give satisfaction, but this remark made her angry, as did the way he was staring at her. She might as well stay at Sevley's as take on another unpleasant employer. 'I wouldn't be in need of a job if my father hadn't wasted all our money and then died leaving us in debt. And I'm wearing this dress because I can't afford to buy any new ones. It's left over from *better days*, when I did have the right to call myself a lady. Which I don't now. However, if you have no job going, I'll take my leave. I certainly can't afford to waste my time.' She only hoped no one told Mr Sevley they'd seen her in town today or she'd lose her present job as well.

As she turned away, Mr Cardwell moved to bar the way. 'I didn't say there wasn't a job going, only that you didn't look suitable.'

'And if I were wearing ragged clothes, I *would* be suitable?'

'Well, at least I'd know I'd get a good day's work out of you. Hunger makes for good workers.'

Emma drew herself up and could not stop her voice from sounding bitter. 'You're not even going to give me a chance, are you?'

'I haven't decided.'

His eyes were on her again, but not in an offensive way, rather as if he were still assessing her. She held her breath. Please, she thought, please let him give me a chance! He may be blunt, but at least he doesn't look at me in that horrible, leering way Mr Sevley does.

Suddenly he stuck out one hand. 'Let's start again, shall we? How do you do? I'm James Cardwell.'

She stared at his hand for a moment, then shook it, surprised at how warm and strong it felt.

'Come in and tell me what you can do, Miss Emma Harper.' He grinned mockingly.

A spurt of anger made her speak as bluntly as he did. 'For a start, I can keep this place clean and tidy for you. I'm amazed you have *any* customers if this is what greets them when they walk through that door.'

'You don't mind getting your hands dirty, then?'

'I don't mind any honest work, Mr Cardwell, if it pays.' She fumbled in her bag to produce the reference from her friend. 'If you'd like to see what—'

'I asked for someone who was good at her work. If Millie Aspinall's sent you, I've no need to read that piece of paper as well.'

A man clumped in from the back, his muddy boots dirtying the bare boards still further. 'I need you outside, James lad.

Young Nat's fell over an' broke his arm so Tim's took him to hospital. But we've still got that stuff to sort out.'

'Damnation! How did the young tyke manage that?'

'Climbing on the pile of green timber.'

'I'll tan his bloody hide for him when he gets back, broken arm or not.'

Emma breathed deeply and concentrated on the wallpaper. It was not for an employee to criticise her employer's mode of speech, not if she wanted the job.

Mr Cardwell let out a long, aggrieved sigh. 'Right, then, Walter. I'll be out in a minute.' He turned to Emma. 'I'll give you a week's trial. A pound a week. *If* you're good enough.' He was already moving towards the back door. 'I'll have to leave you to hold the fort.'

'But – what do you want me to do?'

'Do owt you can until I get back.' He turned to give her another of his cheeky grins. 'Use your initiative, Miss Harper. Prove you've got some. You'll certainly need it if you're going to work for me.'

She stood there in the bare room, feeling stunned and not at all sure now that she wanted this particular job. Mr Cardwell was – well, unlike anyone she'd ever met before. But if he meant what he said, a pound a week was better than seventeen shillings, the princely amount her wages had risen to at Sevley's.

There was a noise from the back yard and she hurried out to see what was happening. She was just in time to see a motor lorry loaded with timber pulling out of some gates at the rear. When it had gone, its chugging fading gradually into the distance, there was no sound and no movement at all.

'Is anyone there?' she called across the yard.

There was no answer.

She shivered in the damp, chill wind and went back inside, turning in a full circle to study the front room. What a dreadful, untidy place! This was no way to greet customers! Feeling like an intruder, she went exploring the rest of the old house. The door she had already gone through led out to the back yard through a narrow passage and there was another room opening out of it, full of boxes and pieces of wooden moulding and who knew what else. The room Mr Cardwell had appeared from was his office. It had drawings of houses pinned to the walls, a big sloping desk by the window and mounds of paper all over the other desk and the floor. She tutted under her breath at the mess.

On the other side, she found another room whose dusty floorboards barely showed beneath boxes of all shapes and sizes. Screws spilled out of one, pieces of sandpaper lay on top of another.

The final door opened on to a second narrow passageway. Stairs led up on one side and at the rear she found a small kitchen, in a disgusting state, with unwashed cups and saucers piled in the sink and on the table, and in one corner a dirty gas stove with a blackened kettle on it. Among the crockery on the table was a cracked jug containing sour milk. She poured that down the sink at once, hating its smell, filling the jug with water from the tap to soak off the yellowing crust.

On the other side of the kitchen another door led out into the big back yard and to the left, just outside, there was a small lavatory. Feeling guilty, like an intruder, she used it while the place was quiet, then went back inside.

When James Cardwell came stamping in two hours later, clearly not in the best of humours, he found the floor swept and Miss Harper sitting behind the table that was supposed to serve as a desk, her neat ankles showing beneath it, her head with its shining, honey-coloured hair bent over a pile of papers which she seemed to be sorting out. The draught of the door opening made some of the top papers shift and she squeaked in dismay as she tried to hold them down.

He nodded his approval. 'Well, I see you're settling in. Any chance of a cup of tea? There's a kitchen at the back.' He jerked his head in the appropriate direction.

'I've already explored the ground floor, Mr Cardwell, and washed up the dirty dishes in the kitchen.' She stood up and used the receipt book and a ruler to hold down the piles of paper. 'I'll bring your tea through to you when it's ready.'

'Walter would probably fancy a cup, too.'

'I'll take one out to him as well, then.'

'We both like plenty of sugar. Three good spoonsful. Oh – and don't forget to make one for yourself.'

'Thank you, Mr Cardwell.'

'And after that,' he grinned at her, his eyes full of mockery, 'you can finish clearing up this desk.'

Her eyes met his and she felt exhilaration course through her. 'Thank you. I'll try to satisfy you, Mr Cardwell. I – I really do need a job. But I'll have to give a week's notice at Sevley's, I'm afraid.'

His smile faded. 'Do you really have to? I need you here.'

'Yes, I do have to. It's only fair.'

'I suppose so.'

'But I can stay and help you today.' A blush stained her cheeks. 'I'm afraid I sent word to Mrs Sevley that I was indisposed.'

He roared with laughter. 'Indisposed! All right, I'll pay you for today's work, then you can let me know when you'll be able to start.' Edith wouldn't like him hiring a pretty young woman to do the office work, but then, his wife didn't like anything very much since she'd had their second child, him included. His lips tightened at the thought of her. She'd brought him money, and ownership of this yard, but she hadn't brought him much joy. And she wasn't even a good mother, either, preferring to go out and have endless cups of tea and eat cakes with her gossipy friends, leaving the children to the maids. Which was probably why they couldn't keep their maids for long.

He banished Edith from his mind, as he usually did at work. He was going to enjoy teasing Miss Emma Harper. So prim and ladylike, though not too ladylike to get her hands dirty. And pretty as well. It'd be a pleasure to have her around.

Lizzie continued to turn to Polly for companionship and the two of them often went for walks together when it was fine, just to get out of the house and away from their mam's sour comments about anything and everything. Polly never said much, but she was a good listener and Lizzie always had plenty to talk about from what had happened in the shop.

'I don't think I'd do very well in a shop,' Polly said thoughtfully one day. 'I'm not quick enough at sums.'

There was no denying that, Lizzie admitted to herself. 'What do you want to do, then?'

Polly stopped walking for a minute to think things over, then decided to confide in Lizzie. 'I think I'd like to go into service, actually.'

'What, do housework all day? I'd go mad.'

'Women do housework all day when they're married,' Polly pointed out. 'And they don't get paid for it then. I like doing housework an' Mam's told me what it was like in service. I think it'd suit me just fine. She says rich folk can't always find maids nowadays, because modern girls don't want that sort of job, so I'd have no trouble getting a place, I reckon. I think I'd like to work in a big house, though, where there were other people to talk to, not get a place as a general. I wouldn't like to work on my own all the time.'

'But you'd have to go away from home if you did that. You'd have to go and live in!' Lizzie was horrified at the mere thought of losing her sister's company.

'I wouldn't mind that – except for missing you.' Polly certainly wouldn't miss her mother shouting at her and slapping her. And she wouldn't miss Johnny, either. He was a sneaky little devil, Johnny was, and she'd caught him trying to break into her savings box the other day. Now, Miss Harper kept it for her up in the attic room and even Mam didn't know where it was.

'Well, I'd mind. I'd miss you a lot.' Lizzie scowled and walked along for a minute or two in silence before cheering up again. 'But you've got a year or two before you have to think about that, Polly. Eeh, you're as bad as our Eva, for planning ahead. You're only just turned twelve now. You might change your mind when you get older.'

Polly shook her head. 'I don't think I will.'

★ ★ ★

While Lizzie and Polly were drawing closer, Eva was feeling more and more distanced from her family. She loved school, and being with her friend and mentor, Alice Blake, but she absolutely hated the time she spent at home.

With her third year at secondary school approaching, Eva had to work out what to do afterwards. What she really wanted was to train as a teacher, but her mother had already started hinting about clerical work.

'I don't fancy office work,' Eva said one day.

'You'll do as you're told, young lady!' Meg snapped. 'I don't know what the world's coming to when uppity young madams,' she scowled sideways at Lizzie, 'cheek their mothers and tell them what they want – *want*, indeed. You should think yourself lucky to have a roof over your head. That secondary school has given you some very airy-fairy ideas. If I had my way, you'd be leaving this year, not next. No! I don't want to hear any more cheek from you. Just get that table cleared, then do the darning.'

'But I have some homework to do.'

'Well, it'll have to wait, won't it? Sometimes you must do things for others, instead of expecting them to do things for you all the time. I work my fingers to the bone for you children, I do that. It's a poor look-out if I can't have an hour off now and then.' And she slammed the mending basket down in front of Eva and stamped up the stairs to get ready to go out with Fanny Preston. They always sat together in the Hare and Hounds, making disparaging comments about the world and exchanging gossip. Whenever Sam came in, he'd buy them a half of stout each. Otherwise they'd make one or two glasses last all evening.

'I'll help you with the mending, Eva,' Polly said, coming in with her hands still damp and reddened from the washing-up. 'I don't mind.'

Lizzie came to sit at the other side of the table. 'When's the homework due?'

'Tomorrow.'

'I'd offer to help as well, but Mam would soon notice the difference between my darning and yours.'

'Go and do your homework,' Polly urged. 'I like mending. It makes me feel peaceful.'

'Thanks,' Eva said gruffly. 'You're all right, you two.'

'Tell that to Mam,' Lizzie said sourly.

'There's no telling anything to her.'

CHAPTER EIGHT

1911–1912

Emma Harper found working for James Cardwell disconcerting. It was a while before she thought of a word that satisfied her, but that one did.

'Ah, you're here at last!' was the greeting he gave her the first day.

'What do you mean "at last"? It's not quite nine o'clock.'

'Well, we start work in the yard at eight o'clock, so I expect you to be here by that time, too.'

She took off her coat to give herself a moment to think and by the time it was neatly folded over her arm, had decided not to take any bullying from him. 'You said nothing about hours, so I assumed it'd be the standard nine o'clock start. Perhaps you'd like to discuss the hours with me now? And am I to work in here?' She gestured around her then looked pointedly at her coat.

He looked round, really looked. 'Mmm. It's a right old mess, this place. Put that coat back on. We'll have to go out.'

'I beg your pardon?'

'Put – your coat – back on!' He took it off her arm and shook it at her.

'But where are we going?'

'To buy some new office furniture.'

She snatched her coat back from him and put it down on the desk. 'Before we go out, shouldn't we make a list of what we need?'

He scowled. 'Are you looking a gift horse in the mouth, Miss Harper?'

'I'm suggesting we work out what we need before we buy anything. I shan't know yet, since I've only spent a few hours here. But if you know what furniture and equipment to buy, that's fine by me.' She picked up a pencil and found a scrap of paper.

He perched on a corner of the desk, grinning. 'Oh. I thought you'd know all that – being such a superior sort of clerical worker.'

'Sarcasm is unnecessary, Mr Cardwell. I shall probably know a lot more by the end of the week. Though,' she frowned at the desk, 'with this being in such public view, a modesty panel would be useful.'

'*Modesty* panel?'

'Yes, a board across the front, so that I don't need to sit with my knees pressed together all the time.' She couldn't help smiling at his expression.

He bent to study the desk. 'I'll fit something temporary. But we'll get you a new desk – put it on your list. Item: one desk. Large and imposing, to impress clients. And you'd better put chairs for customers on your list, too. Sometimes they arrive before I'm ready for them, then the lad has to scrabble round to find them chairs from the kitchen.'

Emma picked up a piece of paper and scribbled on it. 'Anything else?'

He shrugged. 'A plant maybe. A picture for the wall, too. *Not* the King and Queen! Whatever we need to make this place look more attractive. You're a woman – you should have a few ideas about that. *Don't sit down!*'

She froze, wondering what on earth had got into him now.

'I've got a bit of wood panelling which'll be just right for your modesty panel.' He chuckled. 'If you go and get us all a cup of tea, it'll be finished by the time we've drunk it – well, nearly. I'll give it a coat of varnish just before I go home tonight.'

'Who's "us all"?'

'Me, Walter, Tim – no, he's out on a job – and young Ned.'

'Right.' Emma walked through to the kitchen, which was in nearly as bad a state as the first time she'd come here. Clicking her tongue in annoyance, she put the kettle on and automatically began to clear up. She and Blanche had learned early on in their stay with the Kershaws that the only way to stay comfortable in cramped surroundings was to keep tidy all the time. Now, it was second nature to her.

When banging noises echoed from the front room, she went to peer through the door and found James Cardwell on his knees in front of her desk attaching a cross piece to the legs. A big panel of wood lay on the floor.

He looked up as she came in. 'This be all right for a temporary job? Modest enough for you?'

She ignored that gibe. 'It'll be fine, thank you, Mr Cardwell.'

When she brought the tea, Walter, who seemed to be a man of few words, tasted it cautiously, then relaxed. 'Good.' He took a loud slurp.

James grinned. 'You'll win his heart yet, Miss Harper. Great one for his cuppa, is our Walter.'

She sipped her own tea, still feeling like a stranger. 'I hope my duties will include more than making cups of tea and lists of furniture?'

'They certainly will. And when young Ned's arm is better, you can teach him to make a decent brew-up instead. Your time is more valuable to Cardwell's. Oh, and will you put an advert in the paper for someone to clean here regularly?'

'Well . . .' She looked at him cautiously.

'Spit it out.'

'There may be no need to spend money on an advert. One of my landlady's neighbours works as a cleaner. Mrs Holden has a personal hatred of dirt, though she's a bit of a gossip.' Lizzie still hated the Holdens, but Emma thought the mother was an honest soul and struggling like many others to keep her unruly family decent. The eldest daughter had just had to get married and young Mary was boy-mad – unlike Lizzie, who was very immature still in some ways.

'Tell her to come and see me, then. Anything to save myself the cost of an advert.'

Mr Cardwell was mocking her again. He seemed to have a very wayward sense of humour. She wasn't sure she liked that. 'Very well.'

'But before you do, you'd better decide how often we'll need her services and how much I'm to pay her.'

Emma inclined her head and took another sip of tea.

Walter gave the panel a kick by way of indicating that it was firmly fixed. 'Bit o' varnish tonight.' Nodding to Emma, he put his cup and saucer on the table and shambled out towards the back.

'Welcome to Cardwell's, Miss Emma Harper!' James said softly, lifting his cup in a mock toast. 'I hope you enjoy working here.'

'I hope I do, too.' She wasn't at all sure about that, but she was prepared to give it a good try. 'Perhaps you'll explain some of my duties now?'

The Kershaws celebrated Lizzie's sixteenth birthday in March 1912 with a cake made by Polly and a few presents. Lizzie felt it appropriate to put her hair up from now on, a sign she considered herself grown-up. She had experimented with hairstyles and, with Polly and Emma Harper's help, had found a way of fastening her hair neatly on the crown of her head. She was very pleased with the result.

'You look lovely,' Polly said admiringly when her sister came down to show it off on the Sunday after her birthday.

Meg Kershaw stared at Lizzie with a sour expression. 'Who said you could put your hair up?'

'I'm sixteen now.'

'Well, I don't want you putting your hair up yet. You're too young.'

Lizzie gave her a long, level look, but said nothing.

Meg let out a scornful laugh. 'And besides the fact that I haven't given you permission, it'll soon fall down and look messy. Your hair always does. Besides, it doesn't suit you like that, makes your face look even narrower. So you can just take it down and tie it back with a ribbon again.'

'I like it up.' Lizzie stared right back at her mother. 'And I'm not taking it down.'

'You'll do as you're told.'

'I don't see why it makes any difference to you. You don't usually care what I do. You're just saying that to hurt me.' Fine birthday she was going to have with her mother in this sort of mood.

'How dare you speak to me like that? Who do you think you are?'

When her mother raised her hand, Lizzie stepped back and said quickly, 'If you hit me again, I'll hit you back.' And had to prove that. Which made her mother shriek for Percy.

He came running in from the front room, to find Lizzie, cheeks dead white, with a fierce look in her eyes, standing rigid next to the kitchen table, Polly sobbing quietly in one corner and his mother collapsed in a chair weeping hysterically. He chose to deal with his mother first. 'Wait for me in the front room, young lady,' he snapped at Lizzie.

She shrugged and walked out.

'Polly, can you go and play out or something?'

She chose to go upstairs and listen from the landing.

He sat down next to his mother, holding her hand and patting it gently while Meg told her tale. Percy was quite horrified at what she had to say.

When he found Lizzie, sitting in the front room staring stonily into the empty hearth, he burst out, 'What on earth got into you? To hit your own mother. Shame on you!' even before he had closed the door behind him.

She didn't shout at him, or cry, just stared at him.

'Lizzie? Answer me.'

'I will if you're going to listen to my side of the tale. Or have you judged me guilty and sentenced me to hang already?'

'Anyone would be shocked at a lass hitting her own mother.'

'But not shocked if she hits me?'

'She's your mother. She has the right.'

Lizzie took a deep breath. 'Then perhaps I'd better go and find myself some lodgings, because I'm not putting up with it any more.'

He was bewildered. 'Not putting up with what?'

'Mam's been hitting me for years, Percy, ever since Dad died. You don't realise how often she does it because she's a bit careful who's around when she lets fly. I know she doesn't like me, though I don't know why.' She took another deep breath, fighting off tears. 'When I turned sixteen I promised myself I wouldn't let her hit me any more.' Her eyes were bleak and her voice wobbled as she added, 'She has no right to hit me so hard and so often. *No right!* I don't do anything to deserve it.'

Percy stared at her. 'How often does she hit you?'

'Every couple of days. Hard enough to make bruises, too.' After a moment's hesitation, she unbuttoned her blouse and showed him her shoulder. A large bruise was just turning yellow. 'This one was the final straw, Percy. She had the rolling pin in her hand when she did that. It really hurt and it's been stiff ever since. I had to tell Mrs D I'd bumped myself. Mam only hits me when you're out, and not when our dear lodgers are around, either. So it isn't just anger, is it? It's – it's calculated. She *likes* hurting me.' When he said nothing, she added, 'You don't have to take my word for it, you can go and ask our Polly. Look at her bruises, too. Mam hits her and Johnny as well, but not as much as she hits me.'

It was a moment before he could form any words, so shocked was he by the size of that bruise. 'Why didn't you tell me?'

Lizzie shrugged. 'What would you have done?' She waited for a comment, but now he was the one staring into the empty fireplace. 'Shall I move out? I'd have done it before but,' her voice faltered, 'I don't think I'm earning enough to pay for decent lodgings.'

He raised his eyes and she was astonished to see them full of tears. 'You don't need to move out, Lizzie. This is your home. I'll tell Mam I've given you a thorough scolding, but that you're unrepentant. I'll suggest she asks me from now on if she wants you punished.' He broke off and held out his arms. 'Oh, Lizzie love, I'm sorry.'

She nodded, but did not go to hug him. He wasn't going to tell their mother she was wrong, he was just going to try to stop the beatings. Well, she'd done that already by hitting her mother back. They both knew it. She'd wept about the situation so often, usually sitting out in the lav, that she seemed to have no tears left now. 'I'll do my best to keep the peace, Percy. But I'll hit her back if she lays one finger on me again. I mean that.'

He came across, pulled her stiff body into his arms and gave her a long hug, rocking her to and fro, and though Lizzie held herself stiffly at first, after a moment she leaned against him and then the tears came.

'I thought . . .' she sobbed against him '. . . I thought you'd agree with her. I thought you m–might turn me out.'

'No, love. You've every right to be here. I just try to keep her as happy as I can.'

When Lizzie had dried her eyes, she said quietly, 'It's not fair on you, either. You're stuck with her now until she dies, because she won't marry again. Who'd have her? You should be finding yourself a nice girl and getting married.'

'We both know I shan't be able to do that.'

She sighed and clasped his hand for a minute. 'Life isn't very fair, is it?'

'No. But at least we have enough to eat and a decent roof over our heads, which is more than a lot of other folk have. Pilby's have let a few chaps go lately, but the foreman told me I'm all right. And Mam keeps this place nice for us, you've got to give her that. So we've a lot to be thankful for. And you are happy at work, aren't you, Lizzie love?'

Her face brightened a little. 'Yes. Very happy. Me an' Jack have a bit of fun together. Mrs D doesn't mind us enjoying ourselves an' chatting, so long as the work gets done.'

'I saw you in the park with him last Sunday – with Polly walking behind. It looked like . . . are you getting a bit fond of Jack?'

She didn't pretend to misunderstand him. 'Maybe. I don't know. I feel older than him sometimes, but we're good friends and that's enough for me at the moment. And I've got Polly as well as Jack. Me and her are right good pals now.'

Percy looked relieved. 'I'm glad for you. Friends are a help.'

'Well, you should know. You've got Sam.'

'Yes.' But he had been a bit distant since Percy let him down on that deal. He changed the subject. 'It's been a rotten birthday for you.'

She shook her head. 'No. It's been – useful.'

But from then on her mother did not speak to her at all unless she had to. And Lizzie couldn't pretend that didn't hurt. Before there had been occasional patches where her mother hadn't been so bad with her, but now things were always hostile.

All in all, what with Sam and the situation at home, Percy found it a relief to go out to evening classes. It was his main source of pleasure now and he found that he had not lost his love of learning. Emma had been right about that. He told her so as they walked to and from their classes together.

'I like to keep my brain alive,' she said as they walked back through the moonlit streets.

'Aye.' But his thoughts were on her: her slender ankles, soft hair and dainty ways. She always looked lovely. But he had no right even to think that. So he tried not to look at her too often. And he didn't think she knew how he admired her.

Still upset about his mother's attitude to Lizzie, Percy mentioned the incident to Sam.

'You'll never change your mam. The best thing your Lizzie could do would be to find herself a chap an' get wed,' Sam said at once. 'Then she'd be able to leave home.' He felt rather angry that Mrs Kershaw had been bashing the lass he still intended to marry.

'Oh, Lizzie's found herself someone. But she's in no hurry to wed him.'

'She's found herself a chap?'

Percy was surprised by the sharpness of Sam's voice. 'Aye. It came as a bit of a shock to me, too. They grow up quickly, don't they?'

Sam nodded and forced a smile to his face. 'Yes, they do. Er – who is he?'

'Jack Dearden. And it's nothing definite. They're just good friends at the moment. They're both a bit too young to get serious. But they look happy together. I saw them in the park.'

'I should think they *are* too young. Why, I can still remember her walking along the top of that wall.'

Percy chuckled. 'Aye. Silly little fool. But she seems to have settled down a bit lately. Perhaps putting your hair up is good for your brain.'

'Mmm.' Sam liked the way wisps of soft black hair always fell down the nape of Lizzie's neck, however hard she tried to pin it up neatly. She was getting a womanly look to her now – at last!

He made an excuse to leave the pub early that night and went for a walk round the silent park to think things over. Of course, he wasn't supposed to be in there at that hour, but he often scaled the gates at night. You couldn't have a quiet think in the house when Gran was around, nor could you think at work during the day. And Gran was failing lately, getting that shrunken look to her that he'd seen before when an old person was sliding gently towards the end of life.

I'll wait a bit and see what happens, he decided as he strolled past the little boat pond, too immersed in his own problems to notice the beauty of the moonlight shining on it. Yes, I'll see how Gran goes an' I'll keep an eye on Lizzie. No use rushing into things. Percy may be wrong about the lass courting Jack Dearden. He's not all that smart where people are concerned. He's better with his books and figuring, that one is. Sam chuckled. Why he wants to go to classes to learn about looking after money, I don't know. He'll never have any, that's for sure.

But Sam would. Had quite a bit of cash hidden away already. It made him feel good to know it was there if he ever needed it. And no one had ever caught him at his 'night job', because he was very careful indeed and didn't do places too often – even more careful than Josh, who was a wily bugger.

A little later, as he climbed back over the park wall, he nodded and said aloud, 'But I shan't wait much longer for her. She's mine an' she allus has been, an' no one else is havin' her.' He didn't know why he continued to feel so strongly about Lizzie, but he did, so that was that.

By July of that year, Eva would have spent three years at secondary school, which would qualify her to start training as a teacher. She talked things over with Alice Blake, who had recently had some very good news, and then she asked Percy to speak to them both before she approached their mother.

He walked out to the teacher's little house on the Saturday afternoon, saw Eva's bicycle standing against the wall and found his sister cosily installed in the sitting room, looking more at home than she ever did in Bobbin Lane.

'Take that chair, Percy. It's the one we always give to gentlemen callers.' Eva and her teacher exchanged smiles. There was obviously some joke between them about this.

'It's very comfy.'

Alice smiled at the earnest young man. 'A cup of tea, Mr Kershaw?'

'Thank you. That'd be very nice.'

'And try one of these little cakes. They're Eva's speciality.'

He waited for them to tell him what they wanted. He had already guessed it must be be something that would cause more trouble with his mother. Since the confrontation with Lizzie, Mam was quick to take offence at anything and everything, and he'd noticed Polly's cheek looking reddened once or twice. He'd have to speak out about that if it went on, because Polly wasn't a naughty little lass. But it was hard to take your own mother to task. Well, he found it hard, anyway.

He accepted the cup of tea, ate a couple of cakes and waited.

'It's about my future, Percy,' Eva said at last.

'I thought it might be. Time for you to start training as a teacher in the autumn, isn't it?'

'Yes. I've done three years of secondary school, and now I have to apply to become a pupil teacher – I can get a small bursary for that, which'll help. Then after a year as a pupil teacher, I'll need to go to training college. That'll – well, it'll cost more money. And the brewery won't help any more, nor will Mrs Pilby.' Alice had asked them.

He suppressed a sigh. 'We'll find the money somehow.'

Miss Blake cleared her throat. 'There is an alternative, one which will take the burden off your family and give Eva a better chance to learn how to teach.'

'Oh?'

'I've just been left a small house by an old uncle. It's over the other side of Rochdale and there's some money, too.' More money than she had expected, actually.

'I'm very glad for you.'

'It is rather a nice feeling to have the security. But the thing is, if I go to live there – well, I shall know no one. So I thought maybe I could help Eva and myself at the same time.'

Now he was thoroughly puzzled. 'I don't understand?'

'I've made enquiries and I can get a job as a teacher nearby, but – well, I want to take Eva to live with me.' She'd applied for the job and had also mentioned her 'clever niece' who wanted to become a pupil teacher and been assured by the headmaster, who was delighted to gain such an experienced teacher, that they could find a place for the lass as well. 'Your sister will find it a lot easier to start as a pupil teacher in a place where no one remembers her as a child. And – and I've grown very fond of her.'

'I want to go with Alice,' Eva said firmly, putting one arm round her teacher's neck. 'It's a much better way to arrange things, Percy, because it's so hard to study at home, and I'll have even more studying to do now, as well as lessons to prepare.'

'But—'

'And Mam makes such an atmosphere in the house. Honestly, it's murder when you go out to the pub with Sam. She's always yelling at Lizzie, even though she doesn't hit her any more. That's the only time she says anything to her. The rest of the time she tells me to tell her things, even when Lizzie's in the same room. And Mam hits Polly and yells at her, too. On and on. I don't know how Miss Harper and Miss Emma put up with it. Don't you think,' she hesitated, then asked quietly, 'that Mam's getting a bit strange lately? You know, Percy.'

'Mmm.' He ignored the remark about Mam and let out his breath in a long, weary sigh at the prospect of more trouble. 'I don't think she'll agree to your leaving, Eva love.'

'She may do when she realises how much money it'll save her – well, save you, really. You've been wonderful to us all, Percy. It's about time you had more of your own money to spend, not to mention a life of your own. You work so hard.'

He shrugged. 'Even so, she still won't agree.'

'She will if we insist and keep on insisting. We'll just have to wear her down.'

'And anyway, I'm not sure that I like it, either.' He frowned at Miss Blake, then turned back to his prettiest sister. 'It's like – it's as if you *want* to leave the family.'

Eva avoided his eyes. 'I'll be coming back on visits.'

'How often?'

She flushed. 'In the school holidays.'

His voice was sarcastic. 'Three times a year?'

'You can come and visit me as well.'

'A couple more times a year.' If that. They'd never been a family for gallivanting and even when his father was alive had never gone away on holiday as others did, because his mother preferred her own home.

Eva and Miss Blake began to speak at once, then both stopped.

'I'll say it,' Eva said firmly. 'I hate living at home now, Percy, really hate it. I've not been happy for a long time, but I couldn't see any way out so I just put up with things. Now there is a way out and I'm going to take it, whatever Mam says or does.'

He looked at her face, so set and determined. Like Lizzie, she seemed to have grown up a lot lately, and in fact, although she was a year younger, she looked older, with a plump, womanly figure. There was also a look in her eyes that said she considered herself an adult, not a child, even though she'd not tried to put up her hair yet or lengthen her skirts.

'So the thing to do is to decide how we tell Mam.'

'We?'

She nodded. 'I really do need your help on this, Percy.'

He sighed and sat staring at the folded fan of coloured paper in the empty fireplace. The whole house was full of pretty touches like that. His mam kept their place immaculately clean, but she didn't have a sense of beauty. The Harpers had made the attic beautiful, though. He loved going up there for a cup of tea. It felt so restful, with its soft colours and pictures on the wall.

The two women exchanged glances as he said nothing, allowing him time to think.

'Well, I have to admit it'd be the best thing for you, Eva,' he said at last. 'But I'm going to miss you, love. A lot.'

Relief flooded through her. 'I'll miss you, too. But I won't miss Mam. You don't see the half of it, Percy. You ought to pay more attention to what she's doing.'

Lizzie had said that too. He was puzzled as to how he could do or see more. What with work all day and then evening classes, he had as much on his plate as he could take. Too much. As Lizzie said occasionally, life wasn't fair. Not on any of them. But then, that was how it went. Things just happened and you had to cope with them.

CHAPTER NINE

1912

The next day, after dinner, Percy slipped Lizzie a shilling and told her to take Polly and little Johnny out to the park for the afternoon.

'I don't mind taking Polly, but I don't want *him* tagging along.'

'I need to speak to Mam, love. An' – well, there's going to be trouble. So you'll be best out of it. All of you.'

'It's not about me?' Lizzie still had nightmares about her mother throwing her out of the house and for the first time in her life had started saving money. But the change from the shilling a week she was allowed to keep didn't mount up very quickly.

'It's about our Eva.'

She sighed with relief, then looked at him, head on one side. 'She's found a way to become a teacher, then? How?'

'It'll be best if I don't say anything to you till after we tell Mam, I think. You know how touchy she can get about things like that.'

Lizzie rolled her eyes. 'Don't I ever! All right. What time should we come back?'

'As late as you can. About four, or half-past even.'

But Meg became suspicious when Lizzie and Polly, having finished the washing up, began to chivvy their little brother to get ready to go out. 'It's not like you two to take Johnny with you.'

Lizzie felt the anxiety radiating from Polly, standing beside her, and stepped in. 'Oh, I thought it'd give you a bit of peace. We can go and watch the model boats on the pond.'

With the promise of an ice cream in the park if he went with them, Johnny nodded his agreement.

'There's something going on,' Meg said stubbornly, eyes narrowed as she stared from one to the other. 'I can always tell.'

Eva concentrated on folding up the tablecloth.

Percy looked up from his newspaper and jerked his head at Lizzie and Polly to leave. 'I asked them to go out. Me an' Eva want to talk to you, Mam. We have some good news.'

'Oh?' Suspicion was writ large on her thin face. 'What is it?'

'We'll wait for Miss Blake to come round first, shall we? She's part of it all.'

'I see. You've been plotting with that woman behind my back again.' She glowered at her middle daughter. 'You can be a sly one, Eva Kershaw, when you want something.'

Percy kept his voice calm. 'We've been discussing things with Miss Blake, that's all. Now, let me make you another cup of tea and we'll go and sit in the front room, shall we?'

'I'll make the tea,' Eva said quickly. She delayed completing that task as long as she could, glancing at the clock on the mantelpiece from time to time and praying that her teacher would hurry up. Just as she was setting the teapot on the tray, there was a knock on the front door. 'Thank goodness!' She added another cup to the tray as she heard her brother walk down the hall to answer it.

But it was Sam Thoxby, calling to invite his friend to go for a walk with him.

Percy glanced over his shoulder, hoping Sam's voice had not penetrated to the front room and gesturing to him to keep quiet. 'I need to have a little talk with Mam today, I'm afraid, lad. About our Eva. I've sent Lizzie and the two young 'uns out to the park, so I can't ask you in just now.'

'Ah? Secrets?'

'Things to be decided about our Eva. I'll tell you when it's all settled.'

So Sam walked back down the street and turned towards the park. This would be a good time to check whether Lizzie was meeting that lad. If they looked too cosy together, he'd have to do something about it. Anyway, he'd waited long enough for her now. He wanted to start courting her himself.

Just as Eva was carrying the tray through, there was another knock on the door. Alice Blake this time. 'Do come in.' She gave a quick shake of the head in answer to her teacher's mouthed query about how things were, then picked up the tray off the hallstand and gestured to the visitor to precede her into the front room.

Percy stood up and shook the teacher's hand, worried at his mother's angry expression and lack of welcome. 'Won't you sit down, Miss Blake?'

For a few minutes they made stiff conversation and sipped their tea, then Meg set her cup down with a clatter. 'Well, what's this about, that it needs three of you to tell me?'

Percy tried to speak cheerfully, as if he was about to give her good news. 'It's about Eva's future, Mam. You know she wants to become a teacher and—'

'She's had more than enough favoured treatment already and we can't afford another two years without her paying her way. She could go and do a commercial course like Miss Emma did and be earning in a few weeks. I'm not having—'

Her voice was rising, becoming so shrill that Percy came across to sit beside her and laid his fingers gently on her lips. 'Let us tell you what Miss Blake has offered before you say anything else, Mam.'

She batted his fingers away, but took a few quivering breaths and managed to regain control of herself. 'Well? I'm listening.'

So they told the story again.

And Meg listened in absolute silence, her face a sour mask of disapproval.

'It'd be ever such a good chance for me, Mam,' Eva said when her teacher had finished. 'Don't you think?'

'No, I don't. What I do think is *she* is trying to take my daughter away from me and I'm not having it. So the answer is no.' She gave a hiccuping laugh and added, 'If you want one of my daughters, Miss Blake, you can take Lizzie. I wouldn't miss *her* in the slightest. But you're not having my Eva.'

Percy sighed. He'd known she'd be awkward about this. 'Let me talk to Mam alone now, will you, Eva, Miss Blake?'

'We'll go into the kitchen.'

'I'd be better suited if *she* went back home again and stayed there!' Meg called after the visitor, forgetting her usual awe of teachers in her anger. 'I'm not going to change my mind.'

'I hate her,' Eva tossed into the heavy silence as they stood in the kitchen. She stared blindly down at the tray. 'I really do hate her.'

And Miss Blake didn't check her. For she knew all about how Mrs Kershaw picked on Lizzie, hit the younger children regularly and hung like a heavy weight round Percy's neck. Besides, Mrs Kershaw was right in one way. Alice would be taking a daughter away from her family. Only – the daughter was unhappy there and wanted nothing more than to leave.

In the front room, Meg stared accusingly at her son. 'Nice little plot you've hatched.'

'Mam, it's not—'

'But you're not persuading me this t-time. She's my daughter, *mine*. I b-bore her. Carried her in my belly, here, as I carried you all. And I f-fed her, washed her, did everything for her. *So I'm not giving her away*.' Meg felt short of air and for a moment the room was filled with her harsh, rasping breaths.

'Eva *wants* to go with Miss Blake, Mam,' Percy said when her breathing calmed down.

'Well, she can just w-want. She's not leaving home.'

He looked at her face, grown ugly with spite, remembered her nasty remark about taking Lizzie instead and lost patience with her. 'You haven't asked me what I want.'

'I don't need to. Eva's *my* daughter.'

'Aye, and if you stop her becoming a teacher, *your daughter* is going to hate you for the rest of her life.'

'She can hate all she wants. You won't change my m-mind with arguments like that.' But Meg's voice wobbled as she spoke.

'You don't really have much choice about it, Mam.'

'Oh, yes I do! I have the say for once.' She leaned forward, spittle forming on her lips as rage consumed her and made her shake like a leaf. 'And even threatening to l-leave won't change my mind, Percy Kershaw. Because I'm her mother and I'm *not* giving my daughter away. And anyway, I don't think you would leave.' She'd thought about that a few times and had decided he was too soft to leave her on her own.

'Then we'll have to take it to a magistrate, won't we?'

She was still suddenly. 'What do you mean, take it to a magistrate?'

'Exactly what I say. Which will make it very public.' He waited, hoping that would shake her, but her expression didn't change. 'I told you about that chap I've met at my classes, the one as works in a lawyer's office? Well, I was talking to him about this, because I knew you'd make a fuss.'

'I've a right to make a fuss!'

'It seems he's known a case or two like this before, where a parent tries to spoil a child's chances in life. It's not as unusual as you think. An' what we have to do is take it to a magistrate – me and Eva and Miss Blake, that is. I have to show that I'm the main breadwinner in this house, Eva's guardian, like. And she has to show she understands what's going on. Then Miss Blake speaks her piece and the magistrate decides.'

'I don't believe you.'

He shrugged. It was a complete fabrication, but he hoped it might serve, because his mother usually hated the idea of other people knowing their family's business.

'Why would you d-do that to me?' Her voice became a shrill wail. 'You and Eva are my favourites, always have been. The only two good apples in a bad bunch. And now you're t-turning against me, too. I wish I'd died with my Stanley, I do that!'

The two listeners in the kitchen heard the raised voice, if not the words, and exchanged resigned glances.

When Percy did not answer, Meg yelled again, 'What have I ever done to you, Percy Kershaw, that you'd spite me by giving your sister away to this – this child-stealing spinster?'

'You've done nothing, Mam. It was Dad's accident that messed up our lives – *all* our lives, mine as well. Have you thought that maybe I want a bit more for myself than spending my time and money supporting you and the children? Have you ever thought about that?'

'No.' She was indignant at the very idea. 'And you've never s-said anything before about it, either.'

'Because what good would it have done? Before, I had to think what was best for the others. But now what's best for Eva is best for me, too.' He hated having to speak to her like this, but he had suddenly realised that the words were true. 'And I'm not letting your selfishness spoil things for us all, Mam.'

Her voice was a hiss, her face twisted with anger. 'You can't stop me! She's still under age.'

'I can. I just told you how. Me and Eva can go and see a magistrate.'

She was bewildered, unsure whether to believe him or not. So she resorted to her usual practice and fell into hysterics.

But this time, he simply walked out and left her to it, poking his head into the kitchen to suggest Eva and Miss Blake return to her house for the night. Then he walked along Bobbin Lane and down to the canal, treading blindly along its bank, staring unseeingly into the muddy water. He was tired of all this, tired of his mother leaning on him for everything. *Sick and bloody tired!*

In the park, Lizzie and Polly were standing behind their brother, watching indulgently as he chatted to another lad who had a little wooden boat to sail on the shallow water. All three Kershaws had eaten an ice cream and Lizzie intended to split the change from the shilling with Polly later.

'I wonder what Percy wants to talk to Mam about?' She wondered aloud.

'About Eva becoming a teacher, I suppose.'

'But we knew about that already. It's nothing new. Why did he want us out of the house?'

They stood frowning. 'Because whatever he's going to say will upset her,' Polly said slowly and her heart lurched. She hated it when there were fusses and scenes. 'Oh, I wish we didn't have to go back.' She sighed. 'Or that I was old enough to leave school and go into service.'

'I'm glad you're still at home.'

There was silence for a moment then Polly said, 'She's getting worse, isn't she?'

'Yes.' Lizzie nodded. 'She started going funny when Dad died. It turned her brain.' She'd heard people say that sometimes in the shop, and had decided a while back that it exactly described what had happened to her mother. 'We'd better get going.'

'I don't want to go back,' Polly repeated, looking distressed.

Lizzie gave her a quick hug. 'Well, we haven't got a choice, have we? It's the only home we've got. Half-past four, Percy said.' She looked up at the clock, thinking how slowly the hands had moved round this afternoon. She was bored with parks and screaming children. 'I wonder what stopped Jack coming out to meet us today?'

As her sister had wondered that same thing several times already, Polly didn't even try to answer.

Lizzie turned to look at the clock tower. 'Hey, Johnny! Time to go home.'

But their brother had his own ideas and these did not include going tamely back just because his sisters said so. To show off to his new friend, he gave them a mouthful of cheek, not noticing the man approaching.

'That's enough from you, my lad!' Sam said loudly, taking Johnny by the scruff of the neck and shaking him so hard his yelp of shock was cut off abruptly. 'You tell your sisters you're sorry for what you said and don't *ever* let me hear you talking to them like that again!'

Johnny squirmed, but was held fast, and shaken again for good measure when he did not immediately apologise. Fear had now replaced the impudent expression.

'Thanks, Sam. He can be a bit of a handful sometimes.' Lizzie beamed up at their rescuer.

Eeh, Sam thought, that smile lights up her whole face. It's a pity she doesn't smile more often. 'My pleasure, lass.' He turned to look down at the boy. 'I'm still waiting to hear that apology, you.'

Johnny wriggled, but the hand was firm on his neck. 'Sorry.'

'I couldn't quite hear that.'

'I said I were sorry!' He glared at his sisters as he spoke, though.

'Right, then. And don't let me hear you talking to any lasses like that again. Where do you think you are, using such foul language?'

Johnny shrugged.

Sam let go of his collar and turned to offer an arm to each girl. 'May I escort you young ladies home?'

Grateful to be spared a confrontation with her younger brother, Lizzie giggled and dropped him a mock curtsey. 'We'd be delighted, kind sir.' She took his arm.

Polly moved to Sam's other side, but didn't take his arm, just began walking along beside him, staring down at the ground and stealing the occasional glance sideways when he wasn't looking.

'Now, tell me what you've been doing with yourselves?' But it was Lizzie Sam was looking at, Lizzie whom he encouraged to speak, listening with a flattering attentiveness to what she said and asking her questions about the shop.

And for once, she felt happy to see him. This was the first time a man had ever treated her as grown-up enough to be offered an arm and she rather liked the feeling.

Polly didn't say a word the whole way home. But she worried a lot. Why was Sam Thoxby fussing over Lizzie like this? What did he want? Because she'd noticed, if no one else had, that Sam only fussed over you when he wanted something from you.

At the house, they found Emma Harper in the front room, in attendance on their mother who was lying exhausted on the sofa, whimpering from time to time. Percy, who had just returned, was sitting in the kitchen and making no attempt to help. He'd not have come home at all if it hadn't been for the other children being due back and the need to protect them.

Scenting a scandal, Sam accepted Lizzie's invitation to come in and have a cup of tea.

Percy seconded the invitation warmly. 'Could you make us all a cup of tea, love?' he asked Lizzie. 'Mam's had a funny turn. Eva's gone to stay the night at Miss Blake's house. And I reckon you'd better know what it's all about. You see . . .'

'Oh, crikey!' said Lizzie, when he'd finished. 'Mam will never agree to that.'

'I think she will,' Percy said thoughtfully. 'In time.' If not, he'd do something to make her, he would that.

'Well, I wish I could go and stay with Miss Blake for a few days, too. It's going to be murder here with her having hysterics all over the place.'

It took a month to wear down Meg Kershaw's resistance. Eva returned home and everyone tried to behave as if things were normal, but they weren't. Polly often sported a reddened cheek and wept into her pillow. Johnny, too, suffered indiscriminate slaps, but just shrugged them off. And one day Meg raised her hand to Lizzie in the kitchen, but dropped it again when the girl raised her own hand back and glared at her, saying, 'I meant it, you know!'

In the end, Percy went out with Sam and fortified himself with a couple of drinks and some friendly encouragement.

'Your thumping the children has got to stop,' he announced

to his mother from the doorway when he came home. 'If it doesn't, I'll not only leave home, I'll take them with me.'

He'd threatened that before, but he'd never said it in such a forceful way, never looked at her as if he hated her. Fear shivered through Meg. Somehow she believed his threat this time. And she'd never manage without Percy's wages.

'It's all that Lizzie's fault,' she muttered. 'She cheeks me all the time.'

'She doesn't.'

'And now you want to take Eva away from me.'

'She's definitely going.'

Meg sat sobbing quietly into her handkerchief. 'It's all gone wrong since Stanley died. I wish I'd died with him, I do that.' She sometimes thought about killing herself, she really did.

He didn't go over to sit beside her. Sam had said he should give her a slap or two to make sure she understood who was boss, but Percy wasn't like that. He could never have hit a woman. All he wanted was a peaceful life. And the only times he really felt at peace now were when he went off to his evening classes or took tea with the Harpers. Even that caused trouble with his mother, though, who didn't like him going up to the attic.

After a while, when the silence had dragged on and Percy's expression hadn't altered, Meg gave in. 'All right, then. Eva can go and live with that woman.'

'I knew you'd see sense, Mam.' Percy forced himself to take her in his arms, which he knew she wanted, and just held her close for a minute, patting her back gently. 'You always lose your children as they grow up, you know.'

You lose everyone, she thought, everyone who's dear to you anyway. But she'd still got Percy, thank heavens. And would make sure she kept him.

Sam had been heartened to find that Lizzie was not with Jack Dearden in the park, but he kept an eye on the situation and saw the two of them together once or twice on other Sundays. There was a comfortable look to them that made his hands clench into fists, but he had no intention of letting a mere strip of a lad steal a girl who was old enough now to start courting, especially when that lad was Peter bloody Dearden's brother. Sam had waited long enough for Lizzie to grow up. Now it was time to act.

He took to walking in the park himself on fine Sundays. He found a bench which gave him a good view of the main promenade area and would sit there, alone, scowling at anyone who approached. If people ignored the scowl and actually sat down, he found that a fart or belch would soon send them packing again.

One evening, he happened to be passing as Jack Dearden left the shop with a late delivery, so seized the opportunity and followed him. When the lad came out of one of the big houses near the park, Sam deliberately blocked his path. 'A word,' he said and stepped into the alley.

Jack was daft enough to follow him, which was more than Sam would have done if he'd been accosted by someone after dark.

He took up a position which blocked the entrance to the alley, seeing by the light of the street lamp uneasiness creep into Jack's face. He bunched one hand into a fist and saw the lad flinch.

'Got an interest in Lizzie Kershaw, have you?' he asked mildly, examining the clenched fist.

'She's a good friend. What's it to you?'

'I'm a friend, too, a good friend of the whole Kershaw family, an' they're getting a bit worried about things, so they asked me to find out what was going on.' He let the clenched fist thud into his other hand and saw the lad wince.

'I don't reckon it's any of your business.' Jack didn't believe anyone had asked Sam Thoxby to speak to him about Lizzie. That rotten mother of hers didn't care two hoots about what she did. 'And I have to get back to the shop now.' He made a quick dash for safety.

Sam tripped him up, then hauled him to his feet by the scruff of his neck and shook him. 'Dear me! Did you fall over, then?'

Jack tried vainly to push him away. 'What do you want?'

'I want to know your intentions towards Lizzie. We all do. We don't want you mucking that lass around.'

'Intentions?'

'Aye.'

Jack stared at him, this huge man standing half in the shadows. He felt afraid, really afraid. Most people did when Sam Thoxby got that look on his face. Only, Jack had never been afraid in quite that way before. He was tall for his age, though not as tall as his brother Peter, but he was still thin and lacking a man's muscles. Sam towered over him, six foot two of solid manhood. And hostility.

'I asked your intentions, lad. Was you intending to marry our Lizzie, like?'

'*Marry?*'

Sam felt exultation course through him at the shock in Jack's voice. No, of course he hadn't intended to marry her. Sam had seen it all before. A lad and a lass walking out, just enjoying one another's company, then they slipped up and had to get married. Well, no one was slipping up with Lizzie. No one except him, any road.

He held Jack against the wall, enjoying exercising his own strength, enjoying the fear on the other's face. 'I'm very,' he bumped Jack's head deliberately against the wall, '*very* fond of that lass. And I'm *not*,' another thump, 'having her messed around. So, if you're not intending to marry her, you'd best stop seeing her.'

'She's my *friend*, that's all.'

Sam laughed. 'Lads an' lasses your age don't stay friends. Things happen between them. Only they're not happening to our Lizzie, not with you.'

'I'd never—' The words were cut off as Jack was shaken again.

'You'd better not.' Sam let go. 'And I reckon you'd better find yourself another *friend* to walk out with of a Sunday or there'll be trouble. We look after our own in Southlea. *She* is one of our own. *You* aren't.' The lad was looking so stunned,

Sam couldn't help tormenting him a little more. 'Of course, if you were intending to wed her, that'd be different, like.'

He saw the horror on Jack's face and laughed. Stepping back, he brushed his hands against one another as if cleansing them of dirt. 'Think on. It's marriage or nowt with our Lizzie.'

He chuckled as he watched the lad hurry away. That's fixed the young sod. Exultation filled him. Now he was going to start paying attention to Lizzie himself. Sam whistled all the way home and poured himself a big tot of rum to celebrate, raising it in a silent toast to his wife-to-be.

When Gran commented on his good spirits, he just nodded. Tell her what he was planning and it'd be all over Southlea that he was courting Lizzie Kershaw. He didn't want to frighten the lass away.

CHAPTER TEN

Winter: 1912–1913

Cold, rainy weather and fog conspired to keep Jack and Lizzie apart for the next two Sundays, and after that it was the run-up to Christmas so they were both working flat out at the shop, with less time than usual to chat to one another.

Lizzie thought he seemed a little strange, not his usual self, but she was too busy to worry about it. Mr Dearden had had a feverish cold, and it'd been touch and go for a time. Mrs D had nursed him and Peter had taken over management of the shop as well as going round to the posh houses to take the orders. He was nice to work with, Peter was, and just occasionally he'd talk to her about the produce they sold or about a film he'd seen. She felt as comfortable with him as she did with Jack, even though he was a few years older. Peter was like his mother, kind and easy to get on with.

At home things were as bad as ever. Lizzie was missing Eva more than she had expected to and felt jealous sometimes when her sister's letters revealed how happy she was. Eva loved being a pupil teacher, especially as the children were quieter in the country and not nearly as much trouble as the lively youngsters of Overdale. And 'Alice says . . .' All the letters quoted that lady extensively. The Kershaws soon grew sick of the sound of her name.

'Eva's forgotten us already,' Polly said to Lizzie one day. 'You won't forget me when you get married, will you?'

'Me? Get married?' Lizzie nearly fell off her chair laughing. 'I'm not going to get married, not ever.'

'Oh, I expect you will. The lads look at you . . .' Polly frowned, searching for words and finding only '. . . as if they're interested.'

'Who does?'

'Well, Jack used to – only we don't see much of him now, do we? And some of the other lads we pass in the park. They look, too.'

Lizzie shrugged. 'You're imagining things, love.'

'I'm not! And there's Sam Thoxby as well, lately.'

'*Sam?* He's old, even older than our Percy.'

'But he still looks at you.'

'Does not.'

'Does so.'

They repeated the words, each getting louder and louder till they couldn't speak for laughing. It was a habit of theirs, but only when their mother wasn't around. She always said something nasty if she caught them laughing.

But Polly's words stuck in Lizzie's mind and sometimes she couldn't help peeking at Sam, to see if he really was looking at her. And he was. It made a little shiver run down her spine. Lots of girls had set their caps at Sam, including her old enemy, Mary Holden, because he was considered quite a catch in the streets of Southlea, even though he wasn't exactly good-looking. But Polly was right. He didn't pay attention to any other girl but Lizzie. Not that *she* wanted him, certainly not. She still didn't like ginger hair or beefy men. Peter Dearden was her ideal of how a man should look, for Jack still kept getting spots, and anyway he had been funny with her lately, she didn't know why.

But whether she wanted him or not, it was nice to think of Sam looking at her like that. Especially as her mam had said to her once or twice that no one would ever want to marry a scrawny rat like her.

*   *   *

Two days before Christmas, Percy came home from work to find his mother looking even more miserable than usual. 'Something wrong, Mam?'

She gestured towards the mantelpiece. 'That came by second post. Read it.'

He picked up the letter propped behind the clock, a hastily scribbled pencil note, not at all like Eva's usual letters, which were always exactly two pages long and written in immaculate copperplate:

> *Dear Mam and everyone*
> *Alice has got the influenza and she's too ill to get out of bed, so I'm afraid I can't come home for Christmas after all. The influenza's really bad round here with lots of people ill. A man down the street died of it only last week, so I daren't leave Alice to fend for herself, not when she's been so kind to me. And I don't want to pass it on to you people, either, especially you, Mam.*
> *I'll come over as soon as I can and we'll have an extra celebration. I'll save your presents till then. I hope you all have a really happy time.*
> *Love,*
> *Eva*

Percy's heart sank, but he tried to speak cheerfully. 'Well, let's hope Eva doesn't catch it herself.' But if she did, she'd not be really ill, because she hadn't inherited their mother's weak chest like Johnny had. 'And she's right not to risk giving it to you, Mam. You know how badly you always catch things.'

Meg glared at him. '*That woman* has done this on purpose! She's probably only pretending to be ill, trying to stop me seeing my own daughter! And at Christmas, too.'

Rather than telling her not to be silly, Percy drew a deep, slow breath into his nostrils, fingering the moustache he'd grown lately, which his mother hated but which Emma said really suited him. Sometimes recently he had felt like striking out at his mother when she acted so irrationally. Sometimes he . . . Another long, slow breath and he was in command of himself again. After all, he'd had years of practice at biting his tongue.

He could guess, even without being told, that Eva was secretly glad of the excuse to stay away. Each of her visits to Overdale seemed to end in tears and recriminations from their mother, which sent his sister away with a tight, angry look on her face. And for days afterwards there would be snide remarks tossed at Lizzie, scoldings for the two younger children (though she didn't hit them nowadays, thank goodness, or not as much) and weeping sessions in the front room or, if she could catch him, in the arms of her elder son.

'How do you stand it, living here?' he asked Emma bitterly one day when he met her on the stairs after one of these scenes. 'Why don't you two find yourselves some new lodgings?'

They'd considered it a few times, but Blanche had said nowhere was perfect and she had grown quite fond of young Polly lately. 'Oh, we don't hear a lot up in our attic,' Emma told him lightly. 'And we really like our nice big room. Besides, your mother's never rude to us. Your poor little sisters have a lot to put up with, though.'

'Aye. We all do. And I'm grateful to Miss Harper for taking an interest in Polly. It gets her out of the atmosphere downstairs when you invite her up to visit you.'

Emma smiled. 'My sister and yours enjoy their little tea parties enormously. And it leaves me free to visit my friend Millie more often, so I'm grateful to Polly, actually.'

He sought for something else to say to keep her with him. 'She loves the singing lessons.'

'She has a nice little voice.' Emma heard Mrs Kershaw come out of the kitchen and stand at the foot of the stairs. She saw that Percy had heard it, too. They exchanged glances and she repeated, a little more loudly, 'Yes, she has a lovely little voice,' then turned to go back upstairs. It annoyed her to know Mrs Kershaw was eavesdropping. If it had been up to her, they would have left here ages ago and rented a house of their own. But she had realised that Blanche was afraid of making any changes. And not only was their life comfortable here – on the whole – but they were able to save money.

Embarrassed, Percy wished, not for the first time, that his mother would mind her own business. He stood and watched Emma climb the stairs, trim and neat as usual, with the prettiest pair of ankles he'd ever seen. Then he sighed quietly and went back downstairs.

Just after Christmas, Peter Dearden came home one night to find Jack sitting alone in the darkened shop, which was lit only by a nearby street lamp, staring moodily into space.

'What's up with you, sitting out here like a fool in the dark?'

'I – can you spare me a minute, Peter? I need some advice.'

'What about?'

'A girl.' Jack blushed hotly and kept his face averted.

'Oh, yes? You're a bit young to be needing advice about girls. Who is it?'

'Lizzie.'

'*Lizzie Kershaw?*'

'Yes.'

'If you've been messing about with that lass, I'll skin you alive.'

'I haven't been messing around. We're just friends, me an' Lizzie.' But he avoided Peter's eyes as he spoke, glad of the dimness. 'We just go for walks in the park together and – and talk.'

Peter stood over him, taller than Jack ever would be and looking very stern. 'So what's the problem, then?'

'It's – well, a friend of Lizzie's family stopped me in the street one day. He said if I wasn't serious, I should leave her alone.'

Peter considered this for a minute, then nodded. He might have done the same thing himself if someone had been paying undue attention to a sister or cousin. 'And are you serious?'

Jack shook his head. 'No – well, I like Lizzie a lot, but

we're too young to – to think of marriage.' He paused, trying to explain to himself as much as to his brother. 'And anyway, I want to learn to fly planes one day, and – and, well, I don't think she's ready to – to settle down, either. We're just – you know, good friends.'

Peter's lips twitched and he moved back into the shadows, not wanting to reveal that he found this situation amusing. His baby brother walking out with a lass! 'I think if you're not serious, then the family friend is right. You shouldn't see so much of Lizzie. It's not fair on her. Who was it spoke to you?'

'Oh, just someone.' Jack didn't even want to mention Sam Thoxby, because he was ashamed of how afraid he'd been.

'You're sure *she* doesn't think you're courting her?'

'No, of course not.' Well, he hoped she didn't.

'Then you should stop seeing so much of her, I reckon. You'll be in no position to support a wife and family for years, young fellow my lad.'

'No. You're right. And – thank you for listening to me.'

Peter walked away, smiling. Well, at least Jack had good taste in girls. But he hoped Lizzie hadn't had expectations. He didn't want her made unhappy. He enjoyed having her around, all cheerful and willing. She was a lovely young lass.

His well-meaning words had an unexpected effect on his brother.

Jack lay awake for hours that night before he could get to sleep. *Support a wife and family!* That was the last thing he wanted, the very last. He'd seen lads who'd had to marry young, because they'd got a lass into trouble, and they soon started looking unhappy and full of care. One, whom he'd known a little from the group of lads who met sometimes at the corner of the main street of an evening, had said to him bitterly, 'Watch your step, Jack lad. Don't ever get yourself into hot water like I did. You pay for it for the rest of your life.'

There was a lot Jack wanted to do before he got married. Mainly fly planes, though of course he hadn't told his mother and father that yet, only his brother. Which would mean leaving

Overdale and upsetting Mam. But he was still going to do it. Though not yet.

Support a wife and family!

Oh, no! That was the last, the very last thing he needed. He'd miss seeing Lizzie, talking to her, but he wasn't going to mess up his whole life. Not for any girl on earth.

Percy promised to take his mother over to visit Eva after Christmas but she came down with the influenza. No one was at all surprised when she was so bad they had to have the doctor in. James Balloch was a new man to the terraces of Southlea, a stern young Scot with a heart of gold where his patients were concerned, however much he tried to hide it. He gave Polly, who'd stayed at home from school, very strict instructions about looking after her mother and not letting her overstrain her heart while she was ill.

Meg lay back in relief. It was almost worth being ill to have a good rest. No one knew how hard it was for her sometimes to keep going, how tired she got. 'Will you – tell my son that, doctor?'

'Oh, yes. I'll make sure your family look after you, Mrs Kershaw.' Because he'd lost a few patients whose families hadn't looked after them and as a consequence had stopped mincing his words.

At a family conference, it was decided that Polly, now nearly thirteen, should stay home from school to look after her mother for as long as was necessary. She nursed Meg with her usual devotion to anyone in need, and did most of the cooking, while Lizzie and Johnny did the shopping and the two sisters shared the housework, all the time bearing meekly with their mother's complaints. Lizzie tried to make Johnny help them round the house, but it was more trouble than it was worth. So far as he was concerned, housework was women's work and he wasn't having anyone calling him a cissy. Percy lent a hand sometimes, though, and didn't seem to mind it.

The lodgers helped where they could, as well, behaving

more as if they were family members than paying guests. Miss Harper did some cooking and shopping, though she stayed away from the invalid, and Miss Emma also lent a hand after work. But meals were necessarily scrappy affairs, and they all missed Meg's excellent cooking, because Polly (kept dancing attendance on her mother) just didn't have the time or ability to do anything fancy, and Lizzie (who was a better cook) got home from work too late to help in that area.

Meg, enjoying the rest, soon felt better than she had for ages and stretched out her illness as much as she could. She was disappointed when the doctor said she had to get up and start doing a few things. 'Are you sure it's safe?'

'If you stay in bed any longer, you'll lose the use of your arms and legs,' he joked.

'But I still feel exhausted if I do anything, doctor.'

'Your chest is clear now and you must start to build up your strength again. You need to move about, do light work around the house.'

So she went down and sat in the front room, and when anyone tried to get her to do anything, pretended to feel faint. But after a quiet word with Dr Balloch, Percy insisted that Polly go back to school, so Meg had to start taking over her old tasks again. She still did as little as possible, leaving most of the heavy jobs to her daughters when they came home from work and school.

Then Lizzie started looking pale and sounding hoarse.

'Are you all right?' Percy asked one evening.

'Oh, it's just a bit of a cold.'

'Perhaps you'd better take a day off work. We don't want you coming down with the influenza as well.'

The thought of being at home with her mother all day was enough to make her shrug her shoulders and say, 'I'm all right! Just leave me alone, will you?'

But she wasn't all right. And she felt worse the next morning, far worse. As she was lingering over her breakfast, wondering whether to take Percy's advice, her mother said sharply, 'Get off to work, then! I don't want *you* under my feet all day.'

So Lizzie trailed off. But the wind was icy, seeming to cut right through her, and when she arrived at work, shivering and white, Sally Dearden took one look at her and told her to go home.

'You've got the influenza, Lizzie Kershaw, and I don't want you passing it on to us, thank you very much. Go home and get yourself to bed.'

'I don't want to – let you down.' She broke off as a cough erupted and nearly tore her apart. It felt as if someone was sticking knives into her back.

Sally waved one hand dismissively. 'You'll get better more quickly if you rest. Get off with you.'

As Lizzie walked through the streets, the wind was icy and she coughed a lot. She was now feeling so dizzy that she had to stop a couple of times to lean against the nearest wall.

'Eeh, you do look bad,' Fanny Preston said when she met her at the end of the street.

Lizzie hardly heard her. She staggered through the front door, tears of relief trickling down her cheeks, to be greeted by the sight of her mother pottering around the kitchen, looking rosy and happy. She paused in the doorway, trying to pull herself together, wishing her head wasn't thumping.

Meg turned and scowled when she saw who it was. 'What are *you* doing at home?'

'Mrs D sent me.'

Meg clutched her chest in shock. 'You've never lost your job!'

'Of course not. I've got the influenza.' Lizzie began to cough again and had to clutch the doorframe to stay upright. 'She says I'm to go – to go to bed.'

Meg didn't want to share her quiet house with this daughter. 'Just playing your usual tricks, if you ask me. It's a bit of a cold, that's all. And don't expect me to rush up and down those stairs all day, waiting on you! I'm not fully recovered myself, yet.'

Lizzie, who had been going to fill herself a hot water bottle, turned and walked slowly upstairs, shivering at the malevolence in her mother's expression. When she got into her bedroom, which was chilly and felt damp, she scrambled into her nightdress and wrapped an old shawl around her shoulders. As she crept into the bed, coughing, she wished that she had stayed to get that hot water bottle. She huddled all the covers round herself, but couldn't seem to get warm.

Miss Harper heard the sound of coughing from the girls' bedroom and hesitated outside the door, then shrugged and went downstairs to make herself a cup of tea. 'Is one of the girls ill?' she asked Meg.

'It's that Lizzie. She's not bad, just wants to laze around. Ignore her.'

But when Miss Harper carried her cup of tea back upstairs, she heard muffled weeping coming from the bedroom and couldn't ignore that. She tapped on the door and when there was no answer, pushed it open a trifle. 'Lizzie? Are you all right, dear?'

The face that peered back at her from under the bedcovers was bleached white, even the lips looking bloodless, and Lizzie was shivering so hard that Blanche could see it from where she stood. She didn't make the mistake of going into the room, because she was terrified of catching anything herself. 'I'll go and fetch your mother, dear.'

'She w-won't come.'

Blanche went back downstairs. 'Lizzie's really ill, I'm afraid, Mrs Kershaw. I do think you should go up and see her, maybe take her a warm drink. She's shivering and—'

'If she wants a hot drink, she'll have to come down and get it. I've just been ill myself. I have to be careful.'

Without a word, Blanche went back upstairs, listened again to the sound of hopeless weeping, then put on her hat and coat, feeling furious. Only when she was outside did she stop and wonder who to fetch. Polly? No, Mrs Kershaw would just send her back to school. It had to be Percy. Only he had the authority to get something done.

When she got to Pilby's, she hesitated a moment at the gate. It was such a big place, with all those huge workshops and sheds, and it looked so dirty. Almost she turned away, then she thought of the sick girl, lying alone and weeping, and gathered her courage together.

Inside the yard she found her way to the office and asked for Percy Kershaw. 'His sister is very ill indeed, I'm afraid.'

When Miss Harper had explained in a low voice why she'd come, Percy looked sickened. 'Is there no end to her malice?' he whispered before he could prevent himself.

'I'm sorry to trouble you at work, but I daren't care for Lizzie myself, given my own state of health. Your sister seems very bad. I think you should send for the doctor and get someone in to look after her. Perhaps Polly again?'

'I'll go and tell the foreman, then I'll come back with you, sort something out.'

'I, um, think it's best if we don't arrive home together. It'll make your mother even angrier. You could perhaps hint that Mrs Dearden sent a message to you at work?'

'All right.'

He told the foreman briefly what had happened.

Ben stared at him. 'But your mother's at home! Why can't she look after things?'

Percy was sick of hiding the truth. 'Mam hates our Lizzie. She'll not lift a finger to help her.'

'Eeh! What a thing to say!'

'Aye, but it's true all the same. You know I wouldn't ask for time off if it weren't necessary.'

As he walked along to get his coat, Percy nearly bumped into Sam.

'What's the matter with you? You look like you've lost ten bob and found a farthing.'

'It's our Lizzie. She's ill. Really ill, Miss Harper thinks. And Mam is refusing to look after her, won't even take her up a hot drink.'

'Your mother is a wicked old bitch!' Sam snapped.

Percy nodded. 'Trouble is, she's getting worse. I – I worry that she'll do Lizzie real harm one of these days. Since Eva left, she's been so strange at times.' He sighed and finished buttoning up his overcoat. 'What the hell am I going to do about looking after her, though?'

'I'd send my gran over but she's got the influenza herself.' Sam frowned. 'What about getting one of the neighbours round?'

Percy shook his head. 'My mother would go mad if we brought one of them in.'

'Well, you'll have to do something if the lass has got it really bad.' And Sam decided he'd go straight round after work himself to make sure Lizzie was being cared for.

Percy nodded. 'Aye. Well, best I go and see what's what first. No use borrowing trouble till you know what you're facing, is it?'

At home he opened the front door quietly, tiptoed along the hall and found his mother in the kitchen, toasting her feet on the fender and sipping a cup of tea. She looked up, startled to see him.

'Eeh, Percy! You did give me a turn. What on earth are you doing home at this hour?'

'I had a message to say Lizzie was ill.'

Spots of colour burned suddenly in Meg's thin cheeks. 'It'll be that Sally Dearden interfering again. And even if Lizzie *is* ill, why you had to come home from work, I don't know. What will they think at Pilby's? Anyway she's not really ill, just a bit under the weather.'

'I'll go up and see for myself.'

'She's all right, I tell you. Sleeping. You get back to work or they'll dock your wages.'

'They'll dock them anyway now so I might as well see how she's going on. Have you been up to see her lately?'

'Of course not. I'm only just getting better myself.'

He looked at her, not hiding his disgust. 'You didn't even take her a cup of tea, did you?'

Meg avoided his eyes. 'She's asleep.'

'How can you know that if you've not been up to see?'

'There hasn't been any noise. If she was awake, I'd hear the bed creaking.'

He stood over her, anger making a muscle twitch near his left eye. 'Make her a cup of tea now, Mam, while I go upstairs. And fill her a hot water bottle, too.' Then he walked out.

Muttering to herself, Meg lit the gas under the kettle again and went to fetch the flat-based earthenware bottle she always called a 'hot piggie'.

As Percy knocked on Lizzie's bedroom door, he heard a voice muttering inside. His sister was lying half-covered on the bed, tossing and turning, so lost in fever she didn't even notice him.

He tried to tuck her up under the covers but she beat him away, murmuring in delirium. Appalled, he ran downstairs and began to pull on his coat again.

Meg peered out of the kitchen. 'There, I told you she was all right. You get yourself back to work.'

'I'm going to fetch the doctor. She's bad – far worse than you were.'

James Balloch took one look at Lizzie then turned to Percy. 'I think we should get her into hospital. She's seriously ill. Pneumonia, I'm afraid. She must have been coming down with this for a while. Why didn't you send for me sooner?' When patients looked like this, he didn't give a lot for their chances, though he was amazed to see how neglected this lass was. Usually the families had drinks by the side of the bed, and someone nearby keeping an eye on the invalid. 'Who's been caring for her?'

'No one.'

The two men exchanged glances. 'Your mother still playing at being ill?'

Percy nodded.

'But surely even she—'

'Um . . . she doesn't like Lizzie.' It felt awful to have to admit this to a doctor.

Lizzie had begun to shiver violently again and huddled down under the bedclothes, whimpering.

The doctor spoke briskly. 'Well, I've got my motor car

outside. If you'll wrap your sister up in a blanket and carry her downstairs, I'll drive you to both to the hospital and see her admitted.'

For several days, Lizzie hovered between life and death. Sam sent her flowers but the nurses wouldn't put them by her bedside, saying she needed all the oxygen herself. When he was allowed in to see her for a minute, he was shocked by her pallor. He was suddenly terrified he'd lose her. He'd waited so long, so very long, for Lizzie to grow up.

'How much is it for a private room?' he asked abruptly, looking round the long ward with its twenty beds full of wheezing, coughing patients, for the epidemic was at its height.

Percy looked at him aghast. 'We can't afford a private room.'

'I can.'

'What do you mean?'

'I'd better tell you now that I mean to marry your sister one day. I've been waiting for her to grow up and I'm not having her die on me like this. She's mine!'

'But – you haven't even been courting her, Sam.'

'I was just about to. Let's go and see that bloody starched-up head nurse with the silly hat on.'

It was arranged very quickly.

Gran Thoxby fell ill that same day, but she didn't seem too bad so Sam just paid a neighbour to come in and look after her. She grinned at him from the bed and wheezed, 'Treating me like a queen, eh? You're a good lad, Sam.'

When she died quietly during the night, he stood for a long time by the bed before saying abruptly, 'You did well by me, Gran. I'll give you a decent send-off.'

In the morning, after he'd got a death certificate from the doctor and booked the funeral, he went out to the hospital to see Lizzie.

'I'm not having you dying on me as well,' he told her, holding her hand fast in his.

Lizzie blinked up through a fever dream to see a large figure standing by her bed. It seemed to her weak, watering eyes to be haloed in light from the window behind. 'Dad!' she sighed. 'Oh, Dad, I've missed you so.' And after that she started to get better.

Sam couldn't make out what she was mumbling about, but he liked the way she held on to his hand. 'Get better,' he whispered when it was time to leave. 'I've waited long enough, lass.'

CHAPTER ELEVEN

When Lizzie was at last allowed home from hospital, Sam went with Percy to fetch her in their lunch break and insisted on hiring a cab to take her back. She felt shy with him, knowing he had paid for a private room for her though she couldn't imagine why he'd done that. He had been to see her in hospital a couple of times, too. She hadn't known what to say to him and he'd spent most of the time just holding her hand and staring at her. She didn't like to pull her hand away from his, but it made her feel funny to have Sam Thoxby touching her.

'Your gran will be jealous if you keep doing things for me,' joked Lizzie as they jolted along in the cab.

He and Percy exchanged glances, then Sam said, 'Look, we didn't tell you at the time, Lizzie, but my gran died a few days ago.'

'Oh. Was it the influenza?'

'Yes.'

She laid one hand on his arm. 'Oh, Sam, I'm so sorry.'

He didn't want her pity. He wanted her to look at him with bright-eyed interest, as she had looked at that Dearden lad in the park. 'Aye, well, she was over seventy. It was a bit of a surprise, though. She didn't seem to have it all that badly, or I'd have brought her to join you in hospital. I said good night to her, had a bit of a chat, like.' He looked into the distance. 'Then next morning when I looked in on her, she were dead.'

He patted the thin hand that still lay on his overcoat sleeve and dared to hold it in his for a moment.

Lizzie looked at him in concern. She'd never seen Sam Thoxby with quite that expression on his face, never thought to feel sorry for him. 'You must miss her, though. She brought you up, didn't she?'

'Aye. Right from a babby.' He was still surprised, actually, every time he went into the house, not to find Gran there waiting, and sometimes he felt angry that she'd died without saying a proper goodbye to him. 'I gave her a fine send-off, though, with a ham tea for her boozing pals. She'd have liked that.' And there were compensations, as he kept telling himself. He now had Gran's savings to put with his extra earnings. With what he had in the bank, and what he had hidden away, he was about ready to make a few changes in his life.

After a moment, Lizzie looked at her brother and changed the subject. 'Mam didn't come to see me in hospital. Mrs D came, though. Peter brought her in the motor van one morning. It wasn't visiting hours, but the nurse let them come in for a few minutes. She gave me a lovely box of chocolates and said my job was still waiting for me. I really like working for her. And it isn't as if she hasn't got troubles of her own. Mr Dearden isn't at all well. He's that thin, his clothes just hang on him and he coughs all the time. She's really worried about him, you can tell.' Lizzie paused then added sadly, 'But she still came to see me.'

Not for the first time, Sam felt a surge of jealousy towards the Deardens who had so much that he'd never known, with their happy family life, their comfortable income and the easy way they had of making themselves liked. Peter Dearden had gone to school with him and had been tall and good-looking, even as a lad, with dark wavy hair and never a spot in sight. He'd been the most popular kid in the class, the one everyone wanted to sit near or play with. He hadn't been a favourite of Sam's, though. The two of them had clashed physically a few times, with the honours just about even as to who had won those short, fierce bouts of punching and kicking.

The memory of those long-ago fights made Sam's face go still, as it always did when he thought about things that upset him. Bloody Peter Dearden!

Lizzie, seeing that tight expression, decided he must be really upset about his gran dying. Daringly, she reached out and patted his hand again. 'I'm sorry about your gran,' she whispered. 'Really sorry, Sam.'

He tried to keep a sad expression on his face. 'It helps to have friends like you an' Percy. I haven't any relatives now. Not one.'

'Your mother might be alive somewhere?'

He couldn't hide his anger. 'She's dead to me an' allus has been! If I saw her coming down the street towards me, I'd turn an' walk the other way. I would that.'

Percy pretended to look out of the cab window, but watched the pair of them from the corner of his eye. If Lizzie married Sam, it'd get her away from Mam. And his friend was never short of a bob or two, so she'd be well set. The younger ones were leaving home now, one by one, Eva gone and Polly going. In the end, he'd be left alone with his mother.

'Here we are, then!' he said loudly as the cab horse came to a halt and began to drop some dung on to the stone setts of the street. He reached out to help Lizzie from the cab, but Sam was before him, tenderly handing her down and telling her to stand still for a minute while he paid the driver.

'I can walk!' she protested.

'You'll wait for me.'

Within seconds Mrs Preston had nipped out of her house with a shovel and bucket, wanting to pick up the horse dung and put it on the rhubarb which she grew in her little backyard to 'keep me regular'.

Lizzie giggled and whispered, 'She's always the first to rush out when a horse passes by.' She raised her voice, 'Good afternoon, Mrs Preston.'

Fanny nodded a greeting. 'Eeh, lass, you look all wambly. But at least they've let you out of that place. I never could abide hospitals.' But her thoughts were clearly on the pile of steaming manure and as the cab began to move off, she darted forward to claim her prize.

Sam offered Lizzie his arm. 'Come on inside, then, lass. That doctor said you were to rest, remember.'

Percy led the way. 'Polly's got the front room ready for you,

Lizzie. You can sleep in there on the sofa, then you won't have to go up and down the stairs till you're properly recovered.' For she still looked poorly, her eyes dull and sad, not full of life as usual, and from the way she moved she was clearly dizzy.

Sam escorted her into the front room as if she were Queen Mary come among them on a royal visit, then took his leave without even trying to see Mrs Kershaw, who bitterly resented this omission which she ascribed to Lizzie's influence.

The invalid was glad to lie back on the sofa and let Percy tuck a blanket round her legs, then bring her a cup of tea. She tried not to mind that her mother hadn't bothered to come in and see her.

'Polly will be in to look after you as soon as school finishes,' he said, hovering over her. 'She's got a bit of good news for you. I have to get back to work now.'

Lizzie nodded and let herself slide down into a lying position. She felt all swimmy-headed and was annoyed at herself for being so weak.

As soon as Percy had left, Meg came to stand in the doorway and stare at her, a cold, hostile look on her face that hurt Lizzie. 'You're back, then.'

'You know I am. Percy came and told you when he got me a cup of tea.'

'Yes.' Meg gave a bitter laugh. 'Funny, isn't it? To think I'll soon be left with only *you!* Three daughters I bore and you're the one I'm going to be saddled with. Rich, that is.'

'What do you mean, left with only me?'

'Haven't they told you yet? Our Polly's got herself a job. She's as sneaky as you are when she wants something and—'

'What's she going to do?'

Meg snorted. 'Go to Mrs Pilby's as a maid. She'll be starting after Easter. Couldn't try for a place at the works, could she, and live at home? No, she has to get herself a fancy job, so that *we* have to spend good money buying her an outfit. And even then she's not going to give us any of her wages after she's paid us back for that. He spoils you lot rotten, Percy does.'

'But aren't you pleased for Polly? Pleased she's going to be a maid, like you were?'

'You're none of you girls like me – a bunch of cuckoos, you are. I don't know where you get your fancy ideas from. "Honour thy father and mother" it says in the Bible, but I don't get a scrap of respect from any of you!'

Lizzie closed her eyes. 'I'm feeling tired, Mam. I think I'll have a bit of a rest, if you don't mind.'

'Well, don't expect me to run round after you. I had the influenza too, you know. Only they didn't fuss over me like they did over you.' As she went out, Meg deliberately left the door open, smiling as she banged the kitchen door shut.

Lizzie sighed and got up to close the door, shivering in the cold draught from the hall. How would she ever cope with it, being at home all day with a woman who hated her? Even one day was too long. Tears rolled down her cheeks and she scrubbed them away angrily. She'd never felt so weak in her life before. What if she never got better? What if she remained an invalid? The doctor had said it'd be weeks before she recovered fully. She'd go mad lying here like this.

The sound of the front door opening woke Lizzie and she blinked in bewilderment for a moment, then realised that she was at home and sighed in mingled relief and worry. The door opened and Polly came in, rushing over to the sofa to give her a hug and a kiss, and weep a few happy tears over her.

Lizzie blinked away tears of her own as she hugged her younger sister back.

'You did give us all a fright!' Polly scolded. 'And I've missed you. They wouldn't let me and Johnny come and see you in the hospital – said children under fourteen weren't allowed.' She looked down at herself and smiled. 'I don't really feel like a child any more, though, an' I bet I could have got in, but you know what our Percy's like for following rules.' She had grown her figure over the last few months and was now plumpish, like Eva, but without her sister's prettiness. Mrs Preston had once said that Polly would be pretty once she'd grown into her face, for she had the sort of features which would look much better on a woman than a girl, but no one, least of all Polly, believed that.

'You don't look at all like a child,' Lizzie said enviously. 'You and our Eva are lucky. I wish I had proper bosoms like yours. Mine are more like pimples.' She held out one hand, staring at it scornfully. 'And look how thin I've got. I'm like a set of twigs strung together with wire.' She'd been shocked when she saw herself in a mirror at the hospital. She knew she'd never be pretty, but now she looked ugly, really ugly.

'The doctor says we have to feed you up. Would you like a cup of tea an' a piece of cake?'

'I'd love one.'

Polly hesitated. 'Has she come near you?'

No need to ask who 'she' was. 'Only to tell me she wasn't going to wait on me – and to say you'd got yourself a job.'

Polly's face fell. 'She knew I wanted to tell you that myself!'

'The tea can wait. Tell me now. How on earth did you get taken on at Redley House?'

'Well, I went to see the housekeeper a while back to say I'd be interested if a job came up.'

Lizzie sat upright. 'You never said!'

'Miss Harper suggested doing it. She said I had nothing to lose.'

'Ooh, I wouldn't have dared.'

'Well, my knees were knocking together when I called and I didn't think there was much chance. Mrs Frost – that's the housekeeper's name – looked down her nose at me. I nearly ran away then, I can tell you. But I said what we'd decided and gave her a piece of paper with my name on it and Miss Harper's – because she said she'd give me a character reference.

'Then, while you were ill, I got a message to go and see Mrs Frost. So I went after school one day and she took me in to see Mrs Pilby herself – ooh, Lizzie, it was such a lovely room! – and they asked me lots of questions about housework and that. And in the end Mrs Pilby said I could have a month's trial because Miss Harper had spoken very highly of me – wasn't that kind of her? And I'm to start after Easter, just leave school and start. Miss Harper arranged it all for me because Mam said she was too sick to go traipsing across town to see the headmaster. Isn't it exciting?'

Lizzie nodded and tried to smile. 'I'm really glad for you, love. I know it's what you wanted. But will you have to live in?'

Polly lost her excited expression. 'Yes. They insist on all the maids living in. Oh, Lizzie, I'll miss you so much. But I can't turn down this chance, can I? If I get taken on, they'll give me a proper training, then I can get a job anywhere. In London even.' She hesitated then said, 'Mam went mad at me for not trying to get a job at the works and said she wouldn't buy me an outfit, but Percy said I was to follow my heart and if that meant going into service, he'd get me one. And he even backed me up when I said I wasn't sending any money home from my wages. I would do if Mam were short, but she isn't, Lizzie. She has Percy's wages and yours and the money from the lodgers. She's even got some money saved, because her bank book fell out of her bag one day and I saw what was in it.' She noticed Lizzie's astonished expression and looked guilty. 'It'd fallen open and I couldn't resist a peep.'

'How much has she got?'

'Over twenty pounds.'

'Never!'

'She has.'

They were both silent for a minute at the thought of this huge sum, then Lizzie said, 'You're so lucky. It'll be ages before I can start earning again. But I think I'll ask our Percy if I can have more than a shilling a week out of my money once I get back. I've got a bit saved up now, but not much.'

'You never used to save anything.'

'Well, I am doing now.' Lizzie started fiddling with the blanket as she confessed, 'I sometimes worry that she'll chuck me out and I'll have nowhere to go.' That was her worst nightmare. 'I keep the bankbook at work in Mrs D's office. But I haven't got much in it.'

'If you ever need any money desperately, you can always come to me,' Polly said softly. 'I've been saving since I was little. I haven't told Mam how much I've got, though she's asked and asked. She's even looked through my things, but I keep my savings book up in Miss Harper's room. I'd never let you want, you know that.'

'Oh, Polly, you are a love!' And Lizzie had to wipe away another tear.

One morning that same week Emma Harper let herself into the front office, which was her own domain, humming to herself. She loved working here at Cardwell's. How different it was now from the shabby place she'd taken over! She'd helped James Cardwell (she could never think of him as 'Mr Cardwell' somehow) get some nice furniture and a couple of plants, and it had made all the difference. Now she looked up to find him leaning against the doorframe, smiling across at her.

'Someone sounds happy?' he commented.

'I am happy.'

'Then you're going to be even happier. I've decided to give you a rise.'

Emma gaped at him. She'd never heard of an employer giving someone extra money without being asked.

His smile broadened. 'You're worth it. And anyway, I've had one or two other chaps asking me about you. I can see the signs. If I'm not mistaken, you'll be offered jobs elsewhere in the next week or two.'

Emma blushed. 'Well, actually, I have been offered a job elsewhere, but I – I didn't think I'd like it, so I said no.'

'Old Washbourne?'

She nodded, trying not to shudder.

'Wise decision, lass. He'd have his hand up your skirts before you'd been there an hour. Doesn't think decent women go out to work, that one.'

She could feel herself blushing. 'Well, actually, he has tried to—'

James Cardwell's smile vanished abruptly. 'You let me know if he tries owt again. I'm not having him acting like that in *my* office! Who does he think he is?'

'I can manage him.'

'You shouldn't have to.'

She shrugged. 'I found out at Sevley's that such – attentions – are common when one is out at work. And I'm grateful that you've never – you know?'

'Never tried it on.' His expression was suddenly wry. 'Well, it's not because I don't fancy you, lass. Only you've never given me the glad eye and I'm not one to push myself where I'm not wanted.'

Emma was bright red now. 'I think we'd better change the subject.'

'If you like. But if you ever do feel like giving me the glad eye, I won't say no.' And, whistling loudly, he went back into his office.

Emma plumped down at her desk and buried her face in her hands for a moment, then straightened her shoulders and tried to concentrate on the day's work. But it was a while before she could settle. The trouble was, if he were free, she'd not hesitate to give James Cardwell 'the glad eye', as he'd phrased it. He was an attractive man and fun to work with, too, once you grew used to his abrupt ways. He joked and laughed and made the yard a pleasant place to be for all of them. Not that he was there all that much. He was out and about most of the time, supervising jobs or working on them himself. And making big plans, like this row of houses he was building in Maidham Street, which he said would be model homes for the better-off working folk. He'd put a lot of effort into thinking out the design, even asking Emma what women wanted in their houses.

He'd put all his spare money into them. She who kept his accounts was only too aware of how great a risk he'd taken – and she was aware, too, of his wife's continual complaints about the project. If it were left to Mrs Cardwell, he'd still be a jobbing builder, like her father had been, doing repairs and renovations and working for other builders on big projects, but creating nothing to be remembered by.

If only she could persuade Blanche to move into a house of their own, Emma thought sometimes, she'd be perfectly happy. But her sister was afraid of living on her own in one of the terraces of Southlea – for, of course, they couldn't have afforded to move anywhere smarter – and they weren't going to go to their aunt for help. She hadn't contacted them once since their father's death.

Blanche much preferred to live in the attic room in Bobbin Lane, knowing there was always someone nearby in case she needed help. For it had to be admitted that her health went up and down, and that she'd had one or two funny turns. And she also enjoyed Polly's company, the two of them seeming more like aunt and niece nowadays. Though that was obviously going to change when Polly started work.

Emma tried to settle down. She always felt full of energy and was relieved to have a job to expend it on. If she hadn't had to earn money, she'd have had to find a job for other reasons. Though if she'd been able to marry and have children, that would have kept her nice and busy. Oh, drat, why was she thinking like this today? 'Work,' she said aloud. 'Concentrate on your work, you fool.'

But she couldn't concentrate. She had decided last night that she wasn't going to stay in Bobbin Lane for much longer. Mrs Kershaw was getting stranger and stranger, so if Emma had to force Blanche to move, she would. She was just waiting for an excuse to leave. Any excuse. And the sooner the better.

CHAPTER TWELVE

It was nearly a month before Lizzie was fit enough to go back to work. During all that time, she lived in a state of outright hostility with her mother, who ignored her and didn't even cook for her until Percy realised what was happening and had a word with her one day.

'Where's Lizzie's tea?'

'If she's not earning, she can make do with bread and jam. That's what happens in other families.'

'Well, it doesn't happen here.' He turned to his sister. 'Here, take half of mine, love.'

'You can have some of mine, too,' Polly said, pushing her plate towards Lizzie.

Johnny ignored them and continued to shovel food into his mouth.

'No. Thank you. I – I'm not hungry,' Lizzie faltered.

Percy folded his arms and pushed his plate aside. 'If you aren't, then I'm not either.'

Polly followed suit.

'It's not worth it!' Lizzie's voice was pleading. She didn't even want to stay in the kitchen with her mother looking at her like that.

'I mean it.' Percy got up and fetched a clean plate, scraping some food from his plate on to it. Polly added some from hers, then patted her sister's leg under the table, giving her an encouraging smile and ignoring their mother's glare.

So Lizzie ate most of what was put before her and from then onwards was given the same food as the rest of the family.

Percy was so worried about his mother he even went to see

Dr Balloch to ask his advice. 'She's gone downright funny and really taken against poor Lizzie – for no reason. My sister's a nice lass, hard-working—' He broke off, unable to continue for a moment, so upset did he feel.

'Mrs Kershaw is going through a time of life when women sometimes do grow rather strange. Medical science has no answers for this, unfortunately, so you just have to let nature take its course. She'll probably come out of this patch in a year or two.'

'Probably?'

The doctor shrugged. 'We can never tell precisely.' And if truth be told, he, too, found Mrs Kershaw erratic and irrational. Nothing definite, just a feeling you got when people were off kilter. Medical science was powerless to help these troubling cases.

As Percy walked home, he felt even more depressed. He had hoped for something to calm his mother down. Anything. And all he'd been told was that this might go on for years, or even for ever. 'Why me?' he asked the starlit sky, then hunched his shoulders and walked slowly home, bitterness roiling in him.

Later that evening he passed on to Lizzie what the doctor had said and she scowled at the floor. 'Well, I'm not putting up with it for years.' She blinked and turned away, trying not to let him see her eyes fill with tears. She wept too easily since her illness.

Percy pulled her round to face him and wiped away the moisture with one fingertip. 'I'm sorry, love. I've thought and thought, and I can't see what we can do about her.'

'If I earned enough, I'd go into lodgings straight away, but I don't.' Suddenly it all came out, her worst fear, the nightmare that kept her awake sometimes. 'Oh, Percy, what if she chucks me out? What shall I do then?'

'If she does that, I'll go too, and we'll find somewhere to live together.'

She gaped at him. 'Would you really do that?'

He nodded, his heart breaking for her, and all he could do was give her another hug.

★   ★   ★

On the Friday night Sam called for Percy. He always had a word with Lizzie when he came round, bringing her a magazine (time she grew out of those comics), or the occasional bag of sweets, or just a big rosy apple. He never arrived empty-handed and Lizzie's face always lit up at the sight of him. He was definitely making progress with her, he felt.

'Isn't Sam kind?' she said to Polly that Sunday when her sister came home on her day off.

Polly looked at her sideways, opened her mouth, then shut it again.

Lizzie stared. 'What's the matter? Why did you look like that when I said Sam was kind?'

'Don't you know?'

'Know what?'

'About Sam.'

Lizzie frowned. 'What are you on about?'

'He's *courting* you.'

'Sam Thoxby! Courting me? *Me!*' Lizzie nearly fell off her chair laughing. 'He's never!'

'He is. I heard him talking to Percy once. He wants to wed you.'

Lizzie turned first red, then white. 'I don't believe you.'

'Why did he pay for you to have a private room at the hospital then?'

'I —' But she couldn't think of a reason, never had been able to, though she'd racked her brain many a time. Percy had just shrugged when she asked him, so it had remained an ongoing puzzle.

'And he never comes round here without a present. Only for you, not for the rest of us.'

Lizzie was still trying to come to terms with this idea. 'But Sam's much older than me. He's even older than our Percy.'

Polly shrugged.

Lizzie blushed scarlet and stared down at the fabric of her skirt, which was crumpled as usual. After a while she looked up, her expression worried. 'I don't think I'd want to marry him. He's too old. And I've never really liked ginger hair.' She liked dark wavy hair, like the Deardens had. They were a good-looking family all right. She'd seen Peter in the street the other day and he'd stopped the van to ask how she was going on and said how they all missed her at the shop. He was a lovely man, and much better looking than Sam.

'Well, it's your choice who you marry, isn't it? No one can force you.' Polly felt relief surge through her.

'No-o-o. Of course not.'

There was a long silence, broken only by the ticking of the clock and the shifting of coals in the grate as the fire burned down, then Lizzie asked, 'Does Mam know – about Sam courting me, I mean?'

'She must do. Everyone else does. Even Mrs Preston said something about it to me the other day, only I pretended not to understand. And Mary Holden's jealous. She's been after Sam herself.'

'Mary Holden? He wouldn't want someone like her!' For the two girls had continued hostile to one another even after they'd left school. 'And anyway, she's walking out with a fellow from down Peter Street, isn't she?'

'So they say. But she still looks at Sam as if she'd rather have him.'

'Oh.'

More silence, then Lizzie scowled. 'Well, I don't want to talk about him – or even think about marriage. At the moment, I just want to get better and go back to work.'

The next time he came to the house, Sam realised that either Lizzie had guessed what he was up to or someone had told her, more likely the latter. In some ways she was still a child and he liked that. He didn't want a wife who knew it all. He wanted one he could shape to suit his own needs. So long as that one was Lizzie.

'You go on to the pub,' he told Percy, taking a sudden decision. 'I want a private word with your Lizzie.'

'I'm tired. I was just going upstairs,' she said hastily.

He followed her into the hall and took hold of her arm, swinging her into the front room and closing the door behind him with a shove of his foot. 'What's wrong, lass?'

'Nothing.' She pretended to rub her arm, as if he'd hurt her. 'You haven't half got hard hands, Sam Thoxby.'

He reached out to stroke her arm, smiling. 'I didn't hurt you, but I don't mind kissing it better for you, if you like?'

Lizzie gasped and turned away from him, feeling out of her depth with not the faintest idea how to deal with this.

'Someone's told you, haven't they?'

'T-told me what?'

'That I want to court you.'

She gulped and managed a nod.

He eyed her sideways. 'Did it upset you that much?'

'It – it made me feel funny. I've never – never thought of you like that, Sam.'

He watched her face, wishing he dare touch that pale skin, kiss her, do all the things he'd dreamed of lately. He couldn't even approach another woman to relieve his need because he wanted Lizzie so badly, and for some strange reason only her. 'Well, couldn't you try thinking of me like that for a bit, see how it goes?'

'I don't – don't want to – to start courting anyone. I'm too young.'

'You're a woman now.' His eyes lingered on her figure briefly.

'Well, I don't *feel* like a woman. Sam, *please*, can't we just forget it? You've been that kind to me, but I – I—'

He put his finger on her lips. 'Shh! Don't say something you'll regret later.'

She felt a shiver run through her. He was so much bigger than she was, and she wouldn't like to be on the wrong side of him. Everyone said he never forgot a wrong.

He tried to keep his voice gentle, coaxing. 'What I want,

Lizzie, is for you to give me a chance. That's all. I won't rush you, won't do anything you don't like, but surely you can give me a bit of a chance?'

There was a small sound from outside in the hallway and Sam turned, looking suddenly angry. He put one finger to his lips, tiptoed across the room and flung the door open wide.

Meg nearly fell through the doorway, yelping in shock.

Sam took hold of her arm and marched her off towards the kitchen

Lizzie crept across to the door and peered out. They all knew Mam eavesdropped and it served her right if Sam shouted at her.

His voice echoed down the hall, loud and emphatic. 'You won't do that again, will you, Mrs Kershaw? I don't like people listening to my private conversations. I don't like it at all.'

'She's my daughter. I have a right to keep an eye on her.'

'You don't treat her like a daughter, so you have *no* rights so far as she's concerned, none at all. I've spoken to Percy and I have his blessing, so I'm doing the right thing by Lizzie, don't you worry.'

'Our Percy never said anything to me about it.'

'Why should he, given the way you feel about that poor lass?'

'You'd be better off looking elsewhere.' Meg laid one hand on his arm and said coaxingly, 'Sam, she's not worth it. Believe me, she—'

He fairly bellowed, 'You old cow! Fancy talking like that about your own daughter. You make me sick, you do. If you weren't a woman, I'd punch you in the face for saying that.'

Lizzie heard a chair fall over, then a shriek of, 'You keep away from me, Sam Thoxby!' Then silence.

When Sam came back into the front room, Lizzie was sitting on the edge of the sofa, waiting for him, hands clasped in her lap. He closed the door and winked at her. 'I don't think your mam will do that again.'

'You've probably frightened her silly.'

His expression was grim. 'Aye. I hope I have, for your sake, lass.'

Suddenly Lizzie felt better about things. If anyone could protect her from her mother, it was Sam. Percy did his best, but he wasn't – well, he wasn't strong enough. Not in the way Sam was anyway.

He came across and sat down beside her on the sofa, taking her hand and keeping hold of it, patting it from time to time as if to emphasise what he was saying. 'Well, Lizzie Kershaw? Are you going to give me a chance to court you or not?'

She stared down at their linked hands and cast a quick glance sideways at him, feeling warmed by the expression on his face. 'Well – all right. But nothing's settled, mind. It's just – we'll see how we go, eh?'

He beamed at her and gave her a great rib-cracking hug. 'Eeh, I'm that glad.'

She pushed at him, not liking to feel so helpless. 'Get off me, you great daft lump! Someone might see us.'

He planted a quick kiss on her cheek. 'I don't care if they do. I'm proud to be your fellow.'

She flushed scarlet again. 'Sam, we're just seeing how we go, right? So don't tell folks we're courting. Because we're not – not yet.'

'Right, love. But if they see us going out together they'll guess. And I can't help that, can I?' Though, of course, he would tell folk, just to make sure no other snotty-nosed lad tried to take his girl away from him. 'And for a start, let's go out to the pictures on Saturday.' He knew how much Lizzie loved film shows.

Her face lit up. 'Oh, Sam! I'd love that! I haven't been anywhere for ages.'

'You're not working full-time yet?'

'No. Mrs Dearden says I'm not up to it, so I just go in for the mornings.' Which meant she didn't bring home as much money as before. Her mother had tried to take all her wages, saying she still had to pay her way, but again Percy had intervened and so

Lizzie was allowed to keep some. But she didn't have any to spare for cinema visits.

'I'll pick you up at half-past five, so get your tea early. We'll go to the six o'clock show, eh, so you're not too late getting to bed. My treat.' He wasn't sitting in the penny seats, either. They'd do this in style. 'Then I'll buy you some fish and chips afterwards.' He pinched her arm and shook it to show he was worried about its thinness. 'You need feeding up.'

Lizzie beamed at him. 'Oh, it'll be smashing to go out! I do hope there's some funny films on. I'll be ready and waiting.' She looked up at him tremulously. 'And – thank you, Sam. For everything.'

'My pleasure, love.'

When he'd gone, Lizzie went to get herself a cup of tea. Meg turned her head away as the door opened.

You'd think I'd be used to it by now, Lizzie thought, as tears dripped into her cup. But it hurt. It always hurt.

Sam was very careful not to touch Lizzie as they walked into the town centre together on Saturday, but he did take her hand when they were sitting in the cinema in the best threepenny seats. And after a jerk of surprise, she let him keep hold of it, enjoying the warmth, the human contact, the way they could laugh together at the funny bits. There were six different films shown that night, all one-reelers. The third one was so exciting, with the heroine in mortal danger, that Lizzie had to clutch Sam's arm with both her hands till the danger was past.

Afterwards, while the reels were being changed, he leaned towards her. 'By, you've got a strong grip when you're frightened of summat.'

'Did I hurt you?'

'No, of course not. I liked you holding on to me.'

'Oh.' She could feel herself blushing in the darkness and was glad when the next film started; glad, too, that it was a comedy.

Afterwards, he bought her some fish and chips on the way

home, as he had promised, joking that they had to fatten her up, get her strength back. He had a double helping himself and coaxed her into eating most of hers. He didn't like her looking so thin and washed out all the time.

At the door of her house, he took hold of both Lizzie's hands. 'That wasn't so bad, was it?'

'I enjoyed myself.' Honesty compelled her to add, 'A lot.'

'There you are, then. We'll do the same thing next week, if you like? An' how about a stroll in the park tomorrow?'

'Don't – shouldn't we – people will—' She didn't know how to refuse him.

'I'll pick you up at two. You can bring your sister with you, if you like.' He leaned closer and said huskily, 'But I'd rather have you to myself.'

Lizzie swallowed hard as she watched him walk off down the street whistling. She hadn't expected to enjoy herself so much. It had been nice to be spoiled. But she didn't fancy him as a man, not at all. And she still felt a bit nervous in his company sometimes, especially when he looked at her in a certain way.

'Did you enjoy yourself tonight?' Percy asked the following day.

Lizzie beamed at him. 'Yes, I did. Sam was really kind. He bought me a bar of Fry's chocolate cream. An' some fish an' chips afterwards.'

'What were the films like?'

Lizzie launched into an eager description of each film, laughing again at the funny bits, shuddering at the dangerous parts. Her happiness made Percy very thoughtful.

The following week, Mrs D said Lizzie could work full-time, just to see how she went. For some reason, she was suddenly feeling much better.

'I hear you've got yourself a fellow,' Sally said when she and Lizzie were alone in the shop towards the end of the afternoon. Peter had told her – and had expressed his worries about who the fellow was. 'Sam Thoxby, isn't it?'

Lizzie nodded, smiling at the memory of the outing. 'He's a good bit older than you. As old as my Peter.'

'Yes.'

'Be careful, won't you? You might be wiser finding some-one nearer your own age.'

Lizzie flushed. 'I don't – it's not – we're just – you know, seeing how we go.'

'Well, go carefully, lass. You're a long time married.'

'Oh, I don't want to get married for years yet.'

'How's your Polly going on?'

'She loves it at the Pilbys'.'

'You must miss her?'

'Yes. A lot.' It was far worse at home now, without Polly. Lizzie absolutely dreaded going back there each night.

She was wondering whether to go and do some night classes like Percy, who was training to be a bookkeeper now, only she finished work later than he did and didn't think she'd be able to get there in time. And besides she still got a bit tired by the end of the day. But on the nights when he was out, it was very hard going in the house in Bobbin Lane. Lizzie wasn't sure she could stand it for much longer.

The sudden noise of raised voices drifted upstairs to the attic again. Emma exchanged long-suffering glances with her sister. 'I'm not putting up with this much longer, love.'

Blanche sighed. 'No. It's been very difficult lately. And this week, Mrs Kershaw has been particularly sharp with poor Lizzie.'

'More than sharp – vicious.' Emma hesitated, then said, 'So perhaps it's time for us to look for a house of our own to rent, eh?'

Blanche looked round the room she felt so safe in, heard the sound of shouting again and accepted the inevitable. 'Yes. Perhaps it is.'

Emma sagged against the back of her chair in sheer relief.

She had not expected to get her way so easily. 'Do you want to make a start looking during the day?'

'Not on my own. I think we should look together. I – I don't feel very competent to interview landlords, actually.'

'I think it's they who interview you.' Emma stared at the sunset reflected in the big windows. The smoky atmosphere of the little town reflected the light back in a haze of bright colour, which had its own particular beauty. 'I'm going to miss that view, though.'

'Yes, so am I. And I'm not very sure about the cooking and cleaning. I'm not very good at that sort of thing.'

'We'll manage somehow. And we'll get someone in for the rough work. I won't have the time and you're not strong enough. We can afford it now.' After a moment, Emma added thoughtfully, 'I'll go and see Mr Cuttler first, I think. He may have a place that's suitable.'

Blanche's thin face brightened. 'Yes. That's a good idea. And – do you think we should say anything to Mrs Kershaw? About our intentions, you know. So that it doesn't come as too great a shock to her?'

'Certainly not, or she won't hesitate to make our lives as miserable as she does her daughter's – which means *your* life, my dear, as you're the one who spends so much time at home. We only have to give her a week's notice and that's all she deserves.' Another thoughtful silence, then Emma added, 'Or I might ask Sam what to do. He always seems to know.'

Blanche's face cleared. 'Yes. Oh, yes. Do ask his advice. He might even go and see Mr Cuttler for us.'

Emma bit back a sharp comment. She was not afraid of Mr Cuttler, but poor Blanche was nervous about everything.

Sam, invited up to take tea with Miss Harper and Miss Emma, knocked on the front door of number thirty and, when no one came, banged again and walked in.

Lizzie came out of the kitchen, looking as if she had been crying, and he felt anger rise in him again. No need to ask who'd upset her. 'I've come to see your lodgers. Been invited to take tea with them.'

Mrs Kershaw stuck her head out of the kitchen, 'Oh, it's you.' She didn't go back inside, just kept watching them, as if she didn't trust him to behave.

'Aye, missus, it's me.' He gave her a curt nod, for he no longer made any attempt to jolly her along, not with the way she was treating his lass. 'Not got anything to do?' he asked pointedly.

Meg disappeared back into the kitchen, but he noticed she'd left the door ajar. 'Don't let her eavesdrop on us, eh, lass?' he whispered. 'The ladies won't want her poking her nose into their affairs.' When he came down, he'd find out what was the matter with Lizzie today, but he was late for tea so it'd have to keep.

'All right.'

When he'd gone upstairs, Meg opened the kitchen door and found Lizzie standing in the hall studying herself in the mirror on the coat stand. 'What do you think you're doing?'

'Seeing if I suit my hair another way.'

'Well, go and do that in your bedroom an' shut the door on yourself. It looks bad, you standing in the hall to do that.'

'You can see better in this mirror. That one in our bedroom's all spotty. An' anyway, I can stop fiddling around if anyone comes in. If it's Sam you're thinking of, he won't mind.'

'You always have a back word for me, you do!'

'I only answered your question.' Lizzie was determined not to let Mam goad her any more tonight. They'd already had one shouting match because her mother hadn't done Lizzie's washing with the others' things.

'Well, I don't want you lounging around in the hallway like that. It isn't decent with a visitor in the house. Go through into the kitchen.'

'I think I'd rather go and sit in my bedroom.' Lizzie didn't wait for an answer but ran lightly up the stairs and left her bedroom door open.

Meg watched her go, feeling jealous of many things but

at the moment of two things in particular – the agility with which her daughter had gone up those stairs and the fact that Lizzie, her scrawny ungrateful wretch of a daughter, had a man courting her. There was no justice in the world, none. What Meg wouldn't give for a husband again! She'd never stopped missing her Stanley. And it'd been weeks since Eva had last written. Weeks. She'd forgotten her family now, just moved on and forgotten them.

Conveniently forgetting that on the last visit she herself had screamed at Eva to go away and never darken her doorstep again, Meg went to stand in front of the kitchen fire with her skirts raised at the rear, toasting her backside. It might be summer, but it still got cold of an evening. Especially when no one cared whether you lived or died. And why Percy had to do all that studying, she didn't know. He'd never make a bookkeeper, never in a month of Sundays. He was common as muck, her Percy was, and always would be. No one would ever take *him* on for office work.

In the attic, Sam found himself being treated very formally, given a china cup of tea – which looked so fragile, he was terrified of breaking it – and handed some chocolate biscuits from Dearden's, an offer he declined instantly because he didn't want to try to talk with his mouth full. Somehow, he always felt he had to be on his best behaviour with the Harper ladies, for all they'd come down in the world.

After a few minutes, he tired of the silly chit-chat and asked abruptly, 'What's up, then?'

Emma took a deep breath. 'We think it's time to move out of here, Sam.'

'Aaah,' he said softly. 'Now that *is* going to throw the cat among the pigeons.'

'I'm sure you understand why,' she went on quietly. 'You must have noticed the atmosphere here.'

'The old lady's losing her marbles,' he said easily, enjoying the shock on their faces at his blunt statement. Then his face became grim. 'But if she sets one finger on my Lizzie, she'll regret it.'

'*Your* Lizzie?' Blanche queried. Polly had said on her last day off that Lizzie didn't really fancy Sam.

'Aye, *my* Lizzie.' He obviously enjoyed saying that out loud.

'You and she have an understanding?' Emma asked.

He nodded. 'We do. But we're not saying owt to anyone at the moment, so don't spread the word. I want to get wed before the winter, but she's a bit reluctant. Well, she's only young. But I'd make her happier than she is here, I know that.'

'I hope – things go well for you,' Emma murmured. But she just couldn't see him suiting Lizzie.

Silence fell again.

'So tell me about your plans an' how I can help you?' he prompted. Women were all alike. They needed a man to look after them. And it could be profitable being that man, with these two.

'We wondered whether you could give us some advice about finding a new place to live?' Emma asked. 'We're not sure how to set about it?'

'Buying a place or renting?'

'*Buying?* We weren't thinking of buying.' Blanche gaped at him. 'What made you say that?'

Sam smiled. He could add up and knew roughly what Emma earned a week, as well as what Blanche got from that annuity of hers. 'Don't tell me you haven't been saving your pennies,' he teased. 'You've got the annuity as well as your wages.' And they made their clothes last, didn't spend much on anything really.

Emma stared at him. She hoped other people hadn't put two and two together like he had, though of course other people wouldn't know about the annuity in any detail. 'We were thinking of renting, of course.'

'Why "of course"? Your Mr Cardwell's building some new terraces of houses over in Northlea. You might have a look at one of those before you come to any decision.'

'I don't think we'd have enough money for that. It'd cost too much.'

'You might if you had anything else left to sell. Or you could ask that aunt of yours for some help. Make up the quarrel. It'd be worth it if she has as much brass as folk say.'

The two sisters looked at one another, both feeling uncomfortable at how much he'd worked out about them.

'Goodness, I never even thought about buying somewhere,' Emma confessed.

'Well, think about it now. If you bought, you'd have no rent to pay.' And if the two of them had to sell things, he'd be bound to profit.

'Well, we do have one or two bits and pieces of our mother's jewellery,' Blanche admitted before her sister could stop her, 'though they have great sentimental value for us and we'd rather not sell them.'

Sam nodded. He'd wondered about that. She'd liked jewellery, old Mrs Harper had. He'd seen her wearing quite a few different bits and pieces.

Emma frowned. 'But we certainly won't ask our aunt for money. She's never tried to get in touch with us. I doubt she'd even open a letter if we sent one.'

'It'd be worth a try. Only cost you a stamp.'

They both shook their heads firmly.

Too proud to wipe their own arses, he thought scornfully. If he had a rich aunt, he'd be buttering her up till the grease ran off. 'Talk to your Mr Cardwell, then. He might let you pay him a deposit and so much per week.' Sam grinned at Emma. 'Seeing as you're such a valuable employee of his. And if he says yes, well, I can sell some more stuff for you, if you like?'

'We'll have to think about it,' Blanche replied. 'It doesn't do to rush into things.'

'Yes, have a think. But don't take too long. Them houses are goin' to be snapped up once they're offered.' In fact, Sam was thinking of buying one himself. If you didn't have to pay rent, you'd feel very secure indeed. They were very nice houses, quite large, with three bedrooms and good attics as well, and even an indoor toilet and bathroom built on to the back upstairs over a scullery-cum-washroom. One weekend not long ago he'd been to have a look round them, unfinished as they were, and had liked what he saw. Cardwell was a good builder.

When he was leaving, he saw Lizzie sitting in her bedroom and beckoned her out, not wanting to enrage the old sod by being caught inside her daughter's room. 'Feel like a breath of fresh air, lass? It's a lovely evening.'

Lizzie hesitated, then the thought of sitting up here for hours made her say, 'Yes. Why not?'

It was while they were walking along that Sam swung her round against a wall and kissed her for the first time. Lizzie wasn't sure she liked this and it was hard to breathe with his mouth covering hers, but all couples who were walking out kissed one another, so she'd been a bit curious about it.

He felt vaguely disappointed that she hadn't responded to his kiss, but on the other hand, she hadn't protested or pushed him away. When they were wed, he'd make sure she responded properly, he would that. And when she nestled against him afterwards with a sigh, he found himself smiling down protectively at her slight form.

'Are you my girl?' he breathed throatily in her ear.

'I suppose so.'

'Good, 'cos I don't want no one else but you, Lizzie, and never have done.'

She looked up at him doubtfully in the soft light of dusk. 'Don't you, Sam?'

'No, of course not.'

'Do you – love me?'

He didn't believe in that sort of nonsense. A man had his needs and women were there to fill them, and it took two of you to make children – but, on the other hand, there was no one like Lizzie so far as he was concerned, so he supposed it must be love. 'I've fancied you ever since you frit us all by walking along that bloody wall,' he offered. 'You're the only one for me, lass.'

She sighed and nestled against him again. 'It's nice when you cuddle me, Sam,' she whispered. She liked it much better than that wet kissing stuff.

'Aye, I like it mysen.' But he wanted a lot more than cuddling. Still, this was progress, it definitely was.

'Well,' he said after a minute, getting tired of just standing there and worried that if Lizzie felt the hardness he couldn't control pressing against her, she'd take fright, 'I suppose I'd better get you home, or your Percy will be having a word with me about keeping you out too late.'

She chuckled. 'Percy wouldn't worry if you kept me out all night. He trusts you, Sam.'

He chuckled too, but for another reason. Anyone who trusted other people as completely as Percy Kershaw did was a fool. But in this case, the lass was quite safe with him. Because Sam wanted to do things properly and marry a virgin. The idea pleased him for some reason, perhaps because it proved Lizzie was so very different from his mother.

He'd better go and see Cardwell about one of those houses for himself before they were all taken. It didn't occur to him to take Lizzie into his confidence about that. Or to ask her along with him to see what she thought of them.

CHAPTER THIRTEEN

The next day, Emma waited until past her usual time for leaving the office, knowing that James always came back here before he went home, wherever he was working, to make sure that the place was locked up properly.

When he saw her, he stopped whistling and raised his eyebrows. 'No home to go to, Emma Harper?'

'I wanted to see you – if you can spare me a minute or two?'

'Of course.' He yawned, stretched, then looked at his pocket watch.

'If you're too tired today, I could—'

He looked at her sharply, wondering why she sounded so nervous. 'I'm not tired, and of course I can spare you a minute or two. And since I'll already be in trouble for getting home late, another few minutes won't make any difference.' Edith never could understand that work didn't necessarily finish at the same time every day, that sometimes emergencies cropped up or jobs took longer than you expected. Anyway, he wouldn't mind a bit of a sit-down before he went home to the usual evening of complaints and carping. Though it'd mean his children would be in bed and no chance of a romp with them.

'Look, you go and make us a cuppa, eh? My throat's as dry as a ditch in summer. That house I've been doing estimates for is full of dust and cobwebs. I'll just nip out to the back and then we'll lock the front door and sit here like Lord and Lady Muck, supping tea together. You wouldn't happen to have a biscuit or two tucked away as well, would you?'

Emma smiled. 'I might have.' He always seemed hungry, so

she made a point of keeping a supply of his favourite biscuits, buying them from the petty cash, keeping meticulous accounts he never even glanced at before initialling them each month.

When they had settled down on the comfortable armchairs in the waiting area, she fiddled with her cup, trying to think how best to broach the matter.

He looked at her and frowned. 'Good grief! I never thought but – you're not going to give notice on me, are you, Emma Harper?' Let alone she was a most efficient employee, he enjoyed her company around the place, liked teasing her, seeing the delicate colour stain her cheeks sometimes. Most of all, he liked making her laugh, something she didn't do often enough in his opinion.

'What? Goodness, no! That's the last thing I'd want to do, Mr Cardwell.' Emma looked away, afraid of revealing her feelings, for she found him all too attractive, her untidy, warm-hearted boss. 'No, I'm perfectly happy here, especially with my recent rise.'

'What is it, then? You might as well come straight out with it.'

She took a deep breath. 'It's – well, it's those new houses on Maidham Street. I was wondering about' She took a deep breath before putting her fragile dream into words. 'That is, my sister and I were wondering about – well, buying one.'

He leaned back and looked at her thoughtfully. 'And can you afford one of my houses?'

'I think so. My sister and I are very careful with our money. Blanche has a small income of her own, and we have some jewellery of my mother's left we could sell. Just a few pieces but one or two of them are really nice. We're fond of them, but – well, quite frankly we need a house more than we need gold brooches and bangles.'

'I thought your father's things were all sold up?'

Vivid colour flared in her cheeks. 'Mother's jewellery was left to us. It wasn't part of Father's estate. You don't think we should have used it to pay off his debts?' The thought had preyed on both their minds for years, which was one of the reasons why they hadn't tried to sell the jewellery before.

'No, of course not. It was yours, not his.'

Emma let out a long sigh of relief. 'I'm glad you think so. Anyway, we feel the time has come to sell it – if it's going to be enough to help us buy a house, that is.'

'How are you going to do the selling?'

'I expect we'll give it to Sam to sell for us.'

'Sam?'

'Sam Thoxby. He sold some other stuff for us – mostly bits and pieces of furniture, but a few small pieces of jewellery as well. He's been very helpful since our – problems. He was the one who found us our present lodgings. And we've been very happy there, on the whole.'

James sat frowning. He knew who Thoxby was and found he didn't like the idea of letting him handle a valuable sale for two naïve spinsters. James heard things on the building sites and there had been one or two caustic remarks about Sam's sharpness and the fact that he always had stuff to sell. 'I can probably get you more than Thoxby can.' He gave a scornful laugh. 'It comes in useful sometimes, having connections, and my wife's got a cousin who's a goldsmith in Manchester.'

'Are you sure? I wouldn't want to – to trouble you. And, of course, we have to see how much we get for it, to make sure we can afford a house.'

'If you don't have enough, you can pay the rest off at so much per week. It'll be no different from paying rent.' He found he liked the idea of Emma having one of his houses. He was proud of the places he'd built and she was a plucky lass and a bloody good employee, too. Clients liked dealing with her.

'That's very kind of you.'

'Aye, well, that's me, heart of gold. Which house were you thinking of buying?'

She stared down at her hands. 'Any of them. They're lovely houses. Let's just see if we can afford it first.'

He hated to see her like this, so worried. He wished – oh, hell, he didn't know what he wished, and even if he did, there was nothing he could do about it – except help her get a house. He pushed himself to his feet. 'You bring that jewellery in to show me tomorrow – me, not that Thoxby chap, mind – if you give it to him to sell, I won't let you have a house.'

She looked at him in surprise, unsure whether he was joking or not. But his face said he was perfectly serious. 'Thank you,' she said simply. 'I don't know how we'll ever repay you.'

'You've done that already. You're a damn' good worker.'

Emma smiled then, one of those glorious smiles that lit up her face and made her look years younger. 'I really like working here, Mr Cardwell.'

'I do wish you'd call me James. I keep telling you that.'

She shook her head. 'And I keep telling you that it wouldn't be right.'

'Not even when we're alone?'

'No. Not even then.' Especially not then. But it was what she called him inside her head. James. A nice, honest name. She'd always liked it.

The next Sunday was Polly's day off. Lizzie was dying to tell her all the news and decided to go and meet her from work.

'See you tomorrow, love?' Sam asked after the cinema on the Saturday night.

'Not tomorrow, Sam. It's Polly's day off.'

'Well, you can see her in the morning, can't you?'

Lizzie tried to wriggle from his grasp, but could not move an inch. 'Sam, you're hurting me.'

He breathed deeply and let her go. 'See Polly in the morning. I want to take you out and show you something in the afternoon. It's important.' He hadn't meant to show her the houses Cardwell was building yet, but he was determined to break the close link she shared with her sister.

'Another time, eh, Sam?' She watched him warily.

'No. Not another time. I want to see you tomorrow. You're my girl and I like to spend the weekends with you.'

She stopped walking to stare at him. 'Polly only has one Sunday off a month.'

'Well, that's one Sunday too many for me. But if you're so stuck on seeing her, bring her along.'

Lizzie shook her head. 'No. I've got a few things to tell her. I need to see her on my own.'

He felt anger surge through him and for a moment wanted to thump her. When they were wed, he'd not have her paying attention to anyone except him. When they were wed . . . He forced himself to smile. 'Aw, Lizzie, you know how much I look forward to seeing you.'

'Sam, I don't—'

He pulled her to him and kissed her abruptly, right in the middle of the street, not caring who saw them. 'I'm getting impatient,' he growled in her ear. 'I want you, Lizzie.'

She felt something – not fear, but something curiously like it – shiver in her belly. This was what she was afraid of: Sam's appetites. She didn't really know what to call them, but she'd heard tales of men and what they wanted of women. And the tales frightened her. It wasn't just kisses. And it hurt sometimes. Especially at first. And he was so big. 'Sam,' she quavered. 'Oh, Sam, you frighten me sometimes. I don't think we should—'

He realised he was pushing her too hard and folded her in his arms. 'Shh, now,' he whispered into her hair. 'Shh, now. Just let me hold you, lass.'

He felt her relax against him, saw a couple of old biddies staring at them disapprovingly and hid a smile of triumph in her hair. Not long now, he told himself. He was nearly bursting for relief. He should have gone and bought some quick satisfaction, but he couldn't somehow. It was only Lizzie he wanted, though he hated this need she had put upon him. Surely, surely it would get better once they were wed? Once he had her in his power, he could take her whenever he wished. A wife had to obey her husband and he'd make bloody sure Lizzie did that. Though he'd look after her too. She'd never want. Not his wife.

'Say you'll see me Sunday evening, then?' he whispered in her ear.

ANNA JACOBS

'Oh, Sam, all right.'

He let her go. And when he'd taken her home, he got out the bottle of rum and took a few good pulls. Bloody courting! It was designed to drive a man crazy.

Polly came out of the side gate of Redley House and beamed at the sight of Lizzie waiting for her. 'Hello, love.'

The two sisters embraced, then, arm in arm, began to stroll down the hill towards Bobbin Lane.

'How are things going?'

'All right.'

'And Sam?'

Lizzie shrugged.

Polly stopped walking. 'Look, if you're not sure of your feelings, you shouldn't let everyone push you into going out with him.'

Lizzie sighed and frowned. 'No one's pushing me. Well, not exactly. It's Sam – he's just – he's so impatient to wed, Polly.'

'No one can force you to marry him.'

'No. But circumstances can give you a push, can't they?'

'Is she still treating you badly?' No need to say who 'she' was.

Lizzie tried and failed to look unconcerned. 'You'd think I'd be used to it by now.'

'No one should have to get used to that. Oh, Lizzie, I wish—'

'What do you wish?'

'Wish you liked housework! There's a place going at Mrs Pilby's. We could share a bedroom, be together, then no one could force you into marriage.'

There was silence as they started walking again, then Lizzie said abruptly, 'I'd rather marry Sam than do that, Polly.'

A sigh was her only answer.

'He's – he can be lovely. He holds me sometimes, just holds me, and I feel all safe. And we have fun together. We go to the pictures and we walk in the park and he buys me ice creams.'

But Polly could not help noticing that her sister had never said she liked Sam for himself. Not once. 'Well, I suppose we'd better get off home or she'll be complaining again. What shall we do this afternoon?'

'Not go to church.'

Polly laughed. 'Definitely not.' Though their mother would make a fuss about that. She always did. One day, Polly was determined to get a job away from Overdale, far away. She'd miss Lizzie dreadfully, but if she never saw her mother again, it'd not worry her in the slightest. And she didn't even feel guilty about that. Their mother was a spiteful woman who had made Lizzie's childhood a misery, and had bashed Polly and young Johnny, too.

When they got home, they found that Eva had turned up for a visit. 'What are you doing here?' Polly asked in delight.

'Miss Blake wanted to visit her cousin, Miss Pilby, the one who runs the school, so I thought it'd be a good chance to see you lot.'

From behind her, Meg said sourly, 'We only get a visit when her ladyship can spare your sister.'

Eva rolled her eyes at Polly. 'How about a walk in the park later? Three sisters together.'

'How about spending some time with your mother?' Meg said, her voice heavy with sarcasm.

'I'm spending some time with you first, aren't I? And you'll be at church this afternoon, anyway.'

'So should you be, all three of you. Do you ever go, Eva?'

She breathed in deeply. 'Yes, of course I do. Miss Blake and I go most Sundays.'

'You'd cut off your own fingers if that woman told you to.'

'Mam, please, let's enjoy this visit,' Percy said quietly.

'How can I enjoy it when my daughters are all godless, when they won't spend any time with me?'

'Is that something burning?' he asked.

Meg shrieked and rushed across to the cooker, sighing with relief to find everything all right. 'No, of course it isn't. I don't know why you should think that, Percy Kershaw.'

By that time, Lizzie had gone out to the lav and Polly had gone to hang up her coat in the hall.

Eva followed her out. 'She's getting worse. If it goes on like this, I'm not coming here again.'

Polly looked at her anxiously. 'Please keep coming, Eva. She does like to see you, even if she doesn't show it.'

'I sometimes think she doesn't like anyone or anything since our Dad died.'

'Well, it's hard for her. She's the sort of woman who needs a man.'

'It's not that hard. Percy hands over most of his wages, so does Lizzie, and she has the money from the lodgers. It's not hard at all, if you do the sums. She just pretends it is.'

They stood for a moment in silence, then Polly shrugged and led the way back into the kitchen. Lizzie didn't come in to join them for a while.

That afternoon, Sam turned up in Bobbin Lane, determined not to take no for an answer when he wanted Lizzie to walk out with him. But by that time she had gone out with her sisters, and since Eva had to get to the station by three o'clock to meet Miss Blake, they didn't go to the park but went to walk by the canal instead, which was closer to the station.

'Sorry, lad,' said Percy, not inviting his friend in because this was a rare moment when he had the house to himself and could just sit and read in peace. Such small mercies helped him cope with the rest.

When he didn't find Lizzie and her sisters in the park, Sam grew angry again. 'I'm not going on like this,' he muttered as he sat on a bench, scowling at the people promenading in their Sunday best. 'She'll not go off with her sisters once we're wed, that she won't.'

★   ★   ★

That same Sunday, since the weather was fine, Emma persuaded Blanche to go out for a walk, and of course they went to look at the houses being built in Maidham Street.

'I have a key,' Emma said as they stood looking at the end four houses, which were further advanced than the rest. 'Mr Cardwell says it's safe to go into number seven.'

Blanche nodded but didn't move immediately. Even with all the mess of building, she could see what the street would look like. Neat little houses with bay windows and attics. A tiny garden in the front of each. You'd be able to grow flowers. She loved flowers. She looked sideways at Emma. 'Are you sure we can afford it?'

'Yes. Well, fairly sure.'

Blanche took a deep quivering breath and allowed a dream to creep into her heart. Net curtains across the bay window, tied in swags. Flowers. A shiny brass door knocker.

'Just wait until these people have passed,' Emma said suddenly. 'We don't want anyone telling Mrs Kershaw we've been poking around here. She'll get suspicious. We don't want her to know anything until it's all settled.'

'No.' Blanche shuddered. 'Oh, no. And even then – you'll tell her for me, won't you, Emma? I know I'm a coward, but she can be very – intimidating.'

'Leave that to me.'

Inside the house was a long, narrow hall, with just enough room for a hallstand. There was a front room to the right, not large but of harmonious proportions.

'It could look very nice,' Blanche admitted.

Emma, who had already seen the house in the company of her boss, nodded. 'Come and look at the back – see, there's a morning room and then a kitchen and scullery. You can have your piano in the front room and continue to give lessons.'

Blanche nodded.

Upstairs there were three bedrooms, the smallest very tiny.

'I think we could use this one for a sewing room,' Emma

suggested, worried that her sister wasn't saying anything. 'It's too small, really, to use as a bedroom.'

After another silence, Blanche said quietly, 'It's a baby's room. Or a child's.'

They both took a moment to move on. They knew they'd never have children and that knowledge hurt each woman from time to time. It was one thing they never discussed. No use opening old wounds. Better to look to the future, concentrate on what they could have.

Finally, there were two attics, proper rooms, with a dormer window to the rear one and a sort of bay dormer to the front one in line with the bays to the other floors. 'I'd like to take this room for mine,' Emma confessed, standing by the window. 'It's got the best view through that gap between the houses. Would you mind?'

'Oh, no. Not at all. Can we really—?'

'Yes, we can. If we sell Mother's jewellery and use all our savings.'

And suddenly Blanche was weeping in her sister's arms. 'It seems like a miracle, having our own place again. I can't believe it's going to happen, somehow.'

'Well, it is. We'll *make* it happen. That's why we've been so careful these past few years. No one's given us this. We've earned it ourselves.' And she felt rather proud of that.

'What about Aunt Gertrude?' Blanche asked as they stood in the kitchen again, looking out at the small yard.

'What about her?'

'I think we should at least let her know when we move.'

'She's never made any attempt to contact us, though you've written to her every Christmas.'

Blanche shrugged. 'I know. But if we do what's right, then I can sleep peacefully. And she is our only surviving relative.'

'Write to her if you want. And tell her we're doing all right, buying a house.' Emma spun round, arms spread wide. 'Oh, I love it already!'

CHAPTER FOURTEEN

August – October 1913

One week later, Sam called in at Cardwell's on his way home, having seen through the window that Emma Harper was still at work.

She looked up as he entered, her heart sinking when she saw who it was. 'Hello, Sam.'

Removing his cap, he nodded. 'Good evening, Miss Emma. I saw you were still here, so thought I'd just pop in and find out if you'd given buying a house any more thought?'

When he came right up to her desk, looming over her, she pushed back her chair, feeling suddenly uneasy and wishing someone else were around. 'We're still thinking about it.'

'It's just that if you have to sell your jewellery, well, I've met a fellow who can help.'

'Thank you, but we've already sold it.' For a moment, she saw an ugly expression cross his face, too clear to be mistaken, then it was wiped off and replaced by a smile, but not a pleasant one.

'Oh? I thought I was going to help you with that. As I've helped you with other things.'

She shrugged, trying to make light of it. 'I found someone who had better connections – who could get us a higher price.' She felt annoyed with herself for feeling nervous and added sharply, 'Actually, he got us a much better price than you did for the other stuff, too, Sam. Nearly double, at a rough estimate.'

There was a moment's silence during which the only sound was his breathing, always rather stertorous. He's like a pig, she thought now, listening to it in the silence of the large waiting area where her desk was located. No, not a pig, that's too tame. A boar.

'I'm right glad for you, then,' he said.

His smile didn't reach his eyes. Looking at him, she believed what James Cardwell had told her, accepting fully now what she had denied before: that Sam had cheated them, on the furniture and on the jewellery. 'So am I.'

He didn't leave and she swallowed, wishing he would go. He was still much too close.

'You'll be buying a house in Maidham Street, then?'

'Yes. Yes, we are.'

He nodded and his smile was a sneer by now. 'We may be neighbours, then.'

She hoped her dismay hadn't shown in her face, but suspected it had. His eyes went glassy for a moment and the silence seemed to go on for a long time.

Sam took a step backwards, staring round him. 'That's the other reason I came here. To see that boss of yours. Is he in?'

'I'll – um, go and see if he's come back.'

To Emma's relief, James was out in the yard, talking to Walter, gesticulating wildly as he always did. He looked wholesome and healthy. The mere sight of him made her feel better, cleaner somehow.

When she called him over and explained what Sam wanted, he frowned. 'I don't like selling to him. And where the hell did he get that much money on his wages?' He looked at her, lips pursed. 'He must be on the fiddle somehow.'

'There's nothing proved.'

'No. But I still think he diddled you and no doubt he's diddled others, too. Has he been pestering you about something?'

'No. Just asking if we still want him to sell things for us.'

James laid one hand on her arm. 'You'll let me know if he annoys you? Promise.'

She could only nod. But she guessed Sam would do nothing

obvious. 'I could do without him as a neighbour,' she admitted.

'Aye. But if he's got the money, I can hardly turn him away, can I?' Because it was all taking longer than James had expected and they both knew he had to sell one or two of the houses quickly to get more cash to finish the rest. And for all he had offered to let Emma pay off part of her purchase weekly, he was glad the jewellery had provided her and her sister with the money to buy the house outright, because with the best will in the world, he couldn't have subsidised them. 'All right, then. Give me a minute to wash my hands, then show him into my office.'

The following weekend Sam took Lizzie out to the cinema as usual, then on the way home, swung her round into the alley where he still lived in the house he had shared with his gran, keeping a firm hold of her hand as she tried to pull back.

'I have to get home,' she said nervously as he opened the front door.

'We need to talk. In private.'

'Sam—'

He chuckled, scooped her up into his arms and carried her inside, taking her by surprise, so that she could only let out a squeak of shock before the door was closed. 'This is what I want to do for real,' he murmured against her throat as she lay in his arms, trembling a little. 'I want to carry my bride across the threshold an' shut the rest of the world outside.' And then do all the things he had dreamed of.

'Oh, Sam, can't we – wait a bit?'

'Why?'

'I'm only seventeen.'

'Seventeen and a half now. A woman grown.' He set her down, but kept hold of her hand, stroking her fingers with his big rough thumb. 'Aw, Lizzie, I need you to marry me now.' He drew her down on the couch, gritting his teeth against the urge to take her there and then, willing or not. He didn't want to frighten her off. He'd seen over the years how stubborn she could be if she set her mind against something. 'I want to be with you every night,' he growled in her ear. 'You and me, husband and wife. And no bugger else! I want to come home and find you waiting, a meal on the table, a fire burning – not an empty house with dust in the corners.' He waved one hand at the neglected room.

She didn't say anything, but as usual nestled against him.

He hid a smile. This was how to get to her. The cuddling. 'An' don't tell me it's easy for you, Lizzie love, going home night after night to *her* shouting at you.' He felt her shudder against him and pressed his advantage. 'Wouldn't you like to have your own home? No shouting? No fuss? Just you an' me?'

The picture he painted did have its attractions, Lizzie had to admit. And she loved it when he held her like this. She wished he'd say he loved her, like they did in the stories in the magazines she read now instead of the comics she had loved as a child. She sighed at that thought. She didn't feel like a child, hadn't for ages. But she didn't feel quite a woman, either. 'I suppose so, Sam.'

A quick look of satisfaction crossed his face. 'Can't I at least tell folk we're serious? Eeh, I want to put a big sign on you to warn all the other fellows off.' In a carefully thought-out gesture, he pulled a little box out of his pocket and took a ring from it. 'Can't we at least get engaged? Won't you give me that much, Lizzie Kershaw?'

She stared at the ring in amazement. 'Engaged?'

He held it out. 'Yes. I got this for you. Do you like it?'

'It's beautiful.' It had a softer sheen than brass and the stone had a sparkle to it, catching the light from the one gas fitting overhead. 'Is it real?'

'Aye, lass. It's a real diamond an' the ring's real gold. I'm not havin' *my* wife wearin' a brass one an' going round with a dirty mark on her finger.'

'*Sam!*' She stared at it in awe. 'Oh, it must have cost a fortune!'

'Nothin's too good for my girl. Give us your hand, then.'

He took the ring and slipped it on to her third finger. 'A bit loose. We'll go to Pearson's next Saturday and arrange to have it made smaller. They've got a piece of wood with holes in to show the size of your finger. They'll do the alterations for nothing because I bought the ring there.' He wasn't daft enough to use one of the rings he and Josh picked up sometimes, though it'd have saved him money.

Lizzie sat staring at her outstretched hand, her mouth half-open in shock, then she looked at him and tears filled her eyes. 'Oh, Sam, you really do love me, don't you? You never say it, but you do. Oh, Sam—'

He nodded and picked up her hand, kissing it, then moving on to kiss her mouth, her soft, trembling lips. Go easy, lad, he told himself, as lust clamoured for release. It's working, just as you planned, so don't spoil it now. 'I'm not one for fancy words, love. I reckon actions speak louder any day. But you're my girl an' I want to show the world that you are.'

She nodded, feeling wanted, really wanted, for herself. 'We could get engaged, then,' she said tentatively. 'If you like?'

'I do like, lass, I do. And you won't keep me waiting too long to get wed, will you?'

'Just a little longer,' she pleaded. 'I need to get a bottom drawer ready.' She gave an embarrassed laugh. 'Though you'll be disappointed in me, Sam. I'm a rotten sewer. I can cook and clean and all that, but I can't seem to sew straight to save my life.'

'Who the hell cares about sewing?' He pressed his lips to hers in a long kiss.

Lost in a glow of happiness, Lizzie responded more warmly than she ever had before.

When they drew apart, he was breathing deeply. 'Come on, lass. Better take you home or I'll get carried away.' And anyway, if they were too late, the old hag would start saying things and he wasn't having any dirty gossip about his wife-to-be. He looked at her, with her eyes shining and her face lit up, and said almost in surprise, 'Eeh, you're lovely when you look happy.'

'Go on with you, Sam. I'm not lovely. I wish I were. For you.'

'You're the one I want. An' you've got the prettiest eyes I've ever seen.'

'Oh, Sam!' She sighed and laid her head against his shoulder. 'You're so kind to me.'

As he walked home after leaving her at the front door, his face bore a look of savage triumph. They were going to tell her family they were engaged the following evening, and the old lady could just like it or lump it. After that, everything else would fall into place as he wanted. It always did when he made a plan and stuck to it. But he'd be glad when he didn't need to fuss over her like this, he would that. He'd already had to face a lot of teasing from his mates about the visits to the cinema. It wasn't right, a fellow running round after a slip of a lass. They should be the ones running round after you.

Two months later, in October, Blanche went upstairs and Emma waited in the kitchen after the evening meal. 'Could I please have a word with you, Mrs Kershaw? In the front room, perhaps?' She glanced at Percy, who already knew that she and her sister were about to give notice, and he nodded slightly.

He watched Emma lead the way towards the front room, graceful and elegant as always, followed by his mother, who had surely grown thinner this past year? Certainly her expression had grown sourer and she'd had a bad cough last winter that had racked her for weeks.

Lizzie looked at him in puzzlement. What was going on?

Percy saw the question in her eyes, but didn't enlighten her, just sat down and picked up the evening paper. She hesitated, then finished clearing the table. He shook the paper out and hid behind it, though he couldn't read a word, so tense was he about what was going on in the front room. He had promised Emma to stay around, in case his mother made one of her fusses, as they were both sure she would do. It didn't take much to set her off lately, and however tactfully Emma approached the subject of their leaving, Mam would take it as a personal affront.

He sighed and stared blindly at the printed page. After the lodgers left, things would be worse than ever in this house. He would miss Emma so much – their little chats, her pretty face, the warmth of her smile. Eva and Polly had already gone, and now that Lizzie and Sam were engaged, she would soon be leaving as well. And he was glad, for her sake. But his own future seemed very bleak. He stood up, letting the paper slide to the floor, and began fiddling with the things on the mantelpiece as he listened for noise from the front room.

'What's going on?' Lizzie asked, coming in with her hands damp and picking up the downstairs towel that was drying on the fireguard. The hands she was wiping were red from the washing soda and she looked cold – well, that scullery never seemed to warm up in the winter, however much they left the kitchen door open to let the heat from the fire through.

He stared at her as if she'd spoken in a foreign language, then blinked his eyes back into focus and said curtly, 'Emma's giving notice to Mam. She and Miss Harper are leaving next week.'

Lizzie's face fell. 'Oh, no! Mam'll go mad.'

'Aye. That's why Emma asked me to stay in tonight – just in case, like.'

'Why are they leaving? Where are they going?'

'They're getting a place of their own. Buying one of those new houses Cardwell's putting up in Maidham Street.'

'Oh.' Lizzie stared down at the cruet she had picked up from the table so that she could shake the crumbs off the tablecloth, but made no move to complete the task for a moment or two. When she realised she was standing gaping, she clicked her teeth in annoyance at herself, put the cruet set on the sideboard and started gathering the tablecloth together, to take it outside the back door and shake it. That was when she heard her mam's voice raised in shrill protest.

'She's off!'

'I'd better go and stop her making a fool of herself, I suppose,' Percy groaned.

'I'll finish here quickly and nip upstairs. She won't want me around.'

'You spend far too much time in that bedroom of yours. What are you going to do in the winter, Lizzie love?'

She shrugged. 'I don't know. Maybe I'll have moved out by then.' If she married Sam, she'd have her own house. For once in her life, she was trying to think things through, as Eva always did, but she wasn't finding it easy. She knew, from things he'd said, that Sam wouldn't be the sort of husband to help around the home, though he'd probably be a good provider, which was important. But she'd be left doing everything and she'd be on her own all day, too, not like at the shop. She'd miss the company dreadfully.

But she did like babies and children, and she wanted very much to have a family of her own – well, one day she did. She'd love them a lot, cuddle them, play with them as her father had done with her – and not be anything at all like her mother. They'd be happy, her children would, and . . . She shook off the daydream, spread the tablecloth out again, shoved the cruet into the middle and rushed upstairs, wincing at the shrill cries still coming from the front room.

Percy found his mother berating a white-faced Emma, who was standing stiff with outraged dignity in front of the fireplace. It was a moment before he could get Meg's attention and in the end he had to put an arm round her and pull her bodily back. 'Mam, stop this!'

She struggled against him, then gasped and stared at him, looking so wild and strange that his heart sank even further.

'But they're leaving! After all I've done for them, our Percy. *Leaving!*'

'They've got a right to live where they want, Mam. And they're giving you a week's notice, aren't they? That was the agreement.'

It was as if she hadn't heard him. 'I've even let them keep that piano in the front room, let those children trail in for singing lessons – and as well as the noise, it all makes extra work, you know. And who does the work? Me, that's who! They never wipe their feet properly, those children don't, and they leave sticky fingermarks all over the place.' Meg gasped for breath and her voice rose even higher. 'And now they're going, leaving us. *After all I've done!*' She burst into tears, wailing more complaints into his chest.

Percy looked across at Emma, hoping she'd read from his expression how sorry he was about all this. He saw the pity in her eyes and it was the last thing he wanted from her. Tamping down his own feelings, he jerked his head towards the door in an unmistakable signal for her to leave. She nodded and went, as quietly as she did everything else. Unlike this shrieking harridan struggling in his arms.

Upstairs Emma paused outside the door to Lizzie's bedroom, which was open for once. 'You've heard what's happening – that we're leaving?'

Lizzie nodded.

Emma sighed and leaned against the door for a minute. 'I'm going to miss you, Lizzie. Blanche and I are moving into Maidham Street, number seven. I do hope you'll come and see us there sometimes?'

The girl's face brightened. 'I'd like that.'

'Don't forget then. I mean it.'

'I'm sorry Mam's being so – so awkward.'

'We'd rather expected it. But it isn't pleasant.' Emma listened to the sobbing from downstairs and shook her head as she turned to leave. 'I'd better go and reassure my sister that I'm all right. I'm sorry your mother's upset, but I won't be bullied by anyone.' Not even by Sam Thoxby, who had stopped her in the street only today to ask if she needed help moving, though how he'd known that they were about to leave was more than she could tell, for she'd asked Percy not to mention it to anyone else.

★   ★   ★

It took Percy even longer than usual to calm his mother down. She kept hold of him, her bony fingers digging painfully into his flesh as she wept on his chest, beating on it now and then with one clenched fist. Then she would stop her weeping to shout a series of angry accusations about how the lodgers had taken advantage of her, how everyone took advantage of a poor widow who had no one to stand up for her.

After a while, the weeping eased and she said venomously, 'And it's all Lizzie's fault! She has a lot to answer for. She'd do anything to spite me, that one would.'

Percy pushed her to arm's length. 'How on earth can this be Lizzie's fault?'

'*She* brought Sam into the house that evening. That's when it all started. Since then, those two upstairs have been going out a lot and coming back full of themselves. They've been buying new things. I've seen the parcels. I should have realised something was going on. But then I'm always getting taken in. I'm too trusting, I am.' A brief pause for breath and she added, 'If Lizzie hadn't kept watch for him, I'd have found out what was going on then and given them notice to leave before they could do this to me.'

Percy's voice was stern. 'Then I can only be glad Lizzie *did* keep watch. You have no right to spy on your lodgers, Mam, no right at all.'

'I have every right. It's my house, isn't it? I can do what I want in my own house.'

'It's my name that's on the rent book now, actually.'

She brushed that aside, as she always did when things didn't suit her. 'Well, it's the same thing. You can't deny it's my *home*. And if your father hadn't died, it'd be his name on the rent book, not yours, then I'd feel safer. Why was he taken? Oh, God, why was he taken from me? I thought I'd be the one to go first. I *wanted* to go first.'

Percy closed his eyes and prayed for patience as he tried to distract her. 'Do you want to get some more lodgers, Mam?'

She gulped and stared at him. 'Of course I don't *want* to.

I didn't want to get these two, either. It's hard work, having lodgers is. But I *have* to do it, or I won't get the pension when I'm old, then they'll put me in the workhouse.'

A thought had been hovering at the edges of Percy's mind ever since he'd heard the Harpers were leaving and now he voiced it. 'You don't have to take in more lodgers, actually.'

The torrent of words stopped for a moment and she stared at him. 'What do you mean by that?'

'I mean, you don't have to bring money in, don't have to work so hard. I've been thinking about it ever since Emma told me they were leaving.' He saw an accusation forming on her lips and said hastily, 'She was worried you'd be upset. She was thinking of you.'

'That sort only think about themselves. Don't you be taken in by her fancy ways, Percy Kershaw, she's not for such as you.'

He ignored that. 'Look, Mam, you're not strong enough to look after lodgers, and anyway those stairs really give you trouble. I think we should move into a smaller house, somewhere that's easier for you to keep nice.'

Meg let out another of her wails of anguish. 'That's right! Throw me out of my home. I want to die in this house, you know I do. Your father brought me to it when we got married. All my children were born here. We laid Stanley out here, too. I can still see him lying there on that sofa. Bobbin Lane's been my home for years and you have no right to ask me to leave. *No right!* You'd think a son would show more consideration for his widowed mother, but no one cares what becomes of me now. No one.'

Percy's frustration boiled up in a tide of bitterness that nearly scalded his throat. 'You bloody well *are* leaving! I should have made you do it before. You aren't strong enough to look after lodgers and you'll feel a lot better if you've less to do.' Well, he hoped she'd feel better, act more sensibly. 'So I'll go and see Mr Cuttler tomorrow about us getting another house, a smaller one, and—'

'I'm not sharing a room with Lizzie! I'd kill myself first.' She clutched her meagre bosom dramatically.

He stopped short, wondering if she had lost her mind. 'What the hell has that got to do with anything?'

'You'd never swear at me like this if your father were still alive. He wouldn't let you.'

'Answer my damned question!'

But she chose to answer obliquely, contradicting her earlier words, as she often did. 'Do you imagine I haven't thought about finding somewhere smaller? Well, I have. Lots of times. But the smaller ones only have two bedrooms. *She* can't share with you and our Johnny, so she'd have to share with me and *I won't – do – it!*'

'You could get separate beds.' But he knew even as he spoke that it wouldn't work.

'No.' Then Meg's mouth dropped open and a slow smile crossed her face. 'But *she* could move out, of course. Then we'd not have to share.'

'You'll not throw her out.'

She looked at him scornfully. 'Who's talking of throwing her anywhere? She and Sam are engaged, aren't they? With a fancy ring, an' all – she doesn't deserve it, but he won't be told what she's like. So if they're going to get wed, now would be the time for them to do it. That'd suit everyone. I know *he* wants to get wed quickly. Well, he's a man, isn't he? Can't do without it, most of them. I've often wondered what's wrong with you that you don't run after the lasses.'

Percy made an inarticulate noise of protest at this unfair gibe on top of everything else, but she didn't even notice.

'I've heard her saying "not yet", the silly little fool! She'll lose him if she goes on like that. He needs a woman to look after him, doesn't he, as well as needing the other thing? Though he'll soon regret marrying her, by heck he will.'

Suddenly Meg was eager to leave this place, glad the lodgers were going because it would mean she could get rid of Lizzie once and for all. She beamed at Percy. 'You can tell Lizzie. Well, you should tell Sam first, I think. He'll help you persuade her to get wed quick. Then I shan't mind moving.'

He was amazed yet again by her mercurial switches of mood.

What she said did make sense in one way, but still he felt uneasy. He knew Sam's feelings, but he also knew Lizzie's reluctance. 'I don't know about that. She's a bit young for marriage.'

'She's old enough. There's many of 'em wed at seventeen.'

'It's one thing to get wed because you want to, Mam, but another thing altogether to do it because someone's pushing you. I'll have a talk with her, certainly, but I'm not forcing her. And you're not to say anything to her till then.'

But Meg wasn't really listening. 'It'll be the best thing for all of us. Just me and my sons. Daughters let you down, but sons don't. I'll feel much better in a smaller house, I'm sure my health will improve.' She sat down on the sofa, tears and tantrums forgotten. 'Pass me the photo album, will you, love? I want to look back at happier days. And then I'll have to think about what we'll be taking with us and what we'll need to sell. We won't get all this stuff into a smaller house.'

He did as she asked, sighing, and left the room. When she started looking at photos of their father, she got very maudlin. She'd be weeping later. Again.

Lizzie wasn't in the kitchen so Percy went upstairs to her bedroom. She was asleep, looking very young and vulnerable in the light from the landing. She'd been looking tired lately, worn down by all the carping. She'd probably be a lot happier away from their mother and in a home of her own; happier than she had been here since their dad had died. Most women wanted their own home.

A little voice whispered in his mind that Lizzie wasn't most women, but he pushed that thought aside as he went back to his newspaper. Things couldn't go on as they were, that was for sure. They'd all have to make concessions to sort this mess out. It could solve all their problems if Lizzie married Sam sooner than planned.

But – he sighed again – he was going to miss Emma. By hell he was! For the first time Percy admitted openly to himself that he was a bit gone on their younger lodger. He knew he'd never have had a chance with her, of course he did, but that didn't stop him enjoying her company, fancying her, dreaming a bit. But that was all he'd ever have: dreams.

Suddenly he got up and went to fetch his cap and overcoat. He'd go down to the pub this very minute. Bound to catch Sam at one place or the other. He could have a quiet word. No time like the present. And he'd get out of the house for a bit.

Emma and Blanche moved out of Bobbin Lane the following Saturday, a fine sunny day. Mr Cardwell helped them with the removal, bringing along his motor lorry. Percy and Harry Preston from across the road helped him carry their stuff down from the attic.

Meg stayed in the kitchen with the door shut, angry that her son was wasting his time helping *them*. Trust a woman to take advantage of a young man's strength. She nibbled on her fingernails, worrying about that. Percy hadn't shown any signs of dangling after girls, so far, but you never knew, so she'd better keep a careful eye open from now on. She wasn't taking a back seat to anyone. Percy was her son and it was his duty to look after her. That's what Stanley would have expected.

Polly came back to say goodbye to Blanche Harper, having begged an hour off work. Mrs Pilby didn't approve of this sort of laxness, but the housekeeper gave her permission. Modern maids insisted on all sorts of privileges and at least Polly Kershaw was a conscientious worker, so Mrs Frost was determined to keep her happy.

When the lorry had gone, Polly popped into the kitchen for a quick word with her mother.

'Seen them off in style, have you?' Meg sneered. 'Didn't think of me sitting here all on my own, did you?'

'Look, Mam, I have to get back to work. I just came in to say hello.'

'I don't know why you even bothered to come round today.' Her mother's voice took on a whining edge. 'Sucking up to them won't do you any good now. You've had the last of those silly singing lessons – proper waste of time those were. Your voice is nowt above the ordinary. They won't want to have anything to do with you from now on. See if I'm not right.

They'll find themselves some fancy new friends and ignore those who've looked after them all these years.'

'I have to go now, Mam,' Polly repeated. 'Will you be all right?'

'What? Of course I'll be all right. Especially now *they* have gone.'

When the door had closed behind Polly, Meg wandered round the house. 'Glad to have it to myself,' she said as she went into the front room and stared at the space where the piano had been. And, 'A fine mess they've made of this,' she said scornfully in the attic, looking at the marks on the wall.

Percy found her still up there when he came home a couple of hours later. She was standing gazing out of the windows, muttering to herself, and jumped like a startled rabbit when he spoke to her, staring at him wildly as if she didn't recognise him.

He put a hand on her shoulder, suddenly afraid. 'Mam, are you all right?'

She jerked and as she focused on his face, the strangeness left her eyes and she reached out to pat his cheek. 'Of course I'm all right, son.'

But on the way downstairs, she stopped again and told her reflection in the mirror at the top of the stairs, 'And I'll be even better when we've got rid of that young madam. Oh, yes.'

Then he knew for certain that the best thing he could do for Lizzie was to get her free of their mother, not for Sam's sake, though his friend was pleased at the thought of an earlier marriage, but for his sister's own sake. And whatever the doctor said, he didn't think this was just a phase due to Mam's age. She was – he faced the fact squarely – not quite right in the head, especially about her eldest daughter. 'I'll talk to Lizzie tonight about Sam.'

'Good lad.' Meg went to sit in front of the fire, staring into it and crooning to herself. It was a full half hour later before she started clearing up the kitchen and only when she looked more like herself did he dare leave her alone.

CHAPTER FIFTEEN

November 1913

Lizzie stared at Percy and swallowed hard. 'Say that again.'

'I said, I think you ought to name a day now, love. You'll be eighteen in four months. You're engaged to Sam, so you must want to marry him. Why delay any longer?'

She stared down at her hands, then stood up and went to look out of the window of the front room, into which he'd taken her after tea 'for a quiet talk'.

He was worried by the expression on her face. Surely that hadn't been fear? Patiently he waited for her to respond. If she was afraid of marrying Sam, or anyone else, then he'd have to find another way out of this situation.

'Why are you saying this now?' asked Lizzie at last, walking over to fiddle with the ornaments on the mantelpiece. 'When you've been telling me to take my time?' She put down the photograph of her father and turned to stare at him.

He shrugged his shoulders, avoiding her clear green eyes which seemed to see deep into the uncertainties within him. 'Because Mam isn't up to looking after any more lodgers and really this place is too big for her, with her being so fussy. So I thought we'd move out – and Mr Cuttler says he'll keep an eye open for a nice place for us. But it'll likely have only two bedrooms, not three, and so—'

'So there'll be no place for me?'

'If you weren't getting married, it'd be different. We'd either stay here or find somewhere with three bedrooms. I'd never see you thrown out of your home, love, you know that. But you're engaged and – well, it seems sensible all round for you to get married now.'

Lizzie's voice was curiously flat. 'Yes, I suppose it does.' Then she realised why Sam had been looking so smug and secretive for the last couple of days. 'You've already spoken to Sam, haven't you?'

'Well, yes.'

There was silence as she reflected on the way men stuck together and never told you anything. Then she said sadly, 'And, of course, Mam would love to get rid of me.'

Percy couldn't deny it.

Lizzie had the feeling she was hurtling towards the edge of a cliff. Terror filled her for a moment, then ebbed away. Sam wanted her, even if her own mother didn't. She shrugged.

'Does that mean yes?'

She looked at her brother, his kind gentle face full of concern. She wasn't the only one to have suffered since her father's death. Percy didn't complain, but he looked sad and worn sometimes. Just now, he couldn't hide his relief.

'You should be married yourself with kids by now, Percy. I've seen you stop and smile at babies in the street.'

His laughter was shamefaced for he adored small children and had a way with them, he knew. 'It's that obvious, is it? I'll have to be more careful from now on, then.' He went across and gave her a quick hug. 'Eeh, lass, you'll be better off away from her. She's getting a bit – a bit—'

'Strange. Yes, I've noticed.' Lizzie managed a smile. 'I'll have to talk to Sam, won't I, sort out a date? We can have a quiet wedding, just us two, you and Polly, and—'

'No. You'll have a proper send-off and I'll see she does the right thing by you – in public at least.'

'Well, a proper wedding will stop all the old biddies thinking I'm having a baby, at least. I'll go round and see if I can catch Sam in now, shall I?'

Percy walked with her to the front door, where he held her back for a moment to ask, 'You are sure, aren't you?'

'As sure as I'll ever be.' Lizzie walked quickly away before he could see the doubt in her face. She knew she wasn't really ready to marry Sam, but she had never been able to work out why.

Sam answered the door and beamed when he saw her. 'Well, you're a sight for sore eyes!'

He was still in his work clothes, looking tired and rumpled. She let him shepherd her inside and presented her cheek for a quick kiss, drawing away when he tried to capture her in his arms.

'You sit down in the kitchen, love and I'll just nip out to the scullery and have a bit of a wash. I've not long been home.' He'd stopped off at the Carter's Rest for a sup of ale. He got thirsty after a day's work.

She sat and stared at the empty fireplace, thinking how lonely it must be to come home to an empty house, and how bad he was at coping with housework. Without taking a conscious decision, she started picking things up and then took the poker to the fire. By the time he came back, it was burning brightly. She had always had a gift for managing fires.

'Eeh, that looks a bit more cheerful, lass. I'll just go upstairs an' put a clean shirt on.'

It seemed strange to be so intimate with him. Lizzie watched him walk out, his back strong and muscular, the skin of his newly washed neck bright pink against the ginger of his hair. As his footsteps echoed up the stairs, she began to carry out the dirty dishes that were dumped here and there and pile them in the scullery. The fire hadn't had time to heat the water, so she put the kettle on the gas stove and when he came down again, she was washing up. Piles of stuff, there were. Everything in the place was dirty, it seemed.

'You can wipe up for me, if you like,' she called.

Sam came to stand in the doorway, frowning. 'No.' His voice was very flat and emphatic. 'I don't do stuff like that. Mrs Wright from next door is supposed to come in and clean for me, but she's been ill.'

'What if I were ill after we'd got married? Would you do it then?'

'No. I'd get some other woman in. I'm a man, an' dishes are women's work.'

Lizzie stared down into the water. Well, she couldn't say she didn't know where she stood with him, could she? 'I see.'

He came over to stand beside her. 'I'll provide for you, lass, an' provide well, but I'm not a cissy an' I'm not doing the housework as well as bringing in the wages. Not even with the curtains closed.' They both knew of one man down the street who helped out in secret. Lizzie thought him a lovely fellow and his wife obviously thought so, too. Men like Sam scorned him.

She plunged another pile of plates into the water. 'I see.'

He watched her busy hands as he talked, enjoying the sight of her working for him. 'Percy said your mam wants to move to a smaller house?'

'An' she wants to get rid of me.' Lizzie blinked her eyes rapidly, but couldn't prevent a tear from rolling down her cheek and plopping into the water. Her hands were gripping the edges of a plate so tightly that her knuckles showed white. 'I'll make sure my children always know they're loved,' she said with sudden savageness. 'So if you aren't going to love our children, don't marry me, Sam, because I won't have a child of mine brought up like I've been since Dad died.'

'I want children an' I'll look after them properly.' His voice was husky. 'I've been without parents myself an' I know what it's like.'

'Yes.' She looked at him, a long, steady look which made her seem older. 'So – when do you want to get married?'

'As soon as possible.'

'Three weeks, it takes, I think. They have to call the banns and—'

'I were thinking more of a register office.'

She stilled and stared down at the water. 'I know I won't have a fancy wedding dress, but Percy says we should get married in church and – I'd like that. A register office wouldn't feel quite as respectable, somehow.'

Sam thought about it for a moment, then nodded. Yes, she had a point. He wanted everything to be done properly too. 'An' you *will* have a fancy wedding dress. Perhaps not one of them white things, because I can't see much sense in spending a lot of hard-earned money for one day's wear, but a good dress, one you can be proud of and wear on Sundays afterwards. I'll buy it for you as a wedding present.' He nodded, pleased with the idea of making a bit of a splash, showing folk that he was well set up. About time he got some enjoyment out of his money. He'd taken quite a few risks to get it, risks that soft sod Percy hadn't dared face. 'And we'll have our photographs took afterwards, too. And I'll get you a bouquet of flowers to carry. Why not?'

He picked her up, wet hands and all, and swung her round, laughing as she squealed in shock. When she flung her wet arms round his neck to give him a hug, he kissed her. He felt gentle inside, for once, not raging with a need for sex.

When he set her down, Lizzie laughed and set to work on the dishes again, leaving them to drain on the wooden board at the side of the slopstone. She finished quickly, with him standing admiring her efficiency, then he led her through into the kitchen, to sit cosily together at the table, writing down all the things they'd have to arrange.

'Could we have my sisters as – not as bridesmaids exactly but, you know, as attendants, I think they call 'em, and – and could they have smaller bouquets?' she asked wistfully. 'It'd make it so special.'

'Why not?' He'd had a good month or two lately.

'And Percy can give me away.' Lizzie was very definite about that.

'I wanted him for best man.'

They laughed.

'Can he do both things?' she wondered.

Sam frowned, then shook his head. 'No, I'll have to ask Josh to do it instead. He'll jump at the chance.'

'Josh?'

'A mate of mine. I do a bit of business with him from time to time.'

'All right. Oh, Sam—'

'What?'

'Isn't it exciting?'

'Aye.' He smiled at her. Soon she'd be his. Then she'd find out what exciting meant!

Lizzie was to realise long afterwards that this was the closest they were ever to get; that it was as close as it was possible for anyone to get to Sam Thoxby. She was to realise a lot of things afterwards. But just then she thought mainly of escaping from her mother, and doing it in an honourable way, so that folk wouldn't talk about her afterwards and laugh at how she'd been thrown out and had to scramble into marriage.

The next evening they went to see the Minister at her mother's church about getting married there and although he gave them both a lecture about not attending regularly, he did agree to marry them 'for the sake of your poor mother'. But only on condition they attended church every Sunday from then on.

'Boring old sod!' Sam growled as they walked home.

'Wait till you hear his sermons. You'll have trouble staying awake!'

Sam let out a snort of laughter. 'Well, if I drop off to sleep in church, don't give me a nudge till he's stopped spouting. And any road, it's only till we're wed. Damned if I'm going into one of them bloody places afterwards. Weddings, christenings and funerals, that's all churches are good for.'

'Oh? I thought you'd have me out praying every Sunday?' teased Lizzie.

It took him a minute to realise that she was joking again, then he gave her a perfunctory grin and changed the subject. 'Are you doing owt on Sunday morning?'

'Nothing apart from going to church. We'll get it over with early, shall we, and then we can enjoy the rest of the day?'

'Good idea. And after church, I want to show you something.'

'I was going to come and give that house of yours a good clean-out afterwards. That neighbour hasn't given you good value for money and I can't bear to think of you living in such a tip.' And she was going to speak to Sam about them getting a new bed and a few other bits and pieces, too, before she moved in.

'I need to show you something first.'

'All right.' She peeped sideways at him, glad to see he was recovering his good humour. 'What is it?'

'Wait and see.'

A state of armed neutrality existed in Bobbin Lane from then onwards. Meg was informed by Percy in no uncertain terms that if she wanted to get rid of Lizzie, she was to do right by the lass. And for a while, she even felt a bit warmer towards her – the first of her daughters to get wed. Especially as Sam was buying the bride's dress and the flowers, as well as taking all the family out for a meal afterwards, so she'd not have too much extra work to do.

When Percy gave his mother some extra money to buy herself a new dress and hat, and get Johnny a new outfit, Meg grew even mellower and decided that it was almost worth the fuss. And she was finding life a lot easier without the lodgers.

So Lizzie found her washing done without complaint and her meals more appetising for a week or two.

Meg had viewed and turned down one house, because it had a shared privvy, but Mr Cuttler said another place would come up soon. They always did.

'Your Lizzie's wedding Sam Thoxby, isn't she?' he said as he was leaving. It didn't sound as if he approved.

'Yes, an' she can think herself lucky to get him.'

'Oh, like that, is it?'

'Like what?'

'Needs to get wed.'

'No, she does not! None of my daughters is like that, thank you very much.'

'Pardon me.' But he wondered as he walked down the street what that nice little lass was doing tying herself to such a shifty lout.

On the Sunday, Sam sat and scowled his way through a service he considered a load of claptrap, not even trying to mouth the hymns. But he listened with pleasure to the banns being called and enjoyed the stares as heads swivelled round.

After that, he got out as quickly as he could, refusing point-blank to answer Lizzie's questions about where they were going. He wanted it to be a complete surprise. He wanted to see her face when he showed her the house.

Stopping outside number one, Maidham Street, he waved one hand carelessly towards it. 'There, what do you think of that?'

She stared at it in bewilderment. 'What do you mean, what do I think of it?'

'Do you like it?'

Lizzie shrugged. 'Of course I do. They're lovely houses. Emma Harper and her sister live in number seven now.'

'Yes, I know.' It was the reason he'd turned down number five and paid twenty pounds extra for the end house; that and the knowledge that he'd be able to come and go through the back yard at night with less chance of anyone seeing him. 'Want to go inside?'

'Can we?'

'Of course we can.' Sam pulled a key out of his pocket with a flourish, opened the front door and gestured her inside.

'Where did you get that?' Lizzie was beginning to realise what this might mean.

'From Mr Cardwell, where d'you think?' He gave her a little push inside.

'Ooh, isn't it lovely, all new and clean?' She tiptoed into

the front room. 'Look at that bay window. Doesn't it give the room a stylish air?'

In the kitchen, she voiced unqualified approval of the latest in gas stoves and marvelled at the thought of electric lighting, though it wasn't working yet. Then she turned to him. 'Are you going to rent *this* house?'

'Not rent, buy.'

Her mouth fell open and she gaped at him as if she couldn't believe her ears. Sam enjoyed her surprise. In fact, he was enjoying everything about this visit. It almost made up for that old fart spouting on and on in church.

'*Sam!*' She flung her arms around him. 'I didn't know you had that much money.'

'Well, I've been saving, like. I've allus done extra jobs for folk. An' Gran had a bit put by, too.'

Lizzie stood there, face aglow. 'Our own house. Oh, Sam.' And she hugged him again.

After that, she had to rush upstairs, then go over everything in detail, bubbling with delight at the convenience of it all. 'An inside lavatory and a proper bathroom! Oh, look at that big linen cupboard! And I'll be living close to Emma, as well.'

He jerked her to a halt. 'You'll not have owt to do with them two stuck-up bitches.'

'You mean Emma?' Her joy began to fade.

'Aye,' he mimicked her softer voice, 'bloody Emma Harper.'

'But — I thought — I thought you were friends with them, Sam?'

'Well, I'm not. They cheated me out of a bit of business an' I don't forget anyone as cheats on me. I'll get back at them one day, see if I don't.'

'Sam, I'm sure they'd never—'

'I don't want to talk about them, not now or ever, so just remember — I'm not having you going in and out of their house, tattling over tea cups and wasting your time.'

Lizzie swallowed a hot reply in defence of her friend. Something had upset him, so she'd have to tread carefully for a while. He'd get over it. But her joy in the house was tarnished, somehow, though she tried not to let that show.

Blanche Harper came into Dearden's on the Monday morning and waited for Lizzie to finish serving a customer. 'When I heard the banns called in church, I was so happy for you, child.' Even if it was Sam Thoxby the girl was marrying. 'We – Emma and I – wanted to congratulate you.'

'Oh.' Lizzie blushed. She still hadn't got used to all the fuss. Mrs D had started the day in the same vein. 'Yes, well, thank you.'

Blanche held out a parcel. 'And we wanted you to have this.'

'Oh, Miss Harper, you shouldn't have!'

'It's the little picture you always liked.'

Lizzie's eyes filled with tears. 'How kind of you!' On impulse she hugged the older woman, though it was Emma with whom she'd always been more friendly. 'I wish—' She cut off the words. She wouldn't dare ask them to the wedding, not with Sam feeling the way he did.

Blanche gave her a wry smile. 'It's all right, dear. We know that Sam's not best pleased with us at the moment. Or your mother. We'd have liked to come and see you married, but we shall be there in spirit. Now, I'd better buy something from the shop or your employer will be telling you off. A pound of sugar, please, and some of those caramels Emma likes.'

On the Tuesday evening, Sam called round and was allowed to sit alone with Lizzie in the front room. 'I've made an appointment for you at the dentist's,' he said without preamble.

'At the dentist's?' She gaped at him. 'But there's nothing wrong with my teeth. It's very kind of you, but—'

'It's to have your teeth out.'

She could only goggle at him, too shocked to form a single sensible word.

'One of the fellows was telling me – his wife had hers out before they were wed. Saves a lot of trouble and expense with dentists later.' He grinned.

Lizzie got her breath back. 'Well, you can just unmake that appointment! There's nothing wrong with my teeth, nothing at all.' She'd seen old women without their teeth and the thought of having only pink gums filled her with horror and revulsion.

'I'd rather you had them out,' said Sam, mildly for him.

'Well, I'll not do it.'

Veins swelled in his forehead. 'You'll do as you're bloody well told!'

She bounced away from him on the couch. 'Not when it's something daft, I won't.' Suddenly she felt afraid. 'Sam, don't,' she quavered. 'Don't look at me like that.'

He snorted angrily. 'I want to do what's best for us.'

'But – but why spend money on having my teeth out?'

'I told you – to save money later.' As Lizzie opened her mouth to protest again, he held up one hand. 'I'll call for you at the shop tomorrow and come with you. You've no need to be afraid. I'll be there with you all the time.'

Even through her fear, she could not agree. 'You'll go there on your own then, Sam Thoxby! I'm not doing owt so daft, for you or for anyone.'

He took hold of her and shook her. 'We're doing things properly!'

Percy came in, holding the newspaper. 'Sam, I just read—' He stopped in astonishment, for it was obvious they were quarrelling. And he didn't like to see Sam lay hands on his sister, either. That was no way to settle an argument.

'Tell her not to be so daft,' Sam said, trying to hold on to the remnants of his temper but not letting go of his intended's shoulders.

'Lizzie?' Percy's tone sounded a warning as well as asking a question.

She glared at them both. 'He wants me to have my teeth

219

out. *All my teeth*. Like an old woman! And I'm not doing it, and nothing he can say or do will make me. It's just plain stupid, that is.'

'Sam, lad—' Percy frowned at the black anger on his friend's face. 'Why? I mean, false teeth are expensive and – and our family has good strong teeth. There's nowt wrong with mine and I doubt there's anything wrong with our Lizzie's, either. Even Mam's got most of hers still. It's a waste of good money and—'

'Sid Barnes said—'

Lizzie stood up and stormed towards the door. Men sticking together as usual. 'You two can discuss it all you like. They're *my* teeth and I'm keeping them.' She reached the door just as Sam stood up, and turned to say loftily, 'I'm going upstairs. If you can't talk any sense into him, Percy, the wedding's off.'

But Sam strode across the room, caught hold of her skirt and dragged her back inside. 'Stay here, you! Leave us alone, Percy, will you?'

Lizzie looked pleadingly at her brother, who shook his head and went out. You didn't interfere between man and wife, which was what these two nearly were.

Feeling betrayed, Lizzie turned to Sam, lips tight with determination. 'I won't do it.'

'I'll think about it,' he said. 'But if I decide it's right, you'll do it – this and anything else I tell you to.'

She looked at him with that new, mature expression on her face again. 'I can never do something daft just because someone else tells me to do it, Sam, whether he's my husband or not.' She wished her voice hadn't wobbled, but he looked so big and angry. 'So if I'm not going to be the sort of wife you want, you'd better say so now.'

Too fast, a voice said inside his head. You pushed it too fast this time. 'You're exactly the kind of wife I want. Only, you must learn to mind what I say. It's a wife's duty to obey her husband. That's what they make you promise in that bloody church.'

Lizzie laid one hand pleadingly on his chest, 'Oh, Sam, you wouldn't want a wife so stupid that anyone could persuade her to do anything, whether it was right or not? Surely you wouldn't?'

'A man is master in his own house.' He saw her lips set stubbornly and for a moment was reminded of the little lass who had walked along the top of that wall, so long ago.

She shook her head again. 'Well, I'll still not do something stupid, not even to please you, Sam.' She tried to pull away, but he wouldn't let her go.

Admiring the fire in her eyes, he drew her slowly towards him. 'Eeh, lass, you'd try the temper of a saint, you would. And I'm no saint.'

The air between them was suddenly charged with tension and his mood changed, breathing quickening and that familiar feeling of need tugging at his loins.

She opened her mouth to protest again, but he closed it with his own, kissing her till she could hardly stand upright. He laughed then, all temper gone.

For the first time Lizzie had felt a surge of physical longing and she didn't know what to do. With her usual candour, she gasped, 'Sam – you make me feel – funny.' She indicated her belly. 'Inside.'

'Good. I'll make you feel even funnier before I'm through, lass. Right inside you.'

And seeing the white teeth gleaming in her soft pink mouth, he decided abruptly that Sid Barnes had been wrong. His gran had had no teeth. Her sunken mouth had looked horrible.

Mind you, that didn't change the fact that Lizzie had defied him.

But now wasn't the time for a lesson in obedience, it was a time for lessons in love. He pulled her towards him again, rejoicing that she was at last showing signs of responding as he wanted her to. He knew she was a virgin, and she'd be one till their wedding night, he was determined on that. It was part of his plan to have a wife as unlike his mother as possible. But afterwards, he'd have Lizzie in every way he wanted. And he'd train her to be so tame she'd stand on her head if he told her to.

'Come here,' he said huskily. And this time she did as he told her.

CHAPTER SIXTEEN

December 1913

On the Wednesday before she stopped working at Dearden's, Sam came to collect Lizzie after work and she rushed out to meet him. 'Mrs D says you're to come in. She wants to drink our health and give us our present.'

'But—' The protest that he wouldn't even stop to piss on Peter Dearden's floor died in his throat. Mrs D was already waiting just inside the door, so he couldn't refuse without giving offence or putting himself in the wrong.

'Mrs D, you haven't really met my Sam,' Lizzie said brightly, tugging him through the doorway.

His smile became a sneer for a moment because they had met once when he was a lad. Sally Dearden had clouted him round the ears in the school yard and told him to stop fratching with her Peter. She'd clouted her son, too, and said the same thing to him, which had made Sam snigger afterwards.

A quick glance around revealed there were other people in the shop looking at him so he held out one hand. 'Glad to meet you properly, missus. My Lizzie's been happy working here.'

'She's a good little worker. If ever she needs a job, she's got one here.'

'Oh, she won't need to work again. I can keep a wife in comfort and,' he patted his belly suggestively, 'I hope my lass will soon have other things to keep her busy.'

Lizzie blushed and stared at the ground, wishing he wouldn't say things like this. But he seemed really eager to start a family and had refused even to consider using the preventive methods that Mrs D, in a motherly talk, had told her about. Lizzie would rather have postponed that side of things for a bit.

Sally turned and said brightly to Peter, 'You remember Sam from school, don't you, love?'

'Oh, yes. I'll never forget those days,' he said. 'Never.' Not even for Lizzie, of whom he had grown really fond, could he force a genuine smile to his face.

Sam turned to stare at him. 'Neither will I, lad. Neither will I.'

Sally intervened again, sensing the undercurrents of antagonism. The two of them should have forgotten those childish quarrels by now! 'And you know my other son, Jack?'

He nodded indifferently to the younger lad. 'We've met before. How do?'

Jack nodded, his bearing as stiff as his brother's.

'Well, I'd like to drink your health and give you your present,' Sally said, abandoning the attempt to include her sons in the celebrations. 'I have a nice bottle of port upstairs, if you'd like to follow me, Mr Thoxby? My husband can't get about much at the moment, so he's waiting for us up there. Peter – I can leave you to lock up, can't I?'

He nodded. But he stood and watched them cross the shop and go out at the back before he returned to work. Lizzie looked so small against Sam's bulk, so bright and alive against his heaviness. It was like – like sacrificing a virgin in the old days, offering her to an evil god. How could she ever be happy with that lout? And she deserved to be happy, because she was a plucky lass and always had been. He'd never forgotten the incident of the shoes.

He liked to see her serving in the shop, too. His father could talk about men making the best grocers, but Peter reckoned the customers enjoyed being served by Lizzie, with her wide smile and clever suggestions. He was sure most of them went out with more stuff than they'd intended to buy. And she didn't do it just to sell, but because she took an interest in her work. As Jack never did. He was going to have to have another word with his young brother, he was that. Mooning about, thinking of aeroplanes, when he should be giving the customers his full attention. He'd got some orders mixed up the previous day – again – which had upset their mother.

Upstairs, Sally introduced Sam to her husband, who didn't attempt to get up, just nodded his head and wheezed a greeting. She poured them each a glass of port and solemnly drank the couple's health. Then she handed them her present: a box of crystal tumblers which had Lizzie in raptures, so pretty were they.

After they'd left, Sally poured herself another glass, an unusual indulgence for her, and sipped it slowly. 'That lass is in for trouble,' she confided in Bob. 'Or I've never seen trouble on two legs.'

He watched her sip her port. 'Eeh, you're still a lovely woman, Sally lass.'

She turned to him with a smile. 'Now what brought that on?'

He gestured to himself. 'What do you think?'

Her smile faded. 'Oh, Bob.' She went to sit on the arm of his chair, leaning against him, hating the feel of his thin bony shoulders next to her plump softness. They both knew he hadn't long to live. But what was the use of going on about it? You just had to make the last few months as happy as you could. She forgot Lizzie for a while, just sat there with her fellow.

When Peter came up, he paused at the top of the stairs which led straight into the living room and grinned at them. 'Are you two love-birds at it again?' he teased.

Bob winked. 'Can't keep us apart, son, can't keep us apart.'

And the picture of his parents, juxtaposed against the picture of Sam guiding Lizzie out of the shop, showing the world who was in charge of that couple, haunted Peter's dreams that night. He wished – oh, hell, he didn't know what he wished. Just happiness for Lizzie, perhaps.

*   *   *

In a cosy cottage just outside Rochdale, Lizzie's sister Eva and her friend Alice Blake sat for longer than usual over their tea. 'Two more days and Lizzie will be married,' Eva said. 'I can hardly believe it.'

'She's very young to marry. And he's much older, isn't he?'

'Yes. A year or two older than our Percy.'

'Well, I suppose she must know her own mind.'

Eva wasn't so sure, but the request that she be an attendant at her sister's wedding had delighted her. It was ages since she'd seen her family, and surely her mother would be in a better mood on such a happy occasion? She frowned at the thought.

Alice smiled at her fondly. 'You'll look lovely, dear. That new brassiere really gives you a good shape.'

Eva looked down complacently at her own figure. The brassiere, a waist-length contraption, called the 'Sophronia', did give her a good firm shape, without the constriction of a full corset. It was made of strong, twilled cotton with three ten-inch whalebones which you took out when washing it. And with the large button at the back and bring-round-the-front tapes, there was no worry about its coming undone by accident. She wished sometimes she didn't have such full breasts, but her mother had once said she was exactly like her father's mother in looks. Lizzie, of course, was like their mam, scrawny, without an ounce of fat, and probably always would be.

Eva twisted round to get a side view of herself, for she was still not used to the improvement, since brassieres were quite a new thing. 'It was really kind of you to buy this for me, Alice.'

'You have to look smart if you're to be an attendant.' Alice Blake sighed. 'I wish I could come with you, but your mother is so hostile.'

'I wish you could come, too.' Then Eva brightened. 'But the weekend after, we'll go and have our photo taken together, me in my new dress and you in your Sunday best.'

Alice beamed at her. 'That's a lovely idea. And I'll pay for a copy of the wedding photos for us, too. Tell Sam to order us an extra set.'

'I'll ask him.' Eva had already worked out that you didn't 'tell' Sam Thoxby anything. She thought Lizzie was mad, marrying a man like him. If she had to get married, she should have chosen a gentler man, one she could manage.

Eva had no intention of ever marrying. Even after she had finished her training, she was going to stay here with Alice and have a comfortable life, instead of being a slave to some man. She got enormous satisfaction from teaching children, from helping the bright ones particularly, though there was another sort of satisfaction to be gained from taking a stubborn non-reader and forcing the child into learning its letters properly.

She yawned suddenly. 'Well, I'd better get to bed early tonight, I think. I'm tired out with all these preparations. I'll have to leave straight after school tomorrow and won't get across to Overdale until ten o'clock, so it's going to be a long day.' For it was unthinkable to ask for a day off just to go to a sister's wedding.

In Redley House, the Pilby family had friends round to dinner, which made a lot of extra work for the servants. Polly pitched in as cheerfully as ever, but wished they wouldn't sit drinking until so late. The second Mrs Pilby was a social butterfly and had no idea that some people had to get up early for work. *She* never lifted a finger in the house, not even to pick up a handkerchief she'd dropped in her bedroom, and it wouldn't even occur to her to give her staff a later start after such a late night.

Still, Mrs Frost had given Polly the whole day off tomorrow for her sister's wedding, so she'd be able to take her time dressing. She shivered as the wind rattled the panes of her attic bedroom's dormer window. It looked like the stormy weather was going to continue. Poor Lizzie. Every bride wanted a sunny wedding day. And if it was pouring with rain, how would they get any decent photos taken?

Polly sighed as she snuggled down in bed with her earthenware hot water pig wrapped in its flannel holder. She hoped Lizzie would be happy, she really did. But she could not help wishing the husband were someone else. Sam was always pleasant enough to his fiancée's sisters, but his smile didn't reach his eyes, somehow, and the way he watched Lizzie's every move, the way he bossed her around, upset Polly.

She knew she was being fanciful, that most men wanted to be in charge, but she couldn't help it. She didn't want Lizzie to get into a situation where someone could hurt her again. 'It's all Mam's fault,' she told the darkness. 'She's spoiled Lizzie's whole life.' But she felt as helpless now to do anything for her beloved sister as she always had been.

In her cosy bed in Bobbin Lane, Meg lay and exulted. Her earlier softening towards her elder daughter had quite vanished by now, because she was sick of the fuss everyone was making of Lizzie. Still, not long and that nuisance would be gone, then they'd move to the new house in Carter Terrace, a nice enough place, she had to admit. Percy had told her to leave the moving to him, and she would. Well, most things, anyway. She'd pack up her own things and her good china, but he could deal with the rest.

She frowned and sucked thoughtfully at a hole in one tooth, which was giving her a lot of trouble lately. She hoped the dress she'd chosen didn't wrinkle too badly. It was such a pretty navy tunic, with a peg-top skirt which would make the neighbours stare it was so fashionable, and a pink blouse underneath to brighten it up. Pink had always been her colour.

It had not even occurred to her that the pink of the blouse, which would have suited her in her youth, now contrasted badly with her sallow complexion, or that the fullness of the gathered top of the skirt only emphasised the bony torso above it. It was the nicest outfit she'd ever had and she was quite determined to outshine her daughter, show folk how cheap Lizzie was in everything. Even the hat was special, a felt cloche shape with a wide band of navy ribbon and a new pink pom-pom at one side, which she'd added to match the blouse.

Percy had stared when she'd tried them on for him. And

folk would stare the next day, too. Lizzie's dress was nothing in comparison, nothing.

In the boys' room, Percy slipped into bed and heaved a sigh of sheer exhaustion. He'd had a hell of a week, with Lizzie jittery and on edge, and his mother exuding veiled triumph one minute, making nasty comments about her daughter's appearance the next. To top it all off, he'd had to start the packing for the move, which was to take place in a week's time, and he'd unearthed some of his father's things, which had made him feel really low and depressed. His dad should have been the one to give Lizzie away tomorrow, not him. Eeh, his dad had had such a short life. But at least he'd had children to carry on his name.

Beside Percy, his little brother, who at nine was not so little any more, kicked out and tugged the covers off him. That settled it, Percy decided. Even if it was an extravagance, he was getting them two single beds for the new house. Whatever else fate had denied him, he'd have his own bloody bed, at least.

He lay there and let himself slide into sleep. It was a relief sometimes to close the world off.

Emma sat on for a long time by the fire after Blanche had gone upstairs, staring unseeingly into the glowing embers. She'd passed Sam Thoxby in the street again tonight and his eyes had lingered on her body in a quite disgusting way. His presence in Maidham Street was the only blot on their horizon, for they loved this house and Blanche was proving quite a good cook, given the chance to practise.

Emma had seen Lizzie in the street the other day and tried to stop for a chat, but the girl had cast a nervous glance around and whispered quickly, 'I can't stop. Sam's in a bit of a mood lately and he doesn't want me to talk to you. I'm so sorry.' And had hurried on.

Emma had been sizzling with fury about this, but there

was nothing she could do. Lizzie was going to be Sam's wife. 'When I see men like him, bullying their wives, I'm glad I never married,' she told the winking embers.

Only she wished it wasn't Lizzie he was bullying. That girl didn't deserve it. And Emma could have done with a friend to chat to now and then. It got very quiet sometimes.

On the Thursday, which was Lizzie's last day at Dearden's, the shop was going to close half an hour early and the staff were all staying behind after work for a drink and sandwiches.

'We're sending that lass off in style,' Sally told everyone.

'She's making a mistake,' Peter said to his mother as he passed over the orders he'd taken in the big houses. He'd been saying the same thing for a few months, ever since someone had noticed Lizzie walking out with Sam Thoxby.

'Well, it's her mistake, not yours.' Sally frowned at him. 'And I don't know why you're taking on so.'

He shook his head. 'I don't know, either. Only – she's such a nice lass, and such a willing worker. And he's such a mean ba— er, devil.'

'Her brother says Sam's had his eye on Lizzie for years, so he must be fond of her. That'll make a difference to how he treats her, I'm sure.' But even so, there was something about Sam's smug expression and small, beady eyes that put her hackles up. And Lizzie looked so tiny next to him.

Eeh, she was borrowing trouble! She'd better stop thinking and start getting things ready for the party.

When Sam picked Lizzie up on the Thursday night, she had her arms full of parcels and was in tears. He watched her blub on Mrs Dearden's shoulder, shaking his head in disapproval. She was so damned trusting, Lizzie was. She thought the Deardens were all wonderful. And they weren't. Most folk were rotten inside. If you gave them half a chance, they tried to get the better of you. Which was why he didn't give them even half a chance, why he felt no compunction about taking stuff from rich folk's houses.

After a bit, he got fed up of waiting and stepped forward, taking Lizzie's arm and pulling her away. 'Come on, love. Let everyone get to bed. Have you got everything?'

'Yes. Oh, Sam, look at all the presents and—'

'We'll look at them when we get back.' He tipped his hat to Mrs Dearden and marched Lizzie off, carrying a couple of the bigger parcels and striding along so quickly she had to run to keep up.

At the new house, he inspected the presents, nodding approval. You might as well get what you could out of folk. 'They'll come in handy,' he allowed. 'Very nice.'

'Oh, Sam, I'm going to miss them all so much—'

He leaned forward. 'No, you're not. You'll have me to look after and,' he leered at her, 'I intend to keep you very busy.' If he didn't get a baby on her within the first year, it'd be her fault, not his.

He leaned back again, yawning. 'Well, better get you home, I suppose.' He had a little job to do later. A 'back-gate job', he called them to himself now that he was living in Maidham Street. One of his mates had some stuff for sale.

Lizzie lay wakeful that night. She'd be glad when this fuss was all over, and she could settle down in her own home. Her expression softened. It was such a lovely house. She'd enjoy keeping it nice for her and Sam. This was just last-minute nerves.

But what are you going to do with yourself all day? a little voice asked inside her head, as it had been asking all week. You're not one for embroidery and knitting and that sort of thing. What you like is meeting people, talking to them.

She lay there for a while worrying, then fell abruptly asleep, lying curled up in a tight ball in the middle of the big double bed.

CHAPTER SEVENTEEN

On Lizzie's wedding day it rained non-stop and an icy wind scoured sodden litter and the remains of long-dead leaves from the nearly deserted streets, dumping them in muddy heaps in sheltered corners.

Just after noon, Sam got himself a scratch dinner of bread and jam, eating it standing in the kitchen of Maidham Street, staring glumly out of the window at the rain pelting down into the back yard. He'd been alone in the chill of the half-furnished new house for the past week, ever since he'd taken possession of it from Cardwell's, and he was fed up of it. Somehow, he didn't feel at ease in the quiet streets of this part of town. He was used to the sounds of other people nearby – swearing, shouting, laughing, playing – not silence and polite nods from an occasional passer-by. And the next-door neighbours were an older couple who kept themselves to themselves and hardly even nodded as they passed him.

'Soddin' weather. What rotten bloody luck! Waste of time payin' for flowers and stuff in this. No one's going to see them.' And he'd wanted folk to see them walking to church finely dressed, had wanted to show the world how well Lizzie Kershaw was doing for herself.

His head was still thumping from last night's drunken party with a group of very particular friends, a group which did not include Percy Kershaw. Squinting at the small square of mirror and wishing it were larger, he belched suddenly and cut himself shaving. Blood splashed down the front of his new woollen, long-sleeved vest, making him grunt in annoyance. While he was trying to dab the stains off with the towel, more drops fell on to the vest, so he took it off and used it to staunch the blood, after which he hurled it on the floor of the fancy new bathroom with its black and white linoleum. As he waited for the blood to stop flowing, he went across to piss out his frustration in the lavatory pan. It still felt wrong to him to piss inside a house, unnatural somehow. But you couldn't deny it was convenient in this weather.

He went into the bedroom and peered into the dressing-table mirror. Yes, the cut had stopped bleeding now. He fumbled through the chest of drawers for his other new vest and pulled it on, followed by his new woollen knee-length drawers. That was a bit warmer. By hell, it was a rotten day!

Pulling on his trousers, he smiled at the unmade bed. 'Not long now an' we'll christen you properly.' It was brand-new, that bed, with a good sprung frame under the mattress, and headboard and footboard of dark oak. He'd been tempted to bring Lizzie up here a couple of times, when she was round sorting things out in the house, but had held back because he was going to marry a virgin and that was that.

Suddenly he wished Gran were here to see him getting wed in style. Eeh, she'd have enjoyed it, the old bugger would. She'd have drunk too much, then smacked a kiss on his cheek as she only ever did when she was sozzled.

Breathing deeply, he concentrated on knotting his tie, but had to have three goes before he could get the bloody thing right. Then he pulled on his jacket, sighing in relief, and looked critically in the mirror. Yes, he looked a right toff today. New suit. New shirt. New everything. He grinned and patted his crotch – well, not quite everything.

He clumped downstairs, cut off another thick slice of bread and spread it lavishly with butter and jam, eating it leaning over the table so the crumbs dropped on the cloth and not on him. He'd got eggs and bacon in the pantry and tomorrow Lizzie would be here to cook them for him. Tomorrow and all the other mornings to come.

When he'd finished, he wiped his sticky fingers on the damp dishcloth, dropped that on the table as well and looked

out again at the rain, which was still pelting down. 'Bleedin'
weather!'

After a final cup of the tepid stewed tea left in the pot
on the hearth, he found his headache subsiding and let out a
satisfied growl of a burp. That felt a bit more like. Ignoring the
mess on the table, he went to get his overcoat, bowler hat and
umbrella.

By the time he reached the church, he was chilled through
and his trouser bottoms were soaking. He grunted a greeting
to his mate Josh, nodded approval of the other man's unusually
smart appearance, 'Got your suit out of pawn, I see!' and
slumped down beside him in the vestibule. 'Let's hope they're
not late. It's bloody freezing.'

'We could go inside. Not that it's a lot warmer there. Makes
you wonder why folk bother to come to church in the winter.'
Josh made as if to get up.

Sam dragged him back. 'No, stay here. I want to see her
arrive.' He wasn't going to stand at the front of that church
until he knew Lizzie was waiting at the back to join him.

In Bobbin Lane, Lizzie dressed slowly, with the help of her
two sisters, who had shared the bed with her for a last time
the night before. She slipped into her new underwear –
daring French knickers cut in a pilch shape, made of fine
cotton lawn, and a lace-trimmed princess petticoat – then
put on the dark green skirt of her new suit, looking down
at it in admiration. It was a copy of a fashionable hobble
skirt, such as Mrs Pilby wore, and had cost Sam a lot of
money. Its hem was definitely too tight to stride out in, but
it was not quite as narrow round the ankles as those of really
fashionable ladies. She buttoned up her ivory blouse and then
put on the jacket. Lapels and pockets were in a lighter green to
match the bands of matching material round her skirt at knee
and hem.

'It's a lovely colour, that,' Eva said admiringly. 'I don't think
I've ever seen you look as well.'

Polly beamed at her with over-bright eyes. 'It's ever so smart. The nicest thing you've ever had.'

Lizzie considered herself in the fly-specked mirror over the chest of drawers. Her mother had jeered at her when she'd brought the suit home, saying only a fool would buy a skirt with lighter material at the bottom, where muddy splashes would be bound to stain it. But the outfit came with extra material to re-do the hem as it got worn, and anyway, Lizzie didn't intend to wear it on rainy days. Only – she hadn't counted on her wedding day being so wet and windy.

She stared down at her thin legs, wishing, as she often did, that she wasn't so scrawny. Still, her high-heeled bar shoes did make them look more curvy. 'I wish it wasn't raining. My hem will get splashed and so will the backs of my legs.' She was glad now that she'd decided against wearing cloth gaiters, popular though they were. They'd have shown up the splashes even more.

Eva picked up the hat, holding it at arm's length to admire it. Given the chance, Lizzie had good taste in clothes, something which had surprised her sister. 'Nothing we can do about the weather, except decide not to let it get us down. Here, put this on.'

Lizzie lifted the hat carefully on to her head. It was of black felt, with a narrow brim turned up at the left side, and a band of green grosgrain ribbon around the crown. She had bought the ribbon especially to match the outfit and Polly had sewn it on for her. A large black feather curved along the right side of the brim. She would no doubt change the ribbon again in future to match other outfits, because you didn't buy hats like this very often. It had cost a whole pound.

Sam had taken her to choose it at a shop in on York Road, an establishment she normally wouldn't have dared patronise. He had insisted she must look really special today, which just showed how much he loved her, even if he didn't say the actual words. He said the hat looked good with her heavy mass of hair showing underneath at the back, and it did. So long as the wind didn't blow it off. So long as her hair didn't fall down. So long as they didn't get too wet today.

She turned to her sisters, who were both dressed in grey, with matching pink blouses and cossack hats. 'You look lovely, too.'

'We don't matter,' said Eva, in her usual calm tone.

'It's your day,' Polly said softly. 'Oh, Lizzie, I do hope you'll be happy.'

'It won't be my fault if I'm not.' She banished the doubts that had bedevilled her dreams for the past week and looked out of the window again, hoping the rain would ease off. Instead, it seemed to have grown fiercer, with squalls beating against the panes of glass and wind howling around the houses. She shivered and hoped she'd be warm enough in the church. She didn't want to spoil her smart appearance by wearing a heavy winter coat.

'We'll have to call a cab,' Eva said, in the decisive tone of voice she'd developed since becoming a teacher. 'We can't walk to church in this downpour.' There was a knock on the bedroom door and she went to open it. Percy stood there, looking very smart in his best suit.

'I'm going to call a cab,' he said. 'We can't walk to church in this downpour.'

They laughed that he should echo Eva's words and the tension was broken.

Even as he went back downstairs, a vehicle drew up outside and someone knocked on the front door. When he answered it, he found Peter Dearden on the doorstep holding a huge black umbrella with difficulty as the wind threatened to turn it inside out.

'Hello, Percy lad. My mother thought you might welcome a lift to the church.' He gestured to the delivery van. 'There's shelves in the back you lot can sit on and Lizzie can ride with me in the front.'

Percy beamed at him. 'Eh, come in, lad. That'll be wonderful. Mebbe it'll have eased off by the time we've married our Lizzie off. If not, I'll get a cab to take us on to the pub afterwards.' He knew, they both knew, that it'd be no use Peter staying to offer Sam a lift after the wedding.

There was a noise on the stairs and Meg began to walk down, very self-conscious in her new finery.

Percy, who had seen his mother's outfit before, gulped audibly. Peter sucked in a long, slow breath. Meg looked raddled and sallow, a caricature of a figure in the new brightly coloured blouse. And her expression was as crazy as the rest of her, the coy expression that of a flirtatious young girl in a wrinkled, monkey-like face.

'Well?' she asked brightly as she reached the bottom, pirouetting to show herself off. 'Do you like it?'

'It's a – a really pretty outfit, Mam,' Percy managed.

'Very striking colour,' Peter added.

'Well, I felt one member of the family had to look good today, at least.' She went to simper at her reflection in the hall mirror.

The two men exchanged glances, then each concentrated on his feet.

From upstairs Polly called, 'We're ready.' Then she stepped back and let Lizzie lead the way down.

Self-conscious yet proud, she walked slowly, flushing slightly as she saw the two men watching her. She knew she had never looked as good.

Peter's breath caught in his throat. Somehow she seemed different from the cheerful lass who had worked beside him for so long. Today she seemed – not beautiful, exactly, Lizzie would never be that – but lovely. Her happiness and innocence were shining out of her. Oh, hell! How could her family let this delicate creature marry that twisted sod? And why, why, why had he never before realised how lovely she could look?

His thoughts in a turmoil, he stepped forward to hand her down the last two steps. 'You'll make a beautiful bride,' he said softly.

Her smile was luminous in the dark hallway. For a moment they seemed to be alone together, staring into each other's eyes, then Meg's voice, sharp with irritation, broke the spell.

'Well, aren't we going to make a move? We don't want to be late. He might not wait.'

Percy jerked to attention. 'Lizzie, Peter's brought the van round to give us a lift to the church so that we won't get wet.'

'Oh, how kind!'

'Smashing!' Johnny said from the kitchen doorway, and rushed to peer out of the front door. 'Better than a rotten old horse cab.'

'Good.' Meg followed her younger son to the door. 'I'll ride in the front with you, Peter.' She gave him another of those coy smiles.

'Sorry, Mrs Kershaw, but the bride rides in the front today,' he replied firmly.

'But—'

Lizzie opened her mouth to say she didn't mind riding in the back, but Percy nudged her with his elbow and shook his head. Let alone this was Lizzie's day, he didn't want his mother paraded through town in the front of that van. In fact, he didn't want anyone to see her today, so foolish did she look. 'Mutton dressed as lamb' folk called it. Her face was thickly made up, too. Like an actress. Or a clown.

Polly went over to their mother and linked arms with her. 'What a lovely colour that blouse is, Mam! I do like pink.'

Eva picked up her small bouquet from the hall stand and took her mother's other arm. 'Three beautiful women riding in the back.'

For a moment, Meg hesitated, scowling at the bouquets, jealous that she hadn't got one, or even a flower for her buttonhole. Then she cast a scornful look at Lizzie and nodded. 'Yes. We three will go in the back. *She* can ride alone in the front. Go and get the van doors open, Percy love. We'll have to make a dash for it or we'll be soaked.'

'Don't forget your bouquet, Lizzie!' he called over his shoulder, winking at her.

Peter escorted her to the passenger seat, holding the umbrella over her as well as the wind would allow, and then went round to sit beside her. A partition separated them from the rear and they seemed to be all alone in the cab as he drove slowly into town. He cleared his throat. 'Sam's a lucky man. Very lucky.'

She nodded shyly and stared down at her bouquet. She had never felt shy with Peter before but she did today, and when she peeped sideways and saw how warm his glance was, the blush deepened and she concentrated on the flowers as if her life depended on it.

'Ma sends her love,' he said as he eased the van round a corner, not daring to drive at more than a snail's pace on these slippery roads.

'Tell her thanks.'

'And . . .' He hesitated, but he had to say it for he had no faith in Sam Thoxby making her happy. 'She told me to tell you – and I agree absolutely – that if you ever need anything, need help in any way, well, you can come to us. We're almost like family after all these years.'

Tears were brimming in her eyes. 'Oh, I'm going to miss you all so!'

'And we'll miss you, too, Lizzie love.' The new shop assistant was a quiet older woman, without Lizzie's sparkle. The place just didn't seem the same. Sometimes, it seemed, you didn't appreciate what you'd got until you lost it.

The rest of the journey passed in silence, but Peter stole several more glances at her. And she at him. She wished Sam had dark hair. She still didn't like ginger, especially with a red neck. Peter's skin was nicer, coloured a little by the sun but not clashing with his hair. And his body was nice, too, tall but slim. Then guilt surged through her. Fancy thinking that sort of thing on her way to marry another man. Honestly, she didn't know what had got into her!

Sam watched in annoyance as the Dearden's van with its distinctive gold letters on maroon coachwork drew up outside the church. When his old enemy got out, he found his fists clenching. What was that sod doing here today? *He* wasn't invited to the wedding.

As Peter helped Lizzie out and held an umbrella over her while they dashed towards the church door, anger began to burn inside the bridegroom, but it faded as she waved her thanks and scurried into the porch without a backward glance at *him*. Suddenly Peter bloody Dearden didn't matter, because Lizzie's glowing face was lifted towards her bridegroom.

'Oh, Sam, did you ever see such a day? And wasn't it kind of Mrs Dearden to send Peter with the van?'

Oh, so it had been the old lady's idea, had it? That didn't seem as bad, somehow. 'Very kind. Thanks.' He nodded stiffly at Peter, who nodded back just as stiffly. Sam held out an arm to his bride and escorted her into the back of the church, out of that bastard's sight.

Percy shepherded his mother and sisters inside after them and Peter hovered in the porch for a moment longer, watching as the women adjusted their clothes and straightened each other's hats, wishing – he didn't know what he wished. He turned and walked slowly out to the van, umbrella not up, heedless of the rain in his face, heedless of everything but the memory of Lizzie's happy face as she rushed towards her bridegroom.

Sam had booked a private room at the Hare and Hounds for a wedding meal, but they were late getting there. The photographer had turned up at the church, as planned, but had not been able to take any photographs in such a storm, so they'd had to get two cabs to go to the studio – more sodding expense! – and have the photographs taken there. By that time, Sam was starving hungry and badly in need of a pint.

He had never found old Mrs Kershaw so irritating as he did today; not only the stupid, embarrassing way she was dressed, but the way she kept pushing herself forward. At one stage, when no one was near, he said in a low voice, 'This isn't your wedding, missus, and if you make one more nasty comment about *my wife*, you'll be out of that door so fast your feet won't touch the ground.' He felt intense satisfaction at being able to use the words 'my wife' at last.

After that Meg sat quietly enough, just scowling at Lizzie sideways from time to time.

The meal was good, nice piled plates of steak pie and mash, and after three pints of best bitter, Sam began to feel happier. When Percy banged on the table and said, 'Charge your glasses, everyone!' he asked the waiter for a double tot of rum, impatient now to get the fuss over with and Lizzie back home.

Percy cleared his throat. 'Before I propose a toast to our Lizzie – the new Mrs Thoxby, I mean – I'd—'

Everyone except Meg laughed dutifully and Lizzie beamed at her husband.

'—I'd like to welcome Sam to the family and express a hope that the two of you will have many happy years together.' He turned to his friend. 'Look after our sister, Sam.'

He nodded. *My wife* now, he thought, not so much your sister.

There was a chorus of 'Hear, hear!' from Eva and Polly.

'So without more ado – let's drink to the bride: Mrs Samuel Thoxby.'

Sam raised his glass of rum and grinned at Lizzie as he took a good sup.

She nodded and watched them all drink her health. It had been such a funny day. So cold. So wet. And yet it hadn't prevented the wedding. And now she seemed to have lost all her doubts and worries. She had done the moment she saw Sam waiting for her with that eager look on his face. She caught her sisters' eyes and beamed at them.

The best man stood up self-consciously. 'And now, I'd like to ask you to drink to the bridesmaids. You look very pretty, ladies – very pretty indeed.'

When Josh leered at Eva, she stared glassily back at him, because he'd already pinched her bottom and she had threatened to empty her glass over his head if he touched her again. And she meant it, too. After a moment, he looked away and gulped down the rest of his beer.

A few minutes later, Eva looked at the wall clock and got up. 'I'm afraid I have to leave now to catch my train. Lizzie, Sam, I wish you a long and happy married life! 'Bye, everyone!' She began to walk towards the door.

'Don't you even say a proper goodbye to your own mother?' Meg called out shrilly, making her daughter stop dead in her tracks, back rigid with annoyance. 'I am still alive, you know, however little attention anyone pays to me.'

Eva walked back to kiss the air above the powder clotted in her mother's wrinkled cheeks. She dislodged the thin hands that clawed at her lapels and gritted her teeth as the whining voice begged her 'not to forget her family'.

'Goodbye now, Mam.'

'I've got a big umbrella so I'll see you to the station, Eva love,' Percy said abruptly. 'I'll be back in a few minutes, Mam, to take you home.'

Johnny, who was fed up of all the fuss, got up and hurried out after him. 'I'm coming too. I don't care if I get wet.'

Percy put one hand on his shoulder. 'All right, lad. But slow down a bit and wait for Eva, eh? She can't walk fast in those shoes.'

'Women are silly, wearing them high heels,' he muttered, but shut up as Percy's elbow dug him in the ribs.

Meg watched them go with a sour expression on her face, muttering, 'Oh, don't mind me. No one else does. Just leave me waiting around.'

Sam had had enough of this. He stood up. 'I reckon it's time for me to take my wife home. I'll just go and settle our bill, then I'll come back for you, Lizzie.'

She nodded shyly. Harry Preston, from across the road in Bobbin Lane, would have carried her suitcase with the last of her possessions in it round to Maidham Street by now. This was the end of her time as a Kershaw.

Seeing the undisguised malice on her mother's face, she felt nervousness surge through her. It had been fun to be the centre of attention for once, and to know herself smartly turned out, but now she had to go home to begin a new life with Sam. Lizzie drew in a long, shaky breath and admitted to herself that she wasn't quite sure how tonight would go. If she would disappoint him.

'It'll hurt, you know,' Meg said conversationally. 'You won't enjoy tonight at all, Lizzie *Thoxby*.'

'Mam, stop it! That's a dreadful thing to say!' Polly turned to her sister, horrified to see how white Lizzie had suddenly become.

'But true all the same.' Meg lifted her glass of port and lemon to her lips and sipped slowly, happy to have got a good dig in.

Sam reappeared in the doorway. 'Come on, love. The cab's waiting.' Then he saw Lizzie's face. 'What's the matter?'

She tried to pull herself together. 'Nothing. I just – I felt sad it was all over.'

Polly rushed across to hug her. 'Don't pay Mam any attention,' she whispered. 'She's just saying that out of spite.' Then she turned to Sam. 'Look after my sister.' She held out her hand to him.

He shook it in a perfunctory way, looked suspiciously at Mrs Kershaw, wondering what she had said, and hurried Lizzie out. She was his now and he didn't care if they never saw her bloody family again. Especially that old loony.

When they were alone together, Polly turned on her mother. 'That was a right nasty thing to say. Why do you do such things, Mam?'

Meg scowled and repeated the same old catch phrases. 'It's better to face the truth. Your father spoiled her rotten. And beside, that one will never be any good in bed. You can always tell. She'll never be any good at anything else, either. He'll soon rue this day.'

Polly went to pick up her handbag and gloves, then marched towards the door, calling over her shoulder as she went, 'I'm ashamed of you. Downright ashamed.' She didn't usually speak her mind to her mother, because it didn't do any good, but today she had to say something.

'Hoity-toity!' Meg muttered and reached across for Eva's glass which was still half-full.

When Percy came back, he found her alone, sitting sobbing amid the debris. 'They've left me alone, Percy. Even Polly's left me. No one cares about me any more.'

He didn't know what had happened, but he knew something had. 'Come on, Mam,' he said wearily. 'Let's get you home. I'm still here.'

'Go and call a cab.'

'The rain's stopped now. We can walk.'

'Oh, yes, nothing's too good for her, but *I* have to walk.'

Her voice rose higher on each word and Percy saw a waiter peeping in at the door.

'I'll go and get you a cab, then.' He rushed out, wishing he need never return to Bobbin Lane. Eva had kissed him at the station and promised she'd try to get over more often. Johnny had gone off home, promising to get the fire burning brightly. But if he knew Johnny, the lad would rush off to one of his friends' houses once he'd changed his clothes and forget about the fire. Whatever promises folk made, there'd be only Percy and his mother in Bobbin Lane that night. He was always left to deal with her, and it was getting harder and harder to do it with a good grace.

Lizzie got into the cab with Sam, silent now, her mother's words still echoing in her head. When he took her hand, she clutched him gratefully.

'What did the old bag say to you?'

'Nothing.'

'Don't lie to me, lass. What did she say?'

Lizzie raised troubled eyes to his face, felt a shiver of fear run through her and burst out, 'She said it'd hurt tonight.'

'The old sow!'

'Sam — will it?'

He cast a quick glance towards the cab driver. 'Shh!' Hell, he didn't know how to answer her. He'd never had a virgin before, had he? 'It might. Only a bit. Just at first.'

Lizzie gulped back her fears as best she could and sat quietly, waiting for the horse to clop its way up the gentle incline to Maidham Street. All the glow had gone out of the day, somehow.

When they got out, rain was threatening again and the sky was full of black clouds. Her suitcase was waiting for them outside the front door. Sam paid the cabbie and then came back to open the door with his new key.

She waited for him to pick her up and carry her over the threshold, but another flurry of rain caught them just then and instead he grabbed her suitcase and pushed her inside, shouting, 'Quick!'

She stopped in the hallway and said reproachfully, 'Oh, Sam!'

'What? What's the matter?' He hung his new bowler hat carefully on the hallstand.

'You were supposed to carry me over the threshold.'

'Oh, hell. I forgot.' Then he shrugged. 'Well, it's too late now. I don't fancy going out again in that lot.' The front door was rattling with the violence of the squall. He dumped the suitcase at the foot of the stairs and walked on into the kitchen.

Lizzie followed, still feeling like a stranger here.

He kicked at the grate, scowling at the embers. 'Bloody thing's gone out.' In truth, he'd forgotten to bank up the coals before he left.

She tried to speak cheerfully. 'I'll just go upstairs and change, then I'll see to it. I'm good with fires.' She didn't comment on the mess the table was in, but turned to pick up her suitcase. Sam followed her up the stairs, but he didn't offer to take the case from her as Percy would have done.

'I need to change, too,' he said. 'This bloody collar's nearly choking me.'

When she got inside the bedroom, she couldn't help noticing

the mess there as well. Hadn't he put a single thing away since he'd moved in? She'd straightened things up one day, after they'd gone shopping for food together to stock up the pantry. Now, clothes were strewn everywhere again and the bed was a tangle of sheets and blankets. She looked at him a bit shyly. 'Do you want to change first?'

'Nay, we can both do it at the same time.'

Lizzie had to gulp in air. She hadn't thought – he'd see her every day – it was only to be expected – but still she felt shy of getting undressed with him watching. 'Yes.' Her voice came out small and afraid.

'Want some help takin' your things off?' He smiled, his expression that of a cat watching a bird in the back yard and waiting for the right moment to pounce.

Lizzie wished he wouldn't stare at her like that. 'N-no. I'm fine. I'll just—' She picked up her suitcase and put it on the bed. 'I'll just unpack and p-put on some ordinary clothes, then I'll set to and sort this place out.'

He was still standing looking at her, hadn't moved an inch.

She glanced sideways. 'Is – is something wrong, Sam?'

'Oh, no. Nothing's wrong at all. Only I don't see any point in you lighting the fire downstairs tonight. It's cold and dark, an' we've had a good feed. We may as well go to bed now.'

'But it's only seven o'clock!'

He began to walk towards her. 'Well, it is our wedding night, isn't it? And we can go to bed what time we like in our own house.'

She felt paralysed with fear and didn't enjoy the smell of beer mingled with the sweeter odour of rum that gusted from his mouth as he loomed over her. 'Can't we – take things a bit – a bit slowly tonight? I'm nervous, Sam, and I—' Her words were lost as he pulled her towards him and covered her mouth with his, grinding his lips into hers, so that she couldn't breathe properly.

She felt terror rise up in her, and when he pulled away briefly, she whispered, 'Sam! My new clothes.'

He drew back a little. 'Get 'em off quick, then, because if you don't, I'll tear them off.' His voice was thick and husky and his eyes held such a strange light they frightened her.

She began to fumble for the buttons.

He started removing his own clothes, casting sideways glances at her, predatory glances that sent chills of fear curling through her belly.

One by one, Lizzie set her new clothes carefully on the bedside chair. Then, standing there in her camisole and fancy drawers, her face burning with embarrassment, she asked, 'Could we put the light off now, Sam?'

He threw back his head and laughed. 'Hell, no! I want to see you, every blessed inch of you. You're my wife now, Lizzie Thoxby, an' I mean to make the most of that.'

When she didn't move, he slid down his woollen drawers, kicked them aside and came across to get her.

She couldn't take her eyes off him, never having seen a man in that state before. He was so big – terrifyingly big. Eva had told her that the man put his *thing* inside you, but Lizzie couldn't believe Sam's would fit into her. It would surely rip her apart. With a whimper, she turned to flee, but he was there beside her, one hand holding her fast by the upper arm.

He laughed and then, excited by her fear, ripped the camisole from her and carried her across to the bed. There he pulled down her drawers and slung them aside, after which he started running his rough hands over her body, gloating at its softness. Her breasts were small but firm. He pinched one nipple and ignored her gasp of pain as he pinched the other, then sucked at it experimentally. Nice. When he moved his hands below her waist, she tried to fend him off, but he slapped her away.

She lay there in sheer terror as he continued his exploration, sticking his fingers between her legs, doing things that shocked her rigid. But as he loomed over her, she knew she couldn't fight him, could only lie there and let him do what he wanted. Because a woman had to go through this to be properly married.

But when he pushed his thing at her, it hurt, and so badly that she couldn't help screaming, then screaming again, the shrill sound ripping out of her throat involuntarily.

One big hand came up to cover her mouth and hold it shut as he continued to grunt and push at her. She could only whimper and jerk against the pain from then on.

'Ah!' He let out a shout of triumph. 'Ah, ah!' Then he began to thrust inside her.

A painful eternity later, he stiffened above her, gave a long, dull roar, and collapsed on to her. Lizzie could hardly breathe, even though his hand had now fallen from her mouth.

When at last he rolled off her, she still didn't dare move.

He fumbled for the bedcovers and pulled them over himself. 'I allus wanted to take a virgin,' he muttered. 'Sorry it hurt, love. They say it's better for the woman the second time.' He turned over, let out a long, satisfied sigh and fell asleep.

Lizzie lay there with tears trickling down her cheeks, and not until he began to snore did she slide out of the bed and stumble towards the bathroom. Her mam had been right. It had hurt – a lot. But what had hurt most of all had been Sam's total lack of concern for her feelings. Not once had he kissed or cuddled her or made her feel loved. He had only snatched and grabbed and pinched at her body.

And inexperienced as she was, she knew that holding his hand over her mouth to keep her quiet was not the right thing to do. Couldn't he have been gentler? She'd seen Mrs D cuddling her husband and they'd seemed to enjoy touching each other. Lizzie hadn't enjoyed Sam touching her, not at all.

Sitting on the toilet seat, her head in her hands, all the fears she had been suppressing came rushing back and she whispered, 'What am I going to do?'

But there was nothing she could do. She was married to him and could only make the best of it. Except perhaps try to persuade him be more gentle with her.

In the morning he proved how impossible that was, grabbing her as soon as he woke up and starting to touch her again, prodding her with his thing until he got it inside. And although it didn't hurt as much, it was still not a pleasant experience. But Lizzie managed not to cry out this time. Or to weep. Though she wanted to.

It was a relief when he finished, slapped her bare bottom and sent her downstairs to get his breakfast.

CHAPTER EIGHTEEN

1914

For the rest of her life, Lizzie was to wonder at how unaware they all were, in the year that followed her marriage, of the war that was looming. Oh, they knew there were troubles in the world, but they didn't realise that these particular troubles would hit England so hard and would take so many of their menfolk away. No war before had ever made such a big difference to the lives of ordinary people, even those on what they soon learned to call the 'home front'.

And anyway, she was too engrossed in her own troubles at that point to care about anything else. As the year unfolded, she tried hard to make the best of her marriage. At least in her daily living she didn't want for anything – food or clothes or nice furniture for the house. In fact, she sometimes wondered how Sam had managed to accumulate all this money, for he always had plenty in his pocket, and encouraged her to furnish the house in great style. Her weekly housekeeping money was reasonable and she could manage on it and even put aside a shilling or two – for she still felt insecure enough to need that. Sam knew about the savings she had brought with her, for he had gone through all her things quite openly. He had pounced on the savings book, then thrown it back to her with a laugh.

'If that's all you've managed to save, you've not done very well, lass. Keep your pound or two. I'm not in need of that sort of money.'

But she didn't tell him about her new savings.

No, it wasn't material things but tenderness Lizzie lacked – especially in bed. And he didn't seem to be aware of that, let alone to care. It was as if she were a doll for him to play with, she decided after a few weeks; a possession, not a person. She began to dread the nights and his appropriation of her body, absolutely dread them.

Sam approved of sewing and housewifely duties, but made it plain from the start that he wasn't having her doing things outside the house on her own.

'Which cinema are we going to tonight?' she asked the first weekend, for Overdale now boasted two picture houses.

'We're not.'

'Sam?'

'I've no need to court you now. I've got you, haven't I? An' it'd look silly, a married fellow taking his wife to the cinema. The lads would laugh at me.'

'But—'

He scowled, feeling guilty about the disappointment on her face. 'Shut up about it, will you? I won't put up with nagging. And you're not goin' on your own, neither.'

She bent her head to hide the tears.

He went out on his own. Lizzie sat at home and wept.

He didn't approve of the way she borrowed books from the library, either.

'But, Sam, I need something to do when I'm at home in the evenings.'

'Other women don't borrow books.'

'Other women have children, or families coming round, or friends, and you don't want me to have any callers.'

'No, I bloody don't.'

'So I thought I'd get a book out to read.'

'Mmm. I'll think about it.'

Two days later, he said grudgingly, 'All right. You can go to the library. But if I catch you reading when there's housework to be done, it'll stop.'

She forced herself to say, 'Thank you, Sam.' It had come as a shock how much he insisted on controlling her life. Though not as much of a shock as his approach to their love-making. And she could have accepted his wish to be master, if he'd done it with love, but he didn't. She was beginning to think he didn't love her at all. Didn't even know the meaning of the word.

'Still, you keep the place nice, I'll give you that.' He glanced around proprietorially.

'It's a lovely house.'

'Aye. I've done well by us.'

'*Very* well, Sam. No one else has a house like this. Why, Mary Holden's had to go back to live with her family because her husband's out of work.' Lizzie hated having to say things like this, but if she didn't praise him occasionally, Sam got into a bad mood, for he seemed to think he was an ideal husband.

She made paper covers for the library books, saying it was to protect them, but actually it was to hide the books' own covers which would reveal to him how much reading she really did. It was her only way of filling in the tedious hours or escaping the misery she felt welling up in her sometimes.

Lizzie tried to understand her new life as she cleaned the house and kept it immaculate, which she did more for something to do than because she loved it – because she didn't, absolutely couldn't, love a place where she was so lonely and unhappy. She missed working at the shop quite desperately and often wondered how everyone there was going on. She hated, too, having to pass Emma Harper in the street with a mere nod of the head, when she was longing to talk to someone. But Sam had strictly forbidden her to have anything to do with the Harpers and she soon learned to obey him in things like that.

Percy came round to visit occasionally, but when she asked him why he didn't pop in more often, he looked at Sam and mumbled something about 'not wanting to disturb you'. Then she realised that Sam must have told him not to come round too much.

The high spot of her life was Polly's Sunday off, which Sam allowed her sister to spend with them. Polly was always self-effacing and polite to him. He said once that she was a wishy-washy sort of a lass but he couldn't see any harm in her. He would stay around the house for the morning, which put something of a dampener on their conversation, but usually vanished in the afternoons, often coming home smelling of beer, for his friend Josh kept a good stock of bottles in the house for times when the pub was closed.

Polly seemed to realise without being told how things were in the bright modern house. She didn't ask awkward questions, just talked about the Pilby family, her work, the housekeeper's foibles, the other maids, the clothes she was making for herself – and she started giving Lizzie sewing lessons, so that she could at least keep her own and her husband's clothes in order, though they both agreed with a laugh that she'd never sew well.

One night in March Sam stared at his wife over the tea table and said accusingly, 'You're taking your time falling for a baby.'

'It's not for lack of trying,' answered Lizzie with a flash of her old spirit.

'No.' He smiled complacently. 'No, I'm always ready for my rations. There must be summat wrong with you, the way you are in bed.' For he could tell she didn't enjoy it, and that was a great disappointment to him. Other women had always praised his prowess.

Lizzie was glad she hadn't started a baby yet, because it was all she could do to cope with her own problems and she didn't feel ready to take responsibility for anyone else. Although she'd made a dreadful mistake marrying him, she still hoped they'd settle down after a while and things would get more comfortable. Surely they would?

It was late March before she first realised that Sam's other business activities were not always on the right side of the law, and that shocked Lizzie rigid. He came pounding in the back way one evening, shouting at her to come upstairs at once.

'What?'

'If anyone comes to the door, you're to tell 'em we've

been in bed for an hour an' have been together all evening!' he ordered. 'Come *on!* You'll need to get your clothes off, or they'll never believe you.' He broke up the fire, poured on some water to put it out and tugged her towards the stairs.

She pulled back, gaping at him. 'But Sam—'

That was the first time he hit her, a quick backhander to the face. 'Don't stand staring at me, you fool. Get up those stairs to bed! And don't put the bedroom light on up there, neither.' He shoved her out of the room so hard she fell sprawling into the hall. And by the time she got up, the kitchen light was out and he was standing over her in the darkness, muttering, '*Will* you hurry up, blast you!'

For once he didn't make love, just lay there, listening, and when she tried to ask him what was wrong, hissed, 'Shurrup! Bloody well shurrup!'

Half an hour later, there was a knock on the front door. He stiffened and grabbed Lizzie's arm. 'Wait!' he breathed. When the knock came a second time he pushed her out of bed. 'Go down and answer that. You can put the light on now.'

She pulled on her warm new dressing gown. 'W-what'll I say?'

His voice was a mere thread of sound. 'Act stupid, like you've just been woke up. An' remember, we've been here together all evening.'

Lizzie opened the front door to find a policeman waiting there and her heart began to thump.

'Mrs Thoxby?'

She could only nod.

'Is your husband at home?'

'Yes. He's in bed.'

'How long has he been home?'

'All evening.' She hoped the policeman couldn't see her face turning red. She hoped he believed her, too, because if he didn't, Sam would be furious.

'Ask him to come down, will you, Mrs Thoxby?' The constable's face in the light streaming from the hall was grim.

255

She called up the stairs, 'Sam! There's a policeman wants to see you.'

There was a grunt, then a few thuds before he made his way down to join them. He greeted the policeman with, 'It's a bit bloody late to come calling.'

'No need to swear, Mr Thoxby.'

Sam shrugged. 'Never at my best when I've just been woke up. What can I do for you?'

'Where were you an hour ago?'

'Here.' He put an arm round Lizzie's shoulders and grinned. 'Doing what a good husband should.'

'I see. Would you agree with that, Mrs Thoxby?'

She nodded, then seeing he expected more, managed to force out a 'Yes'.

'And before that,' the pause was quite marked, 'sir?'

'I were reading me own newspaper in front of me own fire.'

The constable cocked one eye at Lizzie and she nodded.

'Right, then. Sorry to have disturbed you.' He started to move away, then turned round to say pointedly, 'You should know, Mr Thoxby, that one of our men has been injured and we don't take kindly to policemen being hurt.' His eyes said he didn't believe a word they had told him. 'Not kindly at all,' he reiterated.

Sam closed the door on him, laughed and turned towards the stairs.

Lizzie didn't follow. 'What happened tonight, Sam?'

He turned to stare at her, his expression forbidding. 'None of your business.'

For once she didn't care if he did get angry. She felt angry, too. 'It is my business if I have to lie for you.'

A scowl darkened his face. 'Shut up and come to bed.'

'What happened, Sam?' she insisted. Surely, surely he hadn't attacked a policeman?

He lunged forward and dragged her towards the stairs. 'So far as you're concerned, nothing – bloody – happened.' He emphasised each word with a shake. 'We were here together all night.'

She tried to resist, pulling back. 'I want to know, Sam.'

A cracking blow across the side of the head threw her across the hall. She slammed into the wall and fall sprawling on the new carpet, yelping in shock and pain. She lay there gasping, unable to move for a moment.

'Get up, damn you!' This was followed by a kick to the ribs and a command to 'Come to bed, you bloody fool.' When she still didn't move, he hauled her to her feet by the back of her dressing gown.

Lizzie was too stunned to protest, and had to concentrate on not being sick as he dragged her up the stairs.

When they got to their bedroom, he shoved her towards the bed.

She moaned as her bruised ribs hit the wooden footboard.

'Maybe that'll learn you to do as you're told in future. I'm the master here an' don't you forget it!'

He got into bed, turned over and ignored her. Slowly she took off her dressing gown, still half-stunned, still unable to believe this was happening.

'Sam?'

'Shut up! I'm knackered.'

When his breathing deepened, she realised he was asleep. She huddled on the far edge of the bed, her arms clasped protectively around her sore ribs, then cold drove her in beside him. But she lay awake for a long time, absolutely terrified about what might happen if Sam was – her thoughts faltered – thieving. That would explain his having plenty of money, though. And – she swallowed hard – she could easily believe it of him, now that she knew what he was really like.

But nothing, nothing could explain or excuse his thumping and kicking her. Lizzie didn't weep but she lay there for a very long time, facing the fact that after just three months of marriage she hated him. Things were far worse than she had thought – and she could see no way of escaping from him. For one thing was very obvious. Though Sam didn't know the meaning of the word love, he was violently possessive of her and had been for years. Why? Why had his fancy settled on her? He had ruined her life. Tears ran down Lizzie's cheeks, silent trickles of pain. She wept for a long time.

In the morning, Sam stared at her bruises, then shrugged. 'Maybe that'll teach you to do as you're told an' keep your bloody mouth shut in future.'

Lizzie turned over instead of getting up to prepare his breakfast.

He hauled her out of bed and dumped her roughly on the floor. 'You have work to do of a morning, seein' to my needs. Go an' get my breakfast. Two eggs today.'

She stared up at him and this time no tears came into her eyes, as they had the other times the two of them had disagreed. This time she felt as if her face was frozen. But she decided to do as he wanted. If ever she chose to defy him it'd be over something more important than making breakfast.

She didn't say a word all the time she was cooking and getting his lunch box ready. Sam made a comment about what he wanted for tea, eyed her bruised face a couple more times but didn't apologise, uttering not a word of regret.

That evening, however, he commented on how quiet she was as they ate their meal.

'I'm doing as you told me,' she snapped. 'Keeping my mouth shut.'

He made an angry sound in his throat, breathed deeply and carried on shovelling in food. When he had finished, he got up, shook out the newspaper and hid behind it in his favourite chair next to the fire.

Lizzie cleared up, then took out the mending basket and darned a pair of socks, making sure they came out lumpy. After that, she put the sewing things away and got out her book, but she didn't take in a single word. She just held it up in front of her face to block out the sight of him. And anger coursed through her, as well as fear, anger not only at him but at her own helplessness. She had no one to turn to for help, not with a family like hers. What was she going to do?

*   *   *

One day soon after that, when Sam was at work, she noticed he had forgotten to lock the cellar door and could not resist going down to peep at what was in there. It'd been locked since the day they got married and he'd not allowed her down, saying a man had to have a workshop of his own somewhere. Though there was precious little work to do around this new house.

As she stared round, she was quite horrified at how many things were stored there, things she had never seen before, clocks and candlesticks, all sorts of objects, nothing very big, but everything of the best quality.

Shivering, she crept upstairs to the kitchen again. It must be stolen stuff. It must. What else could it be? She gulped as another thought inevitably followed — what if the police came to search the house and found it? Would they take her to prison as well, for lying to them?

She didn't say anything about the cellar and neither did Sam. But he never forgot to lock the door again.

The next time Sam hit Lizzie, he bruised her face badly. When she'd got him off to work the following day, she studied herself coldly in the mirror, then put on her hat and coat and went into town, brazenly flaunting the bruise.

She met Mrs Preston in the street and saw how the older woman's eyes went to her face, the look of shock, quickly followed by a look of sympathy.

'Oh, Lizzie love — are you all right?' Fanny Preston reached out to pat her arm.

Lizzie shrugged. 'As you see.'

'Aye. Eeh, lass, it's a bad do.'

Lizzie nodded and walked on into York Road. After hesitating for a minute at the door, she went inside Dearden's, where she intended to purchase some of the biscuits Sam specially liked with his cups of tea — biscuits which were not sold in any other shop in town.

Sally came forward herself to serve her former assistant. Like

Mrs Preston, she stared at the big bruise along Lizzie's jaw in shock. 'Eeh, lass, did you fall over?'

'No. Sam hit me.'

At the back of the shop, Peter froze where he stood. Hell, that bastard had started thumping her now! And there was nothing he could do about it. Nothing. He remained behind a display of biscuit tins, unable to face Lizzie.

Sally's face crumpled for a moment, then she pulled herself together. 'What can I get you, love?'

'A pound of your special shortbread biscuits, please.' Lizzie stood and willed herself not to cry as the tin was pulled out and the biscuits weighed and put carefully into a paper bag. She tendered the correct change and then said goodbye, walking out slowly, aching to run back and throw herself into Mrs D's capacious arms but too proud to do so.

Back in the shop, Sally went searching for her son and found him out at the back, thumping one hand into the other and muttering to himself.

'Did you see her, Peter?'

'Yes.'

'That poor lass!'

'I knew it was the wrong thing for her to do.' He suddenly kicked a box across the yard, then shoved his clenched fists into the pockets of his overall and went to hide himself in the store room. He felt sickened. And helpless. Kept seeing her battered face. Kept remembering what she had looked like when she was happy.

Lizzie strolled slowly along the shopping street, stopping to stare in all the windows, deliberately showing off her injuries, then sat for a while on a bench near a watering trough for cab horses, a place lots of folk passed. She saw people she knew, saw them jerk in shock at the sight of her face, then avoid her eyes and hurry on.

It was all she could think of to do, the only way she could get back at him.

*　　*　　*

When Sam came home from work the following day, he slammed open the front door in a foul mood and roared, 'Where the hell are you?'

Lizzie tensed. 'Here in the kitchen.' She found her hands were trembling, so busied herself with setting the table.

'Why did you have to go out into town for yesterday, with a face like that?' he demanded.

'I had my shopping to do. You'd have soon complained if there'd been nothing for tea.'

'You could have tried to hide your face.'

'You can't hide a bruise like this one.' Lizzie winced and tried to pull away as he drew her to the window and held her face towards the light.

He turned away and his voice was muffled as he said, 'You'll have to learn not to cheek me.' But still he didn't apologise.

'I'm not a child, Sam. I have a mind of my own and a right to my own opinions.'

The veins in his face swelled with anger and she wondered how soon he would hit her again. It had taken only a few months for him to strip her of every illusion she had ever had about him. Now she was fighting back in the only way she could, exposing his nasty ways to the world. And something inside her had grown hard, so that she didn't care what he said, or even if he hit her again. She intended to keep her self-respect at least.

'You're my bloody wife,' he began in a loud voice, 'an'—'

'I'm not your slave, Sam. And I'm fed up of being treated like one. I don't mind looking after the house, but I do mind being thumped. I mind it very much.'

'A man has a right to—'

'You had no right – *and no reason* – to hit me like that.'

He was growing redder and redder, the veins bulging in his temples. Lizzie braced herself for the inevitable as he raised one hand, but she wouldn't let herself cringe away, just stared at him defiantly.

There was a knock on the door, a loud knock, repeated within a few seconds.

Sam's clenched fist dropped to his side and he gave her a shove. 'Go an' bloody answer it. An' tell whoever it is to bugger off. A man wants a bit of peace an' quiet in his own home.'

Percy stood on the doorstep, staring at Lizzie aghast. He turned her face towards the light with a gentle hand and said in a broken voice, 'It was true, then?'

'What was?'

'What Mrs Preston said. That he'd hit you.'

'Yes.'

'Shut your trap, you stupid cow!' Sam roared from the back of the hall.

'Come home with me, Lizzie,' her brother urged. 'Come home now. You don't have to put up with that.'

She gave a bitter laugh. 'It's too late. I'm married to him. It's what you all wanted and—'

Sam dragged her backwards and shoved Percy from the door, slamming it in his face and yelling, 'An' don't come back, you!

'Right then,' he said thickly to Lizzie, giving her a shake. 'From now on, you can tell your bloody family to stay away from here.'

'I'll not.'

His fist bunched again and she stared him unflinchingly in the eyes. He growled, muttered something under his breath, and for the second time that evening his fist dropped to his side without smashing into her. 'Get up to bed now.'

'*Bed?* But it's only seven o'clock. And I haven't—'

'I've got some work to do in the cellar. I don't want you getting in my way.'

'But—'

He propelled her towards the stairs and sent her on her way up with a hard, stinging slap to her bottom. 'An' if you set one foot down here again, I'll beat the rest of you black and blue to match your face. I mean that.'

She went upstairs, but left the bedroom door open, peeping down after a while. She wasn't able to see anything and tried to work out from the sounds what he was doing. It didn't take her long to realise he was clearing the stuff out of the cellar and stacking it in the kitchen. Good. She'd feel better without stolen goods in her house.

When it grew dark, someone came to the back door. Lizzie left the front bedroom light on and tiptoed into the dimness of one of the back bedrooms to peer down into the yard. She saw the kitchen light go out and heard the back door open. There were muffled voices, then sounds of activity. Two people, she saw in the moonlight, carrying things out of the back gate. Once her eyes had grown accustomed to the dimness, there was enough light from the gas lamp at the corner of the street for her to recognise Sam's friend Josh helping him carry stuff out.

'Good riddance!' she muttered and went back to bed, putting the light out and lying in the darkness, dreading Sam's coming up.

That was the second night he didn't attempt to make love to her. Usually only her monthlies stopped him and he grew impatient about that. When she pretended to be asleep, he just got in beside her and settled down as quickly as usual, filling the room with his snoring.

When Percy picked himself up from the pavement where the force of Sam's push had flung him, he found Emma Harper staring at him. 'Oh God!' he said, still shocked rigid. 'Oh God, he's started beating her.'

Her face crumpled and she nodded. 'I heard about the bruise.'

They both looked towards the house, but there was not a sign of life from it.

'You look upset, Percy. Would you like to come in for a cup of tea?'

He nodded. 'Aye. Thanks. I would.' His voice was shaky and he felt like he'd been hit by a ton of bricks, he did that.

Emma walked along the street beside him. 'I don't think there's anything you can do, you know. It's accepted by the courts that a husband has a right to *chastise* his wife. And the police never interfere between husband and wife.'

Percy stopped and looked at her miserably.

She opened the front door of their house and when they were inside, said hurriedly, 'I'll just tell my sister why you're here,' and went ahead of him.

He hovered in the hall, still feeling sick and shocked. Lizzie's face. That bruise. How it must have hurt her. The gossip about it at work. Tears of shame filled his eyes.

'Oh, Percy.'

He hadn't seen Emma come back and couldn't frame a word to her, just shook his head and brushed away the unmanly tears with shaking fingertips.

She gave him a quick hug and put her arm round his shoulders. 'Come and have a cup of tea with us.'

He sat silently in their cosy, neat kitchen. When Miss Harper excused herself to get ready for choir practice, he stirred uneasily in his chair. 'I suppose I'd better go home now.'

Emma looked at him sympathetically. He still looked shocked and white. 'You can stay and keep me company for a bit, if you like?'

He drew in a long, shuddering breath. 'Do you – would you mind? I don't – don't want to go home.' He felt as if he couldn't find enough air to breathe. 'My mother – she's gloating about this, saying Lizzie deserves all she gets.'

Emma closed her eyes. 'Your mother has become very,' she sought for a tactful word and couldn't find one, 'peculiar lately.'

'Yes.' She had recently spent most of her savings on a whole new wardrobe of girlish clothes, had taken to making up her face as if she were an actress going on stage, and was down at the Hare and Hounds most nights drinking port and lemons. Everyone was laughing at her, he knew – or saying she had lost her marbles – but what could he do about it?

Eva had come home for a visit one Sunday, at Percy's request, and had tried to talk to Mam, but Meg had flown into a temper and shrieked at her daughter to leave the house and mind her own business from now on.

Percy realised Emma was speaking and came to attention. Her voice was quiet, musical. He loved the sound of it. Missed her greatly.

'If you ever need somewhere to go – just for an hour's peace – well, you'll always be welcome here, Percy. We both understand what it's like for you. And we don't gossip.'

'Thank you.' Then he looked up. 'Do you ever see Lizzie? To talk to, I mean. When he's not there.'

'Only to pass in the street. He won't let her associate with us.'

'I didn't realise – what he was like, I mean. I would never have – I didn't *know!*' He covered his face with his hands for a moment, then dashed more tears from his eyes. 'I can't think what to do.'

'There isn't anything you can do. She's his wife and that gives him certain – powers.'

After that they sat on in silence for a long time because Emma had her own troubles, notably her growing fondness for James Cardwell. Her employer had said things a few times, hinting that he'd developed similar feelings for her, but she'd ignored his hints. She could not, would not, become someone's mistress. Only she couldn't bear the thought of leaving Cardwell's either. Let alone it was a good job and paid well, she couldn't bear the thought of not seeing him again.

The awkwardness at work, where Sam seemed to take pleasure in sneering openly at him, was solved for Percy the very next week. Ben Symes stopped him during the lunch break and asked, 'How are those studies going? The accounts and such?'

Percy shrugged. 'All right.'

'Mr Pilby is looking for someone to work part-time in the office. He wants someone who knows what happens on the shop floor. Are you interested?'

Percy looked up, unable to believe what he was hearing. 'Yes. Oh, yes. Of course I am.'

'I thought you would be, lad.' Ben clapped him on the back. 'You're to start tomorrow. You'd better come in a suit, with a shirt and tie. They'll try you out for a few weeks, see how you go, and if you do all right it'll mean five bob a week more. When you're not working in the office, Mr Pilby has some other things he wants you to do. You'll be a sort of assistant to him.'

Ben went back inside his little cubicle of an office and Percy sagged against the wall for a moment in relief, before straightening up and making his way to the lunch room, where, to his further relief, there was no sign of Sam.

When he told his mother about his promotion, she just stared at him and looked pointedly at his callused hands. 'I'd have thought they'd want better than you in an office.'

He breathed out hard but didn't say anything. He might have known *she* wouldn't be pleased for him. 'So I'll need a clean white shirt each day. Is the ironing done?'

'Of course it's done. I'm not a lazy slut like your sister. My husband never had to beat me.'

'Lizzie's husband doesn't need to beat her, either. She keeps that house immaculate.'

Meg changed the subject as she often did now, being no longer willing to listen to reason where her eldest daughter was concerned. 'You'll need to buy some new shirts if you keep on working in the office. An' a new suit, too, maybe.'

'Yes. Well, we'll just see how it goes for a bit before we buy anything, eh?'

Meg smiled slyly. 'An' I'll need to buy some new clothes, too, to keep up with you. Going up in the world, aren't we? Me an' my clever son. Not like *her*.' Which was a contradiction of her earlier remarks. But when had she ever cared about logic?

He went out and left her to her mumbling and muttering, and it was inevitable, somehow, that he found his way to Maidham Street and called on Emma to tell her his news. It was good to have people who cared about you, who were pleased for you. Even if they couldn't be more than friends. And it was a relief to be away from his mother.

At the end of his first day in the office, Percy found Sam waiting for him in the street outside Pilby's.

'Got time for a drink, Percy lad?'

He saw a couple of workmates hovering nearby and gathered his courage together, raising his voice. 'If you'll promise not to touch our Lizzie again. I don't drink with wife-beaters.'

Sam noticed the two men and bared his teeth at them, giving a bark of laughter as they moved hastily on, then turning to scowl at Percy. 'Lizzie's *my* wife an' I do what I want in my own home. And if you don't keep your gob shut about that, it'll be her as suffers for it.'

'I'm too ashamed to talk about it. But don't you think folk'll notice the bruises?'

Sam smiled, a nasty sneer of a smile. 'Not if I hit her where it doesn't show from now on.'

'You lousy, rotten bastard!' Not for the first time, Percy wished he were taller and stronger. But he wasn't. He'd always been a poor fighter right from his schooldays and they both knew it.

Sam feinted a punch at his jaw and roared with laughter when he ducked back. 'I were trying to make peace between us. But I'm not fussed.' And he'd only done it because it'd look better if he was still friends with his wife's brother, not because he cared owt for a weakling like Percy Kershaw. 'Well, you can forget about that drink. An' if I hear you've been so much as talking to Lizzie from now on, she'll be the one as suffers.' He laughed aloud at the expression of shock on Percy's face and strode off, still chuckling. Sam Thoxby didn't let anyone speak to him like that, by hell, he didn't!

One day the following week, the housekeeper came to find

Polly. 'There's a fellow at the door for you. Tell him not to call here again. Mrs Pilby doesn't like followers.'

Polly went to the door and found Sam there, leaning against the wall. Her heart sank. Was Lizzie all right? But all she said was, 'Hello, Sam.'

He straightened up and stared at her for a moment, then said brusquely, 'You're not to come round to my house again.'

Polly gasped. 'Not to come round? But – why not?'

'Because I bloody say so.'

'But—'

He leaned across, pushing his face close to hers. 'Lizzie doesn't want to see you any more, that's why not. She doesn't want to see any of her family. Her an' me like to keep ourselves to ourselves. It's a bloody cheek expecting us to have you for a full day every month, just because your batty old mother don't want you at home. You Kershaws are a right funny lot, an' me an' Lizzie will do better without you. An' tell that snooty sister of yours the same goes for her. If she sends another of those letters, I'll chuck it on the fire.'

He turned and walked off before she could say anything.

Polly went to weep in a quiet corner. Something was wrong. Something was dreadfully wrong.

On her next day off, she went round to Bobbin Lane, braving her mother's hostility to find out what was happening. When Percy explained, she sat in stunned horror. 'Poor Lizzie!' she whispered at last. 'Oh, poor Lizzie!'

Meg tittered. 'She's gettin' what she deserves. Maybe he'll knock a bit of sense into her.'

Polly bounced to her feet. 'You're a wicked old woman, you are! Downright wicked. You're no mother of mine from now on.'

Meg gave a scornful laugh, admiring her reflection in the mirror over the mantelpiece. She'd always looked good in yellow. 'Who cares? I shan't be sorry if I never set eyes on you again. Or on those two sisters of yours. An' your father would agree with me if he were still with us.'

With tears in her eyes, Polly put on her coat and hat.

Percy saw her to the door. 'If you like, love, we could meet next month on your day off, go for a walk together, have a cup of tea somewhere. *We* needn't stop seeing one another.'

'Yes.' But it was Lizzie she wanted to see. Polly was worried sick about her. Every time she'd visited Maidham Street, Lizzie had looked thinner, more nervous, and had only relaxed when Sam left the house.

Polly had been puzzling for a while about how she could help. There must be some way. Only, how was she to arrange a meeting with her sister without Sam finding out? That was going to be the problem.

CHAPTER NINETEEN

Summer 1914

As the year passed, Lizzie was more aware of the struggles of the suffragettes than she was of the approach of war. In the mornings, after Sam had gone to work, she would do the main housework tasks, then sit down and read yesterday's newspaper from cover to cover, looking first to see what those brave women she so admired were doing. Sam might scoff at the idea of women getting the vote, but Lizzie had given it a lot of thought – what else had she to do nowadays but think? – and had come to the conclusion that women were just as sensible as men. Only men were stronger, so they stopped most women joining in. Or doing anything interesting.

She often saw mention of troubles in Ireland, too, but couldn't understand all the ins and outs of that. Except it seemed to her that if the Irish didn't want the English running their country, then the English should stop trying to boss them around. Lizzie could sympathise with anyone who got bossed around, that was certain.

Most of all she loved to read about the cinema stars and their doings, and she missed going to the cinema quite desperately. Once or twice she had begged Sam to take her for a treat, but he wouldn't, not even on her birthday. In fact, her birthday didn't seem special at all, because Sam didn't remember it, let alone buy her a present. She was so unhappy – and about other things besides the way he hit her. In fact, she had never been so unhappy in her whole life.

In April, she began to suspect she might be pregnant and Sam, who kept a careful eye on her monthlies, commented one night, 'You're a week overdue.'

'Yes.'

He looked at her in a gloating way. 'So you might be expecting?'

'It's early days yet.'

'But you might.'

'Yes.'

For a while, he didn't hit her much, apart from a rough shove or two when she didn't do what he wanted as quickly as he expected, and he was gentler in bed – though he still demanded his rations nearly every night.

When she got up one morning and had to run to the bathroom to be sick, he was triumphant. 'You *are* expecting!'

'Yes, I think I must be.'

'When?'

'I don't know exactly. About November or December, I think.' If she'd had a mother who didn't walk past her in the street like a stranger, she could have gone and asked her how to work it out.

'You should go and see a doctor, find out exactly.'

'It's a bit early for seeing doctors.'

He didn't press the point, for once.

By the end of May, Lizzie was feeling very pulled down and was sick most of the morning, right through until the early afternoon. One day, fed up of this, she went to see a doctor in her end of town, a new woman doctor, who confirmed that she was pregnant and gave her instructions about resting more and eating well. The doctor also commented on the big bruise on Lizzie's thigh.

'Bumped into the table,' she said hurriedly, but she could see the doctor didn't believe her.

Sam wasn't pleased about this visit. 'A woman!' he said scornfully. 'What does a woman know about doctoring?'

'Dr Marriott has done just the same training as a man and she's very well thought of.'

'Huh! She's not well thought of by me.' He frowned and sat breathing loudly, as he always did when he was thinking.

Lizzie cleared the tea things away as quietly as she could.

'We'll wait another month or two, then you can go and see Dr Balloch. He's a proper doctor.'

'Oh, Sam, I liked Dr Marriott. Please let me stay with her?'

'Don't you cheek me! You'll do as I tell you.'

She subsided into a chair and hid behind a book, feeling wretched. After a while, she got up. 'I think I'll go to bed early, Sam. I'm always tired lately.'

It was heaven to lie in bed on her own, and for once he didn't wake her when he came up.

That same week James Cardwell paused by Emma's desk. 'Can you stay behind for a cuppa after work?'

She nodded. They were doing this quite often now and she was a bit worried that people might talk, though no one could see them from the street when they sat in his office or at the kitchen table. Blanche hadn't said anything, but Emma knew her sister suspected her feelings and had even asked if she wouldn't like a change of job. A suggestion she had dismissed, of course.

When everyone had gone home, Emma and James went and sat out in the back yard with their cups of tea. It had been another fine, sunny day. The best summer for years, people were saying.

'Have you been following the news from Europe?' he asked abruptly.

'Yes.'

'I reckon there's going to be a war.'

'Oh, surely not? I mean, this is the twentieth century. It's all just – just posturing, I'm sure it is. It'll settle down gradually. The government will sort it out.'

'I don't reckon so.' He sighed and sat staring into the distance before jerking back to the present. 'But most folk think like you do. The thing is, if we're at war, the building industry might not be so lively. Well, not my end of it, building houses. I might even have to go away and fight.'

'You? But you're nearly forty! They'll want the younger men to do the fighting, won't they?'

He grinned. 'I'm in the Army Reserve, love, joined the Overdale Volunteers in my youth. Stupid thing to do, really. But now, well, I reckon those of us with some experience will be the first to be summoned to fight for our King and Country, even if it's only to train the new recruits. Well, it stands to reason they won't expect old fellows like me to go into battle.'

Emma sat frozen in shock, her heart thudding slowly in her chest at the thought of his going away. Not to see him every day, chat to him, laugh with him, think over their encounters while she lay in her lonely bed. She realised he was speaking again and forced herself to pay attention.

'And going away would have its good side, think on. It'd get me away from Edith for a while. I doubt she'd miss me.' He cocked one eyebrow at her. 'Would *you* miss me, Emma Harper?'

She stared down into her cup. 'We all would.'

His voice was soft in her ear. 'That's not what I asked, lass.'

She flushed. 'I can't answer that.'

He took her cup and set it down beside the bench, then pulled her towards him, staring into her eyes. 'I know I'd miss *you*. A lot. And it galls me that I can't do anything about the way I feel for you.'

For a moment she sagged against him, weary of controlling her feelings, of being always alone and unloved. 'Oh, James.'

'Emma, my lovely Emma!' he groaned and pulled her against him. 'You don't know how often I think of you, how I've grown to hate Edith and her carping ways. I haven't touched her for years, you know.' And he hadn't touched Emma, either, because it wouldn't be fair to her.

She gulped back a lump in her throat, unable to speak,

unable to pull away. Just once, she wanted to feel what it was like to be in his arms. Just once.

When he gently raised her chin and said, 'If I don't kiss you, I think I'll die on the spot,' she smiled at him, all her love showing in her eyes, she was sure. He had warm lips, surprisingly soft. They moved, devoured, took possession of her. It felt so good, so very good, that she had wrapped her arms round his neck before she had realised what was happening and was kissing him back with everything that was in her. When he pulled away, she laid her head against his shoulder and they simply stood there for a while, heart beating against heart.

It was he who broke the embrace in the end, he who pulled away. 'I promised myself I'd never touch you. I love you too much to treat you like a loose woman.'

'Love me!'

He nodded and his voice was surprisingly diffident as he asked, 'Do you – think the same of me? I'm not mistaken, am I?'

Emma shook her head. 'No. You're not mistaken. I do love you, James.'

Silence hung between them like a gauze curtain, then he said harshly, 'Oh, hell, Emma, get yourself off home quickly before I do something we'll both regret.'

She hesitated, then managed to find the strength to go inside. There, she had to lean against the wall, drawing in one shuddering breath after another, because her legs felt so unsteady. But she didn't allow herself to stay there for long. He was right. She had to leave quickly, because she would definitely regret it if they – She cut off that thought abruptly. He not only had a wife, however much of a shrew she was, but he had two children and Emma would never, ever, do anything that might hurt them.

She walked home slowly in the drowsy warmth of late afternoon, answering greetings from acquaintances automatically, staring unseeingly at the fine display of flowers in the council gardens near the Town Hall. Her thoughts were a whirl of emotions and desires, mingled with cold reason and shame. How could she feel this way for a married man? And yet – how could she not when that man was James Cardwell? She had worked for him for – what? – four years now, and had grown to respect him, as well as love him. He was a fine upright man, a good employer, a builder of integrity and imagination. He was – just James. And that was enough.

And as for her – well, she was clearly doomed to be a spinster for the rest of her life. She just had to face up to that and stop wasting her time on foolish dreams.

On 28 June, the Archduke Ferdinand, heir to the Austro-Hungarian throne, and his consort, Sophia, Duchess of Hohenberg, were assassinated at Sarajevo and suddenly the word 'war' was on everyone's lips. But though the possibility was much discussed, the general consensus was still that it wouldn't come to actual fighting. It was a load of fuss and botheration, but it was all happening a long way away from England, where folk had a bit more sense in their heads than to assassinate royalty.

The Government would sort it all out. Reason would prevail. In England, at least.

'It just goes to show,' Sam said scornfully one evening, tapping his newspaper, 'that you can't trust foreigners. Can you imagine anyone assassinating *our* King?' He was always surprisingly patriotic. 'No!' He thumped the table and answered his own question. 'No, you bloody can't. Because if anyone tried it, every Englishman nearby would step forward and prevent it. That's what.'

Lizzie realised he was staring at her, expecting an answer. 'You're right,' she said placatingly, hating herself for being so cowardly. She had stopped defying him now and lived in absolute terror of him thumping her, doing something to hurt the child. And she worried, sitting here alone in the house, about after it was born – about trying to bring up a child with such a father. What sort of a life would that child have? A life of bullying and thumping like she did, that's what.

Unfortunately, this was one of Sam's more argumentative

evenings. He'd had words with the foreman at Pilby's and for once had not been able to cow Ben Symes into backing off. In fact, Ben had warned him that they were getting tired of this sort of aggressive behaviour at work and he'd better pull his socks up. For reasons Sam couldn't understand, things were slipping and he didn't seem to be able to regain his old position of ascendancy and freedom from the rules at Pilby's.

'What do you know about it?' he asked Lizzie scathingly, slamming his cup down on the table. 'Make yourself useful for once and fill that!'

She got up and went over to the kettle, slipping it on to the burner and praying that it'd boil fast. But the gas was low that night, for some reason, and it took ages. She glanced sideways at him once or twice and her heart thumped in her chest when she saw he had left the table and was sitting scowling into the fire. He hadn't hit her lately, well, not much more than a quick tap, but tonight he had all the signs of a man itching to vent his anger on somebody.

While the tea was brewing, she went automatically to get his biscuits and found to her dismay that the tin was empty. She knew he was watching her and stood there, feeling quite stupid, not knowing how to appease him.

'Have you bloody run out?'

'I'm sorry, Sam! I meant to go down to Dearden's this afternoon, but I was feeling poorly and I – I fell asleep.'

He heaved himself to his feet. 'You've got no *right* to fall asleep when your work isn't finished. Your duty is to look after me! You're just making excuses for your own laziness.'

'It's the baby, Sam. It makes me feel so tired.'

'That's a lame bloody excuse. Other women have babies without all this fuss.' He took a step towards her.

Lizzie could see his hands clenching into fists and edged round the table away from him. When he laughed and followed her, his purpose obvious, she shrieked, 'Sam, think of the baby! *Sam!*' In sheer terror, she started throwing things at him, trying to keep him away.

But they just bounced off him and when he caught her, he

slapped her so hard she was thrown violently sideways, hitting the wall and falling to the ground.

She lost her own temper, then. 'You rotten pig, you'll hurt the baby! Stop it, Sam! *Sam! Have you gone mad?*' For it was murder she saw in his eyes.

'Get down on your knees, then, and beg my forgiveness!'

And, heaven help her, that was the final straw. She couldn't do that, not even to save her baby. She tried to crawl away, but he caught her by the hair and dragged her back.

For a moment they stared at one another, she defiantly now, letting her own anger show, he with rage throbbing in his face.

'Beg!' he roared.

'No. I've done nothing wrong,' shouted Lizzie, past caring, past anything but her own shame at how he had been treating her. 'I'm leavin' you,' she added, suddenly knowing it was the only thing she could do. 'I'm not staying around to be hit for nothing, treated like dirt.'

Shock made him pause for a moment. She could see it on his face.

'You'll never leave me!' he roared. 'You're mine, and if you ever even say that again, I'll swing for you!'

Anger overtook her again. Why should she put up with this? And all for a biscuit. 'I'm definitely leaving.'

He took her by surprise, swinging back his leg and deliberately kicking her, punctuating the blows from his booted foot with, 'You'll – never – bloody – leave – me! Never!'

She screamed, rolling into a ball and trying to protect her belly.

'You soddin' ungrateful bitch!' He took her by the hair and dragged her half across the floor, then yelled as she managed to get free and tried to run for it. She didn't even get to her feet and knew almost as soon as his foot made contact with her belly that she was in trouble, for it hurt so badly she couldn't help screaming, a hoarse animal sound of agony.

He stopped then and staggered across to lean against the wall, panting and muttering.

Pain followed pain, and suddenly everything went black.

When Lizzie regained consciousness, she was lying alone in a corner of the kitchen. It was an effort to raise her head and even as she did so, pain stabbed through her belly. She moaned and as one spasm followed another, felt a wetness between her legs and sobbed aloud.

'Sam! Help me!'

But there was no answer and the house had an empty feeling to it.

She knew then that he had left, for he often slammed out of the house after they'd had arguments. She also knew she had to get help, so began to crawl towards the front door, pulling herself upright by holding on to the handle and nearly blacking out again for a moment.

How she got out of the house and along the street, she never knew, but somehow she did, making her way through the last of the sun's mocking rays towards the Harpers' house. Only when Emma opened the door did Lizzie surrender to her pain and collapse at her feet.

When she awoke, it was night and she was in hospital. A nurse in a big starched hat was sitting by the bed.

'Ah, you're awake, are you, Mrs Thoxby?' She took hold of her patient's wrist and felt her pulse, saying 'Shh!' when Lizzie tried to speak. 'You need to lie still, my dear.' She saw Lizzie clutch her stomach and said gently, 'You've lost your baby, I'm afraid, but the doctors think no permanent damage has been done, at least. Though your face is a bit – bruised.' It was one of the worse cases of wife beating she'd ever seen and in her opinion, the man should be taken out and hung. But of course, no one wanted to know her opinion.

Tears flowed down Lizzie's face and she put up one hand to cover her eyes. Her weeping was no less painful for being silent.

There was a stir at the foot of her bed and she looked up to see Sam standing there. Terror filled her and she grabbed the nurse's hand and screamed, 'Don't let him near me! Keep him away! He killed my baby!'

Someone came and ushered him away. Lizzie couldn't stop sobbing and shaking. When the nurse raised her a little and told her to drink, she obeyed without question, tears dripping into the cup. Soon the world began to fade.

If she had died there and then, Lizzie wouldn't have protested. She had had enough. She had lost her baby. Just then, she couldn't face anything else, not even thinking.

CHAPTER TWENTY

Emma Harper came to the hospital the next morning, bringing a clean nightdress of her own, some sweet-smelling soap and a bunch of flowers. Lizzie looked at her through lack-lustre eyes. What did she care about flowers? Or fancy soap? *Her baby was dead.* But Emma was trying to be kind, so she roused herself a little to thank her and was surprised at how weak her voice sounded.

It was a relief when her visitor left.

A little later, the nurse came to tidy Lizzie up for the doctor's rounds. 'Now, is there anything you need, Mrs Thoxby?'

'Can you keep my husband away from me?' Lizzie asked. 'I'm terrified of him.'

Sympathy softened the nurse's professional cheerfulness for a moment. 'I'm afraid that's not my decision.'

'But look what he's done to me!' They'd refused to bring her a mirror, but her face hurt and she could feel how swollen it was. 'And he's killed my b-baby. I never want to see him again. I'm leaving him.'

The nurse came to hold her hand for a minute. 'The almoner will be coming to talk to you this afternoon. You can tell her about it. She's here to help people.'

'No one can help me.' Lizzie clamped her mouth shut. This time she had to help herself by running away. Only she had that power. And she would do it, too. She couldn't think now why she'd stayed with him for so long.

The doctor was in a hurry. After a perfunctory examination, he said, 'Yes, you're out of danger now, Mrs Thoxby. Time will soon heal you. But we'll keep you in for a few days.'

Then he walked on to the next bed without waiting for an answer.

Lizzie lay back and listened to him going round the ward. She felt tired. So very tired. But although she dozed off, she couldn't stay asleep because every time anyone came into the ward, she jerked upright for fear that it might be *him*.

The almoner was a brisk woman with posh clothes and a fancy accent. Lizzie took an instant dislike to her patronising smile and sugary voice.

'I'm Miss Terrent, dear. The almoner. I try to help our poorer patients who have problems.' She turned to draw the curtains round the bed.

Lizzie felt shame flood through her at being classed as a 'poorer patient' and tears threatened for a moment as the almoner sat down in the hard visitor's chair.

Miss Terrent cleared her throat and said in a low voice, 'I believe your husband has been beating you, Mrs Thoxby.'

'Yes.'

'Does he do this often?'

'Yes.'

'Would you like me to talk to him? The police could have a word, perhaps?'

Lizzie could just imagine what Sam would do to her if the police came round. 'What I'd like,' she said in a low voice, 'is never to see him again as long as I live. The only way I can be safe is by leaving him.'

'My dear, he's your husband. You took him for better or for worse, I'm afraid. When you've had time to recover, you'll have to go home again. But I do think someone should have a word with him first.'

It was at that moment Lizzie realised her only hope was to run away from the hospital, before anyone expected her to, and she would do it, too – just as soon as she could stand up without feeling dizzy. Perhaps Eva would take her in for a while till she could find herself a job and lodgings? No, Sam would go and look for her there. But she could stay with Eva for one night, perhaps, borrow some money for train fares and be away before he arrived. Yes, that would be the best thing to do. But she needed money to get to Eva's. 'Could you send word to my brother, do you think? He may be able to help.'

'That's an excellent idea. I'm glad to see that you're being sensible.' Miss Terrent took down Percy's particulars and went away.

Lizzie scowled as she watched her go. 'I'm *not* going back to Sam,' she muttered under her breath. 'I'm not.'

When Percy came to visit her that evening, he was unable to hide his shock at the sight of her battered face.

Lizzie clutched his hand and wept, though she had promised herself not to. 'Can you lend me some money?' she said at last, when she had control of her voice again. 'Please, Percy, I'll pay you back.' She saw that he was looking puzzled and added, 'I need to get away.'

He stared at her in utter horror. 'You're going to leave him?'

'Wouldn't you? He killed my baby yesterday, Percy. If I go back, he'll kill me one day as well.' Lizzie was utterly certain of that now, for Sam seemed to be getting moodier, whatever she did to keep him happy. And she hated his stealing, absolutely hated it.

'But – where would you go?'

'To Eva's first, then as far away as I could get.'

'Eeh, lass, that's a bit drastic, isn't it?'

'If you don't help me, I'll kill myself. I swear I will. I'm not going back to him.'

Her voice had risen and Percy suddenly found a nurse by his side.

'Best if you go now, Mr Kershaw. Your sister needs to rest.'

Another nurse appeared. Lizzie fought off the hands that were trying to hold her and force some liquid down her throat, calling, 'Promise me you'll bring me some money tomorrow, Percy! *Promise!*'

He nodded.

Only then did she give in.

That night, Percy knocked on the door of his erstwhile friend, the brother-in-law he had come to despise.

Sam opened it, swaying and smelling of beer.

'I'll come back when you're sober.'

'No. Come in, lad. Come in.'

Percy hesitated, then followed him inside.

In the kitchen, Sam gestured to a chair. 'Have you seen her?'

'Yes.'

'They wouldn't let me in.'

'That's hardly surprising.'

Sam glared at him, then remembered that he needed to gain some sympathy. 'I didn't mean to hurt her. It was just the once. She got me so mad.'

'It wasn't just the once. You've hit her before. Several times. How could you have thumped her when she was carrying your child?'

'I didn't mean to make her lose the baby. You must believe that.' Sam's face crumpled and he dashed away a tear. He'd wept for his son last night, wept bitterly. And he wished – oh, sod it, he didn't know what he wished. 'How – how is she?'

'Bad. You've really hurt her. Have you seen her face? Seen what you've done?'

Sam went to stand with his back to the room, staring down into the fire. 'They won't let me in,' he said in a hoarse voice. 'She has to let me say I'm sorry. I'll promise not to do it again.'

'But do you really mean that?'

Sam turned round. 'Of course I bloody do! I want sons, like any other man. I was a fool to let my temper go, but it won't happen again.'

Percy hesitated. 'Well, I'm going to see her tomorrow night. I'll tell her you're sorry. Maybe if I go with you the day after that? She should be feeling a bit better by then.'

Sam came and shook his hand. 'Thanks, lad. That means a lot to me.'

When Percy had left, Sam went and got another bottle of beer out of the pantry. Sodding women. Weak as piss, they were, and stupid with it. Why didn't she just do as he told her? Why was she so stupid? She'd made him do it. But, stupid or not, he needed her. And anyway, Lizzie was his, always had been. 'I'll have to watch meself, be a bit more careful from now on,' he admitted aloud. Then he snorted. 'But so will she. I'm havin' no more talk of her leavin'.'

Polly went to see Lizzie the next afternoon, having begged time off work to do so. She was horrified at the sight of her sister's face, with one eye puffy and blue, her lip split. 'Oh, Lizzie, you poor thing. He's a brute!'

She shed tears all over her sister, then realised that Lizzie was just lying there, staring dully into space, and pulled herself together. 'What can I do for you, love? Do you need anything washing? I've brought you some fruit, but do you need anything else?'

'I need some money. Quite a bit, actually.'

Polly didn't pretend to misunderstand. 'You're going to leave him?'

Lizzie nodded.

'Good. How much do you need?'

'You'll lend it me, Polly? Really?'

'Of course I will. You can have all my savings. Every penny.'

Then Lizzie wept in sheer relief, but quietly so as not to bring the nurse down on them. After a bit, she pulled herself together and tried to make plans in a low voice. If only her head didn't hurt so much! If only she could think straight!

Polly sat frowning. 'When are they letting you out?'

'They said not for a few days. But I thought – if I just walked out of the hospital one day, before anyone expected it, well, perhaps I could get away while he's at work.' Because she wasn't going back to him, she wasn't. That thought was keeping her going.

'Good idea. If you tell me when you want to leave, I'll come and help you.'

Lizzie managed a faint smile. 'I'll pay you back one day.'

'You don't need to. Just stay away from *him*.'

'You've never liked him, have you?'

Polly shook her head.

'Why didn't you say?'

'It wouldn't have made any difference then.' Someone rang a bell, so Polly squeezed her hand and walked out with the other visitors, turning at the door for a final wave.

'Looking a little brighter today, Mrs Thoxby,' the sister said when she did her next round. 'I'm sure it'll all work itself out, you know. He'll have realised how wrong he was, be ashamed of how he's behaved.'

Lizzie just shrugged. It was clear the people here didn't understand and could do nothing to help her, so she'd have to help herself.

When Percy came to see her that evening, he brought no money with him and asked her to consider very seriously going back to Sam. 'I've had a talk to him and I really think he's sorry for what he did.'

Lizzie stared at him in dismay. Percy was too soft. He'd believe anything, he would. Well, she wasn't soft. Not any more. 'The only thing he might be sorry for would be losing his child. He *likes* hitting me!'

'No, no! He's just got a hasty temper.'

'He likes hurting people,' she insisted. 'And I'm *not* going back to him.'

'Couldn't you just see him for a few minutes? Talk it over before you do anything you'll regret.'

'The minute he walks through that door, I start screaming for help.'

'But he's promised me he'll not hit you again.'

'He could promise all he liked, but I wouldn't believe him and anyway, he wouldn't be able to stop himself when he gets in one of his black moods.' Percy tried to pat her hand and she pulled it away from him angrily. 'I was counting on you!'

'Nay, lass, he's really upset. He had tears in his eyes when I was talking to him.'

She stared at him stonily. 'Did you bring any money for me? If not, you can just go away and leave me in peace.'

He fumbled in his pocket for something to appease her. 'I've got a few bob, but I'm a bit short this week.' His mother had gone into town and spent all the housekeeping money on some garish jewellery yesterday. 'I'll have to go to the savings bank tomorrow. And I really do think you should see Sam before you decide to do anything rash.'

She gave a bitter laugh that turned into a sob. 'That's what the almoner said. I married him for better, for worse, she said. Only it's all worse, Percy. There is no better with Sam.' Then she turned her head away and covered her eyes with one arm. When she looked up, the nurse was whispering in Percy's ear and he nodded, raised one hand in farewell and left.

The following afternoon, Miss Terrent appeared suddenly with Sam behind her, bowler hat in hand, looking all spruced up and respectable in his Sunday best.

'I don't want to see him!' Lizzie said at once. 'If he comes one step nearer, I'll scream.'

Miss Terrent sighed, beginning to feel some sympathy for the poor man, who had been most contrite. 'He's your husband, my dear. Just let him stay for a few minutes and talk to you. He won't move from the foot of the bed, will you, Mr Thoxby? There, you see. You'll be perfectly safe. And, I promise you, I'll only be down at the end of the ward with sister.'

Before Lizzie could protest, she had left them together,

drawing the curtains round the bed to give them some privacy – as if everyone in the ward wasn't listening as hard as they could.

'I'm sorry, lass,' Sam offered.

Lizzie just glared at him.

'I am sorry.' In truth, he was horrified at the sight of her. He couldn't even remember doing so much damage. He took a step forward and moved hastily backwards again as she opened her mouth to cry out. 'I don't know what came over me.'

'The same thing as came over you all the other times you hit me. Only this time you've killed our baby as well as hurting me badly.'

'Shh!' He looked round, embarrassed by her loud words.

'I won't shut up. I don't want to see you and I'm not coming back to you.'

With a great effort, he controlled his anger. 'Look, lass—'

'Go away! Leave me alone!'

He reached out towards her and she screamed, thinking he was going to hit her again. 'Nurse! Nurse! Help!'

There was a clatter of footsteps along the ward and Miss Terrent erupted into the makeshift cubicle, followed by the sister. 'Keep your voice down, please, Mrs Thoxby.'

'Get him away from me! He was going to hit me again.' Lizzie cowered away from Sam, who stood frozen in astonishment.

The sister noted that he was not even close enough to touch his wife and exchanged a glance of sympathy with him. Clearly the woman was a hysteric. 'Best to leave now, Mr Thoxby.'

Three days later, Lizzie bundled her clothes together and crept along the ward during the nurses' dinner break. As a nurse appeared in the corridor, she ducked behind the curtains round the end cubicle and put one finger to her lips, looking pleadingly at the occupant.

The patient lying there nodded and said nothing.

When the footsteps had moved past the ward and the nurse

had disappeared into the distance, the woman in the bed asked, 'Running away from him?'

'Yes.'

'Good luck to you, lass! Don't you ever go back to him neither. They never change, that sort don't.' She gestured to her nose. 'Mine broke this, an' a few other bones as well. I were glad when he died. So if you can get away from yours, I say good luck to you.'

Lizzie nodded, checked that the coast was clear and tiptoed into the public toilet on that floor. She was horrified by the sight of her face in the mirror, but turned resolutely away and shut herself into a cubicle where she removed her nightwear, dressed herself with painful slowness and put on a headscarf Polly had brought her, pulling its folded edge forward to hide her face. Then, keeping her head down, and holding the bundle of night things under her arm, she left quietly, expecting at every step to be stopped.

By the time she got down the hospital stairs, Lizzie was feeling faint and dizzy. She sighed with relief when she found her sister waiting for her in the public area, sitting on a bench in a corner, clutching a full shopping bag and looking anxious.

Polly hurried towards her. 'Thank goodness! Come on, love! There's a train leaves at half-past one.'

Lizzie nodded, but a spasm of dizziness had her clutching her sister's arm.

Polly was worried by how pale she looked. 'Let's link arms. And keep your head down. That way you'll be all right.' She led the way out of the hospital, trying to keep between her sister and anyone they passed. 'We've plenty of time to catch the train. Don't worry.'

At the gates to the hospital grounds, Lizzie stopped, swaying. 'I can't. Polly, I can't go any further.'

Polly looked at her in concern. Beneath the puffiness and bruises, Lizzie's face was bone white. Worried, she looked round, sighing in relief as she saw a cab waiting near the gates, its horse munching from a nose bag. She coaxed Lizzie across to it. 'Can you take us into town, please, to the station? My sister's been ill and she's not fit to walk.'

The driver sprang forward to open the door. 'You make yourselves comfortable. Eeh, love, whatever happened to your face?'

'A bad fall,' Polly said hastily.

As the horse clopped along the road towards the station, Lizzie leaned her head against her sister's shoulder. 'I'm sorry, Polly, but I don't think I can manage.'

Polly didn't think so either. 'You don't have to manage. I'm coming with you to Eva's.'

'You can't. You'll lose your job.' Lizzie began to sob. 'I can't ask you to do that! Take me back to the hospital. They may not have noticed I've gone.'

'Shh, love. I'll send a message to the housekeeper. I won't lose my job. Mrs Frost is very understanding.'

'But—'

Polly looked at her sternly. 'I'm not leaving you on your own, even if I do lose my job.'

Lizzie sniffed and gave her sister a watery smile. 'I love you, Polly Kershaw.'

Polly felt tears come into her own eyes. 'Shut up, you daft ha'porth and save your strength to stagger on to that train.'

At lunch time that day, Sam asked the foreman if he could take an hour off to visit his wife in hospital.

Ben stared at him thoughtfully, then nodded. 'But only an hour, mind, and I'll have to dock your wages.'

'Thanks.'

He strode out of the works, ignoring scornful glances from the men he passed and the growling of hunger in his stomach as well. He had to see her. He didn't know what had got into him to hit her like that. He'd never do it again, never. But maybe he'd not have to. Surely, surely, she'd do as he told her from now on and stop all that foolish daydreaming? Other women were satisfied to stay and quietly mind their homes, why not Lizzie?

Then he remembered the child she had lost and he stopped for a moment as pain shot through him. His child, too. He'd killed his own child. Oh, hell, what had got into him? He had to see her and tell her he'd never hit her like that again. He *had* to. He began to walk more quickly.

All too soon the cab arrived at the station. As Polly paid the driver, she saw him looking at Lizzie with sympathy and understanding, and asked if he could possibly take a message for her.

'Aye.'

'Just let me find somewhere for my sister to sit.' When she had found a bench for Lizzie inside the station, out of sight of the street, Polly ran back to the cab. 'I need to write a note. Can you wait while I go and buy a postcard?'

He nodded. Business was very slack, and he didn't mind helping these two. Whoever had hurt that lass should be hung, drawn and quartered, in his opinion. If she'd been his daughter, he'd have done something about it, he would that. Given the sod a dose of his own medicine.

'You won't take another fare?'

'I've said I'll wait, haven't I?' He got down and went to slap one hand against his horse's neck. 'An' Betsy here doesn't mind the odd rest.'

Polly ran across the road to a stationer's, bought a postcard and borrowed a pencil to scribble a note to Mrs Frost. She gave it to the driver and tried to offer him another sixpence for his trouble, but he brushed that aside with a gruff, 'You go an' look after your poor sister.'

Polly sighed in relief as she watched him drive off. One thing accomplished.

She was so eager to get back to Lizzie that she didn't see Sam stop at the corner and frown in puzzlement at the sight of her. What was Polly Kershaw doing here in town in the middle of the day? And looking so anxious, too. He watched her go into the station, then decided on impulse to follow her and find out what was going on. It never hurt to be in the know. When she stopped at the ticket office, he sidled up to the nearby corner and got close enough to hear her book two tickets to Rochdale.

Two? 'The bitch must be running away!' he said aloud, as the solution suddenly dawned on him. He turned round to look for Lizzie, but couldn't see her.

When Polly turned away from the ticket office window, she saw Sam and froze in horror.

Then he knew that he was right. He went across and took her arm, giving her a shake. 'Where is she?'

She tried to push him away. 'Get off me!'

A gentleman stopped to frown and call out, 'Hey, you! Stop that!'

'Mind your own sodding business!' Sam snarled, without even turning his head.

The man hesitated then walked on, shaking his head and muttering.

Sam dragged Polly into the main station and no one came forward to help her. He caught sight of his wife, sitting hunched up on a bench, looking half dead, and threw Polly aside. 'Ah!'

When she looked up and saw him, Lizzie screamed once then fainted.

He bent to pick her up and Polly darted forward to stop him.

'Gerroff!' He aimed his boot at her.

'You leave her alone, Sam Thoxby! She doesn't want you any more.'

'*She's my wife!*'

A couple of bystanders stopped to watch.

'Don't let him take her!' Polly screamed at them, but no one came forward to help.

Sam thrust his face close to hers. 'You think yourself lucky I don't give you a taste of my fist, too, you interfering bitch. You'll not set foot over my doorstep again.'

Polly began to weep. 'You've nearly killed her once, you rotten bully! Are you taking her back home to finish the job?'

'What I do with her is none of your bloody business. She's *my wife*. She belongs to me.' When Polly didn't move, he pushed her away so hard she fell over, then he picked up Lizzie and walked away without even a backward glance.

For a moment, Polly could only lie there on the ground with tears trickling down her cheeks watching him. As she moved to stand up, she became aware of a hand stretched out to her and a young man hauled her to her feet.

'Are you all right?'

She nodded and tried to wipe away the tears, but they would keep flowing.

'How about a cup of tea?'

She gulped and stared at him. Thin, not much taller than her, but with kind eyes. She found herself nodding agreement.

'Is she his wife?'

'Yes. She's my sister.'

'How did she hurt her face?'

'He bashed her.'

He sucked in his breath in shock. 'That's a bit much.' Then he flushed and said, 'I expect you think me cowardly for not interfering, only I've never been good with my fists and he's a big chap.'

Polly picked up the shopping bag full of things she had meant for Lizzie, then turned to accompany him to the station café. As they walked along, she saw he had a limp. 'Have you hurt your foot?'

He shook his head. 'No. Broke my leg when I was a little 'un. It healed wrong. Doesn't bother me much.'

He opened the café door for her and followed her inside. 'Not much cop, this place, but I have to keep an eye out for my train. Now, what can I get you, miss?'

She watched him walk across to the counter, feeling better to have someone to talk to. He had such a kind face. And she couldn't go back to work and face Mrs Frost, who would have to be told the truth about today if Polly were to keep her job. Not yet.

Lizzie woke up to find herself at home, in bed, with Sam sitting beside her looking grim. She couldn't help a squeak of fear.

'You're not leaving me,' he said immediately. 'You're mine. *My wife*. You're not leaving me, not now or ever.'

She could hardly speak for sobbing. 'If I – s-stay, you'll only – k-kill me. Let me go, Sam! Please. Now, while you can.'

He took several deep breaths, then went to stand looking out of the window. 'I'm sorry, lass, really sorry I hurt you, hurt our baby—'

'Killed our baby. You *killed* it!'

There was silence. Then he said, 'I won't do it again. I promise I won't. But you're *not* leaving me.'

Too weak to argue, Lizzie closed her eyes and began to weep silently. When he came and put his arms round her, holding her close and making slushing noises, she shuddered, but didn't dare try to pull away.

'I won't hurt you again, lass,' he promised. 'I won't.'

She didn't bother to refute that. They both knew he would. It was just a question of time before he hit her again. And a question of how hard, too.

CHAPTER TWENTY-ONE

August 1914

For a long time, Lizzie couldn't seem to pull herself together. Engrossed in her own fears, she spent the days listlessly doing housework, all the time dreading Sam's return from work, then the evenings trying not to upset him. Without money, she couldn't run away. Without money, she was at his mercy. And sometimes she felt herself without hope, too. But then the flame of rebellion would flicker into life again. She was not, definitely not, going to stay with him for ever. She would find a way to leave.

In the four weeks she had been home from hospital, he hadn't hit her, not once. But that didn't stop her expecting a blow, and a few times, on the days something had obviously gone wrong at work, she had seen the veins in his temples bulge with suppressed anger and his hands clench into fists.

One day she'd plucked up her courage, defied Sam and gone round to the back door of Redley House, asking to speak to her sister. Polly, who had outlasted most other maids, was now on excellent terms with the housekeeper.

'You come in for a cup of tea, lass,' Mrs Frost said, staring with undisguised interest at the yellowed remains of the bruising on the visitor's face.

'Thank you.'

'Take the weight off your feet and I'll fetch your sister.'

Polly came rushing into the servants' tiny sitting room, beaming.

'Is it all right me coming here?' Lizzie whispered as they hugged one another.

'Oh, yes. Mrs Frost understands.'

'I owe you some money for the train tickets, but I can't—'

'It doesn't matter.'

'I promise I'll pay you back one day.'

Polly patted her hand. 'I just wish we'd got you away from him. And if you need help again, you've only to ask. I've plenty of money still.'

Lizzie shook her head. 'No, I'll do it on my own next time.' She exchanged a long, serious glance with her sister. 'And there will be a next time, I promise you.' Only not until she had pulled herself together, stopped feeling so tired. Even if she got away at the moment, she would be hard put to fend for herself.

'I'm so glad! I was worried that he'd – well, beaten you into submission.'

Suddenly the old Lizzie was there, eyes flashing, 'No. He'll never do that. *Never!* I didn't realise what he was like when I married him – my own stupid fault. I was such a child then, but I've grown up fast since.' She stared blindly into space for a moment. 'I have to do it right next time, though. I think he'll kill me if I don't.'

Then she sighed and the fire vanished from her face, leaving only exhaustion. 'I'd better go. If he finds out I've been to see you, he'll go mad. I just wanted to thank you, to let you know how I was.'

Polly watched her sister leave, then came back in to find Mrs Frost holding out an envelope.

'The post just came. Who do you know in Outshaw? You've never had a letter from there before. Your sister Eva hasn't moved, has she?'

And Polly couldn't help turning bright, rosy red. For that was where the young fellow she'd met at the station lived. Eddie, he was called. And though he'd promised to write, she hadn't expected him to, hadn't even dared hope. She took the

envelope and examined it carefully. Large, round handwriting.
'Miss P. Kershaw,' she whispered to herself. Then she saw the
housekeeper looking thoughtful and slipped it into her pocket.
'Just a friend. She lives in Outshaw now. I knew her when we
were kids. I met her again in town the other day.'

'You must invite her round to tea the next time she's in
Overdale. You're always welcome to bring your women friends
into the servants' sitting room.'

'Thank you. I'll go and do the bedrooms now, shall I?'

Once upstairs, Polly pulled the sheets off the mistress's bed
and plumped up the feather overlay, then, unable to wait a
minute longer, drew the envelope out of her apron pocket
and opened it carefully.

Dear Miss Kershaw

*I really enjoyed our little chat at the station, so am taking
the liberty of writing to you. I hope you've got over your upset
now and that your sister's all right.*

*I came back to find myself an uncle again and my sister
recovering nicely from giving me a niece – I've already got two
nephews and fine lads they are, but we all wanted a little girl
this time. They live just across the street from us, so we're
always popping in and out to see one another. My brother's
ten years older than me and my sister five, so I'm the 'baby'
of the family. Though there are only two of us now that my
sister's gone to live in Australia.*

*I wondered if you'd be able to get some time off one Sunday?
We could meet in the park if it's fine, or sit in a café and chat if
it isn't. (Even if the tea is awful!) Hope you don't think I'm
being cheeky asking you to meet me!*

*Perhaps you could let me know? I shall wait impatiently
for a letter.*

Eddie Scordale

Polly stood for a moment with her mouth open in shock. No
lad had ever asked her to walk out with him before. Well, she
was plump and if not ugly, definitely not pretty. She re-read the

letter, then stuffed it into her apron pocket and got on with her work. But there was a warmth inside her that hadn't been there before. Eddie Scordale wanted to see her again. He really did. He seemed such a nice lad and he'd been ever so kind to her. And she didn't care about the limp. It was his kindness and his gentle smile that Polly liked.

'I'll go and meet him,' she whispered, clutching a pillow to her bosom. 'Why not?'

Once her body had healed, Lizzie kept trying to make escape plans, for she had no faith in Sam's keeping his fists to himself for much longer. Fortunately he seemed very busy with his other interests, going out often in the evenings and coming back late, using the back door.

She didn't care what he was doing so long as he wasn't with her. She didn't seem to care about anything lately and she still had headaches, still wept at every reminder of the baby she had lost.

So when Sam came home from work one day and asked, 'Have you heard?' she only blinked at him and tried to think what she'd done wrong.

'Heard what?'

'We're at war with Germany.'

'*What?*'

He spoke with heavy sarcasm, as if she were too stupid to understand. 'England – has declared war – on Germany.'

'Oh.' She didn't know what to say.

'Is that all you can say? Oh?' He mimicked her cruelly, then could not resist giving her a shake for good measure.

Lizzie hated her own cowardice, but she couldn't help shrinking away from him. With a muttered curse he let her go and took a step back, thrusting his hands behind him.

'I – I don't know what to say,' she admitted when he still seemed to expect some comment. 'War seems unbelievable, somehow. In this day and age.'

A gloating expression made his face even more unattractive.

'There's money to be made in war, my lass, good money, and I mean to get some of it.' It wouldn't be long now before he could tell those buggers at Pilby's where to stuff their job. He and his friend Josh had been making plans, doing night jobs to build up their funds, going quite far afield sometimes, or selling stuff for others, which also brought in a nice bit.

'Will you have to go and fight?'

Sam threw back his head and laughed. 'Not me! Let them fools as want to get theirsen killed do the volunteering. I'm not that daft. I'll stay behind and look after me and mine, thank you very much.'

Lizzie nodded. She had known that he would say that. So it was still up to her to get away.

He went upstairs to change. Only then did she let out her breath in a long, shaky sigh of relief. What had sent him home in such a bad mood today?

As she finished cooking the tea, it suddenly occurred to her that other men would volunteer. Their Percy probably would! A pang shot through her. Her brother was so gentle, she couldn't imagine him fighting even, let alone killing anyone. No, surely he wouldn't volunteer? He was the breadwinner for Mam and Johnny. What would they do without him? But a lot of other men were going to go away and get killed. Lizzie shook her head in sorrow. War was a terrible thing. She scowled up at where Sam was bumping about, getting changed. So was violence of any sort.

Sam took off his working clothes, hurling them into a corner, still angry at the way Lizzie had flinched away from him. He hadn't hit her since she came out of hospital, had he? No, not even when she deserved it. But Josh had noticed how she cowered away from him the other day and had laughed, saying that was the way to keep a woman – afraid and obedient. Well, he wouldn't comment on Sam's wife again, by hell he wouldn't.

Still feeling angry, Sam went to sluice down his face and

hands in the bathroom. Married life was a bugger, it was that. Not at all what he'd expected. Decent women were no good in bed, no good at all. He looked round. Lizzie did keep things nice, though. He'd give her that. And anyway she was his, allus had been.

Downstairs, Lizzie set a kettle on the stove and stirred the stew. Not until Sam came down to sit by the fire did she run upstairs to pick up his things. She gave them a vigorous shake outside the back door, as usual, then hung them out to air for an hour in the last of the sunshine before the shadows of the next row of houses stretched out to engulf the back yard and darken the scullery.

When he had finished his tea, Sam muttered something, put on his old cap and jacket, and left the house. She breathed a sigh of thankfulness and began to clear up.

'I'm not going on like this for the rest of my life,' she told the fire, poking it into a cheerful blaze. She was saving for her escape, penny by penny, because he still gave her adequate housekeeping money at least. The little hoard was hidden in the pantry, in a jar that said PICKLES on it. He didn't share her taste for vinegary things, so he'd never open it. Well, he never went in the pantry anyway, just ordered her to get him what he wanted.

She stared dreamily into the flames. One day, she'd go to some town far away, a place where he'd never think of looking for her – somewhere in the south, maybe. She'd book a ticket to Manchester and from there, she'd go to London. In a big city like that, they'd never manage to trace her, especially if – she suddenly remembered a story she'd once read – she changed her clothes in the Ladies' Waiting Room. She'd go wherever fate took her, find herself a job and another life, rent a little room and live there in peace. The thought of it made her sigh in anticipation.

As for him, he'd come home from work one day and she'd be gone – just like that, without a word of warning. And she wouldn't leave a note, either, though she'd write to let Polly and Eva know. She dreamed about that day often, how happy she'd feel, and it helped her keep going. But she hadn't yet got enough money to do it.

It'd be hard leaving her family, though, Polly especially, but it was the only way. Lizzie had come to see that now. No one must know where to find her. No one at all. That way there'd be absolutely no risk of Sam's finding out by chance where she was. Because if he did, he'd come after her and this time he'd kill her for sure.

'It's started,' James called from his office when he heard Emma open the front door. 'They've declared war now.'

She came to the doorway and looked in at him. 'I know. I heard.'

'I'm expecting a summons from the Army any day.'

'So quickly?'

'Yes. They'll have had contingency plans prepared.'

'You don't think the Germans could win?'

He looked at her soberly. 'Not until all us Englishmen have been killed.'

She clutched her chest. 'Oh, James.'

He smiled, but he didn't get up, because if he did, he'd be unable to resist kissing her. 'It's only the good who die young, Emma love. I'm too ugly and far too wicked as well.' Especially when he thought about her. 'Now, about Cardwell's . . .' Best concentrate on business matters. But she looked lovely this morning in that thin, summery dress, which clung to her figure more than she realised and showed off a very neat pair of ankles, too.

She blinked. It obviously hadn't occurred to her before that her job might be at risk. 'Oh.'

He tapped the papers on his desk. 'I want to get these signed today. All right if I put you in charge of running the business?'

'You and your jokes!'

'No joke, love.'

'Put me in charge?' Emma clutched at the doorframe, gaping. '*Me?* But surely your wife——?'

'Can't run a house without the help of servants, and even then mucks things up every time she pokes her nose into what they're doing.' And anyway, if he put Edith in charge here, she'd find an excuse to sack Emma. He knew how his dear wife's jealous little mind worked. She didn't want him herself any more, but she didn't want anyone else to have him, either. 'I'll send young Nat round to my lawyer's with these notes on what I want, and you and I will take a little stroll into town later to sign the papers Mr Finch draws up.'

He grinned at her shocked expression. 'So don't go away, Emma. If we run out of stamps, or anything else, never mind. Today I want you handy.' He bent to his work again, then realised she was still there and looked up. 'Something wrong?'

'James, I don't know enough to run a business like this.'

'You know more than you think. Any road, you won't be on your own. You'll have Walter to help you. At fifty-eight, he's a bit too old to go to war.' He smiled at the apprehension on her face. 'But unless I mistake things, business will slow right down. Nat's too young to enlist, but Tim will probably join the Army. They'll be needing more men – a lot more. The British standing army isn't all that big, you know. Not nearly big enough to fight the nasty old Kaiser.'

'I suppose quite a few of the younger men in the town will volunteer?' She was thinking of Percy Kershaw as she spoke.

'They will. And a lot of them will get killed, too. Modern weapons can do a lot of damage to soft human bodies.' He saw the horror on her face and cursed himself for being so blunt. 'Folk won't be wanting to build houses now, but barracks and munitions factories. You'll mostly have to deal with alterations and repairs, I reckon. You and Walter can handle those. And if anyone does want a whole house built, you can always say no, can't you?'

Emma's face brightened. 'But couldn't you get an exemption? To build these barracks and things, I mean. You'd be more use to them doing that, surely?'

James shook his head, impatient to get on with things. 'No. They'll not want barracks in a place like Overdale, nor munitions factories, either. We're too small, too far off the beaten track.'

'How do you know so much?'

He couldn't keep the bitterness out of his voice. 'Because I have nowt better to do of an evening than read the newspapers from cover to cover and think about what's going on across that Channel.'

'Oh.'

He looked at her, so fresh and lovely. 'Besides, I *want* to play my part, serve my country, as any decent Englishman would.' They'd be fighting for lasses like her. And kids like his two young devils. That was what it was all about.

Then he bent his head to his writing, slashing the black ink across the paper in his impatience to get this done. He had to make sure Emma and her job were safe while he was away before he could concentrate on other things. It was all he could do for her.

That same day, the House of Commons voted to increase the Regular Army by half a million men. Emma thought of James's words as she read about it in the newspaper the following day. It was soon followed by appeals to young men to volunteer.

Two days after that, James Cardwell left Overdale for a destination unspecified and Emma moved into his office. It all happened as quickly as that.

As she walked to work the following week, she stopped in astonishment at the sight of a long queue of young men outside the Town Hall, all looking excited. 'What's happening?' she asked Dan Temple, the butcher, who was standing in his doorway, watching.

'Them silly sods are going to volunteer for the Army,'

he said, then realised he was talking to a lady. 'Sorry for the language, love, but my daft son's over there with them and how I'm to manage without him in the shop, I don't know.'

When she arrived at work, she went into James's office. It still smelled of him, she thought, as she hung her hat and coat up.

Within a minute, Walter poked his head through the door. 'I've just made a pot of tea.'

'I'd love a cup. Why don't you bring yours in here and we'll discuss today's work?'

When they were sitting sipping tea, he sighed and said in his hoarse, scratchy voice, 'It makes me feel old, you know, all this fuss. Too old to be of use.'

'Would you volunteer if you were younger?'

He nodded. 'Aye. I reckon I would.'

'Well, they'll need people to hold the fort here, so you'll still be playing your part. I certainly couldn't manage without you.'

'Mmm.'

'I wonder where he is now – James, I mean.'

Walter shook his head, his brief spate of words at an end. But he sat with her until they'd both finished their tea, and his presence was a comfort.

When he stood up, he said, 'I'd welcome your help later, Miss Harper, on some estimates for a couple of jobs. I'm not the best at figures. James always used to go over them with me.'

'My pleasure. And Walter, call me Emma, please!' He'd always refused to do that before.

He nodded slowly. 'I reckon I can now. Seeing it's just us two to hold Cardwell's together. All right, Emma love.'

Led by Ben Symes, marching with the precision of an ex-soldier, a group of mainly unmarried young men from Pilby's walked, shambled or tried to march down the main street together to enlist. Among them was Percy Kershaw. He smiled all the way, for this was his chance to escape. Volunteering was his duty, even. They said he could arrange to have his pay sent home to his mother, so she wouldn't suffer, but for probably the only time in his life he would have a valid excuse for getting away, one he needn't feel guilty about.

Excitement filled him and he clapped one of the other men from the office on the shoulder as they walked down to the Town Hall together. 'Be a bit of a change, eh, Rob lad?'

'It will that.' Rob looked round, scanning the group of men. 'It's true, then?'

'What's true?'

'Sam Thoxby refused to come with us.'

'He never!' Percy also had a quick squint round.

'Mmm. The rotten sod said he had better things to do with his life than play at soldiers.'

'He *is* a married man.'

'Hasn't got any children, though. Not even expecting one, now.'

Percy sighed. Useless to hope that piece of information wouldn't leak out. A few of the fellows had made their scorn for Sam very plain since he'd put his young wife into hospital.

Rob was not one to let a juicy subject drop. 'He'd be better off bashing a few Germans, that one would, than hitting women.'

'Well, you can't force him to volunteer, can you?'

Rob spat into the gutter. 'No, but he's going to find himself even less popular at work from now on. Big strong fellow like that. It's his bloody duty to enlist, if you ask me.'

At the Town Hall, they filled in their papers, had their hands shaken by the Mayor and a cup of tea poured for them by the Mayor's wife. After which, they took their written acknowledgements away and waited for a summons.

When she heard what Percy had done, Meg hit the roof, weeping and wailing all evening till he slammed out of the house and went down to the pub. Johnny followed him along the road, saluting and looking proud.

Percy was dying to leave, but it took over a week for the Army to arrange something. Then word went out that Dr Balloch was to check out the men before they went away, to weed out the ones who weren't fit enough to fight.

Once again, Pilby's was left only half manned. Once again, men streamed into town from all sorts of places, waiting patiently outside the Town Hall in another long line, joking with one another. And back at the works, Ben Symes, who was angry that he was nearly sixty and couldn't fight, glared at Sam Thoxby, who could fight but wouldn't.

When it was Percy's turn, Dr Balloch listened to his chest, frowned and listened again. Then he gestured to a door at one side. 'Could you wait in there, please, Mr Kershaw? I need to check you over again.'

Percy stared. 'What's the matter? There's nothing wrong with me, you know. I'm never ill.'

Dr Balloch's expression gave nothing away. 'Just go through there, please. I'm sorry to keep you waiting, but there's only me to do this.' For it was unthinkable that a woman doctor should examine all these strapping young males.

Inside the next room, Percy found three glum men, two rather old to be enlisting and a weedy fellow his own age, who looked unfit.

'What's wrong with thee, lad?' one of the older men asked. 'Thou doesn't look badly.'

'Buggered if I know.' Percy sat down in a chair.

It was over an hour before Dr Balloch came in, looking tired. 'Right, I'd like to listen to your chests again.'

The two older men were sent away, with one word scrawled across their papers: '*Unfit*'.

The younger fellow, who had an irritating cough, was given a letter for his own doctor and his papers were also labelled '*Unfit*'.

Dr Balloch listened carefully to Percy's chest, then put away his stethoscope and gestured to a chair. 'Sit down a minute, will you?'

Puzzled, Percy obeyed.

'I'm afraid you have a murmur in your heart, so I can't recommend you for active service.'

Stunned, Percy could only gape at him. 'What does that mean exactly? Am I ill?'

'No, you're not ill at all. The murmur just means that you have a small hole in one wall of your heart – many people have the same thing without knowing.' Sympathy on his face, he added quietly, 'It's just – you're not fighting material, Mr Kershaw.' He scribbled that fateful word on Percy's papers, then began to gather his things together.

Percy couldn't move, so shocked was he.

Dr Balloch paused. 'You can live a long and useful life, Mr Kershaw, marry, have children, do all the normal things a young man does, but you're not fit enough to fight.' He looked at Percy shrewdly. 'Surely you've had some warning – an occasional pain in the chest when you've over-exerted yourself?'

And Percy remembered several incidents over the years, little things that he'd dismissed as the simple result of doing too much, too fast. He nodded reluctantly. 'I never thought owt of it.'

'Well, it needn't make a big difference to your life.'

Dejected, Percy finished buttoning his shirt and walked out of the building. It had made a huge difference to his life already. A dreadful difference. Alone, he made his way back to Pilby's.

'What kept you, lad?' Rob asked as he came back into the office.

'Unfit,' Percy said dully, showing him the paper.

'Nay!' There was silence, then, 'What's wrong?'

'Something to do with my heart. It's not bad enough to stop me living a normal life, but it makes me too much of a risk for the bloody Army.' He went and busied himself at his desk, hunching his shoulders against the world, so bitterly disappointed that he felt like weeping. 'You tell the lads for me, will you? I'm a bit upset, like.'

At the end of the day, Rob hesitated. 'Some of us are going

out for a drink, to celebrate. Do you want to come? After all, you did *try* to volunteer!'

Percy shook his head. 'No. I'll just get off home.' But he did nothing for a while, only sat staring out of the window blindly. His one chance to get away from her, ruined. Tears came into his eyes and he had to blink hard to clear them.

When he turned round, he found Mr Pilby himself standing in the doorway. 'I heard you'd been turned down, Kershaw. Mind telling me why?'

So Percy explained again.

His employer nodded. 'Well, lad, these things happen. I just wanted to say – you can still do your bit, you know. We shall be depending on you to keep things going in the office here while the other lads are away.'

Percy frowned at him. 'What?'

'You'll be second in charge here now, lad.'

It was an effort to say, 'Yes. I see.' He stood up. 'I'm sorry, sir. I'm still getting used to it. I'll get off home now, if you don't mind?'

Pilby nodded as he watched him go. A decent young fellow, Kershaw. Had tried to do his duty. And was showing promise in the office, too. A bit of luck for Pilby's, him not being fit to fight. You wanted to do your bit, but you couldn't run a company if everyone rushed off to war.

Percy couldn't face the thought of going straight home. Instead, he called in at Cardwell's and had a cup of tea with Emma. She didn't ooze sympathy all over him, just nodded acceptance when he told her, then got out a bottle of whisky to lace his tea, sitting quietly with him as he sipped.

'Thanks,' he said, when he felt up to facing his mother.

'I didn't do anything.'

'You were there.'

She laid one hand on his shoulder. 'Percy, you did your duty. You volunteered. No man can do more. You shouldn't blame yourself.'

He gave a shamefaced grin. 'It's not just that – I know it sounds silly, but I was actually looking forward to getting away.' He didn't need to add 'from her'.

CHAPTER TWENTY-TWO

August to November 1914

Every day seemed to bring more war news and there was an atmosphere of feverish excitement in the town, with people gathering in small groups to discuss the latest rumours. Mothers threatened their children with 'The Kaiser will get you!' if they misbehaved. Children played war games with sticks for guns. Those who had seen service in the Boer War were much sought after for opinions.

On 12 August, Britain and France declared war on Austria-Hungary.

'Where will it end?' some people asked.

'It'll end when Britain has defeated those scoundrels,' others said stoutly.

On the fifteenth, there was news of a battle the previous day between French and German forces on the frontier between the two countries. People who had never previously had a good word for any foreigner were suddenly cheering the French on and talking about 'our gallant allies'.

Peter Dearden was torn between a wish to volunteer and do his bit and a need to help his mother, who was spending most of her time caring for her dying husband and was little seen by customers these days. He hung a big map of Europe in the window of the shop and small groups gathered around it at regular intervals, pointing fingers and earnestly discussing the fate of countries they hadn't heard of since their schooldays.

No one had blamed Peter for not enlisting, as they did Sam

Thoxby, because everyone knew that Bob Dearden hadn't long to live. Besides, his brother Jack had gone off to volunteer almost as soon as war was declared, not lining up at the Town Hall like the others but going off with a hastily packed bag to find a way of getting into the Royal Flying Corps.

His mother wept over the letter he left. And wept again when she got an excited letter saying he'd been accepted because of his knowledge of planes and flying.

'It makes you realise how lucky we are to live on an island,' Blanche Harper said over tea one night. 'It'll be a lot harder for the Huns to invade us here than it was for them to crush poor little Belgium.'

Funny how patriotic Blanche had suddenly become, Emma thought. 'Yes. We are lucky.' She stared down at her plate. She wasn't really hungry, but if she didn't eat something, her sister would notice and worry. Wherever James was, Emma hoped he wasn't involved in fighting. But she wouldn't know. That was what made it all so hard. She had no right even to expect a letter.

'Have you seen Percy lately?' Blanche asked, with a coy look on her face.

'No. Why? Should I have?'

'Oh, I just thought – you and he seem to have grown very friendly lately. Look at the way he came round to see you when he found he was unfit to serve.'

'Percy is just a good friend. Nothing more, dear, so don't start speculating.'

'The way he looks at you sometimes is more than friendly. And – I'd like to see you happy.'

'I can only hope you're mistaken about the way he looks at me because I don't think of him like that.' She cared too much about another man. 'And anyway, I'm happy here with you.' She started talking about her day at work and the account books she'd brought home to study, relieved when nothing more was said about Percy.

*　　*　　*

Lizzie did not find out that Sam was being shunned by most of the other men left at Pilby's until a woman stopped her in the street, blocking her way, arms akimbo. 'You want to tell that husband of yours to do his duty.'

'I don't understand what you mean?'

'A big, strong fellow like that should be in the Army, helping defend his country against the Huns. My Will's only a little feller, but he's gone.'

Lizzie gave a short, bitter laugh. 'If you think Sam listens to anything I say, you're wrong. He goes his own sweet way, my husband does.'

'Well, you should be persuading him to enlist. That's a woman's duty.'

Lizzie stared her right in the eyes. 'He put me in hospital for a week last time I spoke out of turn.'

The woman met her gaze for a moment, then her eyes fell. 'So it's not you who's holding him back, then?'

'No. I'd be delighted for him to go.'

The woman looked surprised at this bluntness, then her expression became sympathetic, but she didn't say anything, just nodded and stood aside.

Lizzie hurried away. She hated it when people pitied her.

She couldn't help stopping to stare at the recruiting poster outside the Town Hall and wishing Sam would heed its message. There were posters everywhere. He must see them every day. If the war went on, surely he'd have to enlist? Then she gave a snort of laughter. Her husband put his life at risk for other people? Never.

When Sam came home that night, he was in such a foul mood Lizzie's heart gave a lurch.

'Isn't tea ready yet?'

She lowered her eyes. 'It'll be ready as soon as you've changed.'

'You make sure it is.'

Later, as he sat shovelling food into his mouth, making the snorting, snapping noises she hated, he said savagely, 'Well, it won't be long before I leave that bloody place.'

Hope flickered for a minute. Was he thinking of enlisting? But she kept her eyes down, not wanting to say the wrong thing.

He leaned forward and thumped the handle of his knife beside her plate, making her spill the peas from her fork. 'I said, it won't be long before I leave that bloody place. Are you deaf?'

Lizzie risked a glance sideways at him. 'Pilby's, you mean?'

'Of course I mean Pilby's. Where else have I been working these past few years?'

'W-what will you be doing instead?'

'Working for meself. Making some real money.'

'Doing what?'

'Never you mind.' He stabbed his fork towards her. 'And think on, you're not to mention that to anyone.'

'No, Sam.'

'Have you started your monthlies?'

'Yes.' Thank goodness. She didn't want a child any more, not *his* child, anyway.

He glared at her. 'You can't do nothing right, can you?'

Rage swelled in her because he was the one who'd killed their unborn child, but she held it back. No use earning herself another beating.

After the meal, as she was bringing his cup of tea across to him, she tripped on the edge of the rug and nearly fell, spilling tea into the saucer and splashing his trouser leg.

One fist thumped down on the arm of his chair. 'Clumsy bitch. Get that wiped up or—' He shut his mouth and breathed deeply, his expression furious.

Then she knew that he would hit her soon. He was brewing up for a release from anger. Panic fluttered in her breast. Would he hurt her badly, put her in hospital again? Even – kill her?

He looked at her and gave a slow smile. 'Frightened, are you?'

She could only swallow and look at him.

'Come here!'

'I've got the t-tea things to clear up.'

His voice grew even softer. 'Come here when I tell you.'

He held her at arm's length and deliberately slapped her face. Just one quick slap, but it brought the terror throbbing back through her, the terror that seemed to sap her will to resist.

With a laugh, he flung her to the floor. 'Useless, that's what you are. Your mother's right.'

There was a knock on the back door and Josh came in without waiting to be invited. He looked at the woman sprawling on the rug, his eyes knowing, but didn't comment.

'Sit down, lad,' said Sam genially, suddenly in a good mood again. 'Get him a cup of tea, you. Then go and clear up the bathroom.'

Her hands were shaking as she carried the cup over to Josh. He noticed that, too.

In the bathroom, she turned the tap on and sank down on the floor, burying her face in her hands. She couldn't go on like this much longer. She just couldn't. If only she could save money more quickly.

Strangely enough, Sam didn't hit her again for a while. He and Josh were plotting something and he seemed preoccupied, hardly sparing a glance for her. Lizzie no longer cared that they were probably thieving, so long as they didn't involve her in whatever it was.

Then one evening Sam came in scowling and after that he started on her again – just a slap here and a brutal pinch there – enough to make her shiver with fear every time she heard him return from work. But he was very careful not to mark her where people might see it. And she could hardly go into Dearden's and roll up her sleeves to show them the bruises, let alone lift up her skirts to show them the blue pinch marks on the tender white flesh of her thighs.

One night in early November, Lizzie gasped and stood motionless for a moment as she took off her wedding and engagement rings to wash up. The rings! She could pawn them! Real gold and diamonds, he'd said, and they had the marks on them to prove it. So she didn't need to save as much money as she'd thought. She stood with her hands poised over the enamel bowl of steaming water, tears of sheer relief in her eyes. *She could pawn them!*

So many women were doing the same thing, because the Army wasn't sending families the allowances it had promised, even though their husbands had signed the forms and they'd produced marriage certificates and been interviewed by the local committees. With rent to pay, children or elderly parents to feed, coal to buy, they were getting desperate. She had seen women go into Pettit's carrying all sorts of things, dejection and shame in every line of their bodies. She'd also seen the pawnbroker with his eye glass, haggling over the price of the wedding rings as she passed the dark cluttered shop with its three balls outside. She wouldn't go to him, though, because he was a mean old devil, and anyway someone might see her. She'd pawn her rings in Manchester or London, going round several shops to get the best price – and she'd be glad to get rid of them, too. And of everything else that reminded her of Sam. Her spirits began to lift.

That night she lay in bed, listening to the rain dripping along the gutters and trickling down the drainpipes. It seemed to be raining all the time lately. On his way home from work, Sam had encountered a group of women, who'd harangued him about enlisting, and he had come in sizzling with fury. Tonight, she'd seen that wild light flaring in his eyes again. So tomorrow or the day after, she was going away and never coming back. Never.

As the hours passed, she began to wonder why he was later

than usual. It was well after midnight, from the distant chiming of the Town Hall clock.

When she heard the key turning in the back door, she tensed. Here he was. Probably soaked, chilled to the marrow and wanting his rations. He usually did want her body when he'd been out doing whatever it was he and Josh did together, and he was rougher with her at those times, too. Apart from the fact that she hated him even touching her, she worried now that she might get pregnant again and not be able to run away.

When he came into the bedroom, Lizzie pretended to be asleep, but he shook her awake. 'If the police come, I've been here with you all evening.'

She didn't protest, just lay there in the dark, wondering what had happened now.

'The soddin' bobbies nabbed Josh tonight,' he said abruptly, taking off his soggy clothes and dropping them on the lino with wet flopping sounds. 'I don't think he'll give me away, but you can never tell.'

'They – they might not believe me – if he does tell them about you being there,' she whispered.

Sam grabbed her arm, holding it so tightly she gave a squeak of protest. 'You'd better make sure they do believe you.'

For once he didn't want to touch her. Which was a small mercy.

The next day Sam didn't go to work. Lizzie could have wept in disappointment. She had intended to sort through her things, deciding what to take and what not to take. Instead, she had to do her housework with him sitting there, glowering at her.

'Won't they think it's funny – you not going to work today, I mean?' she asked at last.

'Sod what they think!' He went to get himself a bottle of beer from the cellar.

Lizzie decided to clean out the front room to get away from him. They never used it, for they had no visitors at all nowadays, but she still liked to keep it looking nice. He came to peer through the doorway an hour or so later, but to her relief went away again without saying anything. When she had finished cleaning, she decided to go shopping. Anything to get away from that lowering gaze. 'What would you like for tea, Sam?'

He pursed his lips, head on one side, thinking. Just as he was about to speak, there was a knock on the front door.

They exchanged glances, then he gave her a shove. 'You go and answer it. If anyone asks, I'm poorly.' He tiptoed up the stairs and stood at the top, flapping one hand at her and hissing, 'Go on, you dozy bitch. Answer that bloody door.'

Heart thudding in her chest, Lizzie went, her hand trembling as she turned the handle. She let out a soft 'Oof!' of relief when she found not a policeman but a scruffy lad on the step.

'Message for Mr Thoxby.' He glanced down the street, as if he expected someone to be following him.

She held the door open. 'You'd better come in, then.'

He doffed his ragged cap and came inside, staring round at the hallstand, the mirror on the wall, the bright new carpet runner, as if he wasn't used to such luxuries.

'It's a lad with a message for you, Sam!' she called up the stairs.

He came clattering down. 'Fred! What the hell are you doing here?'

'Dad got a message out. He said you'd give me sixpence for bringing it an' sixpence for the fellow as passed it on.'

'After I've heard it.'

Lizzie knew better than to linger so she went into the kitchen but pressed her ear to the door. If something was wrong, she wanted to know at once. The boy's voice was shrill and carried clearly, thank goodness.

'Dad says he'll hold off telling them till tomorrow. But no longer. He says you'd better get away while you can.'

Sam swore and thumped one massive fist into the other. 'Hell, fire and damnation! Can't he even keep his big mouth shut?'

'He said to tell you they already knew who was with him. They've been watching you for a bit.'

'How did they know?'

The lad shrugged. 'I dunno, Mr Thoxby. A fellow as was in for drunk and disorderly brang the message round to our 'ouse. I'm just passin' it on to you. Oh, ta!' He slipped the two sixpences into his pocket and edged towards the front door.

Sam slammed the door shut after him and came to fling himself down at the kitchen table. He cocked one eyebrow at Lizzie. 'You heard that?'

She nodded. No use denying it. 'What will you do?'

'I don't know. Have to think.' He picked up the newspaper, shook it open then stared at it. A minute later, he exclaimed, 'Oh, hell! That's it.'

Lizzie paused in her preparations.

He let out a string of oaths.

She began to sidle towards the scullery door, afraid of him turning on her.

'Don't go!'

She swallowed hard and stayed where she was.

He looked at her, a sour expression on his face, then gave a snort of bitter amusement. 'Well, this'll please all the old biddies who've been stopping me in the street and telling me to enlist. It bloody will an' all!'

'What do you mean, Sam?'

He flicked the newspaper with one fingertip. 'I mean, there's only one place where the police won't bother to come after me — in the bleeding Army.'

Lizzie could only goggle at him.

'So you'd better put your hat an' coat on, Mrs Thoxby. You're just about to escort your dear husband down to the Recruiting Office. And unlike your Percy, I'm fit as a flea, so the buggers will welcome me with open arms.'

'Are you s-serious?'

'Of course I am. Do you think I'd join the bloody Army for any other reason?'

★   ★   ★

They walked into town arm-in-arm. Half way there they met Miss Porter, a spinster lady of uncertain years who'd made it her mission to confront those unmarried young men who hadn't enlisted and urge them to join up. She had a particularly shrill voice and men had been known to dive into alleys or crouch behind motor cars to avoid her.

Today Sam stopped her in the street. 'Well, Miss Porter, you're looking at a man on his way to the Recruiting Office. I've got things sorted out at home now, so I can go an' do my duty.'

She beamed at him. 'Good man! Good man!'

He tipped his bowler hat to her and sauntered on.

Lizzie glanced back and saw Miss Porter already in conversation with one of her friends, pointing after them and nodding her head emphatically.

Sam's fingers bit into her arm. 'Try to look more like a proud wife, eh? You're not going to a bleeding funeral.'

Lizzie was having difficulty hiding her exultation. He was leaving! He really was leaving!

At the Recruiting Office, Sam let go of her, went to the head of the queue and pushed his way inside.

'Here, join the back of the line, you!' one man called. 'We've come in from Wallingby today to join up.'

'An' half you buggers'll be sent back to Wallingby again, too. You couldn't raise a good sneeze between the six of you.'

There was muttering, but no one else challenged him.

The Recruiting Sergeant's eyes lit up at the sight of Sam. 'You look like a strong young fellow. You've come to the right place, lad.'

Lizzie, who had followed him in, noticed her husband's smile go a bit glassy, then she heard him breathe deeply and say, 'Well, where do I sign?'

She couldn't hold in one long shuddering sigh of relief. Then she had control of herself again.

*   *   *

That afternoon, Sam sat morosely in front of the kitchen fire. 'Last night of freedom.'

'Yes. But – but you're doing the right thing, Sam, I know you are. I mean – we are at war and – and they do need men.'

'Hah! Last thing I wanted was to join the sodding Army.' He spat into the fire, then took another slurp of beer from the jug he'd sent her to fetch from the Hare and Hounds.

Usually Lizzie hated fetching him beer, but tonight she didn't care about anything. He was to leave tomorrow. She could take her time about running away now. Maybe – maybe he'd even get killed. Men did in wartime. But guilt shot through her at that, followed by a cynical thought that wicked men didn't get killed, only good ones.

Later, as she was carrying a second jug of beer back up the street, a policeman stopped her. 'Is it true, Mrs Thoxby?'

'Is what true?'

'That your husband has enlisted.'

'Yes.'

'When does he leave?'

'Tomorrow.'

'Ah. Well, personally I'll believe it when I see it, but my Sergeant will be very interested in that news, very interested indeed. I reckon we'll all come to see him off.'

When he let go of her arm, Lizzie hurried on. Not as stupid as Sam thought, the police.

At the house she mentioned the encounter, but Sam only grunted and said, 'It's stopped them coming after me, then.' She went upstairs and busied herself getting his things ready, laying them out on the bed in neat piles.

She spun that job out as long as she could, then came down. 'Do you want to see what I'm packing? I've found everything on that list they gave you.'

'Whassat?'

She saw with dismay that he was already affected by the drink.

'I've got your clothes and things laid out, ready to pack,' she repeated. 'Do you want to come and check them?'

'No, I don't want to come and check them. What I want is my rations.'

'But—'

He glared at her. 'No buts. Get your knickers off.'

'Here?'

'Why not?'

When he had finished, he rolled off her and gave her a shove. 'Useless bloody lump, you are. No good at pleasuring a man.'

Lizzie bit back the obvious response that she only knew what he had taught her – which was definitely not how to please one's partner.

When he was dressed, she poured him another beer and asked, 'What shall I do for money while you're away, Sam?'

That made him think. 'They say the Army will send on my pay, but I've seen no sign of that with other folk, so I'm not signing mine over to you. Besides, I'm going to need that money myself. There must be a few fiddles I can get in on, even in the Army.'

She stared at him in horror. 'But what about me?'

'Oh, I'll give you something to keep you going. Enough for a few weeks. They're bound to let me have leave by then. I'll give you some more next time I come back.'

'But what if they don't—'

He cracked her across the face. 'Bloody well shut up and let a man enjoy his last night of freedom, will you?'

Eventually, she went up to bed, leaving him still drinking, but she couldn't sleep. After a while, she heard him go into the front room. He seemed to be in there a long time, then there was the sound of a bottle clinking. Her heart sank. He must have been fetching the rum he kept for special occasions.

She crept to the top of the stairs, shivering with cold but worried about what he would do. When there had been no noise for a while, she tiptoed down to find him snoring in front of the dying fire, with the bottle of rum standing by his feet, nearly empty. She banked the fire up carefully with a big cob of coal and some slack, then went back to bed, to sleep uneasily.

In the morning, Sam was sitting in the kitchen when she went down, scowling into a blazing fire. He didn't even look up to greet her. 'Have you got my stuff packed?'

'Yes, Sam.'

'Get me a good breakfast while I have a wash.' He glanced at the clock, then back at her bruised face. 'You'd better not come with me into town today. And stay indoors till that mark has cleared up. If anyone asks, tell them you had a fall.'

As if anyone in the whole town would believe that! But she nodded anyway.

A little later, she gathered her courage together to ask, 'What about the money, Sam? I need something to live off.'

He nodded. 'I've got it out for you. There!' He pointed to the mantelpiece.

As Lizzie went to count it, she wondered where he'd got it from. She knew he didn't keep that much on him, because she often had to clear his pockets out before she hung up his things. So he must have a supply hidden somewhere. 'There's only five pounds, Sam. That won't last long. I'll have the gas bill to pay and the coalman and—'

'Make it last. Women don't eat as much as men. I'll send you some more later.'

She didn't dare argue.

At half-past eight, he stood up, collected his suitcase from the hall, then turned at the door to waggle one thick finger at her. 'If I hear you've so much as spoke to another fellow while I'm away, I'll do more than mark your face. An' tell your family to stay away from my house.'

And that was his farewell.

When the sound of his footsteps in the street had died away, Lizzie fumbled her way towards a chair and sat down with a thump. The house felt empty. Delightfully empty. She couldn't believe he'd gone, that she'd be on her own in that big bed tonight, that there'd be no one to shout at her.

She looked at the five crumpled pound notes on the table. They wouldn't last long.

Then she realised suddenly that until she saw him go, actually saw him leave Overdale, she'd not really feel secure. She hunted for the old shawl she wrapped round herself in winter when she sat reading in bed, draped it carefully over her head so that it hid most of the bruise, then slipped out through the back yard.

Hidden behind the corner of the Town Hall, she watched as half a dozen men were lined up outside the temporary Recruiting Office, Sam among them, then ordered into an open-backed lorry where some other men were already sitting.

As it drove away, she sagged against the wall. He'd gone. He'd really gone. She was free, for the first time in over a year.

She couldn't understand why she was weeping, but she couldn't stop and had to lean against the wall, so shaky did she feel. When someone touched her arm, she jumped in shock, then saw it was Peter Dearden staring at her.

'Are you all right, Lizzie?'

She nodded, but she was still unable to stop weeping. 'S–Sam has just left.'

He stared in the direction the lorry had taken, amazed that she was so upset.

She could tell what he was thinking and choked with laughter. 'I'm not sorry – I just can't believe I'm free.'

His expression showed he understood exactly why she'd said that. 'Oh, I see. Look, let me take you home in the van.'

She looked round, saw no one nearby and nodded, sinking gratefully into the front seat of the big maroon and gold van with DEARDEN'S on the side in fussy gold letters. She didn't notice anything on the way back, just sat slumped in the corner, drained of energy, until they turned a corner near Maidham Street. 'Stop here! Quick!'

He braked to a sudden halt. 'What's wrong?'

'If you take me right home, someone will notice. I'll get out here. An' thanks, Peter.'

But he put out one hand to prevent her getting out. 'If you need anything . . .'

'I'm all right. Give my love to your mother. I'm sorry your dad's so ill.' She hid her face with the shawl and hurried off down a back alley.

In her own kitchen, Lizzie looked at the almost empty bottle of rum and on a sudden impulse took a gulp of it, enjoying the warmth as it slid down her throat. Then she locked the doors and stumbled upstairs to bed. Not caring that it was still quite early in the morning, she lay down, pulled the blankets and quilt up and let herself sink into a delicious doze.

Free of Sam's presence, she slept more soundly than she had since she first came to this house and didn't wake up until the middle of the night.

Then she went down and made herself a picnic in the chilly kitchen, eating the bread and jam with relish before going back upstairs and laughing aloud from sheer joy to find the bed unoccupied. She fell asleep again almost immediately, sighing like a carefree child.

CHAPTER TWENTY-THREE

November – December 1914

Apart from one postcard in the second week, Sam didn't write and he certainly didn't tell Lizzie where he was so that she could write to him.

Two weeks after he'd gone, she heard that Sally Dearden's husband, Bob, had died at last and sat staring into the kitchen fire for a long time, feeling sorry for Mrs D, who had loved her husband, but also feeling envious of her, for having such a warm loving family. Outside it was raining again. Inside it was chilly and damp-feeling, because Lizzie didn't dare be extravagant with coal.

When she heard a few days after the funeral that Peter had followed Jack's example and enlisted, and that Mrs D was managing the shop, she wasn't surprised. Her former employer was a strong woman and knew as much about the grocery trade as any man.

As Christmas drew nearer, the money Sam had left dwindled to a few shillings and Lizzie began to worry about how she was going to eat. She wished now that she had left Overdale when he went, but she had worried about being pregnant so had delayed. But she wasn't pregnant, thank goodness. Only, by the time she knew that, the weather was so cold and rainy that she had kept putting off her departure and somehow the money had slipped through her fingers. Soon she would have to dip into her savings, just to buy food.

So when she met Sally Dearden in town one day and

was offered a job in the shop, Lizzie took it eagerly. Sam wouldn't like it, but he hadn't sent her any more money and she had to live, didn't she? And she'd be glad to get out of the house. She was nearly going mad on her own there.

As she walked home, for the first time in ages she felt happy. She stopped to say hello to Blanche Ingram and on impulse added, 'I'd love to pop round and have a natter with you both one night, just for an hour, you know. Only,' she blushed, 'I'd have to come in the back way in case someone told Sam I'd been visiting you.'

Blanche looked at her with great sympathy. Lizzie looked years older than eighteen, and not only older but worn. 'Why not come round tomorrow evening? Have tea with us?'

'That'd be lovely. Only I'll be a bit late. I'm working at Dearden's again.'

'We'll wait for you.'

That same day, Lizzie wrote a letter to Polly to tell her to come round on her next Sunday off, but to use the back door, so that no one would see her.

As she was slipping the letter into the post box, she met Miss Porter.

'Writing to your husband, dear? That's the thing to do, keep our boys happy.'

Lizzie didn't contradict her, but she felt like saying it was hard to write to someone who hadn't sent you an address.

The next day's post brought a letter from Sam with an address in Derbyshire on it. Lizzie saw the envelope lying in the hall when she got home from Dearden's, tired but happy, clutching some bacon for her tea and a loaf of bread.

She picked it up and dropped it on the table, reluctant even to touch it. Then, angry at herself for being so cowardly, she tore it open. The letter was short, but it had a pound note in it, at least.

Dear Lizzie
    Camp is lousy. The Army is lousy, too. We still haven't

got our full uniforms or enough blankets and the food is shocking.
Good job I have my overcoat with me.

Here is some more money to keep you going. I've been
making a bob or two lending to other fellows. I hope to get
some leave soon. Make sure you keep yourself to yourself. I
don't want your family trailing in and out of my house while
I'm away. Your bloody brother doesn't know how lucky he is
staying out of the sodding Army.
Sam

She threw the envelope into the fire and put the letter with the
address on it behind the mantelpiece clock. He'd expect a reply.
She didn't want to write, but she'd better. Or should she take
the pound and just run away now? With a sigh, she admitted to
herself that she didn't really want to leave Overdale, especially
not now she was working at Dearden's again, seeing all her
old customers, enjoying herself as she had not done since her
marriage.

In the weeks that followed, even though she knew it was
risky, she kept putting off her departure.

Christmas came and went. Lizzie visited the Harpers and
Percy called in to see her with a present. Polly had also given
her a present, but Sam hadn't even sent a letter. Percy didn't
stay long. 'Mam's making a lot of fuss about us all spending the
day together.'

'All' obviously didn't include Lizzie. 'Does she know you've
come to see me?'

He nodded, looking embarrassed.

She changed the subject. Even at Christmas, her mother
didn't want to see her, knew she was on her own and hadn't
invited her round.

On Boxing Day Polly popped in for an hour, blushing and
confessing that she was walking out with a fellow she'd met at
the station on that dreadful day Lizzie had failed to escape.

'Are you going to stay with Sam now?' Polly asked hesitantly
as conversation turned to Lizzie. 'Have you changed your mind
about leaving him?'

'I was just going when he joined up. I – I don't know what to do now. Trouble is, I'm enjoying working at Dearden's.'

Just at that moment the front door opened. Only one person had a key. Lizzie's heart plummeted and she turned to face the hall as Sam walked in.

He stared at Polly, eyes narrowed. 'I might have known you'd start coming round here again,' he said sourly, then turned to Lizzie. 'Well, no welcome for your husband?'

She made herself walk across and give him a peck on the cheek. She could smell rum on his breath. He'd clearly not come straight home.

Polly looked at her sister, uncertain what to do.

Lizzie managed a smile. 'I'll see you next month, then, love.'

At the front door, Polly gave her a hug and whispered, 'Are you sure you'll be all right?'

'Yes. I'm used to it.'

Lizzie went back into the kitchen. 'You should have let me know you were coming, Sam. I'd have got more food in.'

'I'm more interested in getting my rations than in food,' he said, throwing his overcoat on to a chair and starting to unbutton his flies.

'I'd rather do it in bed,' she said, trying not to show how the thought of his touching her upset her. 'It'll be warmer.'

But by that time, he had reached out and grabbed her. 'Here.'

When he had finished jerking and roaring like an animal, she set her clothes to rights and went to put the kettle on.

He pulled his trousers back up and went to sprawl in a chair by the fire. 'I heard you'd gone back to working at Dearden's.'

'I ran out of money.'

He grunted and scowled at the fire, then asked, 'What have you got to eat?'

'Not much.'

He gave a sneering laugh. 'What? You working at Dearden's and not bringing food home?'

'There's only me, so I don't need much. If you'd let me know you were coming, I'd have got extra in. I've only got a chop here.'

'That'll do for starters.'

She didn't make the obvious comment that it had been intended for her own tea.

He sawed off a piece of bread, slathering it with butter and cramming it into his mouth. 'Hurry up, then! I'm starving.'

She put some potatoes on to boil and began frying the chop.

'How long has your sister been coming round here?'

'This is the first time. I thought — being Christmas—'

'And your brother? Has he been round, too?'

Best stick to the truth. 'Yesterday. Just for a few minutes.'

'All you Kershaws sticking together,' he sneered.

'They're family.'

'Aye. Well, so long as you don't have other fellows coming round.'

'I'm too busy working to have fellows round, even if I wanted them.'

'Jam.'

She'd forgotten what it was like, how he used to fire orders at her. She went to get the jam and resisted a sudden urge to slam it down on the table. 'So you don't mind me working at Dearden's?'

He shrugged. 'You wouldn't be doing it if I were at home — or if that sod Peter Dearden hadn't enlisted. But as it is, it's all right. It'll save me sending you any money home. No cake?'

'I don't bother making them when there's only me.'

'Well, I want one to take back. It's the least you can do for me.'

'How long do you have?'

'Two soddin' days, that's all. Got to leave again tomorrow.'

'I'll go round to the back door of Dearden's. Mrs D will sell me the stuff for a cake.'

'I'll come with you. Show everyone you're still my wife.'

And when they got back he demanded his rations again.

Lizzie set her teeth to endure, but it was clear now that she couldn't put off leaving much longer.

When Sam had gone, Lizzie waited one day, going to work and pretending things were all right. She tried to catch Mrs D on her own, to tell her she was leaving, but it was a busy day and there simply wasn't an opportunity. And after work, another of the women caught their employer, weeping as she talked, so Lizzie walked off and left them.

At home, she packed her things, intending to leave on the milk train next morning, tears trickling down her face as she filled the old suitcase she'd bought at the market. Then she hesitated and, knowing she couldn't leave without telling Mrs D, went round to the back door of the shop. To her surprise, Peter opened it.

'Oh! I didn't know you were on leave.'

'I started after Christmas.' He held the door open. 'Come in.' Tactfully, he didn't comment on her tear-stained face. 'You'll be wanting to see Mum.'

She explained what was happening to Mrs D, ending, 'I'm that sorry to let you down.'

Suddenly she was folded in a pair of arms and given a big hug. 'You're doing the right thing, I reckon.' Then Mrs D drew her into the shop and pulled some money out of the cash box. 'Here. Take this.'

'I can't.'

'You can. You're going to need it.'

Lizzie hesitated, then said, 'Thanks.'

When she got home, Lizzie let herself into the house and looked at the clock. Only three hours to wait, then she'd be off.

'Been seeing your fancy man, have you?' a voice snarled.

'Sam!'

He stood in the back doorway, nearly filling it, and the look on his face was terrifying.

For a moment she froze, then she turned and started running, terror setting her heart thumping with a rhythm that filled her whole body. She got out of the front door by the skin of her teeth and was off down the street, running faster than she ever had in her life before.

He pounded along behind her, bellowing her name.

From somewhere, Lizzie found the strength to run faster. With a vague idea of going to Polly for help, she fled towards the better part of town, but although Sam didn't overtake her, he stayed behind her, pounding along, following the beat of her footsteps on the paved paths. And she was getting tired now.

Think! she urged herself. *If he catches you, he'll kill you.* She took a sudden left turn and heard him run past the street, then stop and listen. She stood motionless, but when he started moving in her direction, she panicked and set off running again.

Next time she swerved, she chose the park, with its soft grass. She had always been able to slip through the fence in one particular spot, so praying that she still could, she made for it. As she wriggled through, she heard Sam getting nearer and for one dreadful moment, thought she was stuck.

But with a final desperate wriggle, she got through and was off across the lawn, knowing she showed up clearly in the moonlight, but not caring, because it'd take him a while to get over the railings.

In the shadow of some trees, she stopped and glanced back to see him climbing the railings. Flitting along in the darker patches, she changed direction, heading back towards the gap she'd just come through. When she had heard him blunder off into the distance, she risked the short patch of open ground again, tearing off her coat as she ran and slipping through the hole more easily.

Then she was off again, running through the streets, coat flapping in her hand, trying hard to think. All she had was the money Mrs D had given her, no clothes, no suitcase. And her rings. She needed help. Polly? No, it'd take too long to wake her sister. That left only one place. Dearden's. If they wouldn't hide her, she'd throw herself into the canal.

By the time she got there, breath was rasping in her throat and her legs felt leaden. The upstairs light was still on. She hammered at the back door, terrified that Sam would turn up and catch her.

Peter opened it.

'Sam's after me,' she said simply. 'He came back and caught me leaving.'

He held the door open and she almost fell through it.

A little later, when Sam hammered at the front door of the shop, Peter went to answer it in his pyjamas and dressing gown, his mother behind him. If that man tried to attack her son, she was going to grab a tin of ham and clout him over the head.

'Where is she?' Sam demanded, shoving the door wider.

'Who?' Peter blinked and tried to look as if he'd just woken up.

'My bloody wife, the one as came round to see you here tonight.'

Sally stepped forward. 'Your wife came to see me, not my son. She didn't even know he was home.'

Sam turned to sneer at her. 'If you think I'll believe that, you must think I'm stupid.'

'You *are* stupid, ill-treating that poor lass, and even more stupid if you think she's got another fellow, let alone my Peter. She works here, that's all.'

'I want to see.'

'Pardon?'

'I want to come in and see that she's not here.'

'Of course she's not here.' But Sally stepped back and gestured to him to enter.

Sam tramped round the whole house and shop, taking great care that no one could slip from one place to another behind his back, and going over some areas a couple of times, to make sure.

Sally held Peter back when he began to get angry and simply let Sam go where he wanted. He'd never find the hidden cupboard where they kept their valuables and the shop takings. It had been very skilfully fitted. Lizzie would be cramped in there, but safe.

'Satisfied?' she asked when at last he stopped searching.

'You've got her hidden somewhere,' he accused.

'If she had come round, I'd have got her away at once, not kept her here,' said Sally scornfully.

He jerked towards her, fists clenched, and Peter moved in front of his mother. But although the two men stared each other in the eyes, their hatred clearly visible, the moment of danger passed.

'You'd better leave now,' Peter said. 'We want to get some sleep.'

Sam went outside, made a great play of tramping off down the street, then crept back to keep watch, circling the house from time to time, rubbing his chilled hands, anger keeping sleep at bay. He'd known when he saw that sod was home that she'd go to him. He knew no woman could stay faithful. When he found she'd started working at Dearden's, he'd been prepared for trouble and had lied about the length of his leave. Well, she wasn't going to get away with it. Oh, no!

Inside the house, they made plans, then Peter kept watch at one of the windows while his mother packed some things for Lizzie by the light of a street lamp, and helped her change into some of his father's old clothes.

In the morning, their driver accepted a pound note to drive Lizzie out openly, dressed as a fellow, with her front hair cut into a fringe and flour brushed through to make it seem grey.

When Sam stopped the van at the yard gate and insisted on looking in the back, he hardly looked at the old fellow smoking a cigarette in the front. He checked behind the boxes, then waved the van on.

'They'll not get her out without me seeing her,' he muttered to himself.

In the front of the van, Lizzie sat rigid with terror, nearly choking on the cigarette. Peter had said it was best to do this boldly, but she was been so afraid when Sam stepped up to the van that her whole body had gone numb. And still felt numb.

When the van stopped some time later, she couldn't move at first.

'You get out here, love,' the fellow said, looking at her curiously. By, she looked to be in a right state, and no wonder, with a husband like that. He only hoped Mrs D didn't get into trouble for helping her. Thoxby could be a nasty sod when crossed.

When Peter left, going openly to the station, Sam followed him, leaving his friend Josh to keep watch on the shop. He saw Peter climb on the train, muttering, 'I'll get that bastard one day, I will that. I don't know how they hid her, but she couldn't have got away without help.'

As the train chugged out of the station, he went back to Dearden's, going into the shop openly.

'Have you found Lizzie, Mr Thoxby?' Sally asked at once. 'I've been right worried about her.'

'Not yet, missus. But I will.'

Then he had to leave Overdale to go back to the sodding barracks. But he went round to his friend Josh's house first to leave instructions with young Fred – and money, too – to keep watch on the house in case Lizzie came back. As he climbed into a late afternoon train, rage boiled within him. She might have got away for the moment, but he'd find her. And make her very sorry indeed.

Percy didn't discover for a couple of days that Lizzie was missing. When he went round to her house one evening, a strange lad opened the door.

'Is my sister in?'

'She's not here.'

Percy stared at him. 'Who are you?'

'Friend of Mr Thoxby's. Looking after the house for 'im.'

'Tell my sister I called, will you?'

'She's left.' The lad slammed the door shut.

Percy went straight along to the Harper's house. 'Have you seen Lizzie lately?' he demanded, before he even got inside the door.

The two sisters exchanged glances and Emma spoke. 'We haven't seen her for several days. But – well, there was a hubbub one night and she chased off down the street with him following her and yelling at her to come back.'

'I had the toothache,' Blanche explained. 'We don't usually spy on neighbours, but I couldn't sleep and when the noise started, I looked out of the window. But I didn't see her come back.'

'I hope she got away,' Emma said. 'He's a wicked brute.'

Percy went round to Dearden's next, knocking on the back door.

Mrs D opened it, a rolling pin in her hand. 'Oh, it's you, lad.'

'I was looking for Lizzie.'

Sally looked round the yard, then gestured to him to come in. 'She's left him. She came round a few nights ago to say she was going, then later on Sam came round, thinking she was here.'

'And was she?'

'We're not sheltering her,' Sally said obliquely, because she and Peter had decided to tell no one, not even Lizzie's family, any details.

'Where can she be?' worried Percy, then thanked her and left.

She almost called him back to say Lizzie had got away all right, but Peter had stressed that no one should know, so she bit back the words.

*   *   *

Percy knocked at the back door of Redley House next. 'Can I speak to Polly, please? I'm her brother, Percy.'

Mrs Frost nodded, scenting more trouble. 'Just a quick word. It's late.'

Polly was there within the minute. 'Percy? Is something wrong?'

'Have you seen Lizzie lately?'

'Not for a few days, no.'

'She's not in Maidham Street.' He told her all he knew, watching her anxiously. 'I was sure she'd have come to you.'

Polly shook her head. 'No. I knew she was going to leave, but she said she'd do it on her own. Oh, Percy! I do hope she got away.'

'So do I.' He stood there for a minute, worrying. 'You'll let me know – if you hear anything, like?'

She nodded.

But no one heard anything for quite a while.

CHAPTER TWENTY-FOUR

Manchester: January 1915

Lizzie didn't realise the train had pulled into the station in Manchester till one of the other passengers touched her arm. She had flinched away before she realised what she was doing. 'Oh, sorry! I was miles away.'

The young woman frowned, then sat down again and said bluntly, 'You look to be in trouble, love. Would you like to come and get a cup of tea? We could talk. They say two heads are better than one.'

Lizzie blinked and tried hard to concentrate. 'I – I don't know—'

'Let me buy you that cup of tea, then.' The voice was firm and the stranger reached out to pull Lizzie gently to her feet.

'All right.' She picked up the bag of necessities Mrs D had packed for her and stumbled off the train, finding it difficult to put one foot in front of the other. Lying on the sofa in Mrs D's sitting room through the long, dark hours of the night, she had had no sleep, terrified that Sam would break in and get her. Now, she felt stupid and muzzy-headed. Maybe a cup of tea would help.

When they were seated in a corner of the café, with two steaming cups in front of them, the other woman held out her hand. 'I'm Peggy Garrett.'

Lizzie reached out automatically to clasp the hand. 'Lizzie . . . Smith.'

The other woman's smile said she knew the name was false.

'I know I'm interfering, but I can see you're in trouble and maybe I can help.'

'I don't think anyone can.' Lizzie found it hard to say the words, but forced them out. 'I'm running away from my husband. He—' Her face crumpled and she bent her head, too ashamed to finish.

'Ill-treats you?'

Lizzie nodded.

'Then you did right to run away. Got anywhere to stay tonight?'

A shake of the head was her only answer.

'Would you like to come home with me? You'll have to sleep on the floor, I'm afraid.'

Lizzie could only stare at her and ask, 'Why should you – I mean –' Her voice tailed away.

'He beats you, doesn't he?'

'Yes.'

'My father used to beat my mother. I like to help women in the same sort of trouble when I can. I couldn't help Mam, you see.' There was silence for a moment, then Peggy glanced at the clock. 'Look, I have to catch a train in ten minutes' time. Do you want to come and stay with me for a night or two or do you have other plans?'

'No plans. I just ran. And some f-friends helped me get away.'

'Come home with me, then. I promise you I don't bite – though my friends tell me I do tend to organise other people.'

Then, for the first time, Lizzie noticed the knot of green, white and purple ribbon in the stranger's lapel. 'You're a suffragette!'

'Yes. Does that upset you?'

'Oh, no! I think you're right about votes for women.' She felt reassured, somehow, by that knowledge. 'And – and if you really mean it – I'd be so grateful for your help. I can't seem to think straight today.'

'Come on, then. Drink up. We'll have to buy you a ticket.

I live on the outskirts of Manchester, in Murforth. I work in a munitions factory there.'

At the ticket office, when the stranger reached for her purse, Lizzie said, 'I have some money. I can pay for my own ticket.' Thanks to Mrs D. 'But I don't have many c–clothes.'

'That's all right. The girls will lend you some things. Come on! We'll have to hurry!'

The hard floor didn't prevent Lizzie from sleeping soundly because she felt so safe with Peggy. In the morning – well, it must have been morning, but it was still dark – she was woken by stealthy sounds and found her companion trying to get dressed quietly by the light of a candle lamp.

'Sorry, I didn't mean to wake you. I have to go to work. I'm on early shift this week.'

Something crystallised in Lizzie's mind then. Why did she have to go to London? Sam could be posted anywhere in the country. Nowhere was really safe from him. So she might as well stay here, if her new friend didn't mind. 'Are there any jobs going at the factory?'

'Yes. They nearly always need new hands.' Peggy hesitated then added, 'But it's dangerous work. People get injured, though we haven't had anyone killed here yet.'

'How much do they pay?'

'About thirty shillings a week, once you're trained.'

'That much?'

Peggy smiled. 'It's hard work and a seventy-two-hour week.'

'I've never heard of women getting so much money.' Lizzie could surely live well, and even save from that, then she'd be able to pay back Mrs D. 'Are there other lodgings round here?'

Peggy smiled. 'Yes, lots. With so many men away, women are making money any way they can.'

'What time is it?'

'Half-past five. I've told my landlady about you. She'll

give you breakfast later, then you can spend the day here resting.'

'Shouldn't I come in with you to ask about the job?'

'It'll still be there tomorrow. You look as if you need a bit of peace and quiet today.'

Sam was having a bad time of it. He'd never been at his best in the mornings and it nearly killed him to get up so early and do drill before breakfast. Even the food was poor. And though he had earned some money at first by lending to other fellows, a Sergeant had found out about it and put a stop to that. So he didn't have a lot to spare to buy extra food – even if he'd been able to get away from the camp.

Since he couldn't get back to Overdale, he wrote to Josh's wife and offered her two shillings a week if young Fred would sleep in the house at night, and write to him straight away if Lizzie came home or was seen in the town.

He wasn't surprised when his offer was accepted. With Josh in prison, Dora would be finding it hard to make ends meet.

And then there was the question of paying his rates on the house. After some thought, Sam wrote to the Council saying he'd pay the money he owed next time he was on leave and could get to the savings bank. He got a letter back enclosing a bill and hoping the leave wouldn't be too long delayed.

'Grasping sods!' he muttered.

He had a bit of luck the following week when a young officer left his wallet lying around carelessly. There was an almighty stink about its going missing, but no one found it up the drainpipe and a couple of weeks later Sam was able to retrieve it and send some money off to the sodding Council for the rates.

He applied for leave again and again, but his request was denied and then, to his astonishment, he heard that his battalion was to be sent straight to the Front. He'd counted on getting embarkation leave before this happened, not to mention there being another few weeks' training, but there had been huge numbers of casualties since the war began and it seemed they desperately needed more men out there.

For the first time it occurred to him that he might be killed, which put him in a foul mood and got him in further trouble with the Sergeant. He hadn't made friends here because the others were a bunch of bleeding fools. Listening to them eagerly looking forward to 'doing their bit' made Sam want to puke. He'd do as little as he could, by hell he would! They weren't going to find it easy to kill him.

He wrote a long letter to Dora, giving her orders about keeping an eye on the house, then he gloomily concentrated on rifle practice. He'd taken to guns straight away, loved the feel of them in his hands and was determined to become accurate enough to make sure he could get the Huns before the bastards got him.

To his amazement, he got pulled out the next day and commended.

'You're beginning to show the right spirit now, Thoxby,' a weedy young officer told him. 'And you've got a good eye.'

'Yessir.' Stupid git, Sam thought, even as he smiled. You don't know what time of day it is. I'm doing this for me, not you!

The Monday following her arrival in Murforth, Lizzie started work in the munitions factory. It was a large, one-storey building, laid out in individual work areas, she learned later, for safety reasons. It seemed huge to her, with yards and buildings labelled A, B and so on.

'You didn't tell me it was so big!' she gasped.

'Over three hundred workers here,' Peggy said proudly. 'Mostly women. I reckon they can do anything the men can.'

Which was a new idea for Lizzie.

Peggy left her outside the supervisor's office and when the new shift had started work, Doreen showed Lizzie what to do. First she had to clock in, then Doreen took her to the dressing room and gave her a cap, fireproof overalls and rubber shoes. It felt strange to wear trousers, but there was a freedom to it after long skirts. She looked down in wonder at herself, then realised Doreen was still speaking and jerked to attention.

'You have to wear this cap at all times. Make sure it covers your head. No hair allowed to show. If I were you, I'd get my hair cut short. A lot of the girls are doing that. It's so much easier to manage. And you're not to wear any pins, brooches or rings – no metal of any kind. It's dangerous.'

Lizzie nodded, feeling funny in the stiff overall.

'Here, let me fix your cap.' Doreen smiled encouragingly. 'I know it all seems strange, but you'll get used to it in no time.' Then her voice became severe. 'The main thing is to follow the safety regulations. You'll get fired straight away if we find you being careless. And, worse, you could kill or main yourself and others if you cause an accident, so it's very important indeed to follow the rules.'

Lizzie nodded. She'd be very careful indeed. She didn't want to lose this job.

They walked down a long corridor to the room where Lizzie was to work. Another girl called Ivy showed her what to do and Doreen did a quick tour of the room to check progress while Lizzie had her first lesson.

'These brass bits are for fuses,' Ivy explained. 'You have to check them. If any aren't up to standard, you chuck 'em out.'

Lizzie noticed that many of the girls had bandages on their hands and wondered if they had been careless. Within a few minutes she had found out the reason, because the brass parts, small and harmless-looking as they were, had sharp edges that cut your fingers, however carefully you handled them. And these had to be filed off.

At first she felt very much the outsider. It was a large room with dozens of women working in it, all exchanging cheerful comments and some moving round here and there, though Lizzie couldn't at first understand what they were doing. But first one then another smiled at her and gradually she began to relax.

When it was time for the dinner break, Ivy said cheerfully, 'Come on! I'll show you where the canteen is. They do a decent meal here, meat and veg, plus a pudding, for ninepence, and a penny extra for tea or coffee.'

Lizzie found that for the first time in ages she was starving hungry.

By the end of the week she felt settled in, both at work and at her new lodgings with Mrs Bailey, an elderly widow whose only son was serving at the Front. But she still felt lonely, still missed her family, and when Peggy invited her round for tea on the Sunday, she accepted gladly. She'd found out by now that her new friend was a deputy supervisor as well as a union representative, and was very well thought of by the other women. It seemed fate had been kind to Lizzie for once. What would she be doing now if she hadn't met Peggy at the station?

As she walked home from her new friend's house through the darkness of a chilly March night, she breathed a sigh of thankfulness. She wished she knew how her family were going on, but she wasn't going to get in touch with them for a while. And when she did, she'd have to find a way to get the letter posted from somewhere else, because she wasn't giving them her address. One careless word and Sam would be after her. And next time, he'd kill her for sure.

In late May, James Cardwell was sent home to recover after being wounded. He strolled into the office one day, grinning broadly, his arm in a sling.

Emma surprised herself by bursting into tears of sheer relief and throwing herself into the shelter of his good arm. They'd all heard of the Second Battle of Ypres and the way the Huns were using poison gas, and she'd been terrified for him. She'd tried to ask Mrs Cardwell for news when that lady paid one of her visits to the office to try to bully everyone, but Mrs Cardwell had looked down her nose at Emma and Walter and simply said her husband was fighting bravely at the Front, and that was all they needed to know.

Now, Walter winked at his employer and made himself
scarce, so James drew Emma into his office and shut the door
on the world. 'Nay, lass, don't take on so!'

'I'm sorry! But I've been so worried for you. And you'd
been wounded and she didn't even tell us.'

'I suppose by "she" you mean dear Edith?'

Emma nodded.

'Been giving you any trouble, has she?'

'A bit. But I just listen quietly, agree with whatever she
says, then ignore her instructions.'

He grinned. 'Aye. She's a bit put out that she hasn't been
able to bully you. Been nagging me to change how I've left
things. But I shan't. I'd as soon trust my son Frank to run the
place as her – sooner!'

Emma loved the way he spoke so proudly of his children,
of whom he was very fond. She tried to wipe her eyes, realised
she was still cradled in his arms and blushed furiously as she
pulled away.

'Denying a man a bit of comfort,' he teased.

She looked at him then, her heart in her eyes, worried
by how thin he had become. She opened her mouth to say
something light to defuse the situation then shut it again and
shook her head blindly. 'I wish I could offer you some comfort,'
she said softly.

He muttered, 'Don't tempt me.' Then he took a deep breath
and said briskly, 'Well, let's have a look at the books, then. How
are things going?'

He stayed there all day, though he was looking tired out by
tea-time.

'You should go home,' Emma urged.

'What for? To get another ear bashing?'

'Then go and lie down upstairs. There are some piles of
painters' drop sheets. They should be fairly soft.'

He yawned and nodded. 'Why not? "It is better to dwell
in a corner of the house-top, than with a brawling woman
in a wide house". *Proverbs*, but don't ask me the chapter
and verse.'

Emma chuckled. 'Don't tell me you've taken to reading the Bible?'

He smiled at her. 'It has some beautiful words and poetry in it. And anyway,' he shrugged, 'there isn't much else to read out there. We carry ammunition and food, not books.' His smile faded and he added, 'Besides, when you see young lads getting killed and maimed around you, blown to pieces in front of your eyes, it starts you thinking of your own mortality.' He suddenly saw how white Emma had become and took her in his arms again. 'Sorry, love. I wasn't thinking. We don't usually talk about the gory details when we're back in Blighty.'

This time she didn't pull away. 'But you have to face things like that – every day?'

'Yes.'

They stayed close to one another for a long time and only the opening of the outer office door made them move apart.

'You'll stay behind after work?' he breathed in her ear.

And, heaven help her, she nodded.

Eva looked at her friend and mentor one night as they were finishing their tea. 'Oh, Alice, I do wish we knew where Lizzie was. I worry about her.'

'Wherever she is, she's better off away from that man.'

'I know, but I still wish . . .' Her voice trailed away. After a moment, she said, 'Mr Buckley spoke to me today. He said I could stay at school as a full teacher next year, now I've finished my course.'

'Yes, he told me.'

Eva looked very solemnly at the older woman. 'Dear Alice, I owe you so much. How can I ever repay you?'

'You've more than repaid me by doing well. You're a superb teacher, my dear. And I enjoy your company. Do you – er – want to stay on here, continue living with me?'

'Of course I do.' Eva stole a quick glance sideways. Her friend was being strangely diffident tonight. Was something wrong?

Alice was fiddling with the fringe on the tablecloth. 'The thing is, Eva, I don't want you to feel tied to me, now that you'll be earning enough to live on.'

'Oh, is that what's worrying you? Look,' she tried to explain, 'I've been calling you Auntie Alice ever since we arrived here.' It had seemed the best way to explain why she wasn't living with her family in Overdale. 'Now – well, I feel as if you really are my auntie.'

Alice beamed at her. 'I'm so glad. I've been afraid you might – well, want to go and do war work.'

'No. I'm not very adventurous. I enjoy teaching and I think that's important, too. And at least our school hasn't been taken over to house troops, though it is a tight fit with the extra children crammed in from Westbury School.'

Once the tea things had been cleared away, they sat on at the table peacefully, each with her own preparations to do for the next day's lessons, then later went to relax in the easy chairs by the fire, Miss Blake taking out her embroidery and Eva her library book.

'I do wish I knew where Lizzie was, though,' the girl sighed again as they got ready to go up to bed. 'Surely one day she'll let us know?'

It was not until July that Lizzie found a way to write to her sisters without betraying where she was. Only a genuine fear for her family's safety had made her keep quiet for so long. It wasn't just her own that was in question. If Sam thought they had helped get her away, he would find some way to hurt them. He'd always boasted that he never let anyone get the better of him.

When Peggy said she was going to spend a week in London during her summer holiday, meeting the people at union headquarters and sleeping on the sofa of one of the women organisers, Lizzie suddenly realised that here was her chance.

'Could you post a couple of letters for me while you're there?'

'Of course. Why?'

'I want to let my family know I'm all right.'

'Haven't you done that yet?'

Lizzie looked down at her hands, avoiding Peggy's eyes, which were too knowing. She didn't like talking about her past, didn't even like thinking about her time with Sam, still had nightmares about him discovering where she was and coming to get her. 'No. I don't want to risk Sam finding out where I am. He might hurt them as well as me.'

'Is he so bad? You never talk about him.'

Lizzie nodded and managed to say, 'Worse,' in a hoarse voice. She'd ask Polly to let her brother know about her quietly. She wasn't going to write directly to Percy, because if her mother got hold of the letter, she might tell Sam.

The letter arrived at Redley House a week after Polly had left it to marry Eddie. Why wait? he'd said. He had the promise of a house – only a small place and rather tumble-down, but near his family. He earned enough to support her and had a secure job.

She'd agreed at once, feeling no ties now to Overdale. Percy had got very quiet lately, and sad-looking. He spent all the hours he could at work. And her mother was so strange that people talked openly of her being 'batty' and laughed at her in the street for her girlish clothes. It was so embarrassing to hear tales of her mother's silly doings that Polly had come to hate going into town.

Mrs Frost kept meaning to forward the letter but things were frantic at the big house for she'd not managed to replace Polly yet. So it was two weeks before it got sent on.

Polly burst into tears when she read it. Lizzie had not given her any address to write back to, but someone called Peggy had put the letter in an envelope and scribbled a note saying that if Polly wanted to write to her sister, she should send it to this address in London and write PLEASE FORWARD TO PEGGY on the top left-hand corner.

'What's up?' Eddie asked, when he came home and found his young wife with reddened eyes.

'I've heard from our Lizzie. She's safe. And – and I've burnt your chops!' Polly burst into tears again and found great comfort in his thin but reassuring arms.

'Eeh, lass, I'm that glad for you. Where is she?'

'She doesn't say, but she's got herself a job in munitions and she's made some friends and says she hasn't been as happy for years.' And Polly sobbed all the harder in sheer relief. 'Oh, I do wish I could see her.'

One day after work, Peggy caught up with Lizzie and held her back from the group of girls who lived in the same part of town and always walked home together, tired after their long shift. 'I've got something for you.' She flourished an envelope. 'Recognise the handwriting?'

Lizzie stopped dead in the middle of the pavement, her heart thumping. 'It's Polly's. But how did you—?'

'I got my friend Helen at union headquarters to forward it to me. I had to tell her why, but she's on your side and won't give your address to anyone else. And if you send letters to her, she'll post them to your family for you. So now you do have a way of writing to your sister.' She had to guide Lizzie into a side street and stand with her till the tears had ceased. 'Well, aren't you going to open it?'

'No, I'll save it for later.' Lizzie gave her a tremulous look. 'I'll only cry again when I read it.' Then she threw her arms round Peggy and gave her a big hug. 'I don't know how to thank you! You've been a wonderful friend to me.'

It seemed as if everything in her life had changed for the better since the day she'd met Peggy in the station in Manchester. She had a job, friends, lodgings with a motherly woman, and she was even saving money. After the war, she knew she'd have to think what to do, perhaps emigrate to Australia or somewhere Sam could never find her, but for the moment this suited her fine. And anyway, like most other people, she wanted to do her bit for her country.

CHAPTER TWENTY-FIVE

Spring and Summer 1917

Lizzie saw her twenty-first birthday pass with a sense of unreality. She had been away from Sam for over two years now, and yet still she felt his shadow looming over her. The birthday, which no one else knew about except her, was followed by the month everyone was soon calling 'Bloody April', when the enemy had success after success against British aircraft on the Western Front.

To add to the gloom, Polly wrote to tell her that Jack Dearden had been killed in one of those air battles – indeed, it was a wonder he'd lasted so long – and Lizzie shed a few tears for the happy-go-lucky lad she'd walked with in the park. How long ago that all seemed now. She had been a mere child. Well, at least he'd got to fly his beloved planes.

She wrote a letter to Mrs D expressing her condolences, but still did not dare send it direct from Murforth. Only Polly and Eva knew her address here, for as the months passed without a sign of Sam finding her, she'd relented and told them where she was. She wouldn't let them pass the address on to Percy, though, and she wouldn't let them visit her. It would only take one accident, one person finding out where she was, for Sam to trace her.

As spring lengthened into summer, Lizzie began to feel weary. She was an experienced worker now, having spent time in several of the departments at the munitions factory, moving from one low sprawling work area to the next, learning to know her way through the maze of yards and store-rooms and despatch areas. Peggy, who was now a senior union representative, was trying to get her interested in helping her fellow workers through union activities, but Lizzie knew that sort of thing wasn't for her. Let alone she wasn't clever enough to think things out as Peggy did, and deal with the bosses, she knew that as soon as the war was over she had to get out of the country. Fast.

She had thought and thought about her situation and had come to realise that so long as he was alive, Sam would never willingly let her go. The first thing he'd do when he got out of the Army would be to come looking for her, she was sure. So she had settled on Australia as a destination, because the Australians were sort of like cousins to the English. Well, they were fighting against the Huns side by side, weren't they? And a lot of them came from England originally. So they must be all right. Though the thought of going so far away all on her own terrified her, and sometimes, even living here in Murforth, she was just plain homesick for Overdale and all the people she knew, like Mrs D and Emma Harper.

But she'd not go till after they'd won the war. She was making a difference to the war effort in her own way. She was quite proud of that, proud even of the long scar on one forearm from an accident at the factory. Once the war was won, she'd leave and again tell no one where she was going, not even Peggy. Only this time she'd not write to them. She just couldn't risk it, not if she wanted to feel safe. Sam was a dangerous man when his temper was roused, a very dangerous man. She sometimes wondered if she should even have told Polly and Eva her new address.

On those nights when she still woke from terror-filled nightmares, she would lie there trying to trace the pattern of Sam's obsession with her from the time she'd first walked on the wall, for it had all seemed to start that day, right through to when she was very ill with the influenza – and he had been good to her then, there was no denying that – and then to the way he'd later persuaded her to marry him. Could she have avoided it all? She didn't know. But what puzzled her most, what she could never really understand, was why, if he'd wanted her so badly, he had hurt her so much? Maybe it was some darkness inside him, for other women at the factory talked with fondness of their husbands, never showed any signs of bruising and wept when their fellows were killed.

It seemed to Lizzie now that in the past she had just let herself drift, but she wasn't going to do that again. From now on, she would make her own plans and choose her own path.

In the meantime, the war had brought all sorts of food shortages to complicate daily life, and rumours had it that Britain had only a few weeks' supply left. People were encouraged to have 'meatless days' and most accepted this cheerfully. Lizzie had never been a fussy eater, so she just polished off what was set before her, both by her kindly landlady and in the canteen at work where supplies were slightly better than average, since the girls in the factory were doing such important war work. And anyway, other rumours said Germany was in a far worse state for food. They all took comfort from that thought.

Her landlady had a small back garden planted with potatoes, as did many of their neighbours. They compared progress and exchanged ideas for growing more vegetables. Posters said things like 'Eat Less Bread – save the wheat and help the fleet'.

Mrs Bailey was a bit put out by this. 'I don't know what they expect us to do. If we can't eat meat and we're not to eat as much bread, what *can* we eat? We can't eat potatoes all the time. Or cabbage. And do you know how long I had to queue yesterday to get some margarine, Lizzie? Three-quarters of an hour. It's a bit much, it really is. I know there's a war on, but people still have to live, or why are we fighting?'

Lizzie just made soothing noises and soon they got talking about Mrs Bailey's daughter and her little grandson.

In April, too, the Germans staged a naval raid on Ramsgate, which made everyone furious that civilians, especially children, could be attacked like that. Wanton slaughter, that's all it was. It just went to show the depths to which the enemy would sink when they would fire on innocent citizens not directly involved in the combat. Which was why they had to be stopped.

In May the fighting in France became more desperate and casualty lists grew longer and longer. One or two more of the women at work lost their fellows and that made everyone feel a bit down.

Lizzie couldn't help wishing Sam were among them and she always studied the casualty lists in the papers very carefully. You'd notice a name like Thoxby. But it was never there. She'd feel glad if he died, glad and relieved, even if that was a sinful way to think. But men like him seemed to be protected by the devil and if she knew him, he'd probably come out of the war better off than he went into it. He usually did manage to turn things to his own advantage.

She wrote to Polly from time to time. Her little sister was carrying her first child, which made Lizzie think of her own loss and weep for it again. It was hard not to go and see Polly at this important time, hard too that she talked of little but Eddie and the coming baby in her letters.

In June, Polly wrote to say she had heard from Percy that Sam was still alive and had come back to Overdale on leave, though of course she hadn't seen him herself because she rarely went into town and kept right away if she ever heard he was there. Well, it was no hardship, for her mother was getting barmier by the month and she hated to see her parading round town looking like a scarecrow dressed in party clothes. But it was nice to see Percy now and then. He'd been over to Outshaw a few times now and got on very well with dear Eddie.

As the summer days grew warmer and the sunshine made her itch to get outside, Lizzie allowed herself to be persuaded to spend a day in Manchester with two of the girls from work. They had all been working on night shift for a while and Peggy, now head supervisor, said they needed a break before starting day shifts again, so told them to take a week's holiday and go out and enjoy themselves.

Lizzie felt that with his last visit so recent, Sam couldn't possibly be coming back to England for a while yet, so surely it'd be safe to go? She'd really welcome a change of scene and had never visited Manchester before, except for the railway station where she'd met Peggy.

The city seemed very large and she lagged behind the other girls as they walked from the station through the busy town centre, feeling quite bewildered by it all. There were still fashionably clad ladies around, but they all wore their skirts much shorter than before the war. Her companions pointed and giggled at some of the fussy, draped creations they saw, but Lizzie was more interested in the working women wearing uniforms. A postwoman, a conductress on an omnibus, even a policewoman. How things were changing! Peggy was right – women could do anything the men could. Well, almost anything.

Oh, there were shortages in Manchester, of course, and many shops bore signs asking you to remember there was a war on and only to buy what you needed. Still, there seemed an incredible choice of things for sale after Murforth, though the higher prices made the three young women gasp.

Suddenly, as she was lingering behind the others to stare at some materials in a shop window, since she needed a new summer dress, a voice called out, 'Lizzie! It's Lizzie!' and she swung round, her heart thumping in panic, ready to flee.

But it was Peter Dearden, his hand heavily bandaged, beaming at her from across the street. Without thinking, she ran across the road and flung herself into his arms, so delighted to see him, she didn't even notice the angry shouts of a motorist, some cyclists ringing their bells and a man driving a cart laden with boxes shaking his fist at her.

Neither did Peter. 'You do look well.' He stared down at her, his good hand resting lightly on her shoulder. 'Better than I've ever seen you look, I think. Oh, Lizzie, it's so *good* to see you! And that short hair suits you, it really does.'

She'd given up trying to curl her hair now and had it in a jaw-length bob, with a straight fringe.

'You look well, too,' she said softly, beaming up at him.

At the same moment, they both became aware of his arm around her shoulders, the way their bodies were pressed together, and she jerked away. He took a step backwards, his eyes still devouring her. Why had he not remembered how piquant her face was, how her eyes sparkled with life, how her lips curved so easily into a smile? 'Thank you for writing when Jack got killed. It meant a lot to Mother.'

Tears filled her eyes. 'I felt so sad when Polly told me.' She still couldn't believe that she'd never see Jack's cheeky grin again.

'We were glad to hear from you, and to know that you were getting on all right. You only sent a short note when you repaid the money. You didn't need to do that, Lizzie. We were happy to help you in any way we could and we're not short of money.'

'I needed to pay it back, for my own self-respect.' It was very important to her now that she managed her money well and had some decent savings to help her escape after the war. She looked round for her friends but couldn't see them, and with him standing next to her, so tall and attractive, found she didn't really care.

'Have you time for a cup of tea with an old friend?'

'Of course I have.' She abandoned all thought of finding Mary and Jen. She could make her own way back to the station later. The others would understand when she told them she'd met an old friend who was now a soldier and had been wounded. Everyone wanted to do their best for the boys on leave.

'Come on, then, let's find somewhere really nice.'

It was only when they'd sat down that she realised. 'You're an officer!'

'Only a Lieutenant.'

'Oh, but you must have done well to get promoted from the ranks.'

His face took on a shadowed look. 'Yes, I suppose so. But I'm standing in dead men's shoes, as it were.' He changed the subject quickly. Some things you didn't discuss with civilians. 'What are you doing with yourself nowadays? You didn't say in your letter. Sam hasn't found you, I gather?'

'I'm working in munitions, actually. Doing my bit for the war as well.'

'That doesn't surprise me at all. Have you ever been back to Overdale?'

'No, never.' Not even to retrieve her clothes.

'Mother says your old house is still empty, though *he's* been back a couple of times on leave.' Those visits had coincided with a brick thrown through the window of the shop and a fire lit in the outhouse, but Peter didn't tell Lizzie that. The guilt wasn't hers.

She told him about the munitions work and how she was currently using a press to make detonators, a job where you had to be really careful because one wrong move could cause an explosion and a girl had lost two fingers a few weeks previously. But Lizzie had learned to be very careful during her years with Sam Thoxby and she'd had no trouble so far at the factory. Well, not much.

'You're not yellow,' he teased. 'Not turned into a canary girl, then?'

'No. The chemicals made me ill and I can't stomach milk, which they give you to help with the poison when you're testing the springs, so they took me out of the spinning room after a week.'

'I'm glad. I don't want you getting hurt.'

She looked across the table and found him gazing at her seriously, but with a tender expression on his face, as if he liked what he saw, as if he really did care what became of her. A warm feeling stirred in her stomach. She liked all the Deardens. Then she felt sad as she remembered that there was only him and his mother left now.

'I've often thought about you, Lizzie, wondered how you were getting on,' Peter said softly. 'Do you think – when I go back to the Front – you could write to me? We do look forward to letters from home and Mum's not much of a correspondent.'

Lizzie knew she shouldn't, because there was no future to it, but she nodded anyway. Letters from home helped soldiers endure the horrors of war, for everyone had heard the tales from those who returned permanently, men glad to have copped a Blighty, an injury bad enough to get them out of the Army. One woman at the factory had left suddenly to care for a husband who no longer had any legs and whose lungs had been partly destroyed by mustard gas.

Lizzie and Peter spoke at once, then both laughed. 'Give me your address before we forget,' he said. 'I'll write first, if you like?'

'All right, but I'm called Smith now.'

'I won't forget that, young Lizzie Smith.' He liked it better than Lizzie Thoxby, that was certain.

They borrowed pencil and paper from the sympathetic waitress, who slipped them an extra pot of tea with an admiring glance at Peter.

That made Lizzie look at him anew and realise what an attractive man he'd turned into. It wasn't just the uniform, but the air of assurance he had now. And although he'd never be exactly handsome, his whole face reflected his innate kindness. That had always made folk warm to him and she'd seen several women turn their heads to look at him as they'd walked towards the café.

Lizzie felt a funny little feeling inside as she studied him. If things were different, she could warm to this new Peter herself — but she squashed that feeling instantly. Things weren't different and the minute the war was over she had to get as far away from Sam as she could manage.

'A penny for them,' he said softly.

She opened her mouth to speak, but the words wouldn't come out and she got caught up in staring at him, as he was staring at her, as if he'd never really seen her before.

'Ah, there you are, Lizzie!' a voice called, breaking the spell, and the other girls from the factory came across to join them. 'We've been searching all over for you.' And then it was introductions and general conversation, with Peter buying the others a cup of tea and a scone each, smallish scones, limited to two ounces weight per person by the new regulations.

Just as well we were interrupted, Lizzie decided. But she wished he wouldn't look at her quite so fondly in front of her friends. She took a deep breath and set out to make them all laugh, a talent she'd discovered in herself since working at the factory. And she succeeded, too. It distracted the other girls, anyway, but it didn't take the warmth from the way Peter looked at her.

As they were all parting, he pulled her aside and asked urgently, 'Do you think – you wouldn't be able to get out tomorrow and meet me again, would you? You did say you were on a week's holiday.'

'Well . . .' She looked up at him, then decided on frankness. 'Are you sure that's wise, Peter?'

'I'm not sure it's at all wise, but I do want to see you again. Very much. Please, Lizzie?'

She decided she didn't feel very wise that day, either. 'All right. Tomorrow.'

'Meet me here, then?' He raised one eyebrow. 'Ten o'clock?'

She nodded.

He hesitated, then planted a kiss on her cheek.

Lizzie could feel the imprint of his lips all afternoon.

Her friends teased her all the way home about her 'new fellow' and wouldn't believe her denials. And even Peggy heard about it – Lizzie Smith, who never had anything to do with fellows, had met one in Manchester and he was a bit of all right, too. Being Peggy, she came round and asked bluntly who he was.

'Just the son of my old employer,' Lizzie said quietly. 'And before you say anything, I know I shouldn't be seeing him again, but I've missed everyone so. And – well, he's been injured.'

Peggy gave her a quick hug. 'Go and enjoy yourself for a change, girl. You're far too serious normally. The only fun you have, apart from kidding around at work, is when we drag you down to the cinema.' She grinned for it was a joke in their group that Lizzie had seen every film ever made, most of them more than once, and it was usually she who dragged her friends to the pictures.

After that week, during which she went up to Manchester every day, Lizzie didn't see Peter Dearden again for a very long time. But they wrote, stiffly at first, then more comfortably as they grew used to sharing their thoughts. It was strange how alike they were in their attitudes and opinions nowadays. She received postcards from him as well as letters. Some had cartoons on which made her laugh. Others had war scenes and '*La guerre dans le nord*' written under them – scenes showing streets full of rubble and damaged buildings, or stretcher bearers carrying wounded men along trenches. She had to ask Peggy what the French words meant. Lizzie worried a lot about Peter getting killed as she pored over those postcards, trying to imagine what it was really like out there, and even showed the pictures to her landlady who sometimes shared her son's letters.

Lizzie didn't tell Polly about her meetings with Peter and she didn't share news of him with her co-workers as some girls did. Those letters and cards were her treasures, though, and she read them over and over. Peter's fondness for her showed through, even though he said nothing direct about his feelings. She hoped her own growing fondness for him wasn't too apparent. After this was all over, she rather thought she would take the cards and letters with her to Australia. Just to remember him by. Because she had no right to care for anyone. She was still a married woman.

Sam Thoxby continued to be a loner, but as most of the other men in his platoon and many in his regiment were killed, inevitably those who'd been there from the start began to draw closer together as new platoons were formed and re-formed. He was a sharpshooter now, when occasion required, though the young fool of an officer who'd first noticed his skill with a rifle was long dead.

As the killing continued, he found himself making an

improbable friendship with a cheerful young fellow called Ronnie, who seemed impervious to bullets and whose kindly grin and high spirits won over even a dour fellow like Sam Thoxby. Ronnie was happily married and liked nothing better than to talk about his wife and two small children, reading extracts from his Vi's letters to Sam, who nodded dutifully at intervals while listening intently.

For the first time, he began to realise how much more there could be to a marriage. Ronnie spoke most tenderly of his wife. To listen to him, Vi was perfection itself, and yet from her photo she was a lumpy young woman with crooked teeth.

One day Sam couldn't resist asking, 'Did you ever have to – you know, give her a thump? To make her do what you want?'

'Crikey, no!' Ronnie shook his head emphatically. 'I'd as soon stick my head in a gas oven as lay a finger on my Vi.'

'But what if she does something that upsets you, like?'

'She's bound to do that – and I'm bound to upset her – but we just rub along together, taking the rough with the smooth.' Ronnie looked sideways at him, a thoughtful look on his face. 'Is that what you used to do, thump your wife?' By now he knew that Sam's wife had run out on him.

A nod was the only answer.

'I couldn't do that. I'm much stronger than she is, so it wouldn't be fair. And anyway,' he grinned, 'I reckon she'd take a rolling pin to me if I ever tried it.'

Sam pursed his lips and changed the subject. He didn't sleep well that night. He kept seeing Lizzie's face as it had been against the white hospital pillow, the bruises on it – bruises he'd made – and he kept remembering that he'd killed his own unborn child. Maybe that was why he was a bit more careless the next day and got his first wound. Not a bad one, just a bullet going through the fleshy part of his thigh, but it was deep enough to get him sent back from the Front to a hospital, which gave him more time to think.

He even got some home leave to finish off his recovery and gave young Fred a thorough telling-off about the state he'd let the house in Maidham Street get into. Dora was pleased to come in and clean things up, but she didn't do as good a job as Lizzie had. Nor did she cook very well, either. Lizzie had been a good little cook. And she'd always had everything sparkling clean. And he'd never even said how much he liked that.

It all made him think. You could think too bloody much, that was the trouble. In a strange way, Sam was glad to go back to the Front. And this leave he didn't chuck a brick through Deardens' window, though he had intended to. Well, he had too much on his mind to bother with them snooty sods.

Back in France, he was utterly delighted to see Ronnie still alive. They pounded each other's backs and called each other all the insulting names under the sun, as men will when they're happy to be reunited. And, of course, he had to catch up on Vi's doings and see pictures of the children. Yet again, it made him wish desperately that he had a child of his own. If he was killed now there'd be no one to carry on his name and blood. He'd never thought about that before, not till Ronnie said soberly one night, 'At least I've got a son, so the Rotsons won't die out, whatever happens to me.'

The Thoxby name would die out if he didn't find Lizzie, Sam thought glumly. He'd tried several times to relieve himself with whores, but somehow his heart wasn't in it and he'd failed even to get a proper hard on. Sodding women. They got into your blood. You grew used to them. Sodding everything. Especially this war. Would it never end?

He roused himself to start a chorus and banish the pictures of Lizzie that kept taunting him.

> *O-o-oh, why did we join the Army, boys?*
> *Why did we join the Army?*
> *Why did we come to fight in France?*
> *We must have been bloody well barmy!*

The others joined in, as they always did, and soon the song was ringing down the trenches.

*   *   *

Percy had met Sam in the street while he was home on leave and had stopped for a chat. You couldn't refuse to speak to a soldier who had been wounded in the service of his country. Meg was furious with him for not inviting Sam round for a meal, but he wouldn't do that. It would seem disloyal to Lizzie somehow.

A few days later Percy went round to call on Emma, but she was a bit distracted and Blanche kept watching her secretly, as if worrying about her. So he didn't stay long, just went home to his mother, who had been a little better lately.

'I want to go and see Polly and my grandson,' she announced one night over tea. 'On Sunday. Will you take me?'

'I don't know.' He knew perfectly well that Polly wouldn't be glad to see their mother.

'Well, if you won't come with me, I'll go on my own. It's a poor look-out if I can't see my own grandchild, the only one I'm ever likely to get. It is, that.'

He sighed and when he failed to persuade her out of it, wrote a quick letter to Polly warning her to expect them on Sunday.

In fact, the visit went quite well, though things were a bit stiff at first. Mam was on her very best behaviour and Percy began to relax a little. After a nicer dinner than usual, because food was more plentiful in the country, Polly suggested a walk into the village.

'I'll stay here and have a bit of a nap, I think,' Meg said, snuggling down in Eddie's big armchair. 'I'm not as young as I used to be.'

She looked so sleepy that they all went out together, with Percy pushing the pram, for a treat, and beaming down at his nephew.

When they'd gone, Meg opened her eyes and smiled. She tiptoed round the room, as if they could still hear any noise she made. After a while, when she didn't find what she was seeking, she went upstairs to the little bedroom. There, she went through Polly's drawers, being most careful not to disturb

363

anything. And her search was rewarded for she found some letters from Lizzie.

'Ah!' she breathed. 'I knew they'd be writing to one another. Disloyal cow, she is, running away from a fine man like Sam.'

Carefully she memorised the address, then went back downstairs and settled herself for a real nap. She'd got what she'd come for. They all thought she was batty but she wasn't. She was smarter than they were. And poor Sam deserved some support from his wife's family, indeed he did. Why, he'd even stopped to say hello to her in the street the leave before last and had slipped her a bob to have a drink on him. A fine figure of a man he made in his uniform. Not as handsome as her Stanley had been, but still better than Lizzie deserved.

When the others got back, Meg was snoring gently and Polly, who'd been uneasy about leaving her mother in the house alone, felt relieved to see this hadn't been a ploy. Her mother was looking a lot older lately and had stopped wearing such girlish clothes, settling now for dark garments and calling herself 'a poor widow' in a tremulous voice whenever she wanted to make people pity her.

It was a relief to everyone when Percy said it was time they caught the bus home.

'Your mother's quietening down,' Eddie said, coming to put his arms round his wife after everyone had left.

'She's still a nasty piece.' Polly frowned. 'I wonder why she wanted to come here? She hardly even looked at our Billy.'

'Likely she wanted to be able to boast to her friends about visiting her daughter.'

Polly sighed, but didn't contradict him. His family were so loving that he always thought the best of others. But she wouldn't trust her mother as far as she could throw her. Still, no harm had been done by this visit.

But when there were no more visits, not even a hint of her mother wanting to come and see them again, Polly began to worry. She grew more and more certain that Meg had had some ulterior motive and kept worrying about whether it was something to do with Lizzie. Eddie said she was being silly, but she knew she wasn't. She just knew it.

CHAPTER TWENTY-SIX

Autumn 1917 – December 1917

Sam went back to face the Third Battle of Ypres, which people were afterwards to call by the name of its final objective: Passchendaele. Mud, blood and boredom, they said, and made up little jingles about it. Even Ronnie's cheerfulness was dimmed by now, and for all of them each day, each hour, of this interminable conflict was a matter of grim endurance, worse than ever before somehow. If they had any doubts about who would win this marathon, they didn't voice them, though, just tried to hang on.

In another part of the same battle, James Cardwell was injured – badly enough to be sent home to Blighty, but not badly enough to threaten his life. A bullet thumped into one forearm, breaking the bone, and another bullet zipped a furrow in his cheek.

'You've been lucky, my old son,' the doctor said cheerfully. 'They seem to like hitting you in the arm. I prescribe two months back home with your wife. There's nothing complicated about your injuries, though you'll be left with a scar on that cheek. You just need time to heal and you might as well do that at home.'

Afterwards, James lay there quietly on the narrow hospital cot, but it wasn't his wife he was thinking about. The two of them seemed even farther apart than before, and not because of the war – mainly because he and Edith were chalk and cheese. If it weren't for the children, he'd leave her tomorrow. If it weren't for the scandal, and the money he brought in, Edith would leave him, too. She had never tried to write him letters, just sent postcards with love from the children, and he sent only postcards, too. Sometimes the children wrote, though, funny little notes, which he kept in his wallet and re-read often.

He had heard from other sources that Edith had been seen in mixed groups, driving round the countryside in fast cars, drinking in isolated hotels. He simply tossed away the letter from the anonymous 'well-wisher' that hinted at worse. Who was he to cast the first stone when he longed, absolutely longed, to be unfaithful to her? Though he would, he decided grimly, draw the line at bringing up another man's child.

He nurtured a faint hope that Edith would meet someone whom she could love, but it was only faint because he wasn't sure she was capable of loving any man as much as she loved herself. Still, if she did meet someone, he might have a chance of a divorce . . . he did not allow himself to dwell on that hope. Well, only in bleaker moments, when he needed something good to think about.

When he got back to Overdale, James spent a couple of days lying around, enjoying the peace, the decent food, and the wonderful lack of lice, battle noises and cries of pain. Most of all, he enjoyed the company of his children. Young Frank was twelve now, a sturdy lad who looked very like James's father but hopefully had more backbone. And Doris, his 'little princess', was ten. Surprising how Edith's heavy features could be transformed into prettiness and how her daughter could have such a sunny nature.

On the third day, he grew bored and decided to go and see how his business was doing.

'What'll people think?' Edith stormed. 'Home because you're wounded, but well enough to go to work. Let *her* see to things. That's what you pay her for, isn't it? Though a poor job she's making of it, I can tell you . . .'

Letting her shrill voice trail him down the hallway, he walked out of the house without a backward glance, not even bothering to close the door. The fresh, clean air felt wonderful, though the sun had lost its warmth now and the leaves were beginning to turn. He didn't hurry, just strolled through the streets, enjoying Overdale's smallness, the cosiness of its two low hillsides full of houses, and its single street of shops. Most of all, he enjoyed the fact that none of these houses had been reduced to rubble and that folk still had a relatively cheerful look to them. To him, this town was a microcosm of what they were all fighting for: the right to live a decent life in a free country.

He didn't mind how many times he was stopped for a chat as he strolled along. He felt expansive, relaxed. Home was this town, not the house he shared with his wife. Best of all, he was going to see Emma again, dearest Emma, to whom he didn't even dare write for fear of people gossiping, though he had sent regular postcards addressed jointly to her and Walter at Cardwell's.

When he walked into the office, she was busy dealing with a customer, so he sat down in the waiting area and listened to her low, musical voice explaining the obvious for the second time. He grinned. If it'd been him, he'd have been a lot sharper with old Mr Barton.

As the customer left, Emma came to the doorway with him out of politeness, saw James and turned bone white.

He stepped forward hastily, greeting Mr Barton, distracting his attention and gesturing to her to return to the office as he showed the man out and answered yet more stupid questions about life in the trenches. As if a returned soldier wanted to talk about that!

When he went back to join Emma, she was waiting just inside the office, leaning against the wall as if she hadn't the strength to stand upright. She was still pale, but with such a glow in her eyes that the world receded to a great distance and there seemed to be only the two of them together in an oasis of joy.

Her voice said, 'I heard you were back.' Her eyes, though, said a whole lot more as they raked him from head to toe, as if she needed to make sure of every inch of him.

His voice said, 'Yes, I came back a few days ago.' But his eyes, too, spoke of his feelings, he knew, for the love was welling up in him even as he was reaching out for her with his good arm, pulling her towards him, kicking the door shut with his left foot.

Then he had hold of her and could crush her against him and kiss her as he'd dreamed of doing during all those long nights in the trenches; nights where you dreaded yet longed for the morning, whose assault might well see your last moments of life. 'Where's Walter?' he whispered as they drew apart for a moment to catch their breath.

'Out on a job.'

'Any appointments?'

'No.' It was a breath of a word only.

'I'll go and lock up, then.'

'Your arm—'

'Doesn't matter.'

She didn't protest, just subsided on the edge of the desk as if her legs were no longer strong enough to hold her up.

When he came back in, she simply held out her arms to him and gathered him to her breast with a sob of thankfulness, tracing the new red scar across his cheek with one tender fingertip and pressing kisses on it. He was home, he still wanted her and that was enough for the moment.

It was an eternity later, as they were lying back spent, that he realised. 'Oh, hell! I didn't do anything to protect you.'

Emma hadn't even thought of that. 'I dare say one slip won't hurt.'

He planted a kiss on her cheek and shifted awkwardly to favour his broken arm. 'I'll get something before tomorrow.' He grinned. 'But you'll have to put it on for me.'

The next few weeks were a golden interlude. Edith complained fretfully that he was never home, or if he was, he spent all his time with the children. James shrugged and murmured something about, 'Giving everything at the office a thorough checking over.'

Walter found a dozen jobs to keep him out of the yard.

Blanche didn't comment on the long hours her sister was spending at work – or her starry-eyed and slightly dishevelled appearance when she returned home.

And to set the seal on their isolation, a period of heavy rain drove away potential customers – except for a couple whose roofs had sprung a leak.

Even before his convalescent leave drew to an end, Emma had begun to wonder if that first careless love-making had left her with a more tangible proof of James's devotion – but she didn't, couldn't regret that. To have his child seemed a wonderful thing, in spite of all the practical difficulties it would involve.

But she didn't burden him with her suspicions, for he had to go back to war, a war so dreadful that he wouldn't tell her any details or talk about it at all if he could help it. And although Emma suspected that Blanche had guessed her secret, she didn't say anything to her sister, either. For a time, just for a very short and precious time, she wanted to hold the knowledge and the joy of carrying his child close to her heart. The world would tarnish her pleasure all too soon.

In that particular corner of the French landscape, the fighting raged round them all day. Sam cursed his way through it, wondering why the hell the brass wanted to recapture another stupid patch of mud. He managed to stay alive, which was what he cared about most, and managed to kill a few of the enemy, which was his secondary purpose in life.

Just before noon, he got a nick on the forehead which bled for a bit, but that was bugger all. At one point, he helped Ronnie get out of a tight situation; at another Ronnie helped him. The two of them seemed to have grown much closer in the past few weeks.

'Real pals,' Ronnie had said one quiet, moonlit evening. 'That helps most of all out here, doesn't it?'

And Sam had simply grunted his agreement, since he could

never have put that sort of thing into words. But he had grinned at his mate and feinted a blow at his chin.

The only time the two of them had disagreed lately was when Ronnie tried to persuade him not to hit his wife again. The idea had upset Ronnie and he'd referred to it several times. Sam just told him to shut his trap when he got in that sort of mood – usually after a letter from Vi. But he was secretly amazed that something so unimportant mattered so very much to his mate, who had never even met Lizzie.

The following day all hell erupted round them and within an hour of the battle starting something thumped Sam hard in the chest. He felt himself falling and to his surprise couldn't get up. Bullets flew around him and he could only lie there, too astonished to feel any pain.

Ronnie's face appeared above him. 'You stupid sod. You should have dodged that bullet!'

'Am I shot?' Sam murmured, his voice hoarse for lack of water.

'Yes, but we'll soon get you out of here.' And Ronnie proceeded to drag him back towards their own line.

'Look after yourself!' Sam managed. 'Get down lower.'

'I'll look after us both.'

They nearly got back to their own line safely, but some rotten enemy bastard must have been watching and laughing at them as he aimed his rifle, because he waited till they were within a couple paces of the trenches to let fly. Sam felt something smash into his foot and couldn't help a roar of pain.

Above him, Ronnie jerked and staggered, saying, 'I've bought one,' in a tone of astonishment. He crumpled slowly and fell forward, lying with his head resting on Sam's arm.

For a moment the war receded and there were only the two of them in the whole universe.

'Thought I was going to make it,' Ronnie whispered.

'You still will. They'll pull us out in a minute and patch us up. You'll see. Just hold on.'

Ronnie's smile was the sweetest Sam had ever seen. 'Nay, lad, I'm done for. I can feel it – it's all – ebbing away.' He closed his eyes for a moment, then opened them again to stare at Sam. 'There's good in you, lad,' he whispered, 'if you'll only give it a chance.'

Sam stretched out his hand to touch Ronnie's hair and it got covered with red. 'Save your strength,' he ordered. 'Just hold on.'

'Promise me,' the shadow of a voice insisted, 'promise me you'll not hit her again?'

Sam felt a wetness on his cheeks and realised he was crying, he who'd not cried since he was a tiny lad. When he looked at Ronnie's face, he could see death creeping across it. He'd seen it too many times to mistake it. Suddenly it was important that he do one last thing for the closest friend he'd ever had. 'I promise,' he said.

Ronnie's face lit up 'That's my best mate. And,' he was struggling to speak now, blood frothing on his lips, but still he forced a few more words out, 'write – tell Vi – my last thought was of her.'

'I will, lad, I will!' Sam found sobs tearing at his throat and didn't even try to hold them back. When he blinked away the rush of tears, he saw that Ronnie's face was very still – and very peaceful. It almost made him want to go wherever his mate had gone, because he had never felt so at peace in all his life.

He lay there weeping silently for a very long time before anyone came and rescued him. And he wept a lot in hospital, too.

'You've copped a Blighty one, lad,' a young doctor said, standing beside his bed one night, his face nearly grey with fatigue. 'You'll limp for the rest of your life, but I think the rest of you will recover, given time.'

And Sam couldn't even raise the energy to care.

He was in hospital for a very long time, it seemed, and it wasn't till a new nurse came along, a nurse with dark hair and greenish eyes – though they weren't half as bright as Lizzie's – that he began to pick up again.

'You know, you could go home if you had someone to look after you,' she said one night.

Sam, who hadn't been able to sleep the night before for thinking about Ronnie and Lizzie and the whole bloody mess his life had turned into, just glowered at her. All he had left was his money, most of it still safely hidden, and what the hell use was that with no one to spend it on? What the hell use was anything?

'Well, I don't have anyone. There's only my wife an' she buggered off and left me back in '15.'

'Well, shame on her.'

'I'll find her again,' he said quietly, expressing for the first time the determination that had been growing within him as he got better and became used to walking with a limp. 'Lizzie's mine and she's coming back to me. I'll find her and make her.'

The nurse frowned at him. 'You're not going to hurt her, are you?' For he was a large man and several times they had wondered if he was going to thump the orderly for nagging him into doing something he didn't want to.

He let out an irritated growl. 'I promised my mate as he lay dying not to thump her again so I'll not hit her, but I'll drag her back by the hair if I have to.'

'You must love her very much.'

He looked at her, with her la-di-da voice, her shining hair and pink skin, and the next growl was closer to laughter. 'Folk like you call it love, I suppose. I just – she's mine, you see, an' she always has been.'

The nurse felt a glimmer of pity for the wife. He couldn't be an easy man to live with.

When Meg saw Sam Thoxby limping along York Road, her eyes lit up and she hurried across the street to him, nearly getting run down by an omnibus in her hurry. She stopped to exchange insults with the driver, brandishing her fist and screeching at him, then clutched her bosom as another fit of coughing took her.

When it died down, she hid the blood-stained handkerchief hurriedly in her pocket and turned towards where Sam had been standing. To her disappointment he was nowhere to be seen. Funny, that. She'd thought he'd noticed her, but he couldn't have.

Twice she walked up and down the main street, peering at the passers-by and rushing into one shop when she saw a head of ginger hair. But it wasn't Sam so she rushed out again, afraid of missing him.

In the end, she decided he must have gone home and turned in the direction of Maidham Street, feeling distinctly dizzy now. Eeh, those fits of coughing were getting worse. She'd have to get some stronger medicine from the chemist's, she would that. No use going to the doctor's. Doctors didn't know anything, especially lady doctors like that Dr Marriott. Meg wasn't really ill, not her, she just had a bit of a cough. And it was better to be lean than fat, whatever Percy said. The lean ones lived the longest because they had less to carry round with them. She'd outlive him, with his ticky heart, and she'd probably outlive Lizzie, too. Meg scowled, as she always did at the thought of her eldest daughter, then smiled grimly. Well, she'd found out where that young trollop was living. Oh, yes. She'd fooled her family. That Polly had always been slow on the uptake. And now – now she was going to tell Sam where his wife was, as she'd planned to do.

When she fell over in the street, she clicked her tongue in annoyance, but felt so tired she just lay there for a while gathering her strength. Voices hummed around her and she opened her eyes for a moment. 'Bugger off and let a poor widow woman have a bit of a rest,' she said, but the words came out in a jumble.

When she next woke, she was in hospital and there was a nurse fussing with the bedclothes.

'Oh, you're awake, are you, Mrs Kershaw? Let me take your temperature.'

Meg spat out the thermometer. 'Wann – g'home,' she managed. What had happened to her voice?

'I'm afraid you can't go home just now, dear. You're not at all well. But we've sent for your son and he'll be here soon.'

Percy didn't arrive for another hour, by which time Meg was raging with frustration. She'd heard the nurse talking to a doctor who had come to peer at her a few minutes ago. On her last legs, indeed! What did they know about anything? She was just tired. And no wonder. She'd had a hard life, and no help from her three ungrateful daughters. Which reminded her of Lizzie. And Sam. It even made her smile for a moment – till the next nurse came along and pestered her to swallow something she didn't want.

When he saw his mother, Percy stopped dead in shock. She had a shrunken look to her, as if she had suddenly become much smaller, and she was so thin she hardly made a bump under the neatly arranged covers.

'Just a few minutes,' the nurse told him.

Meg clutched Percy's arm. 'Sh'm,' she managed. 'Gorra – see 'um.'

'What? I can't make out what you're saying, Mam.'

She would have shaken him if she'd had the strength. 'Sh'm!' She tried again and at last the word came out clearly. 'Sam!' Her fingers dug into his hand.

He stared down at her. What maggot had got into her now?

'Sam,' she repeated, her face twisting with frustration.

Well, why not humour her? The doctor said she was failing fast. A stroke, and she had lung trouble as well.

'Do you want me to fetch Sam to you, Mam?'

'Esss. Sam.'

He stayed a few more minutes, but she didn't try to say anything else so he left.

*　　*　　*

Sam muttered in annoyance as someone knocked on the door. He limped down the hall and flung it open. 'What do you want?'

Percy nodded a greeting. 'Could I come in a minute? I – I want to ask a favour of you.'

Sam shrugged and led the way through to the kitchen, sinking into a chair because his mangled foot still hurt when he stood on it too long.

'How are you getting on?' Percy asked politely.

'All right. Seen any sign of your bloody sister?'

'No.'

'She's not written to you?'

'No.' Percy didn't say that she wrote regularly to his sisters. He had promised to tell no one that.

'What do you bleedin' want with me, then?'

Percy cleared his throat. It had been silly to come here, but he had to ask. 'My mother's in hospital. She, er, wants to see you.'

Sam stared at him. 'Well, I don't want to see her.' He'd already seen her in the street, looking like a little black scarecrow, but had managed to avoid her.

'She's dying.'

About time, too, Sam thought. 'So? What business is that of mine?'

'She's desperate to see you.'

Then it suddenly occurred to Sam that the old lady might know where her daughter was. If she did, she'd tell him, because she'd never liked Lizzie. 'Oh, all right, then. You'll have to go and get a cab, though. I can't walk far yet.'

'Thanks, lad.'

Sam shrugged. 'Well, we have to help one another, don't we?' A picture of another dying face came back to him suddenly. He'd written to Ronnie's wife from the hospital to pass on his friend's last words, and received a tear-stained note in reply, thanking him for his trouble. And that was that. His best mate just wiped out.

*   *   *

The Sister didn't want to let them in. 'It's not visiting hours,' she declared, hands on hips.

Sam gestured down to his injured leg. 'I can't walk so well since I copped this in France. Couldn't you just make an exception, for once? I promise you we won't make any noise.'

She pursed her lips, then let out a long breath. 'Oh, very well. But only this once. And only one of you at a time.'

Percy sighed. 'I'll wait here for you.'

Meg jerked into wakefulness as Sam sat down beside the bed. Not until she had hold of his arm did she believe it was him, because she'd seen her Stanley a little while ago and he was dead, so she must be feverish. But Sam's arm was warm and solid.

'What can I do for you, then, Mrs Kershaw?'

She tried to laugh, but only a gasp came out. ''Swhat I c'n do f'you.'

He just frowned.

'L'zie.'

'Ah!' He leaned closer. 'Do you know where she is?'

She nodded. 'Murforth.' The word came out all jumbled, so Meg tried again, and this time he repeated it correctly after her.

'Whereabouts in Murforth?'

She tried to say the street name, but her tongue tied itself in knots, so she drew it out on the warm palm of his hand, letter by letter.

'Right. I've got that. Willow Street. What number?'

She drew that out, too.

He leaned forward to grasp her shoulder. 'Thank you, Mrs Kershaw. I'm very grateful.'

She lay back on her pillow, beaming at him, then flapped her hand and tried to tell Stanley to get out of her way but he wouldn't leave. He kept pulling at her arm, wanting her to go with him. She sighed and gave in, as she always had done when Stanley was determined about something.

Sam waited for her to open her eyes again, then something in the stillness of her face made him realise that the old bitch had just gone and died on him. 'Nurse!' he yelled. 'Nurse, come here quick!'

Eva went to Overdale for her mother's funeral and felt absolutely nothing except relief as she watched the coffin being lowered into the ground. Beside her, Polly was calm and tearless, looking thoughtful rather than grief-stricken, for she had heard about her mother calling for Sam and couldn't understand why.

Only Fanny Preston was there, apart from the family, because Meg had alienated her neighbours one by one over the past year or two. When they were walking home, Fanny, who was a bit overawed by how posh Eva talked, mumbled an excuse and went off back to Bobbin Lane, to her own house.

The family sat around drinking cups of tea and eating the sandwiches Polly had prepared. When Johnny, now thirteen, had filled his belly, he went off to visit one of his friends, and then Eddie took Polly to catch a train home.

Eva made no attempt to catch an early train, because she wanted to have a heart-to-heart with her brother, who had sacrificed so much for his family. 'What are you going to do with yourself now, love?'

He shook his head, too tired to think straight. He still kept expecting to hear his mother wailing about something, or flying into a tantrum, or erupting into one of those dreadful coughing fits which had punctuated the last few months. 'I don't know. It happened so suddenly. I haven't got used to it yet.'

'You can have a life of your own now, marry perhaps.'

'No.'

'You're only twenty-eight. You'll meet someone and—'

'No!' Suddenly he had to share it, having held it inside him for too long. 'There is someone only she loves another fellow.' He shrugged. 'You can hardly blame her. I'm no film star. And with my heart . . .'

'You know the doctor told you that if you took things easily, you could live a perfectly normal life.'

He just shrugged, his expression bleak, his eyes looking inwards.

'Who is she?'

'Doesn't matter.'

Eva laid one hand on his. 'Oh, Percy, I'm sorry. So very sorry.'

He roused himself to smile at her, squeezing her hand in reply. 'I'm used to it now. When are *you* going to find yourself a fellow? Pretty lass like you. They should be queuing up at your door.'

It was her turn to shrug. 'I don't want to get married. Look what happened to our Lizzie.'

'Fellows aren't all like Sam Thoxby. And any road, he seems different since he got back. Why, he even came to see Mam in hospital when I asked him.'

'A leopard doesn't change its spots.'

They were both silent for a moment, then Eva said very quietly, 'I think Lizzie's going to go away once the war is over.'

'What do you mean – away?'

'Australia or America. Somewhere *he* won't be able to find her.'

'You and our Polly have never told me where she is.'

'Because you might have let something out by mistake. If Mam had found out, she'd have told *him*.' She hesitated. 'If I told you now, you wouldn't tell him, would you?'

'Never! He doesn't deserve a nice lass like our Lizzie. Even if he has changed, I'd not trust her to him again.' Percy swallowed a sob. 'I've never forgotten – never – what she looked like in hospital after he'd bashed her. And how unhappy she was after he stopped her running away with Polly.'

'She was coming to me, you know. And if she had come, we'd have got her away, Alice and I.'

'You've always had more sense than me. So – where is she?'

'At Murforth. Working in munitions.'

'So close!'

'Yes.'

'I could go over and see her, then.'

'If you were careful that no one was following you, why not?'

'Eeh!' His eyes filled with tears. 'That'd be the best start to next year I could get, seeing our Lizzie again.'

Christmas Eve was one of the nicest times Lizzie could remember. All the girls who had no family got together and had a party. She drank two shandies and felt tiddly, for she had no head for booze, and as they sat round the piano singing, she thought of Peter, whose last letter had said very definitely that he wanted to see her after the war, that he wanted to help her do something about 'the problem standing between us'. There was no future for them – Lizzie acknowledged that even if he didn't – but still it was nice to be wanted by a good-looking man, a Captain now. And if things were different, well – she sighed at the thought – there was no one she'd want more.

Suddenly she had had enough noise, so she slipped out while they were still singing and made her way home alone, enjoying the crisp, frosty night and the hard twinkle of stars shining down from an almost clear sky. Mrs Bailey was away, staying with her daughter who had just had another baby, and the other lodger had gone home to her family for a couple of days, so Lizzie had the house to herself, for once. Which made a nice change.

As she was opening the door, she felt a sudden awareness of someone standing behind her and turned to see her worst nightmare come true. 'Sam!' The word was a whisper, then she fainted clear away.

CHAPTER TWENTY-SEVEN

On Christmas Eve, Blanche finished her meal, then laid one hand on her sister's and said quietly, 'Don't you think it's about time you told Mr Cardwell about the baby? It'll start showing soon.'

Emma stared at her. 'You know, then?' She had begun to wonder, with time passing and Blanche saying nothing.

'We live very closely together, dear. You've missed your monthlies the last few times and you've been looking distinctly queasy some mornings, though you've tried to hide it from me.'

'Oh, Blanche, I was so frightened to tell you!'

They stared at one another for a moment, then Blanche got up and went to put her hands on her sister's shaking shoulders. 'Did you think I'd disown you?'

'I thought — thought you'd despise me. Be ashamed of me.'

'You're my sister, the only relative I care about. If you're in trouble, then I'm here to help you. The question is, what are you going to do? You haven't told him yet, have you?'

'No.'

'I thought not.'

'He has a right to know.'

Emma stared down at the tablecloth, making patterns in the crumbs on her bread plate. 'But what can he do? He already has a wife and family.'

'He can help you financially at least. It's his child, too.'

'I'll write to him after Christmas, I promise.'

'Good. But even if he doesn't see his way to helping, we'll

work things out. We can manage on my annuity and our savings for quite a while, then I could look after the baby if you went back to work and—'

At that, Emma let the worries slide off her shoulders, put her head down and sobbed her heart out. She'd been carrying this burden for two months now and it was such a relief to share it with someone.

When her sister had stopped weeping, Blanche guided her upstairs and put her into bed. 'What you need now is rest. Set your worries aside until after Christmas. We'll sort it all out then.'

At the door she turned to smile. 'Actually, I'm rather excited about becoming an aunt.'

When Lizzie came to, she was lying on the couch in Mrs Bailey's parlour and Sam was sitting beside her, patting her hand. She closed her eyes again, trying to gather her determination together, then opened them and stared at him.

'I'm not coming back to you, Sam, even if you kill me for it.'

'You bloody are, if I have to drag you every inch of the way.'

'That's exactly what you'll have to do, and then tie me up. If you leave me alone for even one minute, I'll start walking away.' She had always promised herself that if he found her, she'd show no sign of fear and she wouldn't give in to him, not in the smallest degree. She held her breath, waiting for him to thump her, but he didn't, just sat there, looking solemn.

When he didn't speak, she didn't either, waiting to see what he would do.

'You're my wife,' he said at last. 'You belong with me. And I *want* you with me.'

'Well, I don't feel like your wife any more, not since you started thumping me – and I'm not coming back to live like that. I'd rather die.' And perhaps she would do just that tonight.

'You've got another fellow,' he accused, his face turning a dusky red with anger.

'No. I've never forgotten that I'm a married woman.'

'If you're a married woman, you belong with your husband.'

'Not any more.'

'Why not?'

'I've told you. Because you thump me – because you don't love me – because you don't even know what love is.'

He frowned and stared down at her ringless hand, which he was holding tightly in his. Then, suddenly, he told her about Ronnie and his promise.

Lizzie listened quietly, then shook her head. 'I don't believe you. You may think you mean it, you may even stop hitting me for a while, but you'll start again.'

'You don't understand – he was my best mate. He was dying!'

'You'll not be able to keep that promise.'

'I *told* you . . .' He broke off, realising that he'd got hold of the front of her dress and was holding her up in the air like a rag doll. He let her drop back on to the sofa. 'I *told* you – that sort of thing is all finished now.'

'Even if it was, I'd not come back to you, Sam. We should never have married. We don't suit. I make you unhappy as well as you making me unhappy.'

Anger exploded in him, throbbing through his whole body, and he had to fight it back, fight the urge to smash his fist into her small, white face for saying something as horrendous as that. But he didn't, no, he didn't thump her as she deserved. He kept his promise to his mate. When he had control of himself, he repeated, 'You're my wife. You have to come back. And I've a right to force you.'

She was lying with one arm covering her eyes, clearly expecting a blow. He stopped speaking to stare at her in bafflement, then at the softness of her arm, the gleam of her black hair, the slight curves of her breasts. Desire began to rise in him for the first time in years. He reached out one hand to touch the nearest breast and Lizzie tried to knock it away. He laughed softly then. He wouldn't thump her. He'd keep his promise to Ronnie about that. But he had a right to her body.

Sam took hold of her as if she were a child and began to take off her clothes, smiling and muttering encouragements to himself. He'd forgotten how small she always felt in his arms, how beautiful the white skin of her body was.

She was sobbing and fighting and pleading with him not to touch her, but he ignored that. He had a right. A husband's right. And he wasn't hitting her.

To his sorrow and annoyance, Lizzie continued to fight him every inch of the way, sobbing and pleading for him to stop. He pulled her to the floor and finished removing her clothes, then held her with one hand while he undid the buttons on his trousers and shrugged out of his braces.

Then he lay down beside her and took her quickly and savagely, exploding into her like one of those bloody shells that crashed into the trenches sometimes. He roared out his pleasure, but as he began to come to himself again, looked down at her angrily, for she was sobbing as if her heart was broken.

'You're my wife, Lizzie,' he repeated quietly. 'You always will be. And I'll *never* let you go.'

Then he pulled her into his arms, waiting for the tears to stop. A little later, as desire rose, he took her again, more slowly. And again, she wept.

On Christmas morning, Sam woke up and smiled to see Lizzie sleeping by his side, tied to his wrist. He lay there quietly and studied her face. She'd grown up. She looked like a woman now, not a girl. He liked that. And she had a scar on one arm. How had she got it? Then he felt that stirring again and was nearly inside her by the time she woke.

'No!' she screamed. 'No, no, no!' For she'd been dreaming that his return was just another of her nightmares. Only he was too big and sweaty to be a figment of her imagination.

Struggle as she might, she was no match for him and he took her at his leisure. Then he made her get dressed and when she at first refused, said simply, 'We're going home. If you don't put your clothes on, I'll drag you naked through the streets, Lizzie. I mean that.'

She bit back a sob and began to pick up her clothes.

He watched her, enjoying the sight of her dainty underclothing, staring out of the window from time to time, for it had started to snow. 'Now get all your things packed. There'll be trains to Overdale this afternoon.'

'I can't go there. I've got a job here, in munitions.'

'You can just forget that. You've a job looking after your husband now. I've been invalided out with this bleedin' foot.'

'Can I just leave them a note?' Maybe Peggy would think of some way to help her, for her friend would understand that she'd never go back to Sam willingly.

'You can send them a letter from Overdale.' Suddenly he was anxious to get home again, anxious for Lizzie's touch in the house. She'd make it shine like it used to. She'd cook him meals and wash his clothes. And he'd prove to her that he'd given up thumping her. It'd take a bit of time, but he'd make it all happen because that was how he'd planned it.

She packed a suitcase, managing to leave Peter's letters in their hiding place at the back of a drawer, and slipping her savings in among her things, hidden in the book she'd hollowed out specially to hide them. Sam was watching everything she did, but he didn't seem to notice anything different about the book, though she'd had to glue the edges of the pages together to make the hiding place.

With him carrying the suitcase and her arm firmly circled by his meaty fingers, she walked along the street beside him, hoping to see one of her friends but meeting no one she knew. Lizzie began to feel desperate. This was like a nightmare and she was still sore from Sam's forcing himself upon her. But, she told herself fiercely, she wasn't going to give in to her fear this time.

She'd meant exactly what she said. Unless he spent every single moment by her side, he'd not be able to keep her with him. If she had to walk barefoot across the moors to Yorkshire to get away from him, she'd do it. Never, ever again, would she just stay passively with him, jumping to obey him.

And anyway, she'd managed to bring her savings with her. The thought of the money was her only consolation at the moment. It might at least give her a start on running away to Australia. She'd not dare to come back to Murforth now.

OVERDALE. She stared at the sign through the train window and Sam had to pull her to her feet. She'd thought about this place so often and now she was back – but not to stay. She was glad to get off the train, which had been crowded with people wishing each other 'Merry Christmas'. When they'd said it to her, she'd just stared at them, unable to form a word in reply. It was the most ghastly Christmas of her life. Hell could be no worse than this.

'My wife's been ill,' Sam had said to the other passengers.

After that, people left her alone, giving her sideways glances as if they thought she was crazy.

He kept hold of her arm all the way home, forcing her to walk with him through the whirling snow, for it was coming down more heavily now. They passed a couple of people she knew, but when they called out greetings and would have stopped to ask how she was, Sam just nodded and hurried her past them.

By the time they got to Maidham Street, she was panting and he was limping badly. The little row of houses looked like a Christmas scene from a magazine, with roofs and window sills covered in white. People had decorations in their windows, bits of greenery, red paper flowers – every house had something. Except hers. Keeping up morale, that was called, or 'giving our boys a taste of home happiness'.

Sam had to thrust her through the front door, and even then Lizzie didn't move till he shoved her roughly along the hall into the kitchen. It was bitterly cold and everything was in a mess. 'I got some food in,' he said. 'I'm bloody famished.'

She sat down on a chair and folded her arms. 'Well, I'm not cooking for you.' She stared into his face. 'I mean it, Sam. I won't be a wife to you in any way. I won't housekeep for you, or wash for you, and you'll have to force me every time you want to do it. I'm never going to live with you willingly again.'

'You'll live with me, willingly or not.'

She just sat there.

He raised his hand to thump her, then let it drop and muttered, 'Sorry, Ronnie.'

Lizzie was hungry and cold, but she'd sit here and freeze before she lifted a finger, she decided. So she just watched as he lit a fire, grunting awkwardly as he knelt and jarred his bad foot. Good. He deserved to be hurt. He'd hurt her already.

He stood up. 'Lizzie, please—'

She just stared at him, not even bothering to shake her head.

He turned round and thumped one fist into the door, cracking a wooden panel. But still he didn't touch her and she found that unnerving. When he looked at her, anger was burning in his eyes, but something else gradually replaced it.

'Well, lass, if you won't do the housework, we'll have to keep ourselves warm in other ways, to take our minds off our hunger.'

When he reached for her, she let herself go limp and tried to slide to the floor. He had to carry her up the stairs. And take her clothes off. The thrusting and hurting seemed to go on for a very long time before he managed to get his release this time.

'Why won't you be a wife to me?' he yelled after he'd rolled off.

'Because I hate you!'

He smashed one hand into the pillow, then sat up again. 'I need a bloody drink.'

When he went downstairs, she got dressed again, as warmly as she could, then tiptoed after him, wondering if she could rush out. But he appeared in the doorway of the front room, with a bottle of rum in his hand, and grabbed hold of her. The bottle was nearly empty.

He dragged her into the kitchen, which was a lot warmer now, and plonked her down forcibly on one of the chairs, then drained the bottle and stared at it in disgust. 'A man needs a drink on Christmas Day,' he muttered.

She wondered if he'd go out to find one. Unless things had changed greatly, he'd only have to knock on the back door of the Carter's Rest to buy another. The landlord there was always ready to make a bit extra. Maybe that'd give her a chance to get away. She pulled her chair up to the table, laid her head on her hands and closed her eyes, exhausted now. 'I'm not getting it for you.'

He put his overcoat on again, keeping the hall door open, never for a minute letting her out of his sight.

She lay still. Maybe if she feigned sleep . . .

Suddenly he was beside her, a length of rope in his hand. 'You didn't think I'd leave you free to run away did you, Lizzie girl?' He chuckled as he tied her up. 'I'm not that stupid.'

'You'll not keep me here with you for ever.'

He grinned. 'No, just till your belly's swelling. Then you'll find it a bit harder to run.' He thrust his face against hers. 'And if you're thinking of that money you've got saved up, I found that this morning when you were in the bathroom and I went through your things.' He fumbled in his pocket and waved the notes at her. 'I left you the change, but this'll come in useful.'

She felt physically sick as she watched him pile coal on the fire, then walk out. The rope was firmly tied, too firmly for her to escape. She looked around desperately, hoping to find something sharp to rub it on, but she couldn't even move the chair, because he'd tied that to the table leg. She was as firmly trussed as any chicken going to market. And as bound for disaster.

Despair swept through her. She had never felt so bleak and unhappy, not even when she'd lived here with him last time, because now she had tasted freedom – and friendship – and the satisfaction of a job well done.

*　　*　　*

Christmas Day was just like any other at the Front. The first year of the war they'd called a truce for the day and some had even fraternised with the enemy, but now there was no question of that. You never knew when the fighting was going to start again, when a sniper's shot would zip past you or tear into your flesh. Only the Americans seemed to have the spare energy to celebrate in any style – and the money.

James Cardwell lay on his stretcher bed in the officers' quarters, unable to sleep, wondering how Emma was. He'd written to his wife; sent little embroidered Christmas cards to both his children, pretty things made by the Frenchwomen who lived around here. Yet all the time he'd been doing that, he'd been thinking of Emma, longing to see her again. So he'd bought her a little embroidered card, too, but had only dared write an innocuous message on it.

When he left Overdale, he'd asked her not to write to him, because if anything happened to him, his wife might find the letters, and though he didn't care about Edith, he did care about his children, who were old enough to understand what was going on. He only wrote to Emma when he was sure he'd be able to finish the letter quickly and get it into the post. Twice he'd screwed the letters up and tossed them on a nearby fire as he'd rushed to arms. He didn't dare risk someone finding a half-written letter to his mistress. You learned to think like that when your life was worth so little.

He'd even changed his will while he was back in Overdale, leaving Emma a share in the business she and Walter had kept going all through the war. She deserved that if anything happened to him. And she'd keep things going so that his children had enough to live on at least. Edith couldn't even manage the housekeeping money.

The shell landed on headquarters in the small hours of Boxing Day, killing every officer there. It was the first shell in a short, sharp barrage, and the only one to make a direct hit. James had fallen asleep by then. Like the rest of the victims, he didn't feel a thing.

*   *   *

Sam returned to the house somewhat the worse for wear and for a time didn't release Lizzie from her bonds. There was something satisfying in seeing her helpless, with her bright green eyes glaring defiantly at him. Eeh, she'd make a fine mother for his children, she would that.

He had to prepare the tea himself and when he untied her, stand over her with a threat of forcing the food down her throat before she'd eat anything. Afterwards, he brought her a cup of tea, hot and sweet.

She hesitated for a moment, then drank it.

He said nothing, just told her to sit down opposite him by the fire, and when, after another moment's hesitation, she did that, he felt a sense of triumph. Little by little he'd win her over. When she saw that he no longer hit her, when she saw that he really wanted her for his wife, well, she'd be bound to come round.

Two days passed. Two long, boring days for Lizzie. She wondered if she'd ever grow used to his fixed stare and even, occasionally, whether she'd manage to hold out against him and refuse to lift a finger in the house. He wanted his rations night and morning, and although she felt cold and unmoved by his attentions, he still got his own satisfaction, as he always had.

'You'll be with child before the spring,' he promised her.

'I'll not. I'll will it not to happen,' she threw back at him.

But he just laughed and stroked her bare breast, laughing as she tried to squirm away.

A few days later, he took Lizzie shopping with him. Before they left, Sam tied her up and went into the front room on his own, fiddling around with something there. Then he came and untied her.

At the market, he bought food lavishly, as if money was no object. It puzzled Lizzie where he got all his money, why he didn't seem bothered about finding himself a job. She knew from what others said that the Government did little to help disabled soldiers and that many were in great want.

Snow still lay on the ground, but dirty now, like piles of muddy washing. In the ruts ice crackled and they had to tread carefully so as not to slip. She saw Sam wince once or twice when his bad foot skidded, but he said nothing. He seemed determined to ignore his limp. In spite of herself, she felt a bit sorry for him. But not sorry enough to spend the rest of her life with him.

When they got home, there was a knock on the door, the first since Lizzie had returned to Overdale. Sam took her arm and dragged her along to answer it.

Percy stood there, staring at his sister. 'They were right, then. You are back.'

Sam kept hold of her and made a quick decision to let her see her family. 'Come in, lad. Have a cup of tea. It's been a long time since you two have seen one another.' He slammed the door with hearty good humour. 'Eeh, it's bad underfoot, it is that. Me an' Lizzie nearly went arse over tit a few times while we were shopping.'

Percy looked at the way Sam was holding her arm, puzzled.

'She's not used to being back yet,' Sam said, shaking his head in mock sorrow. 'Wants to get away from me. But I'm not having that.'

Lizzie didn't say anything, just let Sam drag her along to the kitchen and plonk her down in a chair. When he was busy with the kettle, she said clearly and distinctly, 'I'm not staying with him and he won't be able to watch me every minute of every day and night. I'll get away from him one day.'

Sam came to lean against the door of the scullery. 'I'm doing pretty well so far at keeping you here.' He looked across at Percy with a grin. 'I tie her up when I go out. They taught us all sorts of useful skills in the Army. She won't get away from my knots.'

'Eeh, lad, is it worth it?'

'Aye. She's my wife. An' she's not leaving me.' He hesitated, then said, 'I don't hit her any more. Nor I won't. Whatever she does. So she's got nothing to complain of now. And when we start a family, she'll *have* to stay.'

Lizzie let out a breath rough with irritation and stared into the fire, leaving the two men to make stilted conversation.

Percy looked from one to the other of them, at a loss for words to bridge the gaps that yawned between them all. His sister looked older, more sure of herself somehow, and the determination emanating from her was so fierce, he had to wonder if Sam would ever win her over. She seemed like the old Lizzie again, the defiant young lass who'd walked on the top of the wall and done a dozen other stupid, daredevil things, tossing her head at the world like an untamed young animal.

When he'd finished his tea, he stood up, feeling awkward, and went over to kiss his sister. 'Can't you make the best of it, love? You are his wife.'

Lizzie turned her head away. 'No. And I don't feel like his wife any more. I belong to myself now.'

Sam stared at her through eyes burning with suppressed annoyance, but his words were controlled, as were his movements. 'Let yourself out, lad. I have to keep my eye on Tiger here.'

Percy hesitated. 'You won't – hurt her again?'

'I already said I wouldn't.' He saw the doubt in Percy's eyes. 'Look, I promised my mate as he lay dying that I'd not beat her again, an' I'll keep that promise whatever it costs. But I'll not let her go, neither. She's mine.'

Lizzie spoke suddenly. 'Would you write to my friend Peggy in Murforth for me, Percy? Tell her what's happened? She's a supervisor at the munitions factory. You can send a letter there.'

He looked surprised. 'Why can't you do that?'

Sam grinned. 'She can do it as soon as she promises not to run away.' Then he scowled. 'So don't bother about writing to anyone, Percy lad. I left a note for her landlady. They'll know nothing bad's happened to her.'

But when Percy got home to the quiet little house, he decided to do as Lizzie had asked. So he wrote, explained the situation as well as he could and addressed the letter to 'Peggy, Supervisor', at the munitions factory. As an afterthought, he added Lizzie's address.

CHAPTER TWENTY-EIGHT

Two days after Christmas, the postman brought a telegram to James Cardwell's house.

'Sorry, Mrs Cardwell,' he mumbled.

Edith didn't move, just stood there staring at it in horror as he turned away and walked off down the street.

'No,' she whispered. 'No!' She walked slowly into the house and sat down in the unheated front parlour, but it was several minutes before she could bring herself to open the telegram. She didn't want to be a widow. When she read it and found the news she had dreaded, she began to scream.

The two maids came running in, and behind them the children. For a few minutes it was a flurry of fuss and sobbing and explanations, with the children mostly ignored.

Young Frank saw the telegram and picked it up, his face wooden with the effort not to cry for he had already guessed what it contained. He read the short message and put an arm round his sister, who was reading it beside him.

'Daddy?' she gulped.

'Don't cry!' he hissed, giving her a little shake. '*She* cries and cries, but it doesn't mean anything.' He scowled at his mother, who was lying back letting the maids fuss over her, then turned away and put his arm round his sister's shoulders.

'What'll we do, Frank?'

'Nothing. What can we do?'

When Edith at last looked across the room, she murmured, 'Oh, my poor children, how am I to tell you?' This was a line straight out of one of her favourite pictures, one she had coaxed no less than three of her admirers to take her to, so she knew the screen captions off by heart.

'You don't need to tell us. We've already seen the telegram and heard you crying.' Frank's voice was gruff, angry-sounding, more like a man's. 'We know Father's dead. It doesn't say how he died, though.'

'What does it matter *how?*' Edith buried her face in her hands again, but made no attempt to comfort them.

Doris pressed against her brother's shoulder, feeling comforted by his arm holding her so firmly.

'I'll take my sister up to the nursery,' he said, still in the same wooden voice. 'We'll leave you to recover, Mother.' He had talked to his father on his last leave about his mother, about how she never spent any time with them or seemed to notice what they were doing, and his father had said that wasn't the children's fault, simply that some women didn't make good mothers.

'It's no use being rude to her or shouting,' James had concluded. 'It's not in her to do it. It's like hitting a puppy for barking at a stranger. It's born in the puppy to bark and it's born in your mother to let others rear her children.' He had hesitated then added, 'But I love you both. Very much. You're a fine lad. I couldn't want a better son. And I'm relying on you to look after your sister if – if anything happens to me.'

So now, Frank sat Doris down and held her while she wept, dashing away his own tears when they would fall. Later, he went down to the kitchen and asked the maid how his mother was.

Kath, who had nieces and nephews of her own, looked at him sympathetically. 'I think she's sleeping, Master Frank. She's taken some of that medicine she got last year and she's lying on the sofa.' She wanted to hug him, but he was so stiff and grown-up that she didn't quite like to. 'I'm sorry about the master, I am indeed. He'll be sorely missed.'

Frank gave a quick nod, changing the subject. Nothing anyone said could help, but at least Kath's tears were real, not for show like his mother's. 'Could we have some breakfast, do you think?'

'Yes, of course. But before I get it, I have something for you.' She went into the pantry and reached up to the top shelf.

He stared at the envelope with his name written on it in his father's heavy black writing.

'The master gave it to me before he left. He said if anything happened to him, I was to give it to you, but not to say anything about it to your mother. And I'll bring you a tray up to the nursery directly.'

Frank took the envelope and nodded his thanks. When he went upstairs, he decided to open the letter in his bedroom. What he read made more unmanly tears run down his cheeks, but softened the hard knot of anguish in his chest at least. He'd always treasure this letter.

Later that afternoon Edith Cardwell dressed in black, grimaced at herself in the mirror, because it definitely wasn't her colour, and went down to the builder's yard, bowing her head like a queen at the condolences offered by people she met in the street. She was filled with fiery satisfaction at what she was about to do.

She walked into Emma's office without knocking and said with immense relish, 'You're fired.'

Emma could only gape and wonder if Mrs Cardwell had gone mad. 'I'm afraid you can't—' she began.

Edith interrupted. 'Oh, but I can fire you now. My husband is dead, you see, so I'm the owner of this business and I'd like you to leave my premises immediately.' She leaned across the desk, her face a twisted mask of viciousness. 'And if you think I don't know you were carrying on with my husband, you must be even more stupid than you look.'

Emma gasped and sat down. 'James is dead?' She couldn't control her voice, which wobbled. 'How?'

'None of your business, you trollop! Just get your things together and leave.'

Too shocked and upset even to weep, Emma began to

gather her possessions. When she went out to the storeroom for a box, she found Edith dogging her footsteps.

'I'm making very sure you don't steal anything. And hurry up, will you?'

Just as Emma had finished clearing the desk of her things, Walter came in, staring from one of them to the other. 'What's up?'

Edith turned to him. 'My husband is dead and now that I'm in charge, I'm not having his whore working here.'

Walter swallowed hard. 'James is dead?'

'I just said so. And I'm warning you now that you'd better pull your socks up, too, or *you* will be out of a job as well.'

He folded his arms. 'I wouldn't work for you if you paid me double, missus. Nor will any other self-respecting tradesman if you talk to them like that. Who the hell do you think you are?'

Edith gasped and drew herself up. 'I'm the widow of your late master and now I'm your employer.'

'Nay, that you're not. I'm not sunk so low I have to work for a nasty bitch like you. You made him miserable for years, which is why he turned elsewhere, but you're not spoiling my life.' He turned to Emma, who was trying not to sob as she crammed the last of her things into the box. 'I'll carry that for you, love, then I'll come back for my tools.'

And he put his arm round her shoulders and led her out without a backward glance at Mrs Cardwell, standing in solitary possession of a business she knew not the first thing about.

The morning after his father's memorial service, Frank didn't go to school but hung around in the back yard of the builder's, which stood empty and forlorn-looking. He couldn't understand where Walter was. Or Miss Harper. And why was the front door shut? The yard was never left unattended during business hours.

When his father was alive, Frank had loved coming down here – sawing bits of wood, helping Walter clear up. He wasn't sure what had happened on the day the telegram had arrived, but his mother had come back from the yard in a raging fury and he had overheard her talking about 'that woman' in such tones of anger that it had been a while before he realised she was talking about Miss Harper. And 'that nasty old man' seemed to be referring to Walter.

What had Miss Harper and Walter done wrong, then?

The short memorial service hadn't seemed right, somehow, or the absence of a coffin. It had upset Frank that there was no body to bury. He'd have liked his father to lie in the churchyard with his grandfather and his great-grandfather and all the other Cardwells. He was going to lie there himself one day.

At the service, his mother had leaned against Major Gresham all the time, fluttering her eyelashes and letting him support her. That had sickened Frank. And the Major – who was in charge of a supply depot and had never been to the Front, so didn't count as a real soldier in the boy's eyes – kept saying he'd come round whenever he could to comfort her, help her with the business.

Today Frank was supposed to go back to school and carry on as if nothing had happened. His mother wouldn't even talk to him about the future of the yard. But he wasn't going to school yet. He was going to do as his father had asked first.

When the school bell rang faintly in the distance and he knew there'd be no teachers out on the streets, he left the yard and walked to the rooms of his father's lawyer, prudently taking the back lanes to get there.

He went into the front office and said firmly to the lad, 'I need to see Mr Finch. It's urgent.' The lawyer was going to come round to his house to read the will that afternoon, but his mother had said it was no concern of Frank's, so he might as well go back to school. But his father's letter said differently.

At first they didn't want to let him in, but when he told them about his father and showed them the last paragraph of the letter, they got pitying looks on their faces and changed their minds. He hated people pitying him, absolutely hated it!

Mr Finch was sitting behind his desk, but he got up and

came to join Frank in the big leather armchairs in front of the fire. 'Sit there, lad, and warm yourself a bit. Eeh, I'm sorry about your father. He was a good man.'

'Yes.' Frank was learning not to answer such comments, just push them aside in his head, because they made him feel like weeping and he was the man of the family now, so couldn't let himself be weak.

'I believe your father left you a letter asking you to come and see me?'

'Yes.'

'I was going to see your mother this afternoon, then send for you tomorrow. Your father made certain provisions under his will and I promised him I'd tell you about them myself if – if necessary.'

'Yes, sir.'

'The main thing is that he has left the business and everything he owns to you, my boy, except for a small share that's left to Miss Harper.'

Frank sat and thought this over for a moment. 'Not to my mother?'

'No.'

'Miss Harper wasn't at the service today. Or Walter.'

'Yes. I'm afraid your mother has dismissed Miss Harper. And Walter left with her.'

Another silence. Then, 'But if I own the business now, I can ask them to come back to work for us, can't I?'

'Yes. You can, indeed. Though it'd be better if I did it. I hope you don't mind, but I'm now joint guardian of you and your sister – together with your mother, of course – and trustee of the business till you grow up?'

'If the business is mine what will Mother do, sir? For money, I mean.'

'Well, she already has an inheritance from her father, besides which your father arranged that the business was to pay for household expenses and servants. Your mother will have enough money to live on, believe me. But he expected you to look after her as you get older – unless she remarries. He

– um, seemed to think you would want to work in the business when you left school.'

Frank's face brightened. 'Oh, yes! I love going down to the yard.' After another silence, he added, 'My mother won't like how things are left, will she, sir? She'll get upset.' She'd probably start screeching and wailing. He hated it when she got like that.

'I dare say she will. I'll go and explain things to her while you're at school.'

The boy wriggled uncomfortably. 'I should have gone there this morning. I'll be in trouble.'

'I'll write you a note explaining you had to see me first.'

'Thank you very much, sir.'

Mr Finch sighed as he watched the lad leave. What a fine young fellow Frank was, a real chip off the old block. He sighed again at the thought of what lay ahead. It was not going to be pleasant. Edith Cardwell was a nasty piece and always had been.

And after dealing with her, he'd have to go and see poor Miss Harper. A pleasant young woman, that. But it was going to cause talk James leaving her a share of the business, and they could all guess why he'd done it.

A few days later, as dusk was falling, there was a knock on the front door of number one Maidham Street. Sam dragged Lizzie along the hall to answer it because he had found he couldn't even leave her in the kitchen alone without her trying to run out of the back door – good thing he'd got that padlock on the gate. It was wearing, though, keeping an eye on someone all the time, bloody wearing.

Blanche Harper stood on the doorstep with a parcel in her hand. 'This came for your wife earlier, Mr Thoxby. No one was in, so the postman left it with me.' She hadn't been able to get along to deliver it earlier because Emma was still prostrate with grief and shock.

'Here!' She pushed the parcel into his hands, nodded a

greeting at Lizzie and turned away. She felt sorry for that poor girl, who looked pale and unhappy, but she had her own troubles, for her sister seemed to have lost the will to live.

Sam stared at the parcel, hefting it in his hand, then turned and pushed Lizzie back into the kitchen, muttering in exasperation, for he'd just about reached the limit with her. He'd have to think of some way to settle her hash, because he wasn't putting up with this much longer. The house was a pigsty and she refused to touch it. He had to force her to eat, to do anything.

'Fine bloody wife you are!' he grumbled as he reached the kitchen. He stared at the parcel again, then noticed the postmark. 'Murforth. One of your dear friends sending you a present, eh?' He weighed it in his hand, wondering whether to simply toss it on the fire, then went to get the scissors. Might as well see what it was.

Lizzie stared at the parcel, wondering what it could be and how her friends in Murforth had got hold of her address. Then suddenly a dreadful thought struck her. It was just the same size as – it couldn't be – surely it couldn't be her letters from Peter? The breath caught in her throat, for she could think of nothing else it could be.

Once Sam saw those letters, he'd kill her. She had no doubt about that. Her writing to any man would be enough to send him into a fury, but writing to the man he hated most in the world would surely push him into murder. Her heart began to thump in her chest. Fear curdled her stomach. For all her assertions to Sam, for all her defiance, she didn't want to die.

When Blanche left Lizzie's house, she almost bumped into Percy. 'Oh!' Her hand fluttered to her chest. 'Oh, I didn't see you.'

'Are you all right, Miss Harper?' She looked so white and worried, he stopped for a moment.

'Yes. I just – you startled me. I was miles away.'

'And how is Emma? I heard about Mr Cardwell. It's a sad loss.'

Blanche's face crumpled and she couldn't hold back the tears. For a moment the world spun around her and she swayed dizzily.

He put an arm round her instinctively. 'You're not well. Let me help you back home.'

She clung to him for a moment, then tried to pull herself together. 'It's not me – it's Emma who's not herself. I'm so worried about her.' She didn't dare let go of him because if she did, she might faint right away. There was something warm and solid about him, and he had such a kind face she found herself confiding, 'Oh, Mr Kershaw, what am I to do? She just lies there, weeping, and she'll lose the child if she goes on like this. Oh!' She clapped a hand to her mouth as she realised what she had said, then buried her head in his shoulder, sobbing incoherently.

Percy patted her shoulder soothingly, his thoughts whirling. Emma was expecting a child? Whose? Well, who else's could it be but James Cardwell's? Only he was dead. Not even a body to bring home, they said.

'What am I to *do?*' she wailed against him. 'Emma's all I've got.'

Long experience with hysterical women enabled him to soothe her down. People passed the end of the street and some hesitated, but no one stopped. A woman looked out of her front window, then let the lace curtain drop again.

As Miss Harper began to calm down, he realised how embarrassed she would be by this public outburst and gently guided her back towards number seven. The ground was still treacherous, with the last of the snow having turned to ice, which had melted a little during the daytime and then frozen into glassy patches in the hollows at night. He could go and see Lizzie later, he decided, but he couldn't leave this distraught woman to cope on her own.

And anyway, there was Emma. Maybe – maybe he could do something to help her. If only be a comfort to her in her sad hour.

'Shall I come inside and make you a nice cup of tea?'

Blanche gulped and nodded, dabbing her soggy handkerchief to her eyes and muttering in a muffled voice, 'S-so grateful.'

Inside the house there was no sign of Emma. Percy sat Miss Harper down and raked up the fire. There was something cheering about a good blaze. He glanced sideways. She was just sitting there, defeat in every line of her body.

She caught his eyes on her and whispered, 'I've tried everything, you see. Everything I can think of. But she won't eat or drink. She just lies there. And—' she looked guiltily at him – 'well, there *is* the baby to think of.'

'Cardwell's?'

'Yes.' Shame flooded her cheeks with colour. 'I know it's not exactly – but she's my sister – and it'll be all she's got to remember him by.'

He went and put the kettle on, then got out the cups. He'd been here often enough to know where everything was, for although Emma never looked at him as a man, she did consider him a friend.

'There you are,' he said soothingly. 'Things always look better after a cup of tea. I'll just take one up to Emma, shall I?'

'Oh, she's in bed. I don't think—'

'Maybe I can talk to her, help her face things?'

'Well,' Blanche stirred her tea thoughtfully, then shrugged helplessly. 'Why not? You've always been a good friend to us.'

He was halfway up the stairs when he got the idea, gasping aloud as he realised its implications. He hesitated just for a moment then nodded, squared his shoulders and marched into her room.

'Emma?'

She was lying in a huddle of bedclothes, her face pale and her expression vacant. She looked a mere shadow of the vivacious and energetic woman he knew. His heart twisted with pity.

'Emma, I've brought you a cup of tea.'

She didn't even turn her head.

He set the cup down beside the bed and sat on the edge of the mattress, taking her hand in his. 'Emma, you have to pull yourself together, for the baby's sake.'

Very slowly, her eyes turned towards him. 'You know?'

'Your sister told me. She's very upset. Says you're not eating.'

'Not feeling hungry. Not feeling anything.' She closed her eyes.

He stared at her. Gentleness wouldn't work, so he shook her hard and her eyes flew open again in shock. 'Pull yourself together, woman!'

She tried to push him away. 'Leave me be, Percy Kershaw! What do you know about love?'

'As much as you.' He glared at her. 'I've loved you for years and known you didn't even see me because of him. Don't tell me about love!' He jerked her into a sitting position, stuffing the pillows behind her anyhow. 'And don't lie there full of self-pity when you're carrying his child. If you knew what I'd give to have a child . . . You're blessed, Emma Harper, and lucky, too, because you've got something good left out of all this mess.'

She started to sob then, but he'd seen the light come back into her eyes, so he just reached out and held her, patting her shoulder and letting the storm of weeping bring her back to life. It was short but violent and when it had died down, he sat her up again and offered the cup of tea. 'It's still warm. Get some down you.'

Obediently she sipped, then gulped down the whole cup, as if she had suddenly rediscovered thirst. She was shivering a little.

Percy looked round the room and found a shawl. He brought it across and draped it round her shoulders, then picked up the empty cup. 'I'll be back with another and something to eat.'

As he went downstairs, he heard her cross the landing to the bathroom. When he went back, he carried another brimming cup and a plate of roughly hacked bread and jam – for Miss Harper was of no use to man or beast at the moment, just lying back in an armchair by the fire looking drained of all ability to move.

'Sorry the bread's such a mess. I've never been good at cutting it thinly. Besides, you need something to stick to your ribs.'

Emma toyed with the plate for a moment, then looked at him and managed a watery smile. 'Thank you, Percy. I couldn't seem to – to climb out of the hole – everything seemed so dark and so—' Her voice faded away.

He patted her hand. 'I know.'

'You're a good friend.'

He hesitated, then decided to risk all. 'I'd like to be more than a friend. And you *need* more than a friend.'

She frowned at him, not understanding.

'You're carrying a child. You're not the first, especially since this war started, but the old biddies will soon be tattling about you. What you need is a husband.' He picked up her hand. 'Emma, I know you don't love me, but I love you, and I can't think of anything I'd like better than to marry you. For the sake of the child, could you consider it?'

'But – it's someone else's child.'

'I know.' He started fiddling with the counterpane. 'But I'd be the best father I know how. I love children. I've always regretted – well, you know how things were at our house. I could never have asked any woman to marry me and put up with that.'

She stared at him, feeling as if she'd never seen him clearly. Percy was so different from James, so colourless compared to him. And yet he had his own integrity. He'd stuck with his mother through thick and thin, done his best for his brother and sisters, not complained. She'd always felt comfortable with him.

He didn't meet her eyes as he added in a gruff voice, 'And if you don't want me to touch you – afterwards – well, I won't.'

Silence filled the room.

He waited as she stared down at her steaming cup.

Emma raised eyes brimming with tears and said, 'You're the nicest man I've ever known, Percy Kershaw.'

'And?'

'And I'll give your suggestion consideration.' She lay back against the pillow. 'I need a little time to – to think it over, to come to terms . . .' Her voice faded away.

He nodded. 'I'll leave you in peace, then.'

She reached out to clasp his hand for a moment. 'Thank you, Percy.'

When he left the house, he forgot about going to visit his sister, forgot about everything, for he was consumed by hope, the first hope of real happiness for himself he had seen in a long time. He could ask nothing better than to look after Emma, be with her, raise a child – never mind if that child wasn't his. Children weren't hard to love.

Keeping one eye on Lizzie, Sam unwrapped the parcel carefully. She knew what it was. He'd seen the sudden jerk of recognition then the look of fear in her eyes, though she'd only shot one glance at him before concentrating on her hands, clasped tightly in her lap.

He unfolded the paper and smoothed it back. 'Letters.' He glanced at his wife and waited for a reaction, but got none. She was so still, she might have been as frozen as the icy streets outside. So still he could hardly even see her breasts rising and falling.

'Addressed to you,' he said, picking up an envelope. Then the breath caught in his throat, for the letter was from the Front and the name on the back was one he loathed with an intensity that sat waiting in his belly to unleash itself every time he heard the name Dearden.

But still he managed to control himself. He had promised Ronnie not to touch her. Promised. Moving with extreme care, he pulled the first letter out of its envelope and opened it. 'Nice handwriting.'

Lizzie had closed her eyes and her whole body spoke of waiting for disaster to strike.

He read it slowly. One of many, this, all carefully preserved.

That bugger spoke of missing her, of visits to the cinema together.

Sam heard a rustling sound, heard the air wheezing in and out of his lungs, heard a faint rumble of anger. It was the sounds he clung to, because what he wanted to do was murder her, choke the life out of her. But he had murdered his unborn child and that had hurt him as much as her. If he murdered Lizzie, he realised suddenly, he would have no reason for living himself.

'How long has this been going on?' he demanded sarcastically.

'Nothing's been going on but a few letters.'

'You kept them! You tied them up with ribbons.' He screwed up the first letter and tossed it aside, tearing open the next one, reading part of it, then tossing that aside too.

When he read the third one, however, the words seemed to burn themselves into his brain. This time Peter bloody Dearden didn't only speak of missing her; he spoke of the future, of his hopes that somehow they would solve her problems and find a way to be together.

With a great roar of rage, Sam lost control of himself and knocked her off her chair. Then he picked her up, slapped her face and threw her across the room. The world seemed full of his rage, burning, consuming him, tearing its way out. From far away he heard some animal sounds of pain and that brought him momentarily to his senses. He looked down, still shuddering with great waves of rage, and saw her face, saw his own hands squeezing her throat, saw the bruise on her cheek.

He also saw Ronnie's face.

'Any man would have hit her,' he told it.

'*You promised*,' said the phantom. '*Promised, promised, promised.*'

Sam's hands slackened round her throat and she rasped in some breath. He shoved her aside, then crawled across the room, picked up the letters and hurled them into the fire. After that, knowing he'd kill her if he stayed a minute longer, he rushed out of the house, coatless, hatless, totally unaware of the snow which was falling again, or the ice which made it hard to stay upright.

When he fell, he picked himself up again. When he saw the lights of the pub, he rushed inside. And Ronnie floated beside him all the way, pale face full of accusation.

CHAPTER TWENTY-NINE

It was a while before Lizzie regained full consciousness. She moaned as she tried to swallow, for her throat hurt. Her head hurt, too, and she couldn't move one arm. When she tried to get up, she nearly fainted with the pain. The arm must be broken.

That didn't seem to matter. What mattered was where Sam was. She listened carefully and heard nothing moving inside the house. Then she felt the icy draught from the open front door.

He'd gone out, then!

But he'd be back.

She had to get away while she could. Whimpering, she tried to stand up and had to crawl across to a chair and use that to lever herself upright. She sat on the edge of it for a minute, remembering what had happened. Not just the rage, but the pain in his face. It was then she noticed the pieces of burnt letter in the hearth and that reminded her.

Why was she just sitting here? She had to get away. Only – he'd stolen her money. She couldn't go far without money. He didn't keep it on him, so where had he put it? She had to think.

Her eyes lit on the table and she saw the teapot standing there amid a broken mess of crockery. Suddenly she felt desperately thirsty and heaved herself to her feet, staggering across to fumble with a cup, sobbing with relief to find the pot half full of cold tea. She gulped some down and let out a mew of pain at how much that hurt her throat.

Did Sam think he'd killed her? She hoped so. But if he came back and saw her alive, he would surely finish the job.

'I wasn't unfaithful!' she sobbed. 'I only saw Peter for that one week. It was all letters, Sam. Just letters.'

But even if he'd been here, he'd not have listened to her. And anyway, it was more than letters. It was feelings, hers and Peter's. But she'd always known it'd come to nothing. And she hadn't been unfaithful.

Where had Sam put her money?

She looked round the room, feeling very strange and distant. Not in here, she decided. I'd have noticed it. Then she remembered seeing him coming out of the front room the previous day as she stood on the landing, watching for an opportunity to run away. He'd been putting something in his pocket. And he'd gone into the front room that first day, too. Excitement gave her strength. The money must be in there. It must.

It took a huge effort to stand up and stagger to the door. She clung to the frame for a moment, then launched herself across the hall, holding her broken arm with her good hand, leaning against the wall of the front room just inside the door and staring round. Where could he have hidden the money? She looked from one piece of furniture to another. She'd polished every inch of them when they were first married. She knew there was nowhere to hide money in them. Well, she'd have found it if there was, wouldn't she? Besides, furniture could be moved, taken away. Sam wouldn't have gone overseas and left his savings in a piece of furniture. She was sure of that.

She looked down at her feet, which seemed to be coming and going, wavering. The floor! Excitement filled her, giving her extra strength. It'd be under the floorboards. But she couldn't pull them all up and she'd never heard him moving the furniture, so it mustn't be under anything. She had to think, had to. And act quickly. If she got to Percy, surely he'd help her to get away when he saw how badly Sam had hurt her again?

In town, Sam staggered into the Carter's Rest, looking so wild and strange that men edged away from him. He didn't even notice them. He clumped across to the bar, snowflakes melting on his face, unaware that the cold and wind had chapped his face a mottled red and turned his fingers blue-white.

'Is something wrong, lad?' one of his old friends dared to ask.

'Sod off!' Sam thumped on the bar. 'Pint an' a double rum. An' quick.' He slapped a couple of pound notes on the surface. 'Put this in a pot an' let me know when y'need some more.' He leaned across the bar, breathing loudly and unevenly. 'An' when y'see my glass empty, bring me another.'

He spied a free table in one corner and made his way across to it, weaving to and fro. No one got in his way.

'He's drunk already,' the barmaid whispered to her employer. 'Shall I serve him more?'

'Aye. As long as he's paying.' But he went away to alert a couple of the lads to a possible need for their help in turfing out an unruly customer, and he kept an eye on that corner. Only for once, Sam Thoxby didn't seem violent, just sat there, sipping his drink, looking hunched and miserable.

After a while, the buzz of conversation started up again, but people kept glancing towards the corner, as if expecting trouble. Within half an hour the nearby tables had emptied and Sam was alone.

As he drank, he muttered to himself. A little later, he began to argue with the shade of Ronnie, which seemed to be hovering nearby. 'I couldn't help it!' he protested. 'Any man would've thumped her for that. Anyone!'

'*You promised,*' whispered the shade. '*Promised, promised, promised.*' It had been dogging him ever since he left Maidham Street, going on and on and on.

Contrary to the landlord's expectations, Sam did not grow argumentative, except with himself. He muttered and gesticulated and from time to time turned his shoulder away from an invisible companion, but he caused no trouble. And he paid for one drink after another, pouring them down his throat in great gulps.

When it came time to close the pub, the landlord took

a deep breath and went over to the corner. His two helpers hovered nearby. 'Time for me to close up now, lad,' he said with forced geniality to Sam. When he got no answer, he repeated his statement.

This time Sam looked up. 'Gimme a bottle of rum, then.' He fumbled in his pocket, found no more money and fixed the landlord with a glowering gaze. 'Put it on t'slate. I've never not paid you what I owed.'

'All right, lad.' The publican knew better than to upset a man as drunk as this.

Clutching the bottle, Sam made his way towards the door. Someone opened it for him. Everyone breathed a sigh of relief when he left.

Lizzie sobbed with frustration as she searched in vain for a loose floorboard. Time was passing. If she didn't get away soon, he'd be back. It was by sheer chance that she stumbled and hit the corner of the skirting board with her foot. Even through the pain that caused her, she felt it move. Only a bit, but enough to alert her. She dropped to her knees, yelping and stopping for a moment as she banged her broken arm. When the worst of the pain had passed, she tugged at the corner of the skirting board. It moved, then stuck, then moved again, revealing a recess where a brick had been removed from the inner wall.

Inside were several piles of money, her own quite separate, notes folded just as she had kept them. But there was a lot of other money, too, so many notes she couldn't take it in for a moment. Then she began to laugh, a harsh scraping sound that hurt her throat. It must have been here all the time. Enough money for her to escape, and she'd waited while she scrimped ha'pennies together! The laugh turned into a sob and she nearly allowed herself the luxury of a good weep, but forced herself to stop. No time for that. No time for anything but running away.

Lizzie grabbed a fistful of money and stuffed it in her apron pocket. She had begun to stand up when she realised that Sam would see instantly that she had found his cache, so she bent down again and awkwardly, with her good hand, put the piece of board back again. It seemed to take a long time to get it into place.

Then she staggered out to the hall and fumbled for her coat, moaning in impatience at her own ineptitude. Even as she was trying to put it on and hold it round her bad arm, footsteps sounded outside in the street. For a moment, she flattened herself against the wall, then she turned to run. If she could get out of the back door, perhaps she could still escape, climb over that locked gate. But she bumped her bad arm again on the hallstand and let out a wail of pain, clinging to the stand with her good arm and trying desperately not to let the blackness swallow her up. She'd not be able to climb over anything. She was trapped! He'd really kill her now she'd tried to take his money.

Sam staggered out of the pub, clutching his bottle. Snow lay thick on the ground, muddied by the feet of the departing customers. Within a few paces, he had fallen flat on his arse, and lay there for a moment or two, cursing and groaning. Two men walked past him.

'Gi's a hand up!' he shouted, but they didn't even turn round. 'Soddin' snow,' he told the flakes as they whirled down on him. 'Soddin' women!' he yelled at the world. He looked sideways and saw Ronnie still standing there, quiet now, with a sad expression on his face.

'Bes' mate I ever had,' Sam told him.

Ronnie just stared at him.

'All right, all right, I won't hit her again.' But Ronnie didn't even nod his head, just continued to stare. With a lot of grunting, Sam heaved himself to his feet, discovered the bottle of rum, unbroken, lying cushioned on a pile of snow, and picked it up, crooning to it as he took a good swig. Then he set off home.

It was at the corner of York Road that he slipped and ricked his good ankle. He stood for a minute letting the pain subside. When he could, he continued on his way up the hill, moving slowly now and with great difficulty. In the middle of the street, he nearly dropped the bottle and stopped to get a firmer grip on it. A chap standing on the pavement started yelling at him and waving his arms, so he yelled back, then turned to continue.

He saw the skidding motor omnibus just seconds before it slammed into him.

The world turned black for a few minutes, then Sam opened his eyes and saw his mate. He allowed Ronnie to help him up. Good ol' Ronnie, best mate he'd ever had. They walked off together.

It took Lizzie a minute to realise that it couldn't be Sam at the door, because he had a key. And anyway, the door wasn't locked, so Sam would just bang it open and stamp inside. With a sob, she stumbled down the hallway. Let it be someone who'll help me, she prayed as she fumbled for the handle.

When she opened it, she found a policeman standing there and whimpered in relief.

'Can I come in, love?'

'I'd rather – would you take me to my brother's? I think I've broken my arm – and my husband isn't here and – and I need help.'

'Let me come in first,' he said, his voice gentle. He put one arm round her. 'Let's go through into the kitchen, eh?' He was horrified by her bruised face and neck, the terror in her eyes. He didn't look forward to this task and she didn't look to be in a fit state to cope with what he had to tell her, but it had to be done.

He helped her sit by the fire, easing her down and trying not to hurt the arm, which did, indeed, look to be broken. Then he piled some coal on the fire and shut the door into the hall.

'Why won't you listen to me?' she sobbed. 'I have to get away or my husband will come back and kill me. Who do you think did this to me?'

He knelt in front of her. 'Listen, love.' He held her good hand in his, amazed at how icy it felt. 'Listen a minute.'

Lizzie stopped protesting and stared at him, wide-eyed as an owl, as terrified as a wild creature caught in a trap.

'There's been an accident. I'm afraid your husband's been killed.'

The words didn't seem to sink in at first, and she just stared at him, so he repeated them more loudly. 'I'm afraid your husband's been killed.'

This time, she opened and shut her mouth, staring into his eyes with an intensity he'd only seen before in a madwoman. 'Say that again.'

He obliged. 'Your husband has been killed, Mrs Thoxby.'

'Sam's dead? Really dead?'

'Yes, love. I'm sorry to be the bearer of bad news.'

She sat so still he began to worry, then she asked very softly, 'You're quite sure of that?'

Funny how it took some of them. 'I'm afraid so. He was standing in the middle of York Road. A motor omnibus skidded on the ice and slammed right into him. He didn't even try to move out of the way.' The fellow had been blind drunk, by all accounts.

'He's dead. He's really dead.' She leaned back and let a great shudder of relief run through her body, taking the worst of her terror with it. Then she shut her eyes and murmured, 'Oh, thank heavens! Thank heavens.'

If her husband was the one who'd beaten her up, the policeman couldn't blame her for being glad of his death. Well, even the Sergeant had said Sam Thoxby would be no loss to the town. But it was a rotten way to die, crushed by those heavy wheels, blood splattered across the cobblestones.

When she just sat there, shaking, he took charge, as he had learned to do at such times. 'Let me fetch one of your neighbours, love. You need help.'

After a moment, she managed, 'Number seven. Harpers.'

He nodded. 'You'll be all right if I leave you for a minute?'

She gave him a ghost of a smile. 'Mmm.' She wasn't, she found, glad that Sam had died, only glad to be free of him. He'd been hurt as well as angry when he found out about her writing to Peter Dearden. She was sorry for that. Sorry for everything. But now, oh, heavens, now she didn't need to go away. She could stay here and build a new life for herself.

Relief washed through her again, making her shiver, and it was a moment before she realised that Emma Harper was standing beside her, looking pale and unhappy but there at least.

'Oh, Emma! I don't know what to do.' Then Lizzie let herself slip into unconsciousness, let the pain go away, let everything go, because it was safe to give in now.

Lizzie arranged a decent funeral for Sam, but didn't attend it, sending Percy in her place. She'd stayed overnight in hospital where they'd set her arm and tended her bruises, then had insisted on coming home. Percy had offered to stay with her, and she'd accepted that, because she did need help just now. Johnny came, too, but he seemed a stranger, a rough lad of thirteen who stared at her blankly and seemed to spend most of his time round at his mates' houses.

A week after the funeral, Percy told her he was going to marry Emma Harper – and why.

'I'm glad for you, Percy. I know how you love her. And you'll be able to look after her. She'll need looking after.'

'Will you come to the wedding, be a witness for us?'

She smiled then. 'Of course I will. And, Percy – I hope it works out.'

'I'll make it work out. And she does need me. So will the child.'

So Lizzie went to the register office in her Sunday best, with her arm in a sling, and signed her name shakily with her left hand. Then Percy and Johnny moved into number seven with the Harpers.

It was good to have number one to herself again. But Lizzie still seemed to be frozen, still couldn't think what to do with herself. And she had to pay for help in the house, help with getting dressed in the mornings, too. Fanny Preston, a lot older now, was glad to come in and do that.

But every morning Lizzie still woke with a start, expecting to see Sam lying in bed beside her.

On their wedding night Percy let Emma go upstairs first and get undressed, for they'd both vetoed Blanche's suggestion of a day or two away somewhere. When he tapped on the bedroom door, he found her already in bed, still looking a bit under the weather.

'I'll just go and get undressed in the bathroom.'

'You can get undressed here.' She gave him a faint smile. 'I know what a man looks like.'

He blushed and shook his head. She might know what a man looked like, but he wasn't used to taking his clothes off in front of a woman.

When he came back, she said quietly, 'Come on. The bed's nice and warm.'

He got in and pulled the cord to turn the light out. Then he lay there stiffly, trying not to touch her. He didn't want her to worry that he'd force himself on her.

'Percy.' Her voice was faint and breathy sounding in the darkness.

'Yes, love?'

'Could you just – hold me?'

He gathered her carefully into his arms and suddenly she was weeping softly and helplessly against him, so he patted her shoulder and made soothing noises till she stopped. It was nice to hold a woman. They were so soft. It was nice not to be on his own.

They drifted off to sleep in one another's arms and both slept well, waking to stare at each other in mild surprise the following morning.

'You all right, Emma love?' he asked anxiously.

'Yes, Percy. And – thank you. For – for just holding me.'

'I'll always be there for you.'

She leaned across to kiss his cheek. 'You're a lovely man.'

As they were sitting over breakfast, she said thoughtfully, 'I haven't been down to the yard since – since I heard. Would you come with me today? Walter's gone back to work again and he's looking after things, but he's not so good with the paperwork.'

Percy, with a few days' holiday from Pilby's, nodded immediately. He'd have stood on his head if she'd wanted it. And actually, he found it interesting to sort through the papers and see how a building business was run. He offered a couple of suggestions for improving the account-keeping – he'd learned a lot in the office at Pilby's, by heck he had – and she looked at him thoughtfully.

That night when they went up to bed, Emma said abruptly, 'Leave the light on. I want to talk to you about something.'

So they lay there, propped up by pillows, him wishing he could hold her again and her talking business. It took him a minute or two to understand what she was saying, then he forgot about cuddling her. 'Me? Run Cardwell's?'

'Well, someone has to do it. Walter's a good man, and he knows the trade, but he's no use with customers and paperwork. I own a quarter of the business now. It's in our interest to see it thrive.'

'Well, I'll have to think about that. I'd not thought of leaving Pilby's.'

'You don't have to leave straight away. I can work for a while yet. But when I get too big, well, by then we'll know how things stand. And I'll have had time to show you what to do.'

'All right.'

It was a funny sort of discussion for two newly-weds, he thought, as he switched off the light and slid down in the bed beside her. But at least she did want a cuddle again. And if he worked in the business with her, it'd bring them even closer. Though he'd have a lot to learn. He would that. Eeh, it was funny how things worked out sometimes, it was indeed.

* * *

A couple of weeks after Sam's funeral, Lizzie went shopping in Overdale, more for something to do than because she needed much. The corner shop had supplied her well enough. Only she was going mad staying inside the house.

She hesitated outside Dearden's, then went inside, feeling a mixture of guilt and embarrassment.

Sally's face lit up as she saw Lizzie and she abandoned a customer, coming across to hug and kiss her then hug her again. 'How's your arm?'

'Oh, all right. It was a simple fracture, they said. I'm getting quite good with my left hand now.'

The customer cleared her throat and Lizzie saw how many others there were waiting. She looked round for staff and saw only one harassed-looking young woman. 'You look like you need some more assistants,' she joked.

'I certainly do. It's hard to find people who know the trade.' Though there wasn't the same amount of custom as there had been. Well, how could there be with all the shortages?

Lizzie looked round the shop. 'If it wasn't for my arm, I'd offer to start at once.'

Sally stared at her. 'Why not?'

'What?'

'Why not come and work for me?'

'You must be joking.'

'I've got a lass out the back who's willing enough, but she needs someone to keep an eye on her. And you could take money or fetch things off shelves.' She sighed. 'I'd welcome the company, actually. When you've been used to a family, being on your own isn't much cop.'

Lizzie beamed at her and joy flooded through her. 'All right. I will, then. Where's a pinny?' She had not expected Mrs D to need any help, not expected anything, just wanted to go inside the shop where she'd been so happy, see her old friend.

CHAPTER THIRTY

1918

Three weeks later, Lizzie woke up one morning and had to rush to the bathroom to be sick. Afterwards, she stared at her pallid face in the mirror in horror. Then she had to face the fact that she was carrying Sam's child. She'd been denying this possibility for days, telling herself her monthlies were bound to be upset after all the trouble she'd been through.

She gazed in the mirror again, wondering if it showed, but she looked just the same now that her colour was coming back. Thin face, wiry body, straight black hair. 'I'm having a baby,' she said aloud, then blushed scarlet.

She scrubbed her teeth vigorously, using more tooth powder than usual to get the nasty taste out of her mouth, then got dressed and went slowly downstairs. 'Oh, crikey!' she muttered as she put the kettle on. 'What am I going to do?'

As she put on her hat to go to work, she took a deep breath and told her reflection, 'Well, it takes nine months, so you don't have to do anything yet, do you?'

So she didn't. Even after her arm was better, she carried on working. She didn't think the extra fullness in her breasts would show and the sickness always passed after a few minutes first thing. It helped to have a dry biscuit next to the bed and a drink of water.

After much consideration, she decided not to tell anyone about the baby; not Mrs D, who was enjoying having her around, nor even Percy and Emma, who was definitely showing her condition now. The two of them seemed like old friends, rather than husband and wife, but Percy looked happier than he had for a long time.

Even Johnny was getting a bit friendlier. Now that he was living a few doors away from his eldest sister, he had started popping in for a cup of tea occasionally, all gruff and off-hand about his visits. But Lizzie made him welcome. She wanted very much to get to know her family again.

Johnny said very little, though he ate all her biscuits. He was growing fast, going to be bigger than Percy, and already had a look of their father which made Lizzie remember how things had been once.

How they had changed! Her mother dead – and Sam – and Jack Dearden. So many people killed in this dreadful war, which seemed as if it would never end.

In March, there were massive German attacks on the Western Front and the enemy overran the Allied trenches. Belgium, Picardy, Aisne – the Germans seemed to be everywhere. Some people were even starting to whisper that defeat lay just round the corner, though not in Mrs D's hearing.

In May, she took Lizzie aside one evening after the shop closed. 'You should have told me sooner,' she said accusingly.

'What?'

Sally made a flapping motion with one hand. 'What do you think? About the baby.'

'Oh. That.' Lizzie couldn't think what to say.

'I suppose it's Sam's?'

Lizzie glared at her. 'Of course it is.' Then she sighed. 'He came and found me in Murforth – it was Mam who told him where I was – and, well, he forced himself on me. So I've just been trying to carry on as usual.'

'It's not the baby's fault that the father was so – you know – rough.'

Lizzie smiled. 'I know that.' She patted her stomach. 'Actually, I hope it's a boy. Every man wants a son to carry on his name.' The baby had come to seem like a way of saying sorry to Sam for hurting him, for she had hurt him, she realised now – though not nearly as much as he'd hurt her. She had thought and thought about that last evening and knew there had been pain as well as anger in his eyes.

Sally's voice was gentle. 'You've forgiven him now, then?'

Lizzie shrugged. 'I've forgiven us both for doing something so stupid – marrying one another. We were an ill-assorted pair, weren't we? Me with my head in the clouds, him wanting to own me.'

'Your family were stupid as well, pushing you into it.'

'Well, they thought they were doing their best for me.' Percy had come round one evening to unburden himself of the guilt he felt about his part in her marriage and the two of them had wept together, then become better friends.

'I wrote to tell Peter you were a widow,' Sally said unexpectedly. 'Have you heard from him?'

Lizzie shook her head. 'No.'

'I haven't had a letter for ages, either. I – I don't think I can bear it if I lose him, too.'

What did you say to a remark like that? Some women had lost several sons. Chance struck out blindly and cruelly. And Lizzie hadn't dared think about Peter. Not in that way. Not when she was carrying her dead husband's child.

Sally heaved herself to her feet. 'Well, I must lock up and see about my tea. I'm that hungry! I thought Mrs Fowler would never leave tonight.'

'She's lonely, too,' Lizzie said softly. 'There are a lot of lonely women around.'

In May, Emma had her baby, a little boy who looked remarkably like his real father. She gave birth quite easily in the front bedroom of their house and Percy, brought in by the unsuspecting midwife to see his 'son', was reduced to tears by the miracle of new life.

'You are a lovely man,' Emma said.

'What, me?'

'Yes, you.'

He shrugged. 'What do you want to call him?'

'What *we* want to call him?' she corrected. 'If he's to be yours as well as mine, we both need to share the naming.'

He blinked at her in surprise. She had said this before, but he'd decided to wait and see how she felt when the baby was actually born. 'Are you sure?'

'Of course I am. So – what is it to be? Stanley or Harold or John?' These were all family names, as well as names they both liked.

'Stanley, then. John Stanley Kershaw. Only we'll call him Stan, eh?' At the door, the midwife cleared her throat and frowned at him. 'And now I think you'd better get some rest, love.'

When he'd gone, Emma couldn't stop the tears from flowing. It should have been James standing there, all proud and fatherly. But James was dead.

'There, there, love,' said the midwife, patting her arm. 'Let it all come out. Having a baby takes some of 'em that way.'

So Emma wept for a while, then fell asleep. When she woke, she told herself firmly that she had to get on with living. She was lucky to have Percy, who had been kind to her in a hundred small ways. In return she owed it to him not to dwell on the past. And to her son.

One sunny Sunday in June, Lizzie went over to Outshaw to see Polly. She enjoyed the feeling of happiness in the small house there, and particularly enjoyed cuddling her little nephew. It was like old times to be together, just her and her sister, and she really enjoyed her day out.

Polly had come over to see her soon after Sam's death, but what with Percy being there and Polly's husband Eddie as well – which was the first time Lizzie had ever met him – well, they couldn't really talk.

This time, Polly sent Eddie off to church and the two sisters sat and talked for ages.

'I'm having a baby,' Lizzie said abruptly when there was a pause in the conversation.

'You didn't say! And here was I, thinking you'd plumped up a bit at last.'

'I don't think I'll ever plump up. I'm too much like Mam.'

After a moment's hesitation, Polly asked, 'Are you glad about the baby?'

'Very. And Sam left me some money, as well as the house, so I shan't be short.' He hadn't altered the will he'd made when they married, leaving her everything, though he'd not told her about it. Mr Finch had had to explain things. Lizzie realised Polly was beaming at her and beamed back, feeling very light-hearted today for some reason.

'That's all right, then. When is it due?'

'In October, Dr Marriott says.'

'Plenty of time for us to make plans, then. Of course, I'm coming over to look after you when you've had it.'

'Come before then and give me a few lessons in looking after babies.'

Polly beamed again. 'There's nothing to it. They're lovely, babies are. I wish I could fall for another.'

Another Sunday Lizzie went over to see Eva. That visit was very pleasant, with a generous country tea provided in spite of the food shortages, but there was not the same warmth as there had been with Polly. Alice tactfully left them alone for a while but they weren't really close. In fact, Eva didn't feel much like family now. She spoke so poshly and seemed totally engrossed in her work as a teacher.

Emma Harper felt like family, though, and as for her tiny nephew, Stan, well, he was a 'little smasher'. Percy loved to cuddle him and coo at him and was always bringing him round to see his auntie.

So all in all, things were going well. And why Lizzie should feel so dissatisfied, she couldn't think. She had her freedom and a baby to think of and a job she liked and plenty of money. But – an image of Peter Dearden rose before her. He hadn't written since Sam brought her back to Overdale. He'd written to his mother, who gave Lizzie news of him from time to time, but he hadn't written to her.

You'd think he'd have written.

Lizzie could only assume that he was upset about the baby. That he didn't want to see her again when he got back. Well, she wasn't going to make a fool of herself over him, definitely not. She was managing perfectly all right on her own and would continue to do so.

Then, in July, a counter-offensive on the Marne showed that the Allies were not yet defeated and the newspapers began to sound a bit more optimistic.

'It makes a difference, having those Yanks fighting with us,' people said. 'We've turned the tables on the Hun now.'

And they had. Suddenly the Germans were retreating, giving way, surrendering. As if they'd run out of steam all of a sudden. It all happened so quickly, people couldn't quite believe it was true.

In late July they heard that Peter had been wounded and was being sent home to recuperate. Mrs D went round beaming at everyone. 'It'll all be over by the time he's better,' she kept saying. 'He's got through. I've still got one son left.' Once or twice she added, when only Lizzie could hear her, 'And maybe he'll find himself a nice lass and have some children. I'd like to be a grandma, I would that.'

Lizzie, who hadn't told her about the days she'd spent with Peter in Manchester, or the letters they'd exchanged, bit her tongue. Why raise old ghosts? She knew she wouldn't be able to help seeing him from time to time, but she would manage – somehow – to stay calm, or so she told herself. She'd treat him as a friend – which was all he'd been really – and just be thankful for what she'd got. Peace of mind, a house of her own, money in the bank and a baby on the way.

It was August before Peter arrived in England, by which time Lizzie felt as a big as a house, though Mrs D laughed at her for saying that. 'You've not put on any weight, except for your belly, and you'll be as slim as ever once you've had it – unlike me.' She patted her own generous curves and smiled reminiscently. 'I never did get thin again after our Peter, though I was quite slender when I was a lass.'

A group of volunteers brought Peter home from Manchester one hot day in August in a motor omnibus full of convalescent men. Lizzie was shocked when she saw him. He looked gaunt and ill, and very severe, not at all like the kindly man she remembered.

He limped into the shop on crutches and stood for a moment in the doorway, sniffing. 'It still smells of coffee and spices,' he said in a hushed voice, as if he couldn't quite believe it was all real. 'I dreamed of it so many times.'

Sally came across to hug him to her ample bosom and urge him to come upstairs and sit down. 'I've baked your favourite cake and . . .' Her voice trailed away, for he was staring across the room at Lizzie, his eyes on her swollen belly as if he'd never seen a pregnant woman before, as if her condition were somehow shameful.

Lizzie waited for him to say something, but he just gave her a quick nod and walked on past.

She watched him go into the back, her hand to her mouth, and if it hadn't been for a customer demanding to be served, she'd have burst into tears because that had been revulsion on his face, definitely revulsion. By the time she'd served the old lady, however, she had herself in hand. It was her baby, and there was nothing shameful in having it. Definitely not.

So when Sally came downstairs, full of how tired her Peter had looked, how he'd eaten a piece of cake and fallen straight asleep, Lizzie was able to listen and nod and murmur appropriate responses.

It wasn't until she was alone at home that night that she could stop pretending and let a few tears fall. 'What's the use?' she told the clock as she wound it up. 'It's no good wishing for the moon.'

As she snuggled under the bedclothes, she said firmly, 'I've just got to be sensible about this.'

But she didn't want to be sensible. She wanted to talk to him, see that fond, amused expression on his face as he teased her – and ask why he had changed? Had he met someone over in France? Or on leave in London?

Only she couldn't ask him – *wouldn't* ask him. She had too much pride to do that.

Lizzie's baby was born on 20 September, after a prolonged labour. 'Eeh, it's a big 'un,' the midwife said complacently as she tidied the little boy up. 'You did well to get him out, lass, you being so small. Though you've got decent hips for your size. That'll be what did it.'

Polly, who had been there with Lizzie all the time, smiled at her sister. 'He's beautiful.'

As they laid her son in her arms, Lizzie could hardly breathe for joy, for he was beautiful. He didn't look anything like Sam. He was just – himself.

'What are you going to call him?' the midwife asked. 'Sam for your husband?'

Lizzie shuddered. 'No. I've always had a fancy for Matthew.'

'That's a lovely name,' Polly said softly, patting her arm.

They tried to make her rest in bed, but Lizzie felt fine and very restless. Within a couple of days she was pottering around the house, ignoring the warnings the midwife gave her to lie up. On the fourth day, she sent Polly back home to her family and managed on her own from then on, with a little help from Emma and Blanche.

But within ten days she was going mad spending so much

time alone, so she put the baby in the fine new pram she had bought him with Sam's money and pushed him into town. It was good to get out in the fresh air, and it was a fine day. Everyone seemed very cheerful because the Allied offensive was going well. They were talking again about the war finishing by Christmas, as they had done when it first started. Only this time, maybe they were right.

She didn't see the figure on the park bench until she was nearly past it, then she hesitated and stared into Peter Dearden's unwinking gaze. She saw anger in it, and disapproval, and her own anger rose to meet his. She stopped wheeling the pram, put its brake on and went to stand in front of him, arms akimbo.

'Why are you looking at me like that?'

He scowled at her. 'I can look at you any way I want.' He jerked his head towards the pram. 'Does he resemble his dear father?'

Lizzie shrugged. 'No, actually. He looks like himself.' Still angry, she sat down on the bench beside him. 'I'm not going until you've told me why you keep looking at me as if – as if I'm a worm.'

'Then I'll have to leave you to it, won't I?' Peter stood up hastily and lost his balance, so that she grabbed at his arm and pulled him back to sit beside her.

'Damnation!' He glared at her. 'Let go of me, Lizzie Thoxby.'

'No.' To make sure he didn't go, she nipped the crutches out of his hand and tossed them across the grass.

'What the hell did you do that for?'

'To keep you here. I'll go an' pick them up once you've told me why you look at me as if you hate me.' She wanted to sob, for he was still staring at her like that, but she wasn't going to let it pass. She'd had enough of being cowed by men.

'Why do you think?' he asked.

'If I knew, I wouldn't be asking you.'

He stared down at his hands, then across the grass. 'I thought you'd left him for good.'

'Sam?'

'Yes.'

'I thought I had, too.'

'But when he came for you, you went tamely back to him.' He gestured towards the pram. 'Right back into his bed.'

'He dragged me back – and dragged me into his bed, too. Only he didn't wait to get me to bed, he forced me on the kitchen floor in Murforth the first time.'

Peter breathed deeply, his breaths harsh and painful-sounding. 'But you stayed with him. You *stayed!*'

But Lizzie had heard the pain in his voice and it gave her new hope. 'You didn't get my letter, then?'

'I haven't had a single letter from you since Christmas last.'

'I wrote – after Sam had been killed. I explained what had happened.' And had wept over the paper as she wrote, for it was still painful to her then.

'I never got any letters. Not one. I thought – I thought you didn't care any more.'

Silence fell. She looked at him, caught him looking at her, and said, 'I didn't write again when you didn't answer because I thought you didn't want me to.'

There was silence between them, broken only by the cries of some little children playing at bat and ball.

'It was all so painful,' Lizzie said quietly. She still couldn't think about those last days with Sam without stirring up nightmares again.

She could feel Peter's eyes on her and shook her head, trying to brush the memories away. 'The night he was killed,' she said in a tight, hard voice, 'he found your letters and tried to strangle me. He broke my arm as well.'

Peter could feel his own anger dissipating. 'But Mum wrote to say you'd gone back to him.'

Lizzie looked at him in puzzlement.

'And since your letters had stopped, I thought – that you'd gone back willingly.'

'Never that. You could have trusted me a little, Peter.'

Silence again, then as she looked sideways, she saw he was

weeping, silent tears streaking down his thin, drawn face. 'Oh, love, don't!' She put one hand on his arm.

He gulped. 'I had built up some hope again – hope of a life after the war. I'd lost hope, you see, before I met you that time in Manchester, and you gave it me back somehow. Then – when I thought you'd – it took all the hope away again, you see.'

And she saw then how hurt he'd been by the war. How fragile he was.

'No.' She laid one hand tentatively on his and when he didn't push her away, clasped his fingers in hers. 'I didn't go back to him willingly. He had to tie me to the bed at night to keep me there. I hated him.'

Peter was looking at the pram. 'But you still have his baby. Sam's still with you.'

She let go of his hand, got up and marched over to the pram, picking up Matthew and dumping him on Peter's lap. 'You take a good look at that child, Peter Dearden. He's himself, not Sam. He's *my* son, too, you know. And he's a lovely little lad.'

As if to prove it, Matthew opened his eyes, blinked at the bright sunlight and nestled against Peter, murmuring disapproval of the awkward way he was being held.

'There's the hope you're looking for, hope for the future,' Lizzie said, her voice ringing with confidence. 'Hope lies in the children who'll have better lives than we did. Well, this child is *my* hope, any road. And he can be yours, too, if you'll let him.'

She allowed the silence to continue for a few moments, pleased when Peter at last began to jiggle the baby and murmur nonsense to him. She saw then that for a time, until Peter had recovered, she'd have to be the strong one, the one to take the initiative. She'd heard other women talking at the munitions factory when their wounded husbands had been sent home; heard them saying how the war had marked their men, taken the heart out of them. Now she looked into Peter's brown eyes and saw horror lurking there, too.

'It was bad, wasn't it?' she asked gently.

He nodded.

'Will you have to go back?'

'Maybe. It depends on this leg. It's taking rather a long time to heal.'

'Don't drop him!' Lizzie grabbed at Matthew and deliberately pressed closer to Peter. With one hand she held her son steady, with the other she reached for Peter's head and pulled it towards her. 'You daft ha'porth!' she scolded softly. 'You should have written and asked me what was wrong.'

And they turned all of a sudden into a tangle of baby and kisses and rough khaki jacket.

Lizzie's hat blew off and she chuckled. 'Hold him!' she yelled, letting go of Matthew and chasing after it, coming back breathless and laughing, waving the hat triumphantly.

And Peter couldn't help laughing, too. For suddenly he'd seen hope reborn, not in the child but in her. Oh, she was a lively lass, his Lizzie was. And she was *his* Lizzie, had never stopped being that. Joy surged up in him and he had to fight back more tears.

'Let's go home and get a cup of tea. I'm dying of thirst,' she declared. She had the baby securely tucked in the pram within seconds, Peter's crutches by his side, and was fairly dancing with impatience to be off.

He thought she was the most beautiful sight he'd ever seen in his life. 'I love you, Lizzie. With all my heart.'

'I should hope so.' She grinned. 'And I love you, too.'

He had to kiss her again.

'We'd better get married quickly,' she decided as they pulled apart.

He blinked and stopped short. 'Isn't that my job – asking you to marry me?'

'No. Not this time.' She looked blindly towards the water glinting in the little lake. 'This time I'm doing the choosing, and I'm going to be an equal partner when we're wed as well.'

'I can see I'm going to be a very henpecked husband,' he said with mock sorrow.

She stopped walking for a moment to beam at him. 'You are that.'

Then she was off, rushing the pram down the hill, cooing to the baby and only stopping to wait for Peter at the bottom. 'Come on! Can't you do better than that?' she demanded.

And he laughed back at her. 'No, I bloody well can't.' But he didn't care, because the hope was still there, glowing inside him.

They seemed to spend a lot of time laughing together from then on, as they broke the news to an astonished Sally, arranged a quick wedding and celebrated in style with all Lizzie's family. And it seemed part of their whole joyful new life that the war ended before Peter could be called back to the trenches.

'Eh, our Lizzie's looking like her old self again,' Percy said to Mrs D after the wedding. 'It's years since I've seen her looking so happy.'

'Or my Peter.' She mopped her eyes, as she had been doing all day. 'I'm feeling a bit happy myself.' And started sobbing aloud, yet laughing at the same time. 'Eeh, I'm a right fool, aren't I?' she said, when Emma had calmed her down. 'I don't know what's got into me today. But my Bob would have been that happy to see the two of them. That happy.'

That night, as Lizzie got ready for bed, she lost some of her sparkle. 'I – I'd better warn you,' she confessed breathlessly as Peter limped in from the bathroom, 'I'm not very good at it.'

'Good at what?'

She gestured to the bed. 'At – you know, making a man happy.'

'You make me happy just by being yourself.'

'That's a lovely thing to say, but—'

He stopped her words with a kiss and when it was over, laid her down on the bed and said very solemnly, 'It takes two people to make love, Lizzie, not one. Let me show you.'

Hours later, she was still awake, happily watching the moonlight trace its way across the room. Peter was right.

It did take two people. And when it was done with such tenderness, making love was wonderful.

The last of her worries died away, the fear that she was unnatural. Sighing happily, she slid an arm round his waist and snuggled down to sleep. She was sure — very, very sure — that her life would be happy from now on. She would *make* it happy!

ANNA JACOBS

JESSIE

Jessie Burton is lively and intelligent – and she wants more than the respectable life in service her mother has long planned for her. And times are changing: railways are being built across the land, bringing new freedom and possibilities.

Jessie tastes that freedom when she meets Jared Wilde, an ambitious young navvy newly arrived in Yorkshire. The attraction between them is overwhelming. He introduces her to the primitive, colourful shanty towns that are springing up around the railway works. But in spite of the hardness of life there, she finds happiness with Jared. Until another navvy becomes determined to destroy their future together ...

HODDER AND STOUGHTON PAPERBACKS

A selection of bestsellers from
Hodder & Stoughton

Fields of Heather	Mary Withall	0 340 71746 7	£5.99 ☐
Beyond the Shining Water	Audrey Howard	0 340 71808 0	£5.99 ☐
More Lives than One	Libby Purves	0 340 68043 1	£6.99 ☐
Down Stepney Way	Sally Worboyes	0 340 72876 0	£5.99 ☐
Prized Possessions	Jessica Stirling	0 340 67199 8	£5.99 ☐

All Hodder & Stoughton books are available from your local bookshop or newsagent, or can be ordered direct from the publisher. Just tick the titles you want and fill in the form below. Prices and availability subject to change without notice.

Hodder & Stoughton Books, Cash Sales Department, Bookpoint, 39 Milton Park, Abingdon, OXON, OX14 4TD, UK. E-mail address: order@bookpoint.co.uk. If you have a credit card you may order by telephone – (01235) 400414.

Please enclose a cheque or postal order made payable to Bookpoint Ltd to the value of the cover price and allow the following for postage and packing:
UK & BFPO – £1.00 for the first book, 50p for the second book, and 30p for each additional book ordered up to a maximum charge of £3.00.
OVERSEAS & EIRE – £2.00 for the first book, £1.00 for the second book, and 50p for each additional book

Name _____

Address _____

_____

_____

If you would prefer to pay by credit card, please complete:
Please debit my Visa/Access/Diner's Card/American Express (delete as applicable) card no:

Signature _____

Expiry Date _____

If you would NOT like to receive further information on our products please tick the box. ☐